ROBINSON CRUSOE

Daniel Defoe was a Londoner, born in 1660 at St Giles, Cripplegate, the son of James Foe, a tallow-chandler. He changed his name to Defoe from c. 1695. He was educated for the Presbyterian Ministry at Morton's Academy for Dissenters at Newington Green. But in 1682 he abandoned this plan and became a hosiery merchant in Cornhill. After serving briefly as a soldier in the Duke of Monmouth's rebellion, he became well established as a merchant and travelled widely in England, as well as on the Continent. Between 1697 and 1701 he served as a secret agent for William III in England and Scotland, and between 1703 and 1714 for Harley and other ministers. During the latter period he also, single-handed, produced the *Review*, a pro-government newspaper. A prolific and versatile writer, he produced some 500 books on a wide variety of topics including politics, geography, crime, religion, economics, marriage, psychology and superstition. He delighted in role-playing and disguise, a skill he used to great effect as a secret agent, and in his writing he often adopted a pseudonym or another personality for rhetorical impact. His first extant political tract (against James II) was published in 1688, and in 1701 appeared his satirical poem, *The True-Born Englishman*, which was a bestseller. Two years later he was arrested for *The Shortest-Way with Dissenters*, an ironical satire on High Church extremism, committed to Newgate and pilloried. He turned to fiction relatively late in life and in 1719 published his great imaginative work, *Robinson Crusoe*. This was followed in 1722 by *Moll Flanders* and *A Journal of the Plague Year* (both published in Penguin), and in 1724 his last novel, *Roxana*, appeared. His other works include *A Tour Through the Whole Island of Great Britain*, a guide book in three volumes (1724–6; abridged Penguin edition, 1965), *The Complete English Tradesman* (1726), *Augusta Triumphans* (1728), *A Plan of the English Commerce* (1728) and *The Complete English Gentleman*, not published until 1890. He died on 24 April 1731. Defoe had a great influence on the development of the English novel and many consider him to be the first true novelist.

•

Angus Ross is Reader in English at the University of Sussex. He writes on eighteenth-century and other literature, and has edited Tobias Smollett's *The Expeditions of Humphrey Clinker*, Samuel Richardson's *Clarissa* and *Selections from the Tatler and the Spectator* for Penguins, as well as a number of other texts and anthologies.

THE LIFE
AND ADVENTURES OF
Robinson Crusoe

DANIEL DEFOE

**Edited
with an Introduction
by Angus Ross**

PENGUIN BOOKS

Penguin Books Ltd, 27 Wrights Lane, London w8 5tz (Publishing and Editorial)
and Harmondsworth, Middlesex, England (Distribution and Warehouse)
Viking Penguin Inc., 40 West 23rd Street, New York, New York 10010, USA
Penguin Books Australia Ltd, Ringwood, Victoria, Australia
Penguin Books Canada Ltd, 2801 John Street, Markham, Ontario, Canada l3r 1b4
Penguin Books (NZ) Ltd, 182–190 Wairau Road, Auckland 10, New Zealand

First published 1719
Published in the Penguin English Library 1965
Reprinted 1970, 1971, 1972, 1974, 1975, 1976 (twice), 1977, 1978,
1979, 1980, 1981 (twice), 1982, 1983, 1984, 1985
Reprinted in Penguin Classics 1985, 1986, 1987

Introduction and notes copyright © Angus Ross, 1965
All rights reserved

Made and printed in Great Britain by
Hazell Watson & Viney Limited,
Member of the BPCC Group,
Aylesbury, Bucks
Set in Linotype Juliana

CONTENTS

INTRODUCTION

A SHIPWRECKED sailor on a desert island – the recipe is ready-made for romance and adventure. Yet *Robinson Crusoe*, the classic novel on this theme, is far from being merely a novel of romantic adventure. We do not read it only in order to escape into an exciting world of danger and triumph. We read it rather in order to follow with meticulous interest and constant self-identification the hero's success in building up, step by step, out of whatever materials came to hand, a physical and moral replica of the world he had left behind him. If *Robinson Crusoe* is an adventure story, it is also a moral tale, a commercial accounting and a puritan fable. To understand how it came to be all this, we must look first at the life and character of its author.

In 1719, Daniel Defoe was sixty years old. At a point when many men think of retirement, he could look back on a life which had found time for the writing of several hundreds of books and pamphlets, and for not one but many careers, most of which would singly have earned him a place in the history of his own day. With the publication of *Robinson Crusoe*, however, he started yet another career, as a novelist, this time producing before his death in 1731 the half-dozen works of imagination which have made him more than a mere historical figure and preserved his name to us as one of the great writers of the language. For his role as a creator of fiction, Defoe was uniquely fitted by his varied experience and abilities, but the nature of that experience, some of it clandestine and dangerous, has meant that, though many of the main facts of his life are clear, the interpretation of them is very difficult. This difficulty is increased by Defoe's own reticence about himself. His surviving letters are astonishingly uncommunicative of his own character. Chameleon-like, he blended into the background he thought each correspondent demanded. Even in his non-fiction he successfully hides himself behind hundreds of masks, ranging from that Kara Selym, who in 1717 gave an impartial Turkish comment on schism among the Christians, to Captain Charles Johnson, who briefly appeared in 1724 and 1728 as the knowledgeable economic historian of the pirates, and earned himself a place in the *Dictionary of National Biography*.

Criticism of Defoe's fiction has been influenced by his critics' evaluation of his inscrutable character. Those of his contemporaries who did not like him or his writings commonly represented him as an ill-educated, disreputable scribbler. Victorian critics of his fiction, taking over this picture, often saw him as a rude forefather of the novel, incapable of telling fact from fiction, who showed his real lack of serious purpose by lying, choosing scamps as heroes and writing mainly of low, not to say criminal, life. To such a view, his novels may be a series of entertaining adventure stories, but not much else. The view is still found, but modern readers, more interested in the techniques of writing fiction and shying off the habit of assessing the value of a novel according to the social setting of its characters, have seen in Defoe's apparently artless style a cunning deliberation, a power of irony and a conscious mastery of narrative. His adoption of masks to tell a tale has come to be seen as an outstanding power of empathy, of 'negative capability', almost poetic in its intensity, giving him those insights into the inner life of man which make him a true father of the English novel. The low life of some of his novels, such as *Roxana* and *Moll Flanders*, is seen as the material for a real imaginative re-creation of the life of his age and for a moral judgement of his society also worthy of serious consideration.

It can also be added that Defoe was far from uneducated. Born probably in 1659 in the London parish of St Giles, Cripplegate, he was designed by his father, John Foe, a respectable dissenting tallow-chandler, for the Presbyterian ministry, and educated to this end at the celebrated dissenting academy in Newington. He was thus from a young age brought up in the close self-questioning of a puritan household, with the strong tradition such a household would have in Bible-reading and discussion, and given the most solid and practical formal education afforded by his age. The grammar-school and university courses of the day drew their power from the settled and traditional study of the Greek and Latin classics, combined with a rather barren logical training. The best dissenting academies were run by scholars forbidden by the

Test Acts to teach or study at Oxford or Cambridge; while not neglecting the classics, they strengthened this kind of reading with an infusion of modern European languages, practical matters such as mathematics and navigation, and the reading under instruction of English writings.

At the risk of over-emphasizing the importance of literature, Defoe's life might be considered as a preparation for writing the works of imagination, produced in the last twelve years of his life, which gave him lasting fame. When he left the Newington academy, he abandoned his intention of becoming a Presbyterian minister : he later wrote

... It was my disaster first to be set apart for, then to be set apart from, the honour of that sacred employ.*

He had a brief interlude of service in 1685 with the rebellious army of the Duke of Monmouth. Fortunately, however, he escaped confronting Judge Jeffreys at the Bloody Assizes, but perhaps the experience parallels Crusoe's romantic defiance of his father and his restless adventure-seeking, the centre of much of the imaginative force of the book's beginning. Then followed a time of practical engagement in commerce, as a stocking-factor (not a hosier, he later indignantly insisted), as a merchant trading to Portugal and Spain and as a tile-manufacturer. He was always ready to make his fortune, but his success and luck were not equal to the enthusiasm and rashness he brought to his schemes, and he had to flee from his creditors. Like some unsuccessful practitioners, he started to write theory, and his writings on economics – books, pamphlets and journalism – form perhaps the biggest single section of his fantastic output. His view of trade was personal and deeply held. He saw its workings as the manifestation of one of the laws by which God regulated the universe, and the 'tradesmen' and merchants seemed to him in his more exalted moments the men chosen to put this law into practice. Unless for the specialist, it is not very valuable to use *Robinson Crusoe* to identify Defoe's particular economic theories (in fact he was inconsistent, sometimes an innovator, sometimes a conservative) but it is vital to feel that economics and socio-

* *Review*, vii, 341.

logical observation were of first-class imaginative importance to
him. Defoe's views on religion, tolerant and more or less rational,
had an economic basis; so did his abhorrence of blind and ex-
tremist nationalism. The first landed him in the pillory for being
only too successful in adopting the mask of a High Church bigot,
in *The Shortest Way with the Dissenters*. The fury of the un-
deceived Tories knew no bounds. His most vigorous set of verses,
The True Born Englishman, sets out his judgement on miscon-
ceived patriotism. In 1719, the fusion of several of these interests
with his taste for realistic romance writing produced *The Life and
Strange Surprising Adventures of Robinson Crusoe, of York,
Mariner*.

On 23 April of that year, William Taylor, a printer who
specialized in religious works and books of voyages and travels,
entered in the Stationers' Register his claim to possess 'the whole
share' of Defoe's book. It was published on 25 April and was an
immediate success. A second edition appeared on 12 May and two
further editions by the end of the year. It is said that William
Taylor cleared a thousand pounds by printing and publishing
Robinson Crusoe. Defoe must have been satisfied by whatever
terms Taylor offered him, however, because the two sequels
which he provided to exploit the success of the first volume were
also printed and published by Taylor 'at the Ship in Pater-Noster-
Row'. The two sequels were *The Farther Adventures of Robinson
Crusoe: being the Second and Last Part of his Life*, published in
August 1719 and *Serious Reflections during the Life and Surprising Adventures of Robinson Crusoe: With his Vision of the
Angelick World*, published in August 1720. These two books are,
in comparison with the first part, of diminishing interest and
were so regarded at the time. *The Farther Adventures* sends
Crusoe on his travels again, back to the island as a colonist. The
bulk of the book is an extension of the kind of 'adventures' which
befell him after his rescue in the first book. It had only two
printings in 1720 and a third in 1722. The *Serious Reflections*,
consisting of a series of essay-like sections on honesty, the Voice
of Providence and similar themes, had only one printing in
Defoe's lifetime, and was not reprinted until 1925.

The contemporary reception of *Robinson Crusoe* shows how

Defoe has been depreciated as an imaginative writer. The book came from a printer whose main output was not ephemeral matter, but solid reading. It cost five shillings, making it quite an expensive book. Nevertheless it sold well enough to warrant four editions in its first year. This success provoked jealous comment, dragging up all the usual personal denigration of the writer, as a scribbler, a liar passing off invention for truth, and a man of no education. The next year, Charles Gildon, an old, blind, unsuccessful playwright known for his 'venal quill', but yet a 'gentleman' who could translate the classics, printed an attack called *The Life and Strange Surprising Adventures of Mr D— De F— of London, Hosier, who has lived above fifty years by Himself in the Kingdom of North and South-Britain*. In this book, Gildon makes some valid criticisms of the realism and probability of Defoe's narrative (which have to be admitted), but the tone is obviously one of jealous outrage that Defoe should dare to be a successful writer at all. One of Gildon's jibes is frequently quoted:

There is not an old woman that can go to the price of it, but buys thy *Life and Adventures* and leaves it as a legacy, with *Pilgrim's Progress*, the *Practice of Piety* and *God's Revenge against Murder* to her posterity.

Defoe was not a 'Gentleman' and as a writer is not an 'Augustan'. There is something to be said for the view that the Augustans, writing for a small, closed, homogeneous audience, are the representatives of a perpetually unstable kind of culture, the culture of *Elites*. Hence the pathos and tragic tension of the *Dunciad*, in which Pope, by choice an Augustan writer, correctly sees the future decline in the Europe of his day of this kind of writing, and perhaps unconsciously (as is shown by his imagery and his preoccupation with the vigorous life in the mercantile society he attacks) escapes blind devotion to the hierarchy of the past. But from Defoe (and Bunyan, and writers that lie dimly behind them) springs the possibility of another kind of culture, a more popular culture. Some modern critics have a nostalgic attachment to the noble Augustan ideal. Their interest lies in the very sophisticated techniques of writers like Pope and

Swift. After all, it is easier to write about technique than the value of ideas. A recent American textbook on eighteenth-century literature comments:

Defoe's deficiencies in education and culture are apparent when we compare him with Addison and Steele, who were as deeply interested in the middle class as he, but whose work has a charm and urbanity, a richness of allusion, and a delicacy of thought and phrasing, which we look for in vain in Defoe. He has the limitations of his class, with a leaning towards the plebeian.

This is to take Addison at his own valuation; 'charm' and 'urbanity' are loaded critical terms; 'plebeian' might be a mistake for 'reality of life'.

Of course, the popular appeal of Defoe's fiction had its disadvantages. The rapid sale of *Robinson Crusoe* encouraged piracies. These were not necessarily badly printed, hole-and-corner affairs, but sometimes well produced, more-or-less carefully edited productions, like the 1719 edition printed by George Grierson in Dublin, where the Copyright Act did not run. The printing known as the Amsterdam Coffee-House piracy, which Thomas Cox produced in the same year, is another matter. It is really an abridgement, done with some care, perhaps by Gildon. The nature of the alterations warrants careful study for the critical history of *Robinson Crusoe*. The reflections are cut out and the remainder partly rewritten to produce a more orthodox travel-adventure story. In other words the peculiar imaginative merit of Defoe's work was rejected, in favour of a simple, old-fashioned narrative. 'Because of its popularity among the semi-literate there was a chance that it might sink to the level of the little chap-books sold by itinerant pedlars. The Rev. James Woodforde purchased it with a life of a gypsy, *The Complete Fortune Teller*, and *Laugh and Grow Fat*, from a "travelling man and woman who sold all kinds of trifling books, etc." ' *

A similar kind of mangling of Defoe's story can be found in nineteenth-century sentimentalized rewritings, or in some modern 'simplified' editions for children.

* J. R. Moore, *Daniel Defoe: Citizen of the Modern World* (Chicago U.P., 1958), p. 222.

Such simplifications seize upon an element that is undoubtedly there, but at the expense of the protean force of Defoe's imagination. He created a work which can be seen in a more complex way as one of the prototypes of the modern novel. *Robinson Crusoe* is certainly an adventure story, which exploits the interest readers had in Defoe's day, and still have, in sea-faring and desert islands and the exotic. But the yarn is not spun out into any very elaborate shape : instead the character of Robinson Crusoe, the persona with which Defoe as a narrator invests himself, is elaborated to give the action significances relating the story to a world of religious belief, and to the inner life of the self. In the latter, Defoe shows all the Puritan's intense interest and powerful perception. After all, Crusoe grew up in the Puritan Commonwealth three quarters of a century before Defoe wrote the book for a more rationalistic age. Robinson Crusoe is, of course, not Defoe (though many critics have been tempted to make the easy transition). As a novelist, Defoe appears as that well-known figure, the 'editor' of a fictional history; in fact, he came near to inventing this device for making a romance realistic. Crusoe's world is in many respects, however, Defoe's world. God's hand is everywhere manifest; secret and over-ruling Decrees are everywhere in operation; and every human action must be judged and weighed. Thus, Crusoe notes 'the strange concurrence of days in the various providences that befell' him on 30 September (his birthday), just as Oliver Cromwell was awed by the Providence that gave him all his greatest victories on 3 September. The story is at once realistic (as far as Defoe went, or could go, at this time) and allegorical. The 'significance' is, however, put forward through a powerful imagination and the story consists of more than the dry bones of a parable : it has flesh and spirit.

Defoe himself gives us complete justification for regarding *Robinson Crusoe* as more than an adventure story pure and simple, for giving the story a more particular scrutiny. In the 'Preface' to *Serious Reflections during the Life and Surprising Adventures of Robinson Crusoe*, published in August 1720, he makes Crusoe write that 'the Story, although allegorical, is also historical . . . In a word, the *Adventures of Robinson Crusoe* are one whole scheme of a real life of eight and twenty years, spent in the most wandering, desolate and afflicting circumstances that ever man went through', thus developing (perhaps retrospectively) the puritan's taste for signs, and allegorical and figurative meanings. The allegory may or may not be there; it is in any case probably irretrievable from the complexities of Defoe's biography. The statement, however, suggests that the book was never intended to be taken straightforwardly.

The solitary sojourn on the island is God's punishment for Crusoe's great 'sin': a particularly painful one since he was by nature gregarious, and a peculiarly apposite one because his 'sin' was caused by 'apparent obstinate adhering to my foolish inclination of wandering abroad and pursuing that inclination, in contradiction to the clearest views of doing my self good in a fair and plain pursuit of those prospects and those measures of life, which nature and Providence concurred to present me with, and to my duty.' This inclination caused him to defy his father (God's natural representative in the family), and to seek to evade the calling given him by Providence to 'the upper station of low life', to follow which was his 'duty'. God warns him very soon after he has left home, by the storm in the Humber, but a fine day and a bowl of punch make him forget all his repentance. At Yarmouth, after the second (and worse) storm, the ship's captain with whom he has left his native Yorkshire underlines the divine message:

'Young Man,' says he, 'you ought never to go to sea any more, you ought to take this for a plain and visible token that you are not to be a seafaring man.' 'Why, Sir,' said I, 'will you go to sea no more?' 'That is another case,' said he, 'it is my calling, and therefore my duty: but as you made this voyage for a trial, you see what a taste Heaven has given you of what you are to expect if you persist: perhaps this is all befallen us, on your account, like Jonah in the ship of Tarshish.'

Wandering abroad (as traders, explorers or flag-carriers) is not bad in itself: seafaring is a calling like any other: but both are not for Crusoe and he takes them up at his peril. During his solitary life on the island, he is gradually brought to see his error (by more 'tokens', like the earthquake and his terrible dream) but he is always liable to forsake the way pointed out to him. This may give him the double pleasure of thinking right and doing wrong, but it also makes him human, even though in this he incurs the displeasure of Karl Marx.*

Crusoe's character is romantically portrayed. He knows his disobedience is wicked. So does the reader : but he is drawn on by Defoe to sympathize with Crusoe. There is a real tension between God's purpose and Crusoe's very human impulses. If this had not been the case, the book would have far less interest, and would have shown the imperfection of a humdrum religious tract. In this respect Crusoe is a new kind of hero in fiction: the reader identifies himself with the character. Of course this is true to a certain extent in any kind of fiction. But here the reader is not held at a distance and forced to judge, by the inter-vention of any traditional form (like the epic: or the rogue's confession), or any literary convention (like the elaborate rhetoric of Nashe's *Unfortunate Traveller*). Crusoe is Everyman. 'So,' we say, 'if I had been Crusoe, I should have behaved.' In saying he is Everyman, an obvious link with the old Morality Play can be made. Just as the Morality Play, and later the Elizabethan theatre, was an art enjoyed by many (as opposed to the purely courtly culture), so fiction on the lines sketched by Defoe became a highly popular art. This does not mean 'easily understood by all', but 'not demanding an "inside" knowledge or esoteric orientation for its enjoyment'.

A network of economic doctrine, perhaps even passionate teaching, has long been discerned as a living part of Defoe's achievement in *Robinson Crusoe*; an understanding of this important preoccupation of Defoe as a novelist can help in understanding how his books work, as will be discussed later. Unfortunately professional economists have sometimes tended to use the book merely as a quarry for earlier 'ideas' rather than as a creative picture of part of Life itself, and that kind of analysis is not often of much direct help to the reader of Defoe's work. Karl Marx, for example, wrote a critique of Crusoe's life on the island, as an exposition of a labour-theory of value,* since Robinson Crusoe's exploits 'are a favourite theme with political

*Karl Marx, *Capital* (Moscow, 1961), i. 76-7.

economists'. Marx, however, is much too schematic in his analysis. He sneers at Crusoe for being inconsistent in failing to distinguish between the truly valuable parts of his own theory, so far as his actions can be made most profitable, and the useless or unpractical parts of his theory, illustrated in his religious life, which are merely comforting. This is only to say that Defoe makes Crusoe a man and endows him with life. H. M. Robertson has made some useful comments on the link between Crusoe's behaviour and economic motives, in support of an attack on some of Tawney's historical and economic theories.* Professor Ian Watt has brilliantly synthesized these biographical and economic strands of the book and related them to *Robinson Crusoe*'s place in intellectual history, and as a forerunner of the English novel.†

Perhaps it may be thought that this is giving Defoe's character an overwhelming load of meaning. After all, there was a real Robinson Crusoe, the Scottish sailor Alexander Selkirk, on whose story Defoe drew for his novel.‡

It is interesting, however, to see how even contemporary journalistic accounts of Selkirk's story of his four years on the island of Juan Fernandez contain the mythologizing overtones of crime and punishment and the penitential effects of solitude so well liked by the eighteenth-century reader. Woodes Rogers's account of rescuing Selkirk, and Steele's interview with the returned castaway in London are printed in the *Appendix*.

The events in the book are also given general human and even cosmic significance. This is perhaps because the island on which Crusoe finds himself is treated by the writer as an *environment*, in the full modern use of the word. That is, it is seen as one of a number of possible *kinds* of surroundings. Perhaps it was for this reason, as well as on general grounds of probability, that Defoe shifted the *locale* of the solitary life from the relatively ordinary

* H. M. Robertson, *Aspects of the Rise of Economic Individualism* (C.U.P. 1933), p. 11.

† Ian Watt, *The Rise of the Novel* (Chatto and Windus 1957; Peregrine Books 1963).

‡ Selkirk's life and adventures are discussed in R. L. Mégroz's entertaining and valuable book, *The Real Robinson Crusoe* (Cresset Press 1939).

clime of the temperate Juan Fernandez, to a more exotic, tropical island which he placed off 'the river Oronoque, commonly called the Great River'. Put on this island with some of the goods suitable for other climates and places, Crusoe sets out to subdue his new environment, to construct in his tropical island a standard of living (even a kind of living) equivalent to life in his native England. He masters the new environment to produce the 'norm' he is accustomed to. He does not set out to build a New Jerusalem, nor does he take advantage of his solitude to develop wholly new insights into experience as a Conrad hero would. The imaginative interest of the reader, therefore, in the castaway's adaptability, his ingenuity in improvising, is like the interest of a reader of certain kinds of Science Fiction. How do human beings adapt their normal habits, ideas, standards and equipment to a Martian society, or a Venusian atmosphere? Or, how do they force this new envionment to support them as they are accustomed to live? Here, too, Defoe was something of an innovating forefather.

In Crusoe's new environment, in which he has only himself to rely on, the ordinary processes of everyday English living take on a new and strange aspect for him. He is reduced to first principles and is able for the first time in his life to generalize his ideas (indeed forced to do so). This is, of course, a common feature of eighteenth-century travels and voyages, where the change of scene is often used to make the familiar unfamiliar, and so induce judgement of it. ' 'Tis a little wonderful,' Crusoe writes, 'and what I believe few people have thought much upon, viz, the strange multitude of little things necessary in the providing, producing, curing, dressing, making, and finishing this one article of bread.' Starting as a heedless young man, who had 'never handled a tool in my life', he goes through in a few years all the long history of human technological inventiveness, solving almost every problem from the beginning. Of human inventiveness and technological resource, Defoe was in his way the sincere if clumsy celebrator. So, the book still has life as a generalized comment on all human life and effort.

Perhaps in this way, too, the famous 'realism' of Defoe's style is so haunting; the celebrated 'details', like the last remains sighted of his fellows in the wreck, 'three of their hats, one cap, and two shoes that were not fellows', or the lists of things removed from the wreck. The prosaic writing, the endless details beget a feeling of confidence in so circumstantial (and so patently unsystematic) a writer. But the details in the new and desolate environment are charged with meaning and living force. Of course, Defoe always wrote a prose that, formally, was rather slipshod and clumsy-seeming. But by a stroke of genius, he makes this the most suitable narrative style in the world for an old, not very well-educated trader, recalling adventures long past. The 1719 Amsterdam Coffee-House piracy cleaned up Crusoe's dangling sentences, with a resultant loss of immediacy and even grandeur. (The same damage is frequently done by the modern editor.) Crusoe's rude shock at finding traces of the cannibals is a good instance of the power of this apparently unorganized writing, which presents the feelings as they rise :

When I was come down the hill to the shore, as I said above, being the S.W. point of the island, I was perfectly confounded and amazed; nor is it possible for me to express the horror of my mind, at seeing the shore spread with skulls, hands, feet, and other bones of humane bodies; and particularly I observed a place where there had been a fire made, and a circle dug in the earth, like a cockpit, where it is supposed the savage wretches had sat down to their inhumane feastings upon the bodies of their fellow-creatures.

Parallel to the framework of religious significance in the story, which makes the realism imaginatively powerful, there is a framework of economic doctrine. It is easy to sense this, but (amid the disagreement of experts) it is not so easy to determine what exactly it is.*

The economic framework is made up of two parts. There is a good deal of straight documentation of Crusoe's financial and

* For a discussion of this, based on wide reading in contemporary economic writings, see M. E. Novak, *Economics and the Fiction of Defoe* (California U.P. 1962). In an interesting chapter on *Moll Flanders*, Dorothy Van Ghent in *The English Novel* (Rinehart, New York, 1953; Harper Torchbook 1961) makes a good case for seeing a symbolism of economics as a unifying imagery. *Robinson Crusoe* also has this, although no doubt more crudely handled.

mercantile dealings. He starts out with £40, which he raises (unknown to his father) from relatives in London. He returns from his Guinea voyage with 5 lb. 9 oz. of gold, which sells for almost £300. When he escapes from the Moors, his rescuer (the Portuguese captain) sets him up with a little capital (220 pieces of eight), the proceeds of selling the Moor's boat, the skins of a lion and a leopard, the lump of beeswax and his fellow-slave Xury: and so on, until at the end, presumably with God's help, he is master of 'above £5000' and sells his Brazil plantations for 32,800 pieces of eight (allowing for the deduction of a pension to the Portuguese Captain of 100 moidores per annum for life: and 50 moidores to his son afterwards). This rather precise financial documentation, adding to the 'realism' of the book, seems also to have fascinated Defoe. It is more than an index of Crusoe's success. Defoe had a real imaginative feeling for financial and mercantile success: perhaps this came from his own misfortunes. The religious overtones are seen in the immediate cause of Crusoe's shipwreck, which was his greed, prompting him to 'rise' faster than 'the nature of the things admitted' by going on a slaving expedition to Africa.

Secondly, however, there is a more speculative economic content, put forward as part of the imaginative exploitation of the theme of 'environment'. Crusoe, for example, in a long passage about making planks, says his 'Time or labour was little worth, and so it was as well employed one way as another.' On the fourth anniversary of his landing, he reflected on the plenty in his island, but added, 'All I could make use of was all that was valuable. I had enough to eat, and to supply my wants. . . . The nature and experience of things dictated to me, upon just reflection, that all the good things of this world are no farther good to us than they are for our use'. A drawerful of diamonds was of no value to him, because of no use. This point about the uselessness of precious metal and money had been amusingly made when Crusoe was taking things from the wreck. He says, 'I smiled to my self at the sight of this money. "O drug!" said I aloud, "what art thou good for, thou art not worth all the heap. I have no manner of use for thee, e'en remain where thou art, and go to the bottom as a creature whose life is not worth saving." However, upon second thoughts, I took it away'.

The speculative, economic passages contain several ideas that had long fascinated Defoe. These ideas were drawn from a number of schools of thought among the writers of his day, who discussed the nature of value, money, imports and exports, and so on. Defoe himself had written extensively on them in his more technical works. In *Robinson Crusoe* he puts them into a powerfully imaginative story. The divine sanction of Trade; the puzzling quality of money, which has value only if it can be used in Trade, but dazzles men into thinking it has intrinsic value; the economic analysis of human labour; all these ideas are thrown into a new light by Crusoe's solitary estate on the island. Fused together with this body of doctrine, and the precise documentation of Crusoe's finances, is the constant religious judgement. This is shown in the balance sheet of his condition, 'imperfectly set down like debtor and creditor', which Crusoe makes after he has settled on the island. Such a fusion was the most natural thing in the world for Defoe (as for Crusoe), though some critics have thought that all religious values are exploded if they are shown to have economic aspects. It can be seen how imaginatively damaging it is to cut out the 'moralizing'. Such passages are often necessary for the development of Crusoe's 'character' as well as adding to an exciting story of adventure glimpses into a now unfamiliar body of speculation, the ancestor of many of our own notions of the everyday world.

To the modern reader there are some unpleasant surprises in reading Defoe's narrative. What does the Western (and in particular the English) reader make of Crusoe's view of Xury, the black slave, and of the Indian, Man Friday. Crusoe's scruples at selling Xury, his companion slave and fellow-fugitive, to the Portuguese captain are absolved when the Captain offers to set Xury free after ten years, if he turns Christian. This confident, paternalistic attitude would have been Crusoe's natural one (and was probably Defoe's). Of course Defoe does not make Crusoe view these men so mawkishly as later adopters of his condemnation of the cannibals. Crusoe goes on to say : 'What authority or call [had I], to pretend to be judge and executioner upon these men as criminals, whom Heaven had thought fit for so many ages to suffer unpunished. . . .' Crusoe is of his own day, and though intellectually puzzled, acts towards the Indians in the all-conquering way of the successful, mercantile civilization which Defoe so admired, and which we from time to time realize is still our inheritance. Defoe's imagination, though free for his day, is yet limited by his time in this respect, and *Robinson Crusoe* stands at once optimistically alive and sad, as a monument to an earlier age of Western culture.

*Facsimile of the title-page of the
first edition (1719).*

THE
LIFE
AND
Strange Surprizing
ADVENTURES
OF
ROBINSON CRUSOE,
Of *YORK.* Mariner:

Who lived Eight and Twenty Years,
all alone in an un-inhabited Island on the
Coast of AMERICA, near the Mouth of
the Great River of OROONOQUE;

Having been cast on Shore by Shipwreck, wherein all the Men perished but himself.

WITH

An Account how he was at last as strangely deliver'd by PYRATES.

Written by Himself.

LONDON:
Printed for W. TAYLOR at the *Ship* in *Pater-Noster-*
Row. MDCCXIX.

PREFACE

IF ever the story of any private man's adventures in the world were worth making publick, and were acceptable when published, the editor of this account thinks this will be so.

The wonders of this man's life exceed all that (he thinks) is to be found extant; the life of one man being scarce capable of a greater variety.

The story is told with modesty, with seriousness, and with a religious application of events to the uses to which wise men always apply them, viz. to the instruction of others by this example, and to justify and honour the wisdom of Providence in all the variety of our circumstances, let them happen how they will.

The editor believes the thing to be a just history of fact; neither is there any appearance of fiction in it: and however thinks, because all such things are dispatched,[1] that the improvement of it, as well to the diversion as to the instruction of the reader, will be the same; and as such, he thinks, without farther compliment to the world, he does them a great service in the publication.

I WAS born in the year 1632, in the city of York, of a good
family, tho' not of that country, my father being a foreigner of
Bremen, who settled first at Hull. He got a good estate by mer-
chandise, and leaving off his trade lived afterward at York, from
whence he had married my mother, whose relations were named
Robinson, a very good family in that country, and from whom I
was called Robinson Kreutznaer; but by the usual corruption of
words in England, we are now called, nay, we call our selves and
write our name, Crusoe, and so my companions always called me.

I had two elder brothers, one of which was lieutenant collonel
to an English regiment of foot in Flanders, formerly commanded
by the famous Coll. Lockhart, and was killed at the battle near
Dunkirk against the Spaniards. What became of my second
brother I never knew any more than my father or mother did
know what was become of me.

Being the third son of the family and not bred to any trade, my
head began to be filled very early with rambling thoughts. My
father, who was very ancient, had given me a competent share of
learning, as far as house-education and a country free-school
generally goes, and designed me for the law; but I would be satisfied with nothing but going to sea, and my inclination to this led
me so strongly against the will, nay, the commands of my father,
and against all the entreaties and perswasions of my mother and
other friends, that there seemed to be something fatal in that
propension of nature tending directly to the life of misery which
was to befal me.

My father, a wise and grave man, gave me serious and excellent counsel against what he foresaw was my design. He called
me one morning into his chamber, where he was confined by the
gout, and expostulated very warmly with me upon this subject.
He asked me what reasons more than a meer wandring inclination I had for leaving my father's house and my native country,
where I might be well introduced, and had a prospect of raising
my fortune by application and industry, with a life of ease and

pleasure. He told me it was for men of desperate fortunes on one hand, or of aspiring, superior fortune on the other, who went abroad upon adventures, to rise by enterprize, and make themselves famous in undertakings of a nature out of the common road; that these things were all either too far above me, or too far below me; that mine was the middle state, or what might be called the upper station of low life, which he had found by long experience was the best state in the world, the most suited to human happiness, not exposed to the miseries and hardships, the labour and sufferings of the mechanick part of mankind, and not embarrassed with the pride, luxury, ambition, and envy of the upper part of mankind. He told me I might judge of the happiness of this state by this one thing, viz. that this was the state of life which all other people envied, that kings have frequently lamented the miserable consequences of being born to great things, and wished they had been placed in the middle of the two extremes, between the mean and the great; that the wise man gave his testinmony to this as the just standard of true felicity, when he prayed to have neither poverty or riches.[2]

He bid me observe it, and I should always find, that the calamities of life were shared among the upper and lower part of mankind; but that the middle station had the fewest disasters, and was not exposed to so many vicissitudes as the higher or lower part of mankind; nay, they were not subjected to so many distempers and uneasiness, either of body or mind, as those were who, by vicious living, luxury, and extravagancies on one hand, or by hard labour, want of necessaries, and mean or insufficient diet on the other hand, bring distempers upon themselves by the natural consequences of their way of living; that the middle station of life was calculated for all kinds of vertues and all kinds of enjoyments; that peace and plenty were the hand-maids of a middle fortune; that temperance, moderation, quietness, health, society, all agreeable diversions, and all desirable pleasures, were the blessings attending the middle station of life; that this way men went silently and smoothly thro' the world, and comfortably out of it, not embarrassed with the labours of the hands or of the head, not sold to the life of slavery for daily bread, or harrast with perplexed circumstances, which rob the soul of peace, and the body of rest; not enraged with the passion of envy, or secret burning lust of ambition for great things; but in easy circumstances sliding gently thro' the world, and sensibly tasting the sweets of living without the bitter, feeling that they are happy, and learning by every day's experience to know it more sensibly.

After this, he pressed me earnestly, and in the most affectionate manner, not to play the young man, not to precipitate my self into miseries which nature and the station of life I was born in seemed to have provided against; that I was under no necessity of seeking my bread; that he would do well for me and endeavour to enter me fairly into the station of life which he had been just recommending to me; and that if I was not very easy and happy in the world, it must be my meer fate or fault that must hinder it, and that he should have nothing to answer for, having thus discharged his duty in warning me against measures which he knew would be to my hurt: in a word, that as he would do very kind things for me if I would stay and settle at home as he directed, so he would not have so much hand in my misfortunes as to give me any encouragement to go away: and to close all, he told me I had my elder brother for an example, to whom he had used the same earnest perswasions to keep him from going into the Low Country wars, but could not prevail, his young desires prompting him to run into the army, where he was killed; and tho' he said he would not cease to pray for me, yet he would venture to say to me, that if I did take this foolish step, God would not bless me, and I would have leisure hereafter to reflect upon having neglected his counsel when there might be none to assist in my recovery.

I observed in this last part of his discourse, which was truly prophetick, tho' I suppose my father did not know it to be so himself; I say, I observed the tears run down his face very plentifully, and especially when he spoke of my brother who was killed; and that when he spoke of my having leisure to repent, and none to assist me, he was so moved that he broke off the discourse, and told me his heart was so full he could say no more to me.

I was sincerely affected with this discourse, as indeed who could be otherwise? and I resolved not to think of going abroad any more, but to settle at home according to my father's desire. But alas! a few days wore it all off; and in short, to prevent any of my father's farther importunities, in a few weeks after, I resolved to run quite away from him. However, I did not act so hastily neither as my first heat of resolution prompted, but I took my mother, at a time when I thought her a little pleasanter than ordinary, and told her that my thoughts were so entirely bent upon seeing the world, that I should never settle to any thing with resolution enough to go through with it, and my father had better give me his consent than force me to go without it; that I was now eighteen years old, which was too late to go apprentice to a trade, or clerk to an attorney; that I was sure if I did, I should never serve out my time, and I should certainly run away from my master before my time was out, and go to sea; and if she would speak to my father to let me go but one voyage abroad, if I came home again and did not like it, I would go no more, and I would promise by a double diligence to recover that time I had lost.

This put my mother into a great passion. She told me she knew it would be to no purpose to speak to my father upon any such subject; that he knew too well what was my interest to give his consent to any thing so much for my hurt, and that she wondered how I could think of any such thing after such a discourse as I had had with my father, and such kind and tender expressions as she knew my father had used to me; and that in short, if I would ruine my self there was no help for me; but I might depend I should never have their consent to it: that for her part she would not have so much hand in my destruction; and I should never have it to say, that my mother was willing when my father was not.

Tho' my mother refused to move it to my father, yet as I have heard afterwards, she reported all the discourse to him, and that my father, after shewing a great concern at it, said to her with a sigh. 'That boy might be happy if he would stay at home, but if he goes abroad he will be the miserablest wretch that was ever born: I can give no consent to it.'

It was not till almost a year after this that I broke loose, tho' in the mean time I continued obstinately deaf to all proposals of settling to business, and frequently expostulating with my father and mother, about their being so positively determined against what they knew my inclinations prompted me to. But being one day at Hull, where I went casually, and without any purpose of making an elopement that time; but I say, being there, and one of my companions being going by sea to London in his father's ship, and prompting me to go with them, with the common allurement of seafaring men, viz. that it should cost me nothing for my passage, I consulted neither father or mother any more, nor so much as sent them word of it; but leaving them to hear of it as they might, without asking God's blessing, or my father's, without any consideration of circumstances or consequences, and in an ill hour, God knows, on the first of September 1651 I went on board a ship bound for London. Never any young adventurer's misfortunes, I believe, began sooner, or continued longer, than mine. The ship was no sooner gotten out of the Humber, but the wind began to blow and the waves to rise in a most frightful manner; and as I had never been at sea before, I was most inexpressibly sick in body and terrify'd in my mind. I began now seriously to reflect upon what I had done, and how justly I was overtaken by the judgment of Heaven for my wicked leaving my father's house, and abandoning my duty; all the good counsel of my parents, my father's tears and my mother's entreaties, came now fresh into my mind; and my conscience, which was not yet come to the pitch of hardness to which it has been since, reproached me with the contempt of advice, and the breach of my duty to God and my father.

All this while the storm encreased, and the sea, which I had never been upon before, went very high, tho' nothing like what I have seen many times since; no, nor like what I saw a few days after : but it was enough to affect me then, who was but a young sailor, and had never known any thing of the matter. I expected every wave would have swallowed us up, and that every time the ship fell down, as I thought, in the trough or hollow of the sea, we should never rise more; and in this agony of mind I made many vows and resolutions, that if it would please God here to spare my life this one voyage, if ever I got once my foot upon dry land again, I would go directly home to my father, and never set it into a ship again while I lived; that I would take his advice, and never run my self into such miseries as these any more. Now I saw plainly the goodness of his observations about the middle station of life, how easy, how comfortably he had lived all his days, and never had been exposed to tempests at sea or troubles on shore; and I resolved that I would, like a true repenting prodigal, go home to my father.

These wise and sober thoughts continued all the while the storm continued, and indeed some time after; but the next day the wind was abated and the sea calmer, and I began to be a little inured to it. However, I was very grave for all that day, being also a little sea sick still; but towards night the weather cleared up, the wind was quite over, and a charming fine evening followed; the sun went down perfectly clear and rose so the next morning; and having little or no wind and a smooth sea, the sun shining upon it, the sight was, as I thought, the most delightful that ever I saw.

I had slept well in the night, and was now no more sea sick but very chearful, looking with wonder upon the sea that was so rough and terrible the day before, and could be so calm and so pleasant in so little time after. And now, least my good resolutions should continue, my companion, who had indeed enticed me away, comes to me. 'Well, Bob,' says he, clapping me on the shoulder, 'how do you do after it? I warrant you were frighted, wa'n't you, last night, when it blew but a cap full of wind?' 'A cap full d' you call it?' said I, ''twas a terrible storm.' 'A storm, you fool, you,' replies he, 'do you call that a storm? Why, it was nothing at all; give us but a good ship and sea room, and we think nothing of such a squall of wind as that; but you 're but a fresh water sailor, Bob; come, let us make a bowl of punch and we 'll forget all that; d' ye see what charming weather 'tis now?' To make short this sad part of my story, we went the old way of all sailors, the punch was made, and I was made drunk with it, and in that one night's wickedness I drowned all my repentance, all my reflections upon my past conduct, and all my resolutions for my future. In a word, as the sea was returned to its smoothness of surface and settled calmness by the abatement of that storm, so the hurry of my thoughts being over, my fears and apprehensions of being swallowed up by the sea being forgotten, and the current of my former desires returned, I entirely forgot the vows and promises that I made in my distress. I found indeed some intervals of reflection, and the serious thoughts did, as it were, endeavour to return again sometimes, but I shook them off, and rouzed my self from them as it were from a distemper, and applying my self to drink and company, soon mastered the return of those fits, for so I called them, and I had in five or six days got as compleat a victory over conscience as any young fellow that resolved not to be troubled with it could desire. But I was to have another trial for it still; and Providence, as in such cases generally it does, resolved to leave me entirely without excuse. For if I would not take this for a deliverance, the next was to be such a one as the worst and most hardened wretch among us would confess both the danger and the mercy.

The sixth day of our being at sea we came into Yarmouth roads; the wind having been contrary and the weather calm, we had made but little way since the storm. Here we were obliged to come to an anchor, and here we lay, the wind continuing contrary, viz. at south-west, for seven or eight days, during which time a great many ships from Newcastle came into the same roads, as the common harbour where the ships might wait for a wind for the river.

We had not, however, rid here so long, but should have tided it up the river, but that the wind blew too fresh, and, after we had lain four or five days, blew very hard. However, the roads being reckoned as good as a harbour, the anchorage good, and our ground-tackle very strong, our men were unconcerned, and not in the least apprehensive of danger, but spent the time in rest and mirth, after the manner of the sea; but the eighth day in the morning, the wind increased, and we had all hands at work to strike our top-masts and make every thing snug and close, that the ship might ride as easy as possible. By noon the sea went very high indeed, and our ship rid forecastle in, shipped several seas, and we thought once or twice our anchor had come home; upon which our master ordered out the sheet anchor; so that we rode with two anchors a-head, and the cables vered out to the better end.[3]

By this time it blew a terrible storm indeed, and now I began to see terror and amazement in the faces even of the seamen themselves. The master, tho' vigilant to the business of preserving the ship, yet as he went in and out of his cabbin by me, I could hear him softly to himself say several times, 'Lord, be merciful to us, we shall be all lost, we shall be all undone'; and the like. During these first hurries I was stupid, lying still in my cabbin, which was in the steerage, and cannot describe my temper. I could ill re-assume the first penitence, which I had so apparently trampled upon and hardened my self against: I thought the bitterness of death had been past, and that this would be nothing too, like the first. But when the master himself came by me, as I said just now, and said we should be all lost, I was dreadfully frighted. I got up out of my cabbin, and looked out; but such a dismal sight I never saw: the sea went mountains high, and broke upon us every three or four minutes; when I could look about, I could see nothing but distress round us. Two ships that rid near us we found had cut their masts by the board, being deep loaden; and our men cry'd out that a ship which rid about a mile a-head of us was foundered. Two more ships, being driven from their anchors, were run out of the roads to sea at all adventures,⁴ and that with not a mast standing. The light ships fared the best, as not so much labouring in the sea; but two or three of them drove, and came close by us, running away with only their sprit-sail out before the wind.

Towards evening the mate and boat-swain begged the master of our ship to let them cut away the foremast, which he was very unwilling to: but the boat-swain protesting to him that if he did not, the ship would founder, he consented; and when they had cut away the foremast, the main-mast stood so loose, and shook the ship so much, they were obliged to cut her away also, and make a clear deck.

Any one may judge what a condition I must be in at all this, who was but a young sailor, and who had been in such a fright before at but a little. But if I can express at this distance the thoughts I had about me at that time, I was in tenfold more horror of mind upon account of my former convictions, and the having returned from them to the resolutions I had wickedly taken at first, than I was at death it self; and these, added to the terror of the storm, put me into such a condition, that I can by no words describe it. But the worst was not come yet; the storm continued with such fury, that the seamen themselves acknowledged they had never known a worse. We had a good ship, but she was deep loaden, and wallowed in the sea, that the seamen every now and then cried out she would founder. It was my advantage in one respect, that I did not know what they meant by 'founder' till I enquired. However, the storm was so violent, that I saw what is not often seen, the master, the boat-swain, and some others more sensible than the rest, at their prayers, and expecting every moment when the ship would go to the bottom. In the middle of the night, and under all the rest of our distresses, one of the men that had been down on purpose to see, cried out we had sprung a leak; another said there was four foot water in the hold. Then all hands were called to the pump. At that very word my heart, as I thought, died within me, and I fell backwards upon the side of my bed where I sat, into the cabbin. However, the men roused me, and told me that I that was able to do nothing before, was as well able to pump as another; at which I stirred up and went to the pump, and worked very heartily. While this was doing, the master, seeing some light colliers, who not able to ride out the storm, were obliged to slip and run away to sea and would come near us, ordered to fire a gun as a signal of distress. I, who knew nothing what that meant, was so surprised that I thought the ship had broke, or some dreadful thing had happened. In a word, I was so surprised that I fell down in a swoon. As this was a time when every body had his own life to think of, no body minded me, or what was become of me; but another man stept up to the pump, and thrusting me aside with his foot, let me lye, thinking I had been dead; and it was a great while before I came to my self.

We worked on, but the water encreasing in the hold, it was apparent that the ship would founder, and tho' the storm began to abate a little, yet as it was not possible she could swim till we might run into a port, so the master continued firing guns for help; and a light ship who had rid it out just a head of us ventured a boat out to help us. It was with the utmost hazard the boat came near us, but it was impossible for us to get on board, or for the boat to lie near the ship side, till at last, the men rowing very heartily and venturing their lives to save ours, our men cast them a rope over the stern with a buoy to it, and then vered it out a great length, which they after great labour and hazard took hold of, and we halled them close under our stern and got all into their boat. It was to no purpose for them or us after we were in the boat to think of reaching to their own ship, so all agreed to let her drive and only to pull her in towards shore as much as we could, and our master promised them that if the boat was staved upon shore he would make it good to their master; so partly rowing and partly driving, our boat bent away to the norward, sloaping towards the shore almost as far as Winterton Ness.

We were not much more than a quarter of an hour out of our ship but we saw her sink, and then I understood for the first time what was meant by a ship foundering in the sea. I must acknowledge I had hardly eyes to look up when the seamen told me she was sinking; for from that moment they rather put me into the boat than that I might be said to go in, my heart was as it were dead within me, partly with fright, partly with horror of mind and the thoughts of what was yet before me.

While we were in this condition, the men yet labouring at the oar to bring the boat near the shore, we could see, when, our boat mounting the waves, we were able to see the shore, a great many people running along the shore to assist us when we should come near, but we made but slow way towards the shore, nor were we able to reach the shore, till being past the light-house at Winterton, the shore falls off to the westward towards Cromer, and so the land broke off a little the violence of the wind. Here we got in, and, tho' not without much difficulty, got all safe on shore, and walked afterwards on foot to Yarmouth, where, as unfortunate men, we were used with great humanity as well by the magistrates of the town, who assigned us good quarters, as by particular merchants and owners of ships, and had money given us sufficient to carry us either to London or back to Hull, as we thought fit.

Had I now had the sense to have gone back to Hull, and have gone home, I had been happy, and my father, an emblem of our

Blessed Saviour's parable, had even killed the fatted calf for me; for hearing the ship I went away in was cast away in Yarmouth road, it was a great while before he had any assurance that I was not drowned.

But my ill fate pushed me on now with an obstinacy that nothing could resist; and tho' I had several times loud calls from my reason and my more composed judgment to go home, yet I had no power to do it. I know not what to call this, nor will I urge that it is a secret overruling decree that hurries us on to be the instruments of our own destruction, even tho' it be before us, and that we rush upon it with our eyes open. Certainly nothing but some such decreed unavoidable misery attending, and which it was impossible for me to escape, could have pushed me forward against the calm reasonings and perswasions of my most retired thoughts, and against two such visible instructions as I had met with in my first attempt.

My comrade, who had helped to harden me before, and who was the master's son, was now less forward than I; the first time he spoke to me after we were at Yarmouth, which was not till two or three days, for we were separated in the town to several quarters; I say, the first time he saw me, it appeared his tone was altered, and looking very melancholy and shaking his head, asked me how I did, and telling his father who I was, and how I had come this voyage only for a trial in order to go farther abroad; his father turning to me with a very grave and concerned tone, 'Young man,' says he, 'you ought never to go to sea any more, you ought to take this for a plain and visible token that you are not to be a seafaring man.' 'Why, sir,' said I, 'will you go to sea no more?' 'That is another case,' said he, 'it is my calling, and therefore my duty; but as you made this voyage for a trial, you see what a taste Heaven has given you of what you are to expect if you persist; perhaps this is all befallen us on your account, like Jonah in the ship of Tarshish. Pray,' continues he, 'what are you? and on what account did you go to sea?' Upon that I told him some of my story; at the end of which he burst out with a strange kind of passion. 'What had I done,' says he, 'that such an unhappy wretch should come into my ship? I would not set my foot in the same ship with thee again for a thousand pounds.'

This indeed was, as I said, an excursion of his spirits which were yet agitated by the sense of his loss, and was farther than he could have authority to go. However he afterwards talked very gravely to me, exhorted me to go back to my father, and not tempt Providence to my ruine; told me I might see a visible hand of Heaven against me, 'and, young man,' said he, 'depend upon it, if you do not go back, where-ever you go, you will meet with nothing but disasters and disappointments till your father's words are fulfilled upon you.'

We parted soon after, for I made him little answer, and I saw him no more; which way he went, I know not. As for me, having some money in my pocket, I travelled to London by land; and there, as well as on the road, had many struggles with my self, what course of life I should take, and whether I should go home or go to sea.

As to going home, shame opposed the best motions that offered to my thoughts; and it immediately occurred to me how I should be laughed at among the neighbours, and should be ashamed to see, not my father and mother only, but even every body else; from whence I have since often observed, how incongruous and irrational the common temper of mankind is, especially of youth, to that reason which ought to guide them in such cases, viz. that they are not ashamed to sin, and yet are ashamed to repent; not ashamed of the action for which they ought justly to be esteemed fools, but are ashamed of the returning, which only can make them be esteemed wise men.

In this state of life, however, I remained some time, uncertain what measures to take, and what course of life to lead. An irresistible reluctance continued to going home; and as I stayed awhile, the remembrance of the distress I had been in wore off; and as that abated, the little motion I had in my desires to a return wore off with it, till at last I quite lay'd aside the thoughts of it, and lookt out for a voyage.

That evil influence which carryed me first away from my father's house, that hurried me into the wild and indigested notion of raising my fortune, and that imprest those conceits so forcibly upon me, as to make me deaf to all good advice, and to the entreaties and even command of my father; I say the same influence, whatever it was, presented the most unfortunate of all enterprises to my view; and I went on board a vessel bound to the coast of Africa; or, as our sailors vulgarly call it, a voyage to Guinea.

It was my great misfortune that in all these adventures I did not ship my self as a sailor; whereby, tho' I might indeed have workt a little harder than ordinary, yet at the same time I had learned the duty and office of a fore-mast man; and in time might have qualified my self for a mate or lieutenant, if not for a master. But as it was always my fate to choose for the worse, so I did here; for having money in my pocket, and good cloaths upon my back, I would always go on board in the habit of a gentleman; and so I neither had any business in the ship, or learned to do any.

It was my lot first of all to fall into pretty good company in London, which does not always happen to such loose and un-guided young fellows as I then was; the devil generally not omitting to lay some snare for them very early; but it was not so with me. I first fell acquainted with the master of a ship who had been on the coast of Guinea, and who, having had very good success there, was resolved to go again; and who, taking a fancy to my conversation, which was not at all disagreeable at that time, hearing me say I had a mind to see the world, told me if I wou'd go the voyage with him I should be at no expence; I should be his mess-mate and his companion, and if I could carry any thing with me, I should have all the advantage of it that the trade would admit; and perhaps I might meet with some en-couragement.

I embraced the offer, and entring into a strict friendship with this captain, who was an honest and plain-dealing man, I went the voyage with him, and carried a small adventure with me, which by the disinterested honesty of my friend the captain I increased very considerably; for I carried about 40l. in such toys and trifles as the captain directed me to buy. This 40l. I had mustered together by the assistance of some of my relations whom I corresponded with, and who, I believe, got my father, or at least my mother, to contribute so much as that to my first adventure.

This was the only voyage which I may say was successful in all my adventures, and which I owe to the integrity and honesty of my friend the captain, under whom also I got a competent knowledge of the mathematicks and the rules of navigation, learned how to keep an account of the ship's course, take an observation, and in short, to understand some things that were needful to be understood by a sailor: for, as he took delight to introduce me, I took delight to learn; and, in a word, this voyage made me both a sailor and a merchant; for I brought home 5 L. 9 ounces of gold dust for my adventure, which yielded me in London at my return almost 300l., and this filled me with those aspiring thoughts which have since so compleated my ruin.

Yet even in this voyage I had my misfortunes too; particularly, that I was continually sick, being thrown into a violent calenture[5] by the excessive heat of the climate; our principal trading being upon the coast, from the latitude of 15 degrees north even to the line it self.

I was now set up for a Guiney trader; and my friend, to my great misfortune, dying soon after his arrival, I resolved to go the same voyage again, and I embarked in the same vessel with one who was his mate in the former voyage, and had now got the command of the ship. This was the unhappiest voyage that ever man made; for tho' I did not carry quite 100l. of my new gained wealth, so that I had 200 left, and which I lodged with my friend's widow, who was very just to me, yet I fell into terrible misfortunes in this voyage; and the first was this, viz. Our ship making her course towards the Canary Islands, or rather between those islands and the African shore, was surprised in the grey of the morning by a Turkish rover of Sallee,[6] who gave chase to us with all the sail she could make. We crowded also as much canvass as our yards would spread, or our masts carry, to have got clear; but finding the pirate gained upon us and would certainly come up with us in a few hours, we prepared to fight; our ship having 12 guns, and the rogue 18. About three in the afternoon he came up with us, and bringing to by mistake, just athwart our quarter, instead of athwart our stern, as he intended, we brought 8 of our guns to bear on that side, and poured in a broadside upon him, which made him sheer off again, after returning our fire, and pouring in also his small shot from near 200 men which he had on board. However, we had not a man touched, all our men keeping close. He prepared to attack us again, and we to defend our selves; but laying us on board the next time upon our other quarter, he entred 60 men upon our decks, who immediately fell to cutting and hacking the decks and rigging. We ply'd them with small-shot, half-pikes, powderchests,[7] and such like, and cleared our deck of them twice. However, to cut short this melancholly part of our story, our ship being disabled, and three of our men killed, and eight wounded, we were obliged to yield, and were carry'd all prisoners into Sallee, a port belonging to the Moors.

The usage I had there was not so dreadful as at first I apprehended, nor was I carried up the country to the emperor's court, as the rest of our men were, but I was kept by the captain of the rover as his proper prize, and made his slave, being young and nimble and fit for his business. At this surprising change of my circumstances from a merchant to a miserable slave, I was perfectly overwhelmed; and now I looked back upon my father's prophetick discourse to me, that I should be miserable, and have none to relieve me, which I thought was now so effectually brought to pass that it could not be worse; that now the hand of Heaven had overtaken me, and I was undone without redemption. But alas! this was but a taste of the misery I was to go thro', as will appear in the sequel of this story.

As my new patron or master had taken me home to his house, so I was in hopes that he would take me with him when he went to sea again, believing that it would some time or other be his fate to be taken by a Spanish or Portugal man of war; and that then I should be set at liberty. But this hope of mine was soon taken away; for when he went to sea, he left me on shoar to look after his little garden, and do the common drudgery of slaves about his house; and when he came home again from his cruise, he ordered me to lye in the cabbin to look after the ship.

Here I meditated nothing but my escape, and what method I might take to effect it, but found no way that had the least probability in it. Nothing presented to make the supposition of it rational; for I had no body to communicate it to, that would embark with me; no fellow-slave, no Englishman, Irishman, or Scotsman there but my self; so that for two years, tho' I often pleased my self with the imagination, yet I never had the least encouraging prospect of putting it in practice.

After about two years an odd circumstance presented it self, which put the old thought of making some attempt for my liberty again in my head. My patron lying at home longer than usual, without fitting out his ship (which, as I heard, was for want of money), he used constantly, once or twice a week, sometimes oftener, if the weather was fair, to take the ship's pinnace, and go out into the road a-fishing; and as he always took me and a young Maresco with him to row the boat, we made him very merry, and I proved very dexterous in catching fish; insomuch that sometimes he would send me with a Moor, one of his kinsmen, and the youth, the Maresco as they called him, to catch a dish of fish for him.

It happened one time, that going a fishing in a stark calm morning, a fog rose so thick, that tho' we were not half a league from the shoar, we lost sight of it; and rowing we knew not whither or which way, we laboured all day and all the next night, and when the morning came we found we had pulled off to sea instead of pulling in for the shore, and that we were at least two leagues from the shoar. However, we got well in again, tho' with a great deal of labour, and some danger; for the wind began to blow pretty fresh in the morning; but particularly we were all very hungry.

But our patron, warned by this disaster, resolved to take more care of himself for the future; and having lying by him the long-boat of our English ship they had taken, he resolved he would not go a fishing any more without a compass and some provision; so he ordered the carpenter of his ship, who also was an English slave, to build a little state-room or cabin in the middle of the long boat, like that of a barge, with a place to stand behind it to steer and hale home the main-sheet, and room before for a hand or two to stand and work the sails; she sailed with that we call a shoulder of mutton sail; and the boom gibed over the top of the cabbin, which lay very snug and low, and had in it room for him to lye, with a slave or two, and a table to eat on, with some small lockers to put in some bottles of such liquor as he thought fit to drink; [and] particularly his bread, rice, and coffee.

We went frequently out with this boat a fishing, and as I was most dextrous to catch fish for him, he never went without me. It happened that he had appointed to go out in this boat, either for pleasure or for fish, with two or three Moors of some distinction in that place, and for whom he had provided extraordinarily; and had therefore sent on board the boat, over night, a larger store of provisions than ordinary; and had ordered me to get ready three fuzees with powder and shot, which were on board his ship; for that they designed some sport of fowling as well as fishing.

I got all things ready as he had directed, and waited the next morning with the boat, washed clean, her antient and pendants out,[8] and every thing to accommodate his guests; when by and by my patroon came on board alone, and told me his guests had put off going, upon some business that fell out, and ordered me with the man and boy, as usual, to go out with the boat and catch them some fish, for that his friends were to sup at his house; and commanded that as soon as I had got some fish I should bring it home to his house; all which I prepared to do.

This moment my former notions of deliverance darted into my thoughts, for now I found I was like to have a little ship at my command; and my master being gone, I prepared to furnish my self, not for a fishing business, but for a voyage; tho' I knew not, neither did I so much as consider whither I should steer; for any where to get out of that place was my way.

My first contrivance was to make a pretence to speak to this Moor, to get something for our subsistance on board; for I told him we must not presume to eat of our patroon's bread; he said, that was true; so he brought a large basket of rusk or bisket of their kind, and three jarrs with fresh water into the boat; I knew where my patroon's case of bottles stood,[9] which it was evident by the make were taken out of some English prize; and I conveyed them into the boat while the Moor was on shoar, as if they had been there before, for our master: I conveyed also a great lump of bees-wax into the boat, which weighed above half a hundred weight, with a parcel of twine or thread, a hatchet, a saw and a hammer, all which were of great use to us afterwards;

especially the wax to make candles. Another trick I try'd upon him, which he innocently come into also; his name was Ismael, who they call Muly or Moely; so I called to him, 'Moely,' said I, 'our patroon's guns are on board the boat, can you not get a little powder and shot, it may be we may kill some alcamies (a fowl like our curlieus) for our selves, for I know he keeps the gunner's stores in the ship?' 'Yes,' says he, 'I'll bring some,' and accordingly he brought a great leather pouch which held about a pound and half of powder, or rather more; and another with shot, that had five or six pound, with some bullets; and put all into the boat. At the same time I had found some powder of my master's in the great cabbin, with which I filled one of the large bottles in the case, which was almost empty; pouring what was in it into another: and thus furnished with every thing needful, we sailed out of the port to fish. The castle which is at the entrance of the port knew who we were, and took no notice of us; and we were not above a mile out of the port before we haled in our sail and set us down to fish. The wind blew from the N.N.E., which was contrary to my desire; for had it blown southerly I had been sure to have made the coast of Spain, and at least reacht to the bay of Cadiz; but my resolutions were, blow which way it would, I would be gone from that horrid place where I was, and leave the rest to fate.

After we had fisht some time and catcht nothing, for when I had fish on my hook, I would not pull them up, that he might not see them; I said to the Moor, 'This will not do, our master will not be thus served, we must stand farther off.' He, thinking no harm, agreed, and being in the head of the boat set the sails; and as I had the helm I run the boat out a league farther, and then brought her too as if I would fish; when giving the boy the helm, I stept forward to where the Moor was, and making as if I stoopt for something behind him, I took him by surprize with my arm under his twist,[10] and tost him clear over-board into the sea; he rise immediately, for he swam like a cork, and called to me, begged to be taken in, told me he would go all over the world with me; he swam so strong after the boat that he would have reacht me very quickly, there being but little wind; upon which I stept into the cabbin, and fetching one of the fowling-pieces, I presented it at him, and told him I had done him no hurt, and if he would be quiet I would do him none; 'but,' said I, 'you swim well enough to reach to the shoar, and the sea is calm, make the best of your way to shoar and I will do you no harm, but if you come near the boat I'll shoot you thro' the head; for I am resolved to have my liberty'; so he turned himself about and swam for the shoar, and I make no doubt but he reacht it with ease, for he was an excellent swimmer.

I could ha' been content to ha' taken this Moor with me, and ha' drowned the boy, but there was no venturing to trust him. When he was gone I turned to the boy, who they called Xury, and said to him, 'Xury, if you will be faithful to me I'll make you a great man, but if you will not stroak your face to be true to me,' that is, swear by Mahomet and his father's beard, 'I must throw you into the sea too.' The boy smiled in my face and spoke so innocently that I could not mistrust him; and swore to be faithful to me, and go all over the world with me.

While I was in view of the Moor that was swimming, I stood out directly to sea with the boat, rather stretching to windward, that they might think me gone towards the Straits-mouth (as indeed any one that had been in their wits must ha' been supposed to do), for who would ha' supposed we were saild on to the southward to the truly Barbarian coast, where whole nations of negroes were sure to surround us with their canoes, and destroy us; where we could ne'er once go on shoar but we should be devoured by savage beasts, or more merciless savages of humane kind?

But as soon as it grew dusk in the evening, I changed my course, and steered directly south and by east, bending my course a little toward the east, that I might keep in with the shoar; and having a fair fresh gale of wind, and a smooth quiet sea, I made such sail that I believe by the next day at three a clock in the afternoon, when I first made the land, I could not be less than 150 miles south of Sallee; quite beyond the Emperor of Morocco's dominions, or indeed of any other king thereabouts, for we saw no people.

Yet such was the fright I had taken at the Moors, and the dreadful apprehensions I had of falling into their hands, that I would not stop, or go on shoar, or come to an anchor (the wind continuing fair), 'till I had sailed in that manner five days; and then the wind shifting to the southward, I concluded also that if any of our vessels were in chase of me, they also would now give over; so I ventured to make to the coast, and came to an anchor in the mouth of a little river, I knew not what, or where; neither what latitude, what country, what nations, or what river : I neither saw, or desired to see, any people, the principal thing I wanted was fresh water. We came into this creek in the evening, resolving to swim on shoar as soon as it was dark, and discover the country; but as soon as it was quite dark, we heard such dreadful noises of the barking, roaring, and howling of wild creatures, of we knew not what kinds, that the poor boy was ready to die with fear, and beg'd of me not to go shoar till day. 'Well, Xury,' said I, 'then I won't, but it may be we may see men by day, who will be as bad to us as those lyons.' 'Then we give them the shoot gun,' says Xury, laughing, 'make them run wey'; such English Xury spoke by conversing among us slaves. However, I was glad to see the boy so cheerful, and I gave him a dram (out of our patroon's case of bottles) to chear him up. After all, Xury's advice was good, and I took it. We dropt our little anchor and lay still all night; I say still, for we slept none! for in two or three hours we saw vast great creatures (we knew not what to call them) of many sorts, come down to the sea-shoar and run into the water, wallowing and washing themselves for the pleasure of cooling themselves; and they made such hideous howlings and yellings, that I never indeed heard the like.

Xury was dreadfully frighted, and indeed so was I too; but we were both more frightened when we heard one of these mighty creatures come swimming towards our boat; we could not see him, but we might hear him by his blowing to be a monstrous, huge, and furious beast; Xury said it was a lyon, and it might be so for ought I know; but poor Xury cryed to me to weigh anchor and row away. 'No,' says I, 'Xury, we can slip our cable with the buoy to it and go off to sea, they cannot follow us far.' I had no sooner said so, but I perceived the creature (whatever it was) within two oars' length, which something surprized me; however, I immediately stept to the cabbin-door, and taking up my gun fired at him, upon which he immediately turned about and swam towards the shoar again.

But it is impossible to describe the horrible noises, and hideous cryes and howlings, that were raised, as well upon the edge of the shoar as higher within the country, upon the noise or report of the gun, a thing I have some reason to believe those creatures had never heard before. This convinced me that there was no going on shoar for us in the night upon that coast, and how to venture on shoar in the day was another question too; for to have fallen into the hands of any of the savages, had been as bad as to have fallen into the hands of lyons and tygers;[11] at least we were equally apprehensive of the danger of it.

Be that as it would, we were obliged to go on shoar somewhere or other for water, for we had not a pint left in the boat; when or where to get to it was the point. Xury said, if I would let him go on shoar with one of the jarrs, he would find if there was any water and bring some to me. I asked him why he would go; why I should not go and he stay in the boat; the boy answered with so much affection that made me love him ever after. Says he, 'If wild mans come, they eat me, you go wey.' 'Well, Xury,' said I, 'we will both go, and if the wild mans come we will kill them, they shall eat neither of us.' So I gave Xury a piece of rusk-bread to eat and a dram out of our patroon's case of bottles which I mentioned before; and we haled the boat in as near the shoar as we thought was proper, and so waded on shoar, carrying nothing but our arms and two jarrs for water.

I did not care to go out of sight of the boat, fearing the coming of canoes with savages down the river; but the boy seeing a low place about a mile up the country rambled to it; and by and by I saw him come running towards me. I thought he was pursued by some savage, or frighted with some wild beast, and I run forward towards him to help him, but when I came nearer to him, I saw something hanging over his shoulders which was a creature that he had shot, like a hare but different in colour, and longer legs; however, we were very glad of it, and it was very good meat; but the great joy that poor Xury came with, was to tell me he had found good water and seen no wild mans.

But we found afterwards that we need not take such pains for

water, for a little higher up the creek where we were, we found
the water fresh when the tide was out, which flowed but a little
way up; so we filled our jarrs and feasted on the hare we had
killed, and prepared to go on our way, having seen no foot-steps
of any humane creature in that part of the country.

As I had been one voyage to this coast before, I knew very well
that the islands of the Canaries, and the Cape de Verd Islands
also, lay not far off from the coast. But as I had no instruments
to take an observation to know what latitude we were in, and did
not exactly know, or at least remember, what latitude they were
in, I knew not where to look for them, or when to stand off to sea
towards them; otherwise I might now easily have found some of
these islands. But my hope was, that if I stood along this coast till
I came to that part where the English traded, I should find some
of their vessels upon their usual design of trade, that would
relieve and take us in.

By the best of my calculation, that place where I now was,
must be that country which, lying between the Emperor of
Morocco's dominions and the negro's, lies wast and uninhabited,
except by wild beasts; the negroes having abandoned it and gone
farther south for fear of the Moors; and the Moors not thinking
it worth inhabiting, by reason of its barrenness; and indeed both
forsaking it because of the prodigious numbers of tygers, lyons,
leopards, and other furious creatures which harbour there; so
that the Moors use it for their hunting only, where they go
like an army, two or three thousand men at a time; and indeed
for near an hundred miles together upon this coast, we saw
nothing but a vast uninhabited country by day, and heard
nothing but howlings and roaring of wild beasts by night.

Once or twice in the day time I thought I saw the Pico of
Teneriffe,[12] being the high top of the mountain Teneriffe in the
Canaries, and had a great mind to venture out in hopes of reaching thither; but having tried twice I was forced in again by
contrary winds, the sea also going too high for my little vessel,
so I resolved to pursue my first design and keep along the shoar.

Several times I was obliged to land for fresh water after we had
left this place; and once in particular, being early in the morning,
we came to an anchor under a little point of land which was

pretty high, and the tide beginning to flow, we lay still to go farther in; Xury, whose eyes were more about him than it seems mine were, calls softly to me, and tells me that we had best go farther off the shoar; 'for,' says he, 'look, yonder lies a dreadful monster on the side of that hillock fast asleep.' I looked where he pointed, and saw a dreadful monster indeed, for it was a terrible great lyon that lay on the side of the shoar, under the shade of a piece of the hill that hung as it were a little over him. 'Xury,' says I, 'you shall go on shoar and kill him.' Xury looked frighted, and said, 'Me kill ! he eat me at one mouth'; one mouth-ful he meant; however, I said no more to the boy, but bad him lye still, and I took our biggest gun, which was almost musquet-bore, and loaded it with a good charge of powder and with two slugs, and laid it down; then I loaded another gun with two bullets, and a third, for we had three pieces, I loaded with five smaller bullets. I took the best aim I could with the first piece to have shot him into the head, but he lay so with his leg raised a little above his nose, that the slugs hit his leg about the knee, and broke the bone. He started up growling at first, but finding his leg broke fell down again, and then got up upon three legs and gave the most hideous roar that ever I heard. I was a little surprized that I had not hit him on the head; however, I took up the second piece immediately, and tho' he began to move off, fired again, and shot him into the head, and had the pleasure to see him drop, and make but little noise, but lay struggling for life. Then Xury took heart, and would have me let him go on shoar. 'Well, go,' said I; so the boy jumped into the water, and taking a little gun in one hand swam to the shoar with the other hand, and coming close to the creature, put the muzzle of the piece to his ear, and shot him into the head again, which dis-patched him quite.

This was game indeed to us, but this was no food, and I was very sorry to lose three charges of powder and shot upon a creature that was good for nothing to us. However, Xury said he would have some of him; so he comes on board, and asked me to give him the hatchet. 'For what, Xury?' said I. 'Me cut off his head,' said he. However, Xury could not cut off his head, but he cut off a foot and brought it with him, and it was a monstrous great one.

I bethought my self, however, that perhaps the skin of him might one way or other be of some value to us, and I resolved to take off his skin if I could. So Xury and I went to work with him; but Xury was much the better workman at it, for I knew very ill how to do it. Indeed, it took us up both the whole day, but at last we got off the hide of him, and spreading it on the top of our cabbin, the sun effectually dried it in two days' time, and it afterwards served me to lye upon.

After this stop we made on to the southward continually for ten or twelve days, living very sparing on our provisions, which began to abate very much, and going no oftner into the shoar than we were obliged to for fresh water; my design in this was to make the river Gambia or Senegall, [13] that is to say, any where about the Cape de Verd, where I was in hopes to meet with some European ship, and if I did not, I knew not what course I had to take, but to seek out for the islands, or perish there among the negroes. I knew that all the ships from Europe, which sailed either to the coast or Guiney, or to Brasil, or to the East-Indies, made this cape or those islands; and in a word, I put the whole of my fortune upon this single point, either that I must meet with some ship, or must perish.

When I had pursued this resolution about ten days longer, as I have said, I began to see that the land was inhabited, and in two or three places as we sailed by, we saw people stand upon the shoar to look at us; we could also perceive they were quite black and stark-naked. I was once inclined to ha' gone on shoar to them; but Xury was my better councellor, and said to me, 'No go, no go'; however, I haled in nearer the shoar that I might talk to them, and I found they run along the shoar by me a good way; I observed they had no weapons in their hands, except one who had a long slender stick, which Xury said was a lance, and that they would throw them a great way with good aim; so I kept at a distance, but talked with them by signs as well as I could, and particularly made signs for some thing to eat. They beckoned to me to stop my boat, and that they would fetch me some meat; upon this I lowered the top of my sail and lay by, and two of them run up into the country, and in less than half an hour came back and brought with them two pieces of dry flesh and some corn, such as is the produce of their country, but we neither knew what the one or the other was; however, we were willing to accept it, but how to come at it was our next dispute, for I was not for venturing on shore to them, and they were as much afraid of us; but they took a safe way for us all, for they brought it to the shore and laid it down, and went and stood a great way off till we fetched it on board, and then came close to us again.

We made signs of thanks to them, for we had nothing to make them amends; but an opportunity offered that very instant to oblige them wonderfully, for while we were lying by the shore, came two mighty creatures, one pursuing the other (as we took it) with great fury, from the mountains towards the sea; whether it was the male pursuing the female, or whether they were in sport or in rage, we could not tell, any more than we could tell whether it was usual or strange, but I believe it was the latter; because in the first place, those ravenous creatures seldom appear but in the night; and in the second place, we found the people terribly frighted, especially the women. The man that had the lance or dart did not fly from them, but the rest did; however, as the two creatures ran directly into the water, they did not seem to offer to fall upon any of the negroes, but plunged themselves into the sea and swam about as if they had come for their diversion; at last one of them began to come nearer our boat than at first I expected, but I lay ready for him, for I had loaded my gun with all possible expedition, and bad Xury load both the others; as soon as he came fairly within my reach, I fired, and shot him directly into the head; immediately he sunk down into the water, but rose instantly and plunged up and down as if he was struggling for life; and so indeed he was. He immediately made to the shore, but between the wound, which was his mortal hurt, and the strangling of the water, he dyed just before he reached the shore.

It is impossible to express the astonishment of these poor creatures at the noise and the fire of my gun; some of them were even ready to dye for fear, and fell down as dead with the very terror. But when they saw the creature dead and sunk in the water, and that I made signs to them to come to the shore, they took heart and came to the shore and began to search for the creature. I found him by his blood staining the water, and by the help of a rope which I slung round him and gave the negroes to hawl, they drag'd him on shore, and found that it was a most curious leopard, spotted and fine to an admirable degree, and the negroes held up their hands with admiration to think what it was I had killed him with.

The other creature, frighted with the flash of fire and the noise of the gun, swam on shore, and ran up directly to the mountains from whence they came, nor could I at that distance know what it was. I found quickly the negroes were for eating the flesh of this creature, so I was willing to have them take it as a favour from me, which when I made signs to them that they might take him, they were very thankful for, immediately they fell to work with him, and tho' they had no knife, yet with a sharpened piece of wood they took off his skin as readily and much more readily than we could have done with a knife; they offered me some of the flesh, which I declined, making as if I would give it them, but made signs for the skin, which they gave me very freely, and brought me a great deal more of their provision, which tho' I did not understand, yet I accepted; then made signs to them for some water, and held out one of my jarrs to them, turning it bottom upward, to shew that it was empty, and that I wanted to have it filled. They called immediately to some of their friends, and there came two women and brought a great vessel made of earth, and burnt as I suppose in the sun; this they set down for me, as before, and I sent Xury on shore with my jarrs, and filled them all three. The women were as stark naked as the men.

I was now furnished with roots and corn, such as it was, and water, and leaving my friendly negroes, I made forward for about eleven days more without offering to go near the shoar, till I saw the land run out a great length into the sea, at about the distance of four or five leagues before me, and the sea being very calm I kept a large offing to make this point; at length, doubling the point at about two leagues from the land, I saw plainly land on the other side to seaward; then I concluded, as it was most certain indeed, that this was the Cape de Verd, and those the islands called from thence Cape de Verd Islands. However, they were at a great distance, and I could not tell what I had best to do, for if

I should be taken with a fresh of wind I might neither reach one or other.

In this dilemma, as I was very pensive, I stept into the cabin and sat me down, Xury having the helm, when on a suddain the boy cryed out, 'Master, master, a ship with a sail,' and the foolish boy was frighted out of his wits, thinking it must needs be some of his master's ships sent to pursue us, when I knew we were gotten far enough out of their reach. I jumped out of the cabbin, and immediately saw not only the ship, but what she was, viz. that it was a Portuguese ship, and as I thought was bound to the coast of Guinea for negroes. But when I observed the course she steered, I was soon convinced they were bound some other way, and did not design to come any nearer to the shoar; upon which I stretched out to sea as much as I could, resolving to speak with them if possible.

With all the sail I could make, I found I should not be able to come in their way, but that they would be gone by, before I could make any signal to them; but after I had crowded to the utmost, and began to despair, they it seems saw me by the help of their perspective-glasses, and that it was some European boat, which as they supposed must belong to some ship that was lost, so they shortened sail to let me come up. I was encouraged with this, and as I had my patroon's antient on board, I made a waft of it to them for a signal of distress, and fired a gun, both which they saw, for they told me they saw the smoke, tho' they did not hear the gun; upon these signals they very kindly brought too, and lay by for me, and in about three hours time I came up with them.

They asked me what I was, in Portuguese, and in Spanish, and in French, but I understood none of them; but at last a Scots sailor who was on board called to me, and I answered him, and told him I was an Englishman, that I had made my escape out of slavery from the Moors at Sallee; then they bad me come on board, and very kindly took me in, and all my goods.

It was an inexpressible joy to me, that any one will believe, that I was thus delivered, as I esteemed it, from such a miserable and almost hopeless condition as I was in, and I immediately offered all I had to the captain of the ship, as a return for my deliverance; but he generously told me he would take nothing from me, but that all I had should be delivered safe to me when I came to the Brasils, 'for' says he, 'I have saved your life on no other terms than I would be glad to be saved my self, and it may one time or other be my lot to be taken up in the same condition; besides,' said he, 'when I carry you to the Brasils, so great a way from your own country, if I should take from you what you have, you will be starved there, and then I only take away what life I have given. No, no, Seignor Inglese,' says he (Mr. Englishman), 'I will carry you thither in charity, and those things will help you to buy your subsistance there and your passage home again.'

As he was charitable in his proposal, so he was just in the performance to a title, for he ordered the seaman that none should offer to touch any thing I had; then he took every thing into his own possession, and gave me back an exact inventory of them, that I might have them, even so much as my three earthen jarrs.

As to my boat, it was a very good one, and that he saw, and told me he would buy it of me for the ship's use, and asked me what I would have for it. I told him he had been so generous to me in every thing, that I could not offer to make any price of the boat, but left it entirely to him, upon which he told me he would give me a note of his hand to pay me 80 pieces of eight for it at Brasil, and when it came there, if any one offered to give more he would make it up; he offered me also 60 pieces of eight more for my boy Xury, which I was loath to take, not that I was not willing to let the captain have him, but I was very loath to sell the poor boy's liberty, who had assisted me so faithfully in procuring my own. However, when I let him know my reason, he owned it to be just, and offered me this medium,[14] that he would give the boy an obligation to set him free in ten years, if he turned Christian; upon this, and Xury saying he was willing to go to him, I let the captain have him.

We had a very good voyage to the Brasils, and arrived in the Bay de Todos los Santos, or All-Saints' Bay,[15] in about twenty-two days after. And now I was once more delivered from the most miserable of all conditions of life, and what to do next with my self I was now to consider.

The generous treatment the captain gave me, I can never enough remember; he would take nothing of me for my passage, gave me twenty ducats for the leopard's skin, and forty for the lyon's skin which I had in my boat, and caused every thing I had in the ship to be punctually delivered me, and what I was willing to sell he bought, such as the case of bottles, two of my guns, and a piece of the lump of bees-wax, for I had made candles of the rest; in a word, I made about 220 pieces of eight of all my cargo, and with this stock I went on shoar in the Brasils.

I had not been long here, but being recommended to the house of a good honest man like himself, who had an *ingenio* as they call it (that is, a plantation and a sugar-house),[16] I lived with him some time, and acquainted my self by that means with the manner of their planting and making of sugar; and seeing how well the planters lived, and how they grew rich suddenly, I resolved, if I could get licence to settle there, I would turn planter among them, resolving in the mean time to find out some way to get my money which I had left in London remitted to me. To this purpose getting a kind of letter of naturalization, I purchased as much land that was uncured as my money would reach, and formed a plan for my plantation and settlement, and such a one as might be suitable to the stock which I proposed to myself to receive from England.

I had a neighbour, a Portugueze of Lisbon, but born of English parents, whose name was Wells, and in much such circumstances as I was. I call him my neighbour, because his plantation lay next to mine, and we went on very sociably together. My stock was but low as well as his; and we rather planted for food than any thing else, for about two years. However, we began to increase, and our land began to come into order; so that the third year we planted some tobacco, and made each of us a large piece of ground ready for planting canes in the year to come; but we both wanted help, and now I found more than before, I had done wrong in parting with my boy Xury.

But alas! for me to do wrong that never did right, was no great wonder. I had no remedy but to go on; I was gotten into an employment quite remote to my genius, and directly contrary to the life I delighted in, and for which I forsook my father's house and broke thro' all his good advice; nay, I was coming into the very middle station, or upper degree of low life, which my father advised me to before; and which if I resolved to go on with, I might as well ha' staid at home, and never have fatigued my self in the world as I had done; and I used often to say to my self, I could ha' done this as well in England among my friends, as ha' gone 5,000 miles off to do it among strangers and salvages in a wilderness, and at such a distance as never to hear from any part of the world that had the least knowledge of me.

In this manner I used to look upon my condition with the utmost regret. I had no body to converse with but now and then this neighbour; no work to be done but by the labour of my hands; and I used to say I lived just like a man cast away upon some desolate island, that has no body there but himself. But how just has it been, and how should all men reflect, that when they compare their present conditions with others that are worse, Heaven may oblige them to make the exchange, and be convinced of their former felicity by their experience; I say, how just has it been, that the truly solitary life I reflected on in an island of meer desolation should be my lot, who had so often unjustly compared it with the life which I then led, in which had I continued, I had in all probability been exceeding prosperous and rich.

I was in some degree settled in my measures for carrying on the plantation, before my kind friend, the captain of the ship that took me up at sea, went back; for the ship remained there in providing his loading, and preparing for his voyage, near three months, when telling him what little stock I had left behind me in London, he gave me this friendly and sincere advice: 'Seignior Inglese,' says he, for so he always called me, 'if you will give me letters, and a procuration here in form to me, with orders to the person who has your money in London, to send your effects to Lisbon, to such persons as I shall direct, and in such goods as are proper for this country, I will bring you the produce of them, God willing, at my return; but since human affairs are all subject to changes and disasters, I would have you give orders but for one hundred pounds sterling, which you say is half your stock, and let the hazard be run for the first; so that if it come safe, you may order the rest the same way; and if it miscarry, you may have the other half to have recourse to for your supply.'

This was so wholesom advice, and looked so friendly, that I could not but be convinced it was the best course I could take; so I accordingly prepared letters to the gentlewoman with whom I had left my money, and a procuration to the Portuguese captain, as he desired.

I wrote the English captain's widow a full account of all my adventures, my slavery, escape, and how I had met with the Portugal captain at sea, the humanity of his behaviour, and in what condition I was now in, with all other necessary directions for my supply; and when this honest captain came to Lisbon, he found means by some of the English merchants there, to send over not the order only, but a full account of my story to a merchant at London, who represented it effectually to her; whereupon she not only delivered the money, but out of her own pocket sent the Portugal captain a very handsom present for his humanity and charity to me.

The merchant in London, vesting this hundred pounds in English goods, such as the captain had writ for, sent them directly to him at Lisbon, and he brought them all safe to me to the Brasils, among which, without my direction (for I was too young in my business to think of them), he had taken care to have all sorts of tools, iron-work, and utensils necessary for my plantation, and which were of great use to me.

When this cargo arrived, I thought my fortunes made, for I was surprised with the joy of it; and my good steward the captain had laid out the five pounds which my friend had sent him for a present for himself, to purchase and bring me over a servant under bond for six years service, and would not accept of any consideration, except a little tobacco, which I would have him accept, being of my own produce.

Neither was this all; but my goods being all English manufactures, such as cloath, stuffs, bays, and things particularly valuable and desirable in the country, I found means to sell them to a very great advantage; so that I might say I had more than four times the value of my first cargo, and was now infinitely beyond my poor neighbour, I mean in the advancement of my plantation; for the first thing I did, I bought me a negro slave, and an European servant also; I mean another besides that which the captain brought me from Lisbon.

But as abused prosperity is oftentimes made the very means of our greatest adversity, so was it with me. I went on the next year with great success in my plantation. I raised fifty great rolls of tobacco on my own ground, more than I had disposed of for necessaries among my neighbours; and these fifty rolls being each of above a 100 wt. were well cured and laid by against the return of the fleet from Lisbon: and now increasing in business and in wealth, my head began to be full of projects and undertakings beyond my reach; such as are indeed often the ruine of the best heads in business.

Had I continued in the station I was now in, I had room for all the happy things to have yet befallen me, for which my father so earnestly recommended a quiet retired life, and of which he had so sensibly described the middle station of life to be full of; but other things attended me, and I was still to be the wilful agent of all my own miseries; and particularly to encrease my fault and double the reflections upon my self, which in my future sorrows I should have leisure to make; all these miscarriages were procured by my apparent obstinate adhering to my foolish inclination of wandring abroad and pursuing that inclination, in contradiction to the clearest views of doing my self good in a fair and plain pursuit of those prospects and those measures of life which nature and Providence concurred to present me with, and to make my duty.

As I had once done thus in my breaking away from my parents, so I could not be content now, but I must go and leave the happy view I had of being a rich and thriving man in my new plantation, only to pursue a rash and immoderate desire of rising faster than the nature of the thing admitted; and thus I cast my self down again into the deepest gulph of human misery that ever man fell into, or perhaps could be consistent with life and a state of health in the world.

To come then by the just degrees to the particulars of this part of my story; you may suppose, that having now lived almost four years in the Brasils, and beginning to thrive and prosper very well upon my plantation, I had not only learned the language, but had contracted acquaintance and friendship among my fellow-planters, as well as among the merchants at St. Salvadore, which was our port; and that in my discourses among them, I had frequently given them an account of my two voyages to the coast of Guinea, the manner of trading with the negroes there, and how easy it was to purchase upon the coast, for trifles, such as beads, toys, knives, scissars, hatchets, bits of glass, and the like, not only gold dust, Guinea grains, elephants teeth, &c., but negroes, for the service of the Brasils, in great numbers.

They listened always very attentively to my discourses on these heads, but especially to that part which related to the buying negroes, which was a trade at that time not only not far entred into, but as far as it was, had been carried on by the assientoes, or permission of the kings of Spain and Portugal, and engrossed in the publick, so that few negroes were brought, and those excessive dear.

It happened, being in company with some merchants and planters of my acquaintance, and talking of those things very earnestly, three of them came to me the next morning, and told me they had been musing very much upon what I had discoursed with them of, the last night, and they came to make a secret proposal to me; and after enjoining me secrecy, they told me that they had a mind to fit out a ship to go to Guinea, that they had all plantations as well as I, and were straitened for nothing so much as servants; that as it was a trade that could not be carried on, because they could not publickly sell the negroes when they came home, so they desired to make but one voyage, to bring the negroes on shoar privately, and divide them among their own plantations; and in a word, the question was, whether I would go their super-cargo in the ship to manage the trading part upon the coast of Guinea. And they offered me that I should have my equal share of the negroes without providing any part of the stock.

This was a fair proposal, it must be confessed, had it been made to any one that had not had a settlement and plantation of his own to look after, which was in a fair way of coming to be

very considerable, and with a good stock upon it. But for me that
was thus entered and established, and had nothing to do but go
on as I had begun for three or four years more, and to have sent
for the other hundred pound from England, and who in that
time, and with that little addition, could scarce ha' failed of being
worth three or four thousand pounds sterling, and that encreasing too; for me to think of such a voyage, was the most pre-
postorous thing that ever man in such circumstances could be
guilty of.

But I that was born to be my own destroyer, could no more
resist the offer than I could restrain my first rambling designs,
when my father's good counsel was lost upon me. In a word, I
told them I would go with all my heart, if they would undertake
to look after my plantation in my absence, and would dispose of
it to such as I should direct if I miscarry'd. This they all engaged
to do, and entred into writings or covenants to do so; and I made
a formal will, disposing of my plantation and effects, in case of
my death, making the captain of the ship that had saved my life,
as before, my universal heir, but obliging him to dispose of my
effects as I had directed in my will, one half of the produce being
to himself, and the other to be ship'd to England.

In short, I took all possible caution to preserve my effects, and
keep up my plantation; had I used half as much prudence to
have looked into my own intrest, and have made a judgment of
what I ought to have done and not to have done, I had certainly
never gone away from so prosperous an undertaking, leaving all
the probable views of a thriving circumstance, and gone upon a
voyage to sea, attended with all its common hazards; to say
nothing of the reasons I had to expect particular misfortunes to
my self.

But I was hurried on, and obeyed blindly the dictates of my
fancy rather than my reason; and accordingly the ship being
fitted out, and the cargo furnished, and all things done as by
agreement, by my partners in the voyage, I went on board in an
evil hour, the [first] of [September, 1659], being the same day
eight year that I went from my father and mother at Hull, in
order to act the rebel to their authority, and the fool to my own
interest.

Our ship was about 120 tun burthen, carried 6 guns and 14 men, besides the master, his boy, and my self; we had on board no large cargo of goods, except of such toys as were fit for our trade with the negroes, such as beads, bits of glass, shells, and odd trifles, especially little looking-glasses, knives, scissars, hatchets, and the like.

The same day I went on board we set sail, standing away to the northward upon our own coast, with design to stretch over for the Affrican coast, when they came about 10 or 12 degrees of northern latitude, which it seems was the manner of their course in those days. We had very good weather, only excessive hot, all the way upon our own coast, till we came the height of Cape St. Augustino,[17] from whence keeping farther off at sea we lost sight of land, and steered as if we was bound for the isle Fernand de Noronha,[18] holding our course N.E. by N. and leaving those isles on the east; in this course we past the line in about 12 days time, and were by our last observation in 7 degrees 22 min. northern latitude, when a violent tournado or hurricane took us quite out of our knowledge; it began from the south-east, came about to the north-west, and then settled into the north-east, from whence it blew in such a terrible manner, that for twelve days together we could do nothing but drive, and scudding away before it, let it carry us whither ever fate and the fury of the winds directed; and during these twelve days, I need not say that I expected every day to be swallowed up, nor indeed did any in the ship expect to save their lives.

In this distress, we had, besides the terror of the storm, one of our men dyed of the calenture, and one man and the boy washed over board; about the 12th day the weather abating a little, the master made an observation as well as he could, and found that he was in about 11 degrees north latitude, but that he was 22 degrees of longitude difference west from Cape St. Augustino; so that he found he was gotten upon the coast of Guinea, or the north part of Brasil, beyond the river Amozones, toward that of the river Oronoque, commonly called the Great River, and began to consult with me what course he should take, for the ship was leaky and very much disabled, and he was going directly back to the coast of Brasil.

I was positively against that, and looking over the charts of the sea-coast of America with him, we concluded there was no inhabited country for us to have recourse to till we came within the circle of the Carribee-Islands,[19] and therefore resolved to stand away for Barbadoes, which by keeping off at sea, to avoid the indraft of the bay or gulph of Mexico, we might easily perform, as we hoped, in about fifteen days sail; whereas we could not possibly make our voyage to the coast of Affrica without some assistance, both to our ship and to our selves.

With this design we changed our course and steered away N.W. by W. in order to reach some of our English islands, where I hoped for relief; but our voyage was otherwise determined, for being in the latitude of 12 deg. 18 min. a second storm came upon us, which carry'd us away with the same impetuosity westward, and drove us so out of the very way of all humane commerce, that had all our lives been saved, as to the sea, we were rather in danger of being devoured by savages than ever returning to our own country.

In this distress, the wind still blowing very hard, one of our men early in the morning cry'd out, 'Land!' and we had no sooner run out of the cabbin to look out in hopes of seeing where abouts in the world we were, but the ship struck upon a sand, and in a moment, her motion being so stopped, the sea broke over her in such a manner that we expected we should all have perished immediately, and we were immediately driven into our close quarters to shelter us from the very foam and sprye of the sea.

It is not easy for any one, who has not been in the like condition, to describe or conceive the consternation of men in such circumstances; we knew nothing where we were, or upon what land it was we were driven, whether an island or the main, whether inhabited or not inhabited; and as the rage of the wind was still great, tho' rather less than at first, we could not so much as hope to have the ship hold many minutes without breaking in pieces, unless the winds by a kind of miracle should turn immediately about. In a word, we sat looking upon one another, and expecting death every moment, and every man acting accordingly, as preparing for another world, for there was little or nothing more for us to do in this; that which was our present comfort, and all the comfort we had was, that contrary to our expectation the ship did not break yet, and that the master said the wind began to abate.

Now tho' we thought that the wind did a little abate, yet the ship having thus struck upon the sand, and sticking too fast for us to expect her getting off, we were in a dreadful condition indeed, and had nothing to do but to think of saving our lives as well as we could; we had a boat at our stern just before the storm, but she was first staved by dashing against the ship's rudder, and in the next place she broke away, and either sunk or was driven off to sea, so there was no hope from her; we had another boat on board, but how to get her off into the sea was a doubtful thing; however, there was no room to debate, for we fancy'd the ship would break in pieces every minute, and some told us she was actually broken already.

In this distress the mate of our vessel lays hold of the boat, and with the help of the rest of the men, they got her slung over the ship's side, and getting all into her, let go, and committed our selves, being eleven in number, to God's mercy and the wild sea; for tho' the storm was abated considerably, yet the sea went dreadful high upon the shore, and might well be called *Den wild Zee*, as the Dutch call the sea in a storm.

And now our case was very dismal indeed; for we all saw plainly, that the sea went so high that the boat could not live, and that we should be inevitably drowned. As to making sail, we had none, nor, if we had, could we ha' done any thing with it: so we worked at the oar towards the land, tho' with heavy hearts, like men going to execution; for we all knew that when the boat came nearer the shore, she would be dashed in a thousand pieces by the breach of the sea. However, we committed our souls to God in the most earnest manner, and the wind driving us towards the shore, we hastened our destruction with our own hands, pulling as well as we could towards land.

What the shore was, whether rock or sand, whether steep or shoal, we knew not; the only hope that could rationally give us the least shadow of expectation, was, if we might happen into some bay or gulph, or the mouth of some river, where by great chance we might have run our boat in, or got under the lee of the land, and perhaps made smooth water. But there was nothing of this appeared; but as we made nearer and nearer the shore, the land looked more frightful than the sea.

After we had rowed, or rather driven, about a league and a half, as we reckoned it, a raging wave, mountain-like, came rowling a-stern of us, and plainly bad us expect the *coup de grace*. In a word, it took us with such a fury, that it overset the boat at once; and separating us as well from the boat as from one another, gave us not time hardly to say, O God! for we were all swallowed up in a moment.

Nothing can describe the confusion of thought which I felt when I sunk into the water; for tho' I swam very well, yet I could not deliver my self from the waves so as to draw breath, till that wave having driven me, or rather carried me a vast way on towards the shore, and having spent it self, went back, and left me upon the land almost dry, but half-dead with the water I took in. I had so much presence of mind as well as breath left, that seeing my self nearer the main land than I expected, I got upon my feet, and endeavoured to make on towards the land as fast as I could, before another wave should return, and take me up again. But I soon found it was impossible to avoid it; for I saw the sea come after me as high as a great hill, and as furious as an enemy which I had no means or strength to contend with; my business was to hold my breath, and raise my self upon the water, if I could; and so by swimming to preserve my breathing, and pilot my self towards the shore, if possible; my greatest concern now being, that the sea, as it would carry me a great way towards the shore when it came on, might not carry me back again with it when it gave back towards the sea.

The wave that came upon me again, buried me at once 20 or 30 foot deep in its own body; and I could feel my self carried with a mighty force and swiftness towards the shore a very great way; but I held my breath, and assisted my self to swim still forward with all my might. I was ready to burst with holding my breath, when, as I felt my self rising up, so to my immediate relief, I found my head and hands shoot out above the surface of the water; and tho' it was not two seconds of time that I could keep my self so, yet it relieved me greatly, gave me breath and new courage. I was covered again with water a good while, but not so long but I held it out; and finding the water had spent it self, and began to return, I strook forward against the return of the waves, and felt ground again with my feet. I stood still a few moments to recover breath, and till the water went from me, and then took to my heels, and run with what strength I had farther towards the shore. But neither would this deliver me from the fury of the sea, which came pouring in after me again, and twice more I was lifted up by the waves and carried forwards as before, the shore being very flat.

The last time of these two had well near been fatal to me; for the sea having hurried me along as before, landed me, or rather dashed me against a piece of a rock, and that with such force as it left me senseless, and indeed helpless as to my own deliverance; for the blow taking my side and breast, beat the breath as it were quite out of my body; and had it returned again immediately, I must have been strangled in the water; but I recovered a little before the return of the waves, and seeing I should be covered again with the water, I resolved to hold fast by a piece of the rock, and so to hold my breath, if possible, till the wave went back; now as the waves were not so high as at first, being nearer land, I held my hold till the wave abated, and then fetch'd another run, which brought me so near the shore, that the next wave, tho' it went over me, yet did not so swallow me up as to carry me away, and the next run I took, I got to the main land, where, to my great comfort, I clambered up the clifts of the shore and sat me down upon the grass, free from danger, and quite out of the reach of the water.

I was now landed and safe on shore, and began to look up and thank God that my life was saved in a case wherein there was some minutes before scarce any room to hope. I believe it is impossible to express to the life what the extasies and transports of the soul are, when it is so saved, as I may say, out of the very grave; and I do not wonder now at that custom, viz. that when a malefactor who has the halter about his neck, is tyed up, and just going to be turned off, and has a reprieve brought to him; I say, I do not wonder that they bring a surgeon with it, to let him blood that very moment they tell him of it, that the surprise may not drive the animal spirits from the heart, and overwhelm him:

For sudden joys, like griefs, confound at first.[20]

I walked about on the shore, lifting up my hands, and my whole being, as I may say, wrapt up in the contemplation of my deliverance, making a thousand gestures and motions which I cannot describe, reflecting upon all my comrades that were drowned, and that there should not be one soul saved but my self; for, as for them, I never saw them afterwards, or any sign of them, except three of their hats, one cap, and two shoes that were not fellows.

I cast my eyes to the stranded vessel, when the breach and froth of the sea being so big, I could hardly see it, it lay so far off, and considered, Lord! how was it possible I could get on shore?

After I had solaced my mind with the comfortable part of my condition, I began to look round me to see what kind of place I was in, and what was next to be done, and I soon found my comforts abate, and that in a word I had a dreadful deliverance: for I was wet, had no clothes to shift me, nor any thing either to eat or drink to comfort me, neither did I see any prospect before me, but that of perishing with hunger, or being devoured by wild beasts; and that which was particularly afflicting to me was that I had no weapon either to hunt and kill any creature for my sustenance, or to defend my self against any other creature that might desire to kill me for theirs. In a word, I had nothing about me but a knife, a tobacco-pipe, and a little tobacco in a box; this was all my provision, and this threw me into terrible agonies of mind, that for a while I run about like a mad-man. Night coming upon me, I began with a heavy heart to consider what would be my lot if there were any ravenous beasts in that country, seeing at night they always come abroad for their prey.

All the remedy that offered to my thoughts at that time was to get up into a thick bushy tree like a firr, but thorny, which grew near me, and where I resolved to sit all night, and consider the next day what death I should dye, for as yet I saw no prospect of life; I walked about a furlong from the shore, to see if I could find any fresh water to drink, which I did, to my great joy; and having drank and put a little tobacco in my mouth to prevent hunger, I went to the tree, and getting up into it, endeavoured to place my self so, as that if I should sleep I might not fall; and having cut me a short stick, like a truncheon, for my defence, I took up my lodging, and having been excessively fatigued, I fell fast asleep and slept as comfortably as, I believe, few could have done in my condition, and found my self the most refreshed with it that I think I ever was on such an occasion.

When I waked it was broad day, the weather clear, and the storm abated, so that the sea did not rage and swell as before: but that which surprised me most was that the ship was lifted off in the night from the sand where she lay, by the swelling of the tyde, and was driven up almost as far as the rock which I first mentioned, where I had been so bruised by the dashing me against it; this being within about a mile from the shore where I was, and the ship seeming to stand upright still, I wished my self on board, that, at least, I might save some necessary things for my use.

When I came down from my apartment in the tree, I looked about me again, and the first thing I found was the boat, which lay as the wind and the sea had tossed her up upon the land, about two miles on my right hand. I walked as far as I could upon the shore to have got to her, but found a neck or inlet of water between me and the boat, which was about half a mile broad, so I came back for the present, being more intent upon getting at the ship, where I hoped to find something for my present subsistence.

A little after noon I found the sea very calm, and the tyde ebbed so far out that I could come within a quarter of a mile of the ship; and here I found a fresh renewing of my grief, for I saw evidently, that if we had kept on board, we had been all safe, that is to say, we had all got safe on shore, and I had not been so miserable as to be left entirely destitute of all comfort and company, as I now was; this forced tears from my eyes again, but as there was little relief in that, I resolved, if possible, to get to the ship, so I pulled off my clothes, for the weather was hot to extremity, and took the water, but when I came to the ship, my difficulty was still greater to know how to get on board, for as she lay a ground, and high out of the water, there was nothing within my reach to lay hold of. I swam round her twice, and the second time I spy'd a small piece of a rope, which I wondered I did not see at first, hang down by the fore-chains so low, as that with great difficulty I got hold of it, and by the help of that rope, got up into the forecastle of the ship. Here I found that the ship was bulged,[21] and had a great deal of water in her hold, but that she lay so on the side of a bank of hard sand, or rather earth, that her stern lay lifted up upon the bank, and her head low almost to the water; by this means all her quarter was free, and all that was in that part was dry; for you may be sure my first work was to search and to see what was spoiled and what was free; and first I found that all the ship's provisions were dry and untouched by the water, and being very well disposed to eat, I went to the bread-room and filled my pockets with bisket, and eat it as I went about other things, for I had no time to lose; I also found some rum in the great cabbin, of which I took a large dram, and which I had indeed need enough of to spirit me for what was before me. Now I wanted nothing but a boat to furnish my self with many things which I foresaw would be very necessary to me.

It was in vain to sit still and wish for what was not to be had, and this extremity rouzed my application. We had several spare yards,[22] and two or three large sparrs of wood, and a spare top-mast or two in the ship; I resolved to fall to work with these, and I flung as many of them over board as I could manage for their weight, tying every one with a rope that they might not drive away; when this was done I went down the ship's side, and pulling them to me, I ty'd four of them fast together at both ends as well as I could, in the form of a raft, and laying two or three short pieces of plank upon them crossways, I found I could walk upon it very well, but that it was not able to bear any great weight, the pieces being too light; so I went to work, and with the carpenters saw I cut a spare top-mast into three lengths, and added them to my raft, with a great deal of labour and pains; but hope of furnishing my self with necessaries encouraged me to go beyond what I should have been able to have done upon another occasion.

My raft was now strong enough to bear any reasonable weight; my next care was what to load it with, and how to preserve what I laid upon it from the surf of the sea, but I was not long considering this. I first laid all the planks or boards upon it that I could get, and having considered well what I most wanted, I first got three of the seamen's chests, which I had broken open and empty'd, and lowered them down upon my raft; the first of these I filled with provision, viz. bread, rice, three Dutch cheeses, five pieces of dry'd goat's flesh, which we lived much upon, and a little remainder of European corn which had been laid by for some fowls which we brought to sea with us, but the fowls were killed; there had been some barly and wheat together, but, to my great disappointment, I found afterwards that the rats had eaten or spoiled it all; as for liquors, I found several cases of bottles belonging to our skipper, in which were some cordial waters, and in all about five or six gallons of rack;[23] these I stowed by themselves, there being no need to put them into the chest, nor no room for them. While I was doing this, I found the tyde began to flow, tho' very calm, and I had the mortification to see my coat, shirt, and wastcoat which I had left on shore upon the sand, swim away; as for my breeches, which were only linnen and open knee'd, I swam on board in them and my stockings. However, this put me upon rummaging for clothes, of which I found enough, but took no more than I wanted for present use, for I had other things which my eye was more upon, as first tools to work with on shore, and it was after long searching that I found out the carpenter's chest, which was indeed a very useful prize to me, and much more valuable than a ship loading of gold would have been at that time; I got it down to my raft, even whole as it was, without losing time to look into it, for I knew in general what it contained.

My next care was for some ammunition and arms; there were two very good fowling-pieces in the great cabbin, and two pistols; these I secured first, with some powder-horns, and a small bag of shot, and two old rusty swords; I knew there were three barrels of powder in the ship, but knew not where our gunner had stowed them, but with much search I found them, two of them dry and good, the third had taken water; those two I got to my raft, with the arms; and now I thought my self pretty well freighted, and began to think how I should get to shore with them, having neither sail, oar, or rudder, and the least cap full of wind would have overset all my navigation.

I had three encouragements : 1. a smooth calm sea; 2. the tide rising, and setting in to the shore; 3. what little wind there was blew me towards the land; and thus, having found two or three broken oars belonging to the boat, and besides the tools which were in the chest, I found two saws, an axe, and a hammer, and with this cargo I put to sea. For a mile, or thereabouts, my raft went very well, only that I found it drive a little distant from the place where I had landed before, by which I perceived that there was some indraft of the water, and consequently I hoped to find some creek or river there, which I might make use of as a port to get to land with my cargo.

As I imagined, so it was, there appeared before me a little opening of the land, and I found a strong current of the tide set into it, so I guided my raft as well as I could to keep in the middle of the stream. But here I had like to have suffered a second shipwreck, which, if I had, I think verily would have broke my heart, for knowing nothing of the coast, my raft run a-ground at one end of it upon a shoal, and not being a-ground at the other end, it wanted but a little that all my cargo had slip'd off towards that end that was a-float, and so fallen into the water. I did my utmost by setting my back against the chests to keep them in their places, but could not thrust off the raft with all my strength, neither durst I stir from the posture I was in, but holding up the chests with all my might, stood in that manner near half an hour, in which time the rising of the water brought me a little more upon a level, and a little after, the water still rising, my raft floated again, and I thrust her off with the oar I had into the channel, and then driving up higher, I at length found my self in the mouth of a little river, with land on both sides, and a strong current or tide running up. I looked on both sides for a proper place to get to shore, for I was not willing to be driven too high up the river, hoping in time to see some ship at sea, and therefore resolved to place my self as near the coast as I could.

At length I spy'd a little cove on the right shore of the creek, to which with great pain and difficulty I guided my raft, and at last got so near, as that, reaching ground with my oar, I could thrust her directly in; but here I had like to have dipt all my cargo in the sea again; for that shore lying pretty steep, that is to say sloping, there was no place to land but where one end of my float, if it run on shore, would lie so high, and the other sink lower as before, that it would endanger my cargo again. All that I could do was to wait 'till the tide was at the highest, keeping the raft with my oar like an anchor to hold the side of it fast to the shore, near a flat piece of ground, which I expected the water would flow over; and so it did. As soon as I found water enough, for my raft drew about a foot [of] water, I thrust her on upon that flat piece of ground, and there fastened or mored her by sticking my two broken oars into the ground, one on one side near one end, and one on the other side near the other end; and thus I lay 'till the water ebbed away, and left my raft and all my cargoe safe on shore.

My next work was to view the country, and seek a proper place for my habitation, and where to stow my goods to secure them from whatever might happen; where I was, I yet knew not, whether on the continent or on an island, whether inhabited or not inhabited, whether in danger of wild beasts or not. There was a hill not above a mile from me, which rose up very steep and high, and which seemed to over-top some other hills, which lay as in a ridge from it northward; I took out one of the fowling pieces, and one of the pistols, and an horn of powder, and thus armed I travelled for discovery up to the top of that hill, where after I had with great labour and difficulty got to the top, I saw my fate to my great affliction, viz. that I was in an island environed every way with the sea, no land to be seen, except some rocks which lay a great way off, and two small islands less than this, which lay about three leagues to the west.

I found also that the island I was in was barren, and, as I saw good reason to believe, un-inhabited, except by wild beasts, of whom however I saw none, yet I saw abundance of fowls, but knew not their kinds, neither when I killed them could I tell what was fit for food, and what not; at my coming back, I shot at a great bird which I saw sitting upon a tree on the side of a great wood. I believe it was the first gun that had been fired there since the creation of the world; I had no sooner fired, but from all the parts of the wood there arose an innumerable number of fowls of many sorts, making a confused screaming, and crying every one according to his usual note; but not one of them of any kind that I knew. As for the creature I killed, I took it to be a kind of a hawk, its colour and beak resembling it, but had no talons or claws more than common; its flesh was carrion, and fit for nothing.

Contented with this discovery, I came back to my raft, and fell to work to bring my cargoe on shore, which took me up the rest of that day, and what to do with my self at night I knew not, nor indeed where to rest; for I was afraid to lie down on the ground, not knowing but some wild beast might devour me, tho', as I afterwards found, there was really no need for those fears.

However, as well as I could, I barricadoed my self round with the chests and boards that I had brought on shore, and made a kind of a hut for that night's lodging; as for food, I yet saw not which way to supply my self, except that I had seen two or three creatures like hares run out of the wood where I shot the fowl.

I now began to consider that I might yet get a great many things out of the ship, which would be useful to me, and particularly some of the rigging, and sails, and such other things as might come to land, and I resolved to make another voyage on board the vessel, if possible; and as I knew that the first storm that blew must necessarily break her all in pieces, I resolved to set all other things apart, 'till I got every thing out of the ship that I could get; then I called a council, that is to say, in my thoughts, whether I should take back the raft, but this appeared impracticable; so I resolved to go as before, when the tide was down, and I did so, only that I stripped before I went from my hut, having nothing on but a chequered shirt, and a pair of linnen drawers, and a pair of pumps on my feet.

I got on board the ship, as before, and prepared a second raft, and having had experience of the first, I neither made this so unweildy, nor loaded it so hard, but yet I brought away several things very useful to me; as first, in the carpenter's stores I found two or three bags full of nails and spikes, a great skrew-jack, a dozen or two of hatchets, and above all, that most useful thing called a grindstone; all these I secured together, with several things belonging to the gunner, particularly two or three iron crows, and two barrels of musquet bullets, seven musquets, and another fowling piece, with some small quantity of powder more; a large bag full of small shot, and a great roll of sheet lead. But this last was so heavy I could not hoise it up to get it over the ship's side.

Besides these things, I took all the mens cloths that I could find, and a spare fore-top-sail, a hammock, and some bedding; and with this I loaded my second raft, and brought them all safe on shore to my very great comfort.

I was under some apprehensions during my absence from the land, that at least my provisions might be devoured on shore; but when I came back, I found no sign of any visitor, only there sat a creature like a wild cat upon one of the chests, which when I came towards it, ran away a little distance, and then stood still; she sat very composed and unconcerned, and looked full in my face, as if she had a mind to be acquainted with me. I presented my gun at her, but as she did not understand it, she was per-fectly unconcerned at it, nor did she offer to stir away; upon which I tossed her a bit of bisket, tho' by the way I was not very free of it, for my store was not great. However, I spared her a bit, I say, and she went to it, smelled of it, and ate it, and looked (as pleased) for more, but I thanked her, and could spare no more, so she marched off.

Having got my second cargoe on shore, tho' I was fain to open the barrels of powder and bring them by parcels, for they were too heavy, being large casks, I went to work to make me a little tent with the sail and some poles which I cut for that purpose, and into this tent I brought every thing that I knew would spoil, either with rain or sun, and I piled all the empty chests and casks up in a circle round the tent, to fortify it from any sudden attempt, either from man or beast.

When I had done this I blocked up the door of the tent with some boards within, and an empty chest set up on end without, and spreading one of the beds upon the ground, laying my two pistols just at my head, and my gun at length by me, I went to bed for the first time, and slept very quietly all night, for I was very weary and heavy, for the night before I had slept little, and had laboured very hard all day, as well to fetch all those things from the ship, as to get them on shore.

I had the biggest maggazin of all kinds now that ever were laid up, I believe, for one man, but I was not satisfy'd still; for while the ship sat upright in that posture, I thought I ought to get every thing out of her that I could; so every day at low water I went on board, and brought away some thing or other. But particularly the third time I went, I brought away as much of the rigging as I could, as also all the small ropes and rope-twine I could get, with a piece of spare canvass, which was to mend the sails upon occasion, [and] the barrel of wet gunpowder: in a word, I brought away all the sails first and last, only that I was fain to cut them in pieces, and bring as much at a time as I could; for they were no more useful to be sails, but as meer canvass only.

But that which comforted me more still, was that at last of all, after I had made five or six such voyages as these, and thought I had nothing more to expect from the ship that was worth my medling with; I say, after all this, I found a great hogshead of bread and three large runlets of rum or spirits,[24] and a box of sugar, and a barrel of fine flower; this was surprizing to me, because I had given over expecting any more provisions, except what was spoiled by the water: I soon empty'd the hogshead of that bread, and wrapt it up parcel by parcel in pieces of the sails, which I cut out; and in a word, I got all this safe on shore also.

The next day I made another voyage; and now having plundered the ship of what was portable and fit to hand out, I began with the cables; and cutting the great cable into pieces, such as I could move, I got two cables and a hawser on shore, with all the iron work I could get; and having cut down the spritsail-yard, and the missen-yard, and every thing I could to make a large raft, I loaded it with all those heavy goods, and came away. But my good luck began now to leave me; for this raft was so unweildy, and so overloaden, that after I was entered the little cove, where I had landed the rest of my goods, not being able to guide it so handily as I did the other, it overset, and threw me and all my cargoe into the water; as for my self it was no great harm, for I was near the shore; but as to my cargo, it was great part of it lost, especially the iron, which I expected would have been of great use to me. However, when the tide was out, I got most of the pieces of cable ashore, and some of the iron, tho' with infinite labour; for I was fain to dip for it into the water, a work which fatigued me very much. After this I went every day on board, and brought away what I could get.

I had been now thirteen days on shore, and had been eleven times on board the ship; in which time I had brought away all that one pair of hands could well be supposed capable to bring, tho' I believe verily, had the calm weather held, I should have brought away the whole ship piece by piece. But preparing the 12th time to go on board, I found the wind begin to rise; however, at low water I went on board, and tho' I thought I had rumaged the cabbin so effectually, as that nothing more could be found, yet I discovered a locker with drawers in it, in one of which I found two or three razors, and one pair of large sizzers, with some ten or a dozen of good knives and forks; in another I found about thirty six pounds value in money, some European coin, some Brasil, some pieces of eight, some gold, some silver.

I smiled to my self at the sight of this money. 'O drug!' said I aloud, 'what art thou good for? Thou art not worth to me, no, not the taking off of the ground; one of those knives is worth all this heap; I have no manner of use for thee, e'en remain where thou art, and go to the bottom as a creature whose life is not worth saving.' However, upon second thoughts, I took it away, and wrapping all this in a piece of canvas, I began to think of making another raft, but while I was preparing this, I found the sky over-cast, and the wind began to rise, and in a quarter of an hour it blew a fresh gale from the shore; it presently occur'd to me that it was in vain to pretend to make a raft with the wind off shore, and that it was my business to be gone before the tide of flood began, otherwise I might not be able to reach the shore at all. Accordingly I let my self down into the water, and swam across the channel which lay between the ship and the sands, and even that with difficulty enough, partly with the weight of the things I had about me, and partly the roughness of the water, for the wind rose very hastily, and before it was quite high water it blew a storm.

But I was gotten home to my little tent, where I lay with all my wealth about me very secure. It blew very hard all that night, and in the morning when I looked out, behold, no more ship was to be seen; I was a little surprized, but recovered my self with this satisfactory reflection, viz. that I had lost no time, nor abated no diligence to get every thing out of her that could be useful to me, and that indeed there was little left in her that I was able to bring away if I had had more time.

I now gave over any more thoughts of the ship, or of any thing out of her, except what might drive on shore from her wreck, as indeed divers pieces of her afterwards did; but those things were of small use to me.

My thoughts were now wholly employed about securing my self against either savages, if any should appear, or wild beasts, if any were in the island; and I had many thoughts of the method how to do this, and what kind of dwelling to make, whether I should make me a cave in the earth, or a tent upon the earth: and, in short, I resolved upon both, the manner and description of which it may not be improper to give an account of.

I soon found the place I was in was not for my settlement, particularly because it was upon a low moorish ground near the sea, and I believed would not be wholsome, and more particularly because there was no fresh water near it, so I resolved to find a more healthy and more convenient spot of ground.

I consulted several things in my situation which I found would be proper for me: 1st. health and fresh water I just now mentioned; 2dly. shelter from the heat of the sun; 3dly. security from ravenous creatures, whether men or beasts; 4thly. a view to the sea, that if God sent any ship in sight, I might not lose any advantage for my deliverance, of which I was not willing to banish all my expectation yet.

In search of a place proper for this, I found a little plain on the side of a rising hill, whose front towards this little plain was steep as a house-side, so that nothing could come down upon me from the top; on the side of this rock there was a hollow place worn a little way in like the entrance or door of a cave, but there was not really any cave or way into the rock at all.

On the flat of the green, just before this hollow place, I resolved to pitch my tent. This plain was not above an hundred yards broad, and about twice as long, and lay like a green before my door, and at the end of it descended irregularly every way down into the low-grounds by the sea side. It was on the N.N.W. side of the hill, so that I was sheltered from the heat every day, till it came to a w. and by s. sun, or thereabouts, which in those countries is near the setting.

Before I set up my tent, I drew a half circle before the hollow place which took in about ten yards in its semi-diameter from the rock, and twenty yards in its diameter, from its beginning and ending.

In this half circle I pitched two rows of strong stakes, driving them into the ground till they stood very firm like piles, the biggest end being out of the ground about five foot and a half, and sharpened on the top. The two rows did not stand above six inches from one another.

Then I took the pieces of cable which I had cut in the ship, and I laid them in rows one upon another, within the circle, between these two rows of stakes, up to the top, placing other stakes in the in-side, leaning against them, about two foot and a half high, like a spurr to a post, and this fence was so strong that neither man or beast could get into it or over it. This cost me a great deal of time and labour, especially to cut the piles in the woods, bring them to the place, and drive them into the earth.

The entrance into this place I made to be not by a door, but by a short ladder to go over the top, which ladder, when I was in, I lifted over after me, and so I was compleatly fenced in, and fortify'd, as I thought, from all the world and consequently slept secure in the night, which otherwise I could not have done, tho', as it appeared afterward, there was no need of all this caution from the enemies that I apprehended danger from.

Into this fence or fortress, with infinite labour, I carry'd all my riches, all my provisions, ammunition, and stores, of which you have the account above; and I made me a large tent, which, to preserve me from the rains that in one part of the year are very violent there, I made double, viz. one smaller tent within, and one larger tent above it, and covered the uppermost with a large tarpaulin which I had saved among the sails.

And now I lay no more for a while in the bed which I had brought on shore, but in a hammock, which was indeed a very good one, and belonged to the mate of the ship.

Into this tent I brought all my provisions, and every thing that would spoil by the wet, and having thus enclosed all my goods, I made up the entrance, which till now I had left open, and so passed and re-passed, as I said, by a short ladder.

When I had done this, I began to work my way into the rock, and bringing all the earth and stones that I dug down out thro' my tent, I laid 'em up within my fence in the nature of a terras, that so it raised the ground within about a foot and a half; and thus I made me a cave just behind my tent, which served me like a cellar to my house.

It cost me much labour and many days before all these things were brought to perfection, and therefore I must go back to some other things which took up some of my thoughts. At the same time it happened, after I had laid my scheme for the setting up my tent and making the cave, that a storm of rain falling from a thick dark cloud, a sudden flash of lightning happened, and after that a great clap of thunder, as is naturally the effect of it; I was not so much surprised with the lightning as I was with a thought which darted into my mind as swift as the lightning it self: O my powder! My very heart sunk within me when I thought that at one blast all my powder might be destroyed, on which not my defence only, but the providing me food, as I thought, entirely depended; I was nothing near so anxious about my own danger, tho' had the powder took fire, I had never known who had hurt me.

Such impression did this make upon me, that after the storm was over, I laid aside all my works, my building and fortifying, and apply'd my self to make bags and boxes to separate the powder, and keep it a little and a little in a parcel, in hope that whatever might come, it might not all take fire at once, and to keep it so apart that it should not be possible to make one part fire another. I finished this work in about a fortnight, and I think my powder, which in all was about 240 lb. weight, was divided in not less than a hundred parcels; as to the barrel that had been wet, I did not apprehend any danger from that, so I placed it in my new cave, which in my fancy I called my kitchin, and the rest I hid up and down in holes among the rocks, so that no wet might come to it, marking very carefully where I laid it.

In the interval of time while this was doing I went out once at least every day with my gun, as well to divert my self as to see if I could kill any thing fit for food, and as near as I could to acquaint my self with what the island produced. The first time I went out I presently discovered that there were goats in the island, which was a great satisfaction to me; but then it was attended with this misfortune to me, viz. that they were so shy, so subtile, and so swift of foot, that it was the difficultest thing in the world to come at them. But I was not discouraged at this, not doubting but I might now and then shoot one, as it soon happened, for after I had found their haunts a little, I laid wait in this manner for them : I observed if they saw me in the valleys, tho' they were upon the rocks, they would run away as in a terrible fright; but if they were feeding in the valleys, and I was upon the rocks, they took no notice of me, from whence I concluded that by the position of their opticks, their sight was so directed downward, that they did not readily see objects that were above them; so afterward I took this method, I always climbed the rocks first to get above them, and then had frequently a fair mark. The first shot I made among these creatures, I killed a she-goat which had a little kid by her which she gave suck to, which grieved me heartily; but when the old one fell, the kid stood stock still by her till I came and took her up, and not only so, but when I carry'd the old one with me upon my shoulders, the kid followed me quite to my enclosure, upon which I laid down the dam, and took the kid in my arms, and carry'd it over my pale, in hopes to have it bred up tame, but it would not eat, so I was forced to kill it and eat it my self; these two supply'd me with flesh a great while, for I eat sparingly, and saved my provisions (my bread especially) as much as possibly I could.

Having now fixed my habitation, I found it absolutely necessary to provide a place to make a fire in, and fewel to burn; and what I did for that, as also how I enlarged my cave, and what conveniences I made, I shall give a full account of in its place. But I must first give some little account of my self, and of my thoughts about living, which it may well be supposed were not a few.

I had a dismal prospect of my condition, for as I was not cast away upon that island without being driven, as is said, by a violent storm quite out of the course of our intended voyage, and a great way, viz. some hundreds of leagues, out of the ordinary course of the trade of mankind, I had great reason to consider it as a determination of Heaven, that in this desolate place and in this desolate manner I should end my life; the tears would run plentifully down my face when I made these reflections, and sometimes I would expostulate with my self, why Providence should thus compleatly ruine its creatures, and render them so absolutely miserable, so without help abandoned, so entirely depressed, that it could hardly be rational to be thankful for such a life.

But something always returned swift upon me to check these thoughts, and to reprove me; and particularly one day walking with my gun in my hand by the sea-side, I was very pensive upon the subject of my present condition, when reason as it were expostulated with me t'other way, thus: Well, you are in a desolate condition, 'tis true, but pray remember, where are the rest of you? Did not you come eleven of you into the boat? where are the ten? Why were not they saved and you lost? Why were you singled out? Is it better to be here or there? and then I pointed to the sea. All evils are to be considered with the good that is in them, and with what worse attends them.

Then it occurred to me again, how well I was furnished for my subsistence, and what would have been my case if it had not happened, *which was an hundred thousand to one*, that the ship floated from the place where she first struck and was driven so near to the shore that I had time to get all these things out of her. What would have been my case if I had been to have lived in the condition in which I at first came on shore, without necessaries of life, or necessaries to supply and procure them? Particularly, said I aloud (tho' to my self), what should I ha' done without a gun, without ammunition, without any tools to make any thing, or to work with, without clothes, bedding, a tent, or any manner of covering? and that now I had all these to a sufficient quantity, and was in a fair way to provide my self in such a manner, as to live without my gun when my ammunition was spent; so that I had a tollerable view of subsisting without any want as long as I lived; for I considered from the beginning how I would provide for the accidents that might happen, and for the time that was to come, even not only after my ammunition should be spent, but even after my health or strength should decay.

I confess I had not entertained any notion of my ammunition being destroyed at one blast, I mean my powder being blown up by lightning, and this made the thoughts of it so surprising to me when it lightened and thundered, as I observed just now.

And now being to enter into a melancholy relation of a scene of silent life, such perhaps as was never heard of in the world before, I shall take it from its beginning, and continue it in its order. It was, by my account, the 30th of Sept. when, in the manner as above said, I first set foot upon this horrid island, when the sun being, to us, in its autumnal equinox, was almost just over my head, for I reckoned my self, by observation, to be in the latitude of 9 degrees 22 minutes north of the line.

After I had been there about ten or twelve days, it came into my thoughts that I should lose my reckoning of time for want of books and pen and ink, and should even forget the Sabbath days from the working days; but to prevent this I cut it with my knife upon a large post, in capital letters, and making it into a great cross I set it up on the shore where I first landed, viz. 'I came on shore here on the 30th of Sept. 1659.' Upon the sides of this square post I cut every day a notch with my knife, and every seventh notch was as long again as the rest, and every first day of the month as long again as that long one, and thus I kept my kalander, or weekly, monthly, and yearly reckoning of time.

In the next place we are to observe, that among the many things which I brought out of the ship in the several voyages, which, as above mentioned, I made to it, I got several things of less value, but not [at] all less useful to me, which I omitted setting down before; as in particular, pens, ink, and paper, several parcels in the captain's, mate's, gunner's, and carpenter's keeping, three or four compasses, some mathematical instruments, dials, perspectives, charts, and books of navigation, all which I huddled together, whether I might want them or no; also I found three very good Bibles which came to me in my cargo from England, and which I had packed up among my things; some Portugueze books also, and among them two or three popish prayer-books, and several other books, all which I carefully secured. And I must not forget that we had in the ship a dog and two cats, of whose eminent history I may have occasion to say something in its place; for I carry'd both the cats with me, and as for the dog, he jumped out of the ship of himself, and swam on shore to me the day after I went on shore with my first cargo, and was a trusty servant to me many years; I wanted nothing that he could fetch me, nor any company that he could make up to me, I only wanted to have him talk to me, but that would not do. As I observed before, I found pen, ink, and paper, and I husbanded them to the utmost, and I shall shew, that while my ink lasted, I kept things very exact, but after that was gone I could not, for I could not make any ink by any means that I could devise.

And this put me in mind that I wanted many things, notwithstanding all that I had amassed together, and of these, this of ink was one, as also spade, pick-axe, and shovel to dig or remove the earth, needles, pins, and thread; as for linnen, I soon learned to want that without much difficulty.

This want of tools made every work I did go on heavily, and it was near a whole year before I had entirely finished my little pale or surrounded habitation. The piles or stakes, which were as heavy as I could well lift, were a long time in cutting and preparing in the woods, and more by far in bringing home, so that I spent some times two days in cutting and bringing home one of those posts, and a third day in driving it into the ground; for which purpose I got a heavy piece of wood at first, but at last bethought my self of one of the iron crows, which however, tho' I found it, yet it made driving those posts or piles very laborious and tedious work.

But what need I ha' been concerned at the tediousness of any thing I had to do, seeing I had time enough to do it in? nor had I any other employment if that had been over, at least that I could foresee, except the ranging the island to seek for food, which I did more or less every day.

I now began to consider seriously my condition, and the circumstance I was reduced to, and I drew up the state of my affairs in writing, not so much to leave them to any that were to come after me, for I was like to have but few heirs, as to deliver my thoughts from daily poring upon them, and afflicting my mind; and as my reason began now to master my despondency, I began to comfort my self as well as I could, and to set the good against the evil, that I might have something to distinguish my case from worse, and I stated it very impartially, like debtor and creditor, the comforts I enjoyed against the miseries I suffered, thus:

Evil	Good
I am cast upon a horrible desolate island, void of all hope of recovery.	But I am alive, and not drowned as all my ship's company was.
I am singled out and separated, as it were, from all the world to be miserable.	But I am singled out too from all the ship's crew to be spared from death; and He that miraculously saved me from death, can deliver me from this condition.
I am divided from mankind, a solitaire, one banished from humane society.	But I am not starved and perishing on a barren place, affording no sustenance.
I have not clothes to cover me.	But I am in a hot climate, where if I had clothes I could hardly wear them.

I am without any defence or means to resist any violence of man or beast.	*But I am cast on an island, where I see no wild beasts to hurt me, as I saw on the coast of Africa; and what if I had been shipwrecked there?*
I have no soul to speak to, or relieve me.	*But God wonderfully sent the ship in near enough to the shore, that I have gotten out so many necessary things as will either supply my wants, or enable me to supply my self even as long as I live.*

Upon the whole, here was an undoubted testimony, that there was scarce any condition in the world so miserable, but there was something negative or something positive to be thankful for in it; and let this stand as a direction from the experience of the most miserable of all conditions in this world, that we may always find in it something to comfort our selves from, and to set in the description of good and evil, on the credit side of the accompt.

Having now brought my mind a little to relish my condition, and given over looking out to sea to see if I could spy a ship; I say, giving over these things, I began to apply my self to accommodate my way of living, and to make things as easy to me as I could.

I have already described my habitation, which was a tent under the side of a rock, surrounded with a strong pale of posts and cables, but I might now rather call it a wall, for I raised a kind of wall up against it of turfs, about two foot thick on the out-side, and after some time, I think it was a year and a half, I raised rafters from it leaning to the rock, and thatched or covered it with bows of trees, and such things as I could get to keep out the rain, which I found at some times of the year very violent.

I have already observed how I brought all my goods into this pale, and into the cave which I had made behind me. But I must observe too, that at first this was a confused heap of goods, which as they lay in no order, so they took up all my place, I had no

room to turn my self; so I set my self to enlarge my cave and
works farther into the earth, for it was a loose sandy rock, which
yielded easily to the labour I bestowed on it; and so when I found
I was pretty safe as to beasts of prey, I worked side-ways to the
right hand into the rock, and then turning to the right again,
worked quite out and made me a door to come out, on the out-
side of my pale or fortification.

This gave me not only egress and regress, as it were a back way
to my tent and to my storehouse, but gave me room to stow my
goods.

And now I began to apply my self to make such necessary
things as I found I most wanted, as particularly a chair and a
table; for without these I was not able to enjoy the few comforts I had in the world; I could not write, or eat, or do several
things with so much pleasure without a table.

So I went to work; and here I must needs observe, that as
reason is the substance and original of the mathematicks, so by
stating and squaring every thing by reason, and by making the
most rational judgment of things, every man may be in time
master of every mechanick art. I had never handled a tool in
my life, and yet in time, by labour, application, and contrivance,
I found at last that I wanted nothing but I could have made it,
especially if I had had tools; however, I made abundance of things,
even without tools, and some with no more tools than an adze
and a hatchet, which perhaps were never made that way before,
and that with infinite labour. For example, if I wanted a board,
I had no other way but to cut down a tree, set it on an edge
before me, and hew it flat on either side with my axe, till I had
brought it to be thin as a plank, and then dubb it smooth with my
adze. It is true, by this method I could make but one board out of
a whole tree, but this I had no remedy for but patience, any more
than I had for the prodigious deal of time and labour which it
took me up to make a plank or board. But my time or labour
was little worth, and so it was as well employed one way as
another.

However, I made me a table and a chair, as I observed above,
in the first place, and this I did out of the short pieces of boards
that I brought on my raft from the ship. But when I had wrought

out some boards, as above, I made large shelves of the breadth of
a foot and [a] half one over another, all along one side of my
cave, to lay all my tools, nails, and iron-work, and in a word, to
separate every thing at large in their places, that I must come
easily at them; I knocked pieces into the wall of the rock to hang
my guns and all things that would hang up.

So that had my cave been to be seen, it looked like a general
magazine of all necessary things, and I had every thing so ready
at my hand, that it was a great pleasure to me to see all my goods
in such order, and especially to find my stock of all necessaries so
great.

And now it was when I began to keep a journal of every
days employment, for indeed at first I was in too much hurry, and
not only hurry as to labour, but in too much discomposure of
mind, and my journal would ha' been full of many dull things.
For example, I must have said thus: 'Sept. the 30th. After I
got to shore and had escaped drowning, instead of being thankful to God for my deliverance, having first vomited with the great
quantity of salt water which was gotten into my stomach, and
recovering my self a little, I ran about the shore, wringing my
hand and beating my head and face, exclaiming at my misery,
and crying out, I was undone, undone, till tyred and faint I was
forced to lye down on the ground to repose, but durst not sleep
for fear of being devoured.'

Some days after this, and after I had been on board the ship,
and got all that I could out of her, yet I could not forbear getting
up to the top of a little mountain and looking out to see in hopes
of seeing a ship, then fancy at a vast distance I spy'd a sail, please
my self with the hopes of it, and then after looking steadily till
I was almost blind, lose it quite, and sit down and weep like a
child, and thus encrease my misery by my folly.

But having gotten over these things in some measure, and
having settled my household stuff and habitation, made me a
table and a chair, and all as handsome about me as I could, I
began to keep my journal, of which I shall here give you a copy
(tho' in it will be told all these particulars over again) as long as
it lasted, for having no more ink I was forced to leave it off.

THE JOURNAL

September 30, 1659. I, poor miserable Robinson Crusoe, being shipwrecked, during a dreadful storm, in the offing,[25] came on shore on this dismal unfortunate island, which I called the Island of Despair, all the rest of the ship's company being drowned, and my self almost dead.

All the rest of that day I spent in afflicting my self at the dismal circumstances I was brought to, viz. I had neither food, house, clothes, weapon, or place to fly to, and in despair of any relief, saw nothing but death before me, either that I should be devoured by wild beasts, murthered by savages, or starved to death for want of food. At the approach of night, I slept in a tree for fear of wild creatures, but slept soundly tho' it rained all night.

October 1. In the morning I saw to my great surprise the ship had floated with the high tide, and was driven on shore again much nearer the island, which as it was some comfort on one hand, for seeing her sit upright, and not broken to pieces, I hoped, if the wind abated, I might get on board, and get some food and necessaries out of her for my relief; so on the other hand, it renewed my grief at the loss of my comrades, who I imagined if we had all staid on board might have saved the ship, or at least that they would not have been all drowned as they were; and that had the men been saved, we might perhaps have built us a boat out of the ruins of the ship, to have carried us to some other part of the world. I spent great part of this day in perplexing my self on these things; but at length seeing the ship almost dry, I went upon the sand as near as I could, and then swam on board; this day also it continued raining, tho' with no wind at all.

From the 1st of October to the 24th. All these days entirely spent in many several voyages to get all I could out of the ship, which I brought on shore, every tide of flood, upon rafts. Much rain also in these days, tho' with some intervals of fair weather: but, it seems, this was the rainy season.

Oct. 20. I overset my raft and all the goods I had got upon it, but being in shoal water, and the things being chiefly heavy, I recovered many of them when the tide was out.

Oct. 25. It rained all night and all day, with some gusts of wind, during which time the ship broke in pieces, the wind blowing a little harder than before, and was no more to be seen, except the wreck of her, and that only at low water. I spent this day in covering and securing the goods which I had saved, that the rain might not spoil them.

Oct. 26. I walked about the shore almost all day to find out a place to fix my habitation, greatly concerned to secure my self from an attack in the night, either from wild beasts or men. Towards night I fixed upon a proper place under a rock, and marked out a semi-circle for my encampment, which I resolved to strengthen with a work, wall, or fortification made of double piles, lined within with cables, and without with turf.

From the 26th to the 30th. I worked very hard in carrying all my goods to my new habitation, tho' some part of the time it rained exceeding hard.

The 31st. in the morning I went out into the island with my gun to see for some food, and discover the country, when I killed a she-goat, and her kid followed me home, which I afterwards killed also because it would not feed.

November 1. I set up my tent under a rock, and lay there for the first night, making it as large as I could with stakes driven in to swing my hammock upon.

Nov. 2. I set up all my chests and boards, and the pieces of timber which made my rafts, and with them formed a fence round me, a little within the place I had marked out for my fortification.

Nov. 3. I went out with my gun and killed two fowls like ducks, which were very good food. In the afternoon went to work to make me a table.

Nov. 4. This morning I began to order my times of work, of going out with my gun, time of sleep, and time of diversion, viz. every morning I walked out with my gun for two or three hours if it did not rain, then employed my self to work till about eleven a-clock, then eat what I had to live on, and from twelve to two

I lay down to sleep, the weather being excessive hot, and then in the evening to work again. The working part of this day and of the next were wholly employed in making my table, for I was yet but a very sorry workman, tho' time and necessity made me a compleat natural mechanick soon after, as I believe it would do any one else.

Nov. 5. This day went abroad with my gun and my dog, and killed a wild cat, her skin pretty soft, but her flesh good for nothing: every creature I killed I took off the skins and preserved them. Coming back by the sea shore, I saw many sorts of sea fowls which I did not understand, but was surprised and almost frighted with two or three seals,[26] which, while I was gazing at, not well knowing what they were, got into the sea and escaped me for that time.

Nov. 6. After my morning walk I went to work with my table again, and finished it, tho' not to my liking; nor was it long before I learned to mend it.

Nov. 7. Now it began to be settled fair weather. The 7th, 8th, 9th, 10th, and part of the 12th (for the 11th was Sunday) I took wholly up to make me a chair, and with much ado brought it to a tolerable shape, but never to please me, and even in the making I pulled it in pieces several times. *Note*, I soon neglected my keeping Sundays, for omitting my mark for them on my post, I forgot which was which.

Nov. 13. This day it rained, which refreshed me exceedingly, and cooled the earth, but it was accompany'd with terrible thunder and lightning, which frighted me dreadfully for fear of my powder; as soon as it was over, I resolved to separate my stock of powder into as many little parcels as possible, that it might not be in danger.

Nov. 14, 15, 16. These three days I spent in making little square chests or boxes, which might hold a pound or two pound, at most, of powder, and so putting the powder in, I stowed it in places as secure and remote from one another as possible. On one of these three days I killed a large bird that was good to eat, but I know not what to call it.

Nov. 17. This day I began to dig behind my tent in to the rock to make room for my farther conveniency. *Note*, Three things I wanted exceedingly for this work, viz. a pick-axe, a shovel, and a wheel-barrow or basket; so I desisted from my work, and began to consider how to supply that want and make me some tools; as for a pick-axe, I made use of the iron crows, which were proper enough, tho' heavy; but the next thing was a shovel or spade; this was so absolutely necessary, that indeed I could do nothing effectually without it, but what kind of one to make I knew not.

Nov. 18. The next day in searching the woods I found a tree of that wood, or like it, which in the Brasils they call the iron tree, for its exceeding hardness; of this, with great labour and almost spoiling my axe, I cut a piece, and brought it home too with difficulty enough, for it was exceeding heavy.

The excessive hardness of the wood, and having no other way, made me a long while upon this machine, for I worked it effectually by little and little into the form of a shovel or spade, the handle exactly shaped like ours in England, only that the broad part having no iron shod upon it at bottom, it would not last me so long; however, it served well enough for the uses which I had occasion to put it to; but never was a shovel, I believe, made after that fashion, or so long a making.

I was still deficient, for I wanted a basket or a wheel-barrow; a basket I could not make by any means, having no such things as twigs that would bend to make wicker ware, at least none yet found out; and as to a wheel-barrow, I fancy'd I could make all but the wheel, but that I had no notion of, neither did I know how to go about it; besides, I had no possible way to make the iron gudgeons for the spindle or axis of the wheel to run in, so I gave it over, and so for carrying away the earth which I dug out of the cave, I made me a thing like a hodd, which the labourers carry morter in when they serve the bricklayers.

This was not so difficult to me as the making the shovel; and yet this, and the shovel, and the attempt which I made in vain to make a wheel-barrow, took me up no less than four days; I mean, always excepting my morning walk with my gun, which I seldom failed, and very seldom failed also bringing home some thing fit to eat.

Nov. 23. My other work having now stood still, because of my making these tools, when they were finished I went on, and working every day, as my strength and time allowed, I spent eighteen days entirely in widening and deepening my cave, that it might hold my goods commodiously.

Note, During all this time, I worked to make this room or cave spacious enough to accommodate me as a warehouse or magazin, a kitchen, a dining-room, and a cellar; as for my lodging, I kept to the tent, except that some times in the wet season of the year, it rained so hard that I could not keep my self dry, which caused me afterwards to cover all my place within my pale with long poles in the form of rafters leaning against the rock, and load them with flaggs [27] and large leaves of trees like a thatch.

December 10th. I began now to think my cave or vault finished, when on a sudden (it seems I had made it too large) a great quantity of earth fell down from the top and one side, so much, that in short it frighted me, and not without reason too; for if I had been under it I had never wanted a grave-digger. Upon this disaster I had a great deal of work to do over again; for I had the loose earth to carry out, and, which was of more importance, I had the seiling to prop up, so that I might be sure no more would come down.

Dec. 11. This day I went to work with it accordingly, and got two shores or posts pitched upright to the top, with two pieces of boards a-cross over each post; this I finished the next day; and setting more posts up with boards, in about a week more I had the roof secured, and the posts, standing in rows, served me for partitions to part of my house.

Dec. 17. From this day to the twentieth I placed shelves, and knocked up nails on the posts to hang every thing up that could be hung up, and now I began to be in some order within doors.

Dec. 20. Now I carry'd every thing into the cave, and began to furnish my house, and set up some pieces of boards, like a dresser, to order my victuals upon, but boards began to be very scarce with me; also I made me another table.

Dec. 24. Much rain all night and all day; no stirring out.

Dec. 25. Rain all day.

Dec. 26. No rain, and the earth much cooler than before, and pleasanter.

Dec. 27. Killed a young goat, and lamed another so as that I catched it, and led it home in a string; when I had it home, I bound and splintered up its leg, which was broke. N.B. I took such care of it that it lived, and the leg grew well, and as strong as ever; but by my nursing it so long it grew tame, and fed upon the little green at my door, and would not go away. This was the first time that I entertained a thought of breeding up some tame creatures, that I might have food when my powder and shot was all spent.

Dec. 28, 29, 30. Great heats and no breeze; so that there was no stirring abroad, except in the evening for food; this time I spent in putting all my things in order within doors.

January 1. Very hot still, but I went abroad early and late with my gun, and lay still in the middle of the day. This evening, going farther into the valleys which lay towards the center of the island, I found there was plenty of goats, tho' exceeding shy and hard to come at; however I resolved to try if I could not bring my dog to hunt them down.

Jan. 2. Accordingly, the next day I went out with my dog, and set him upon the goats; but I was mistaken, for they all faced about upon the dog, and he knew his danger too well, for he would not come near them.

Jan. 3. I began my fence or wall; which, being still jealous of my being attacked by some body, I resolved to make very thick and strong.

N.B. *This wall being described before, I purposely omit what was said in the Journal; it is sufficient to observe that I was no less time than from the 3d of January to the 14th of April, working, finishing, and perfecting this wall, tho' it was no more than about 24 yards in length, being a half circle from one place in the rock to another place about eight yards from it, the door of the cave being in the center behind it.*

All this time I worked very hard, the rains hindering me many days, nay, sometimes weeks together; but I thought I should never be perfectly secure 'till this wall was finished; and it is scarce credible what inexpressible labour every thing was done with, especially the bringing piles out of the woods, and driving them into the ground, for I made them much bigger than I need to have done.

When this wall was finished, and the out-side double fenced with a turf-wall raised up close to it, I perswaded my self that if any people were to come on shore there, they would not perceive any thing like a habitation; and it was very well I did so, as may be observed hereafter upon a very remarkable occasion.

During this time, I made my rounds in the woods for game every day when the rain admitted me, and made frequent discoveries in these walks of something or other to my advantage; particularly I found a kind of wild pidgeons, who built not as wood pidgeons, in a tree, but rather as house pidgeons, in the holes of the rocks; and taking some young ones, I endeavoured to breed them up tame, and did so; but when they grew older they flew all away, which perhaps was at first for want of feeding them, for I had nothing to give them; however I frequently found their nests, and got their young ones, which were very good meat.

And now, in the managing my household affairs, I found my self wanting in many things, which I thought at first it was impossible for me to make, as indeed as to some of them it was; for instance, I could never make a cask to be hooped. I had a small runlet or two, as I observed before, but I could never arrive to the capacity of making one by them, tho' I spent many weeks about it; I could neither put in the heads, or joint the staves so true to one another as to make them hold water, so I gave that also over.

In the next place, I was at a great loss for candle; so that as soon as ever it was dark, which was generally by seven-a-clock, I was obliged to go to bed. I remembered the lump of bees-wax with which I made candles in my African adventure, but I had none of that now; the only remedy I had was, that when I had killed a goat, I saved the tallow, and with a little dish made of clay, which I baked in the sun, to which I added a wick of some oakum, I made me a lamp; and this gave me light, tho' not a clear steady light like a candle. In the middle of all my labours it happened, that rummaging my things, I found a little bag, which, as I hinted before, had been filled with corn for the feeding of poultry, not for this voyage, but before, as I suppose, when the ship came from Lisbon. What little remainder of corn had been in the bag was all devoured with the rats, and I saw nothing in the bag but husks and dust; and being willing to have the bag for some other use, I think it was to put powder in, when I divided it for fear of the lightning, or some such use, I shook the husks of corn out of it on one side of my fortification under the rock.

It was a little before the great rains, just now mentioned, that I threw this stuff away, taking no notice of any thing, and not so much as remembering that I had thrown any thing there; when about a month after, or thereabout, I saw some few stalks of something green shooting out of the ground, which I fancy'd might be some plant I had not seen; but I was surprized and perfectly astonished, when, after a little longer time, I saw about ten or twelve ears come out, which were perfect green barley of the same kind as our European, nay, as our English barley.[28]

It is impossible to express the astonishment and confusion of my thoughts on this occasion. I had hitherto acted upon no religious foundation at all; indeed, I had very few notions of religion in my head, or had entertained any sense of any thing that had befallen me, otherwise than as a chance, or, as we lightly say, what pleases God; without so much as enquiring into the end of Providence in these things, or His order in governing events in the world. But after I saw barley grow there, in a climate which I know was not proper for corn, and especially that I knew not how it came there, it startled me strangely, and I began to suggest that God had miraculously caused this grain to grow without any help of seed sown, and that it was so directed purely for my sustenance on that wild miserable place.

This touched my heart a little, and brought tears out of my eyes, and I began to bless my self that such a prodigy of nature should happen upon my account; and this was the more strange to me, because I saw near it still all along by the side of the rock, some other straggling stalks, which proved to be stalks of ryce, and which I knew, because I had seen it grow in Africa when I was ashore there.

I not only thought these the pure productions of Providence

for my support, but not doubting but that there was more in the place, I went all over that part of the island where I had been before, peering in every corner, and under every rock, to see for more of it, but I could not find any; at last it occur'd to my thoughts, that I had shook a bag of chickens' meat out in that place, and then the wonder began to cease; and I must confess, my religious thankfulness to God's providence began to abate too, upon the discovering that all this was nothing but what was common; tho' I ought to have been as thankful for so strange and unforseen providence, as if it had been miraculous; for it was really the work of providence as to me, that should order or appoint, that 10 or 12 grains of corn should remain unspoiled (when the rats had destroyed all the rest) as if it had been dropt from heaven; as also, that I should throw it out in that particular place, where, it being in the shade of a high rock, it sprang up immediately; whereas, if I had thrown it anywhere else at that time, it had been burnt up and destroyed.

I carefully saved the ears of this corn, you may be sure, in their season, which was about the end of June; and laying up every corn, I resolved to sow them all again, hoping in time to have some quantity sufficient to supply me with bread. But it was not till the 4th year that I could allow my self the least grain of this corn to eat, and even then but sparingly, as I shall say afterwards in its order; for I lost all that I sowed the first season by not observing the proper time; for I sowed it just before the dry season, so that it never came up at all, at least not as it would ha' done: of which in its place.

Besides this barley, there was, as above, 20 or 30 stalks of ryce, which I preserved with the same care, and whose use was of the same kind or to the same purpose, viz. to make me bread, or rather food; for I found ways to cook it up without baking, tho' I did that also after some time. But to return to my journal.

I worked excessive hard these three or four months to get my wall done; and the 14th of April I closed it up, contriving to go into it, not by a door, but over the wall by a ladder, that there might be no sign in the out-side of my habitation.

April 16. I finished the ladder, so I went up with the ladder to the top, and then pulled it up after me, and let it down in the in-side. This was a compleat enclosure to me; for within I had room enough, and nothing could come at me from without, unless it could first mount my wall.

The very next day after this wall was finished, I had almost had all my labour overthrown at once, and my self killed; the case was thus: As I was busy in the inside of it, behind my tent, just in the entrance into my cave, I was terribly frighted with a most dreadful surprising thing indeed; for all on a sudden I found the earth come crumbling down from the roof of my cave, and from the edge of the hill over my head, and two of the posts I had set up in the cave cracked in a frightful manner; I was heartily scared, but thought nothing of what was really the cause, only thinking that the top of my cave was falling in, as some of it had done before; and for fear I shou'd be bury'd in it, I ran foreward to my ladder, and not thinking my self safe there neither, I got over my wall for fear of the pieces of the hill which I expected might roll down upon me: I was no sooner stepped down upon the firm ground, but I plainly saw it was a terrible earthquake, for the ground I stood on shook three times at about eight minutes distance, with three such shocks as would have overturned the strongest building that could be sup-posed to have stood on the earth; and a great piece of the top of a rock, which stood about half a mile from me next the sea, fell down with such a terrible noise as I never heard in all my life. I perceived also, the very sea was put into violent motion by it; and I believe the shocks were stronger under the water than on the island.

I was so amazed with the thing it self, having never felt the like, or discoursed with any one that had, that I was like one dead or stupify'd; and the motion of the earth made my stomach sick like one that was tossed at sea; but the noise of the falling of the rock awaked me, as it were, and rousing me from the stupify'd con-dition I was in, filled me with horror, and I thought of nothing then but the hill falling upon my tent and all my houshold goods, and burying all at once; and this sunk my very soul within me a second time.

After the third shock was over, and I felt no more for some time, I began to take courage, and yet I had not heart enough to go over my wall again, for fear of being buried alive, but sat still upon the ground, greatly cast down and disconsolate, not knowing what to do. All this while I had not the least serious religious thought, nothing but the common *Lord ha' mercy upon me*; and when it was over that went away too.

While I sat thus I found the air over-cast and grow cloudy as if it would rain; soon after that the wind rose by little and little, so that, in less than half an hour, it blew a most dreadful hurricane. The sea was all on a sudden covered over with foam and froth, the shore was covered with the breach of the water, the trees were torn up by the roots, and a terrible storm it was; and this held about three hours, and then began to abate, and in two hours more it was stark calm, and began to rain very hard.

All this while I sat upon the ground very much terrify'd and dejected, when on a sudden it came into my thoughts, that these winds and rain being the consequences of the earthquake, the earthquake it self was spent and over, and I might venture into my cave again. With this thought my spirits began to revive, and the rain also helping to perswade me, I went in and sat down in my tent, but the rain was so violent, that my tent was ready to be beaten down with it, and I was forced to go into my cave, tho' very much afraid and uneasy for fear it should fall on my head.

This violent rain forced me to a new work, viz. to cut a hole thro' my new fortification like a sink to let the water go out, which would else have drowned my cave. After I had been in my cave some time, and found still no more shocks of the earthquake follow, I began to be more composed; and now to support my spirits, which indeed wanted it very much, I went to my little store and took a small sup of rum, which, however, I did then and always very sparingly, knowing I could have no more when that was gone.

It continued raining all that night, and great part of the next day, so that I could not stir abroad, but my mind being more composed, I began to think of what I had best do, concluding that if the island was subject to these earthquakes, there would be no living for me in a cave, but I must consider of building me some little hut in an open place which I might surround with a wall as I had done here, and so make my self secure from wild beasts or men; but concluded, if I staid where I was, I should certainly, one time or other, be bury'd alive.

With these thoughts I resolved to remove my tent from the place where it stood, which was just under the hanging precipice of the hill, and which, if it should be shaken again, would certainly fall upon my tent. And I spent the next two days, being the 19th and 20th of April, in contriving where and how to remove my habitation.

The fear of being swallowed up alive, made me that I never slept in quiet, and yet the apprehensions of lying abroad without any fence was almost equal to it; but still when I looked about and saw how every thing was put in order, how pleasantly concealed I was, and how safe from danger, it made me very loath to remove.

In the mean time it occur'd to me that it would require a vast deal of time for me to do this, and that I must be contented to run the venture where I was, till I had formed a camp for my self, and had secured it so as to remove to it; so with this resolution I composed my self for a time, and resolved that I would go to work with all speed to build me a wall with piles and cables, &c., in a circle as before, and set my tent up in it when it was finished, but that I would venture to stay where I was till it was finished and fit to remove to. This was the 21st.

April 22. The next morning I began to consider of means to put this resolve in execution, but I was at a great loss about my tools; I had three large axes and abundance of hatchets (for we carried the hatchets for traffick with the Indians), but with much chopping and cutting knotty hard wood, they were all full of notches and dull, and tho' I had a grindstone, I could not turn it and grind my tools too; this cost me as much thought as a statesman would have bestowed upon a grand point of politicks, or a judge upon the life and death of a man. At length I contrived a wheel with a string, to turn it with my foot, that I might have both my hands at liberty. Note, I had never seen any such thing in England, or at least not to take notice how it was done, tho' since I have observed it is very common there : besides that, my grindstone was very large and heavy. This machine cost me a full weeks work to bring it to perfection.

April 28, 29. These two whole days I took up in grinding my tools, my machine for turning my grindstone performing very well.

April 30. Having perceived my bread had been low a great while, now I took a survey of it, and reduced my self to one bisket-cake a day, which made my heart very heavy.

May 1. In the morning, looking towards the sea-side, the tide being low, I saw something lye on the shore bigger than ordinary, and it looked like a cask; when I came to it, I found a small barrel, and two or three pieces of the wreck of the ship, which were driven on shore by the late hurricane, and looking towards the wreck itself I thought it seemed to lye higher out of the water than it used to do; I examined the barrel which was driven on shore, and soon found it was a barrel of gunpowder, but it had taken water, and the powder was caked as hard as a stone; however, I rolled it farther on shore for the present, and went on upon the sands as near as I could to the wreck of the ship to look for more.

When I came down to the ship I found it strangely removed. The fore-castle, which lay before bury'd in sand, was heaved up at least six foot, and the stern, which was broke to pieces and parted from the rest by the force of the sea soon after I had left rummaging her, was tossed, as it were, up, and cast on one side, and the sand was thrown so high on that side next her stern, that whereas there was a great place of water before, so that I could not come within a quarter of a mile of the wreck without swimming, I could now walk quite up to her when the tide was out; I was surprised with this at first, but soon concluded it must be done by the earthquake, and as by this violence the ship was more broken open than formerly, so many things came daily on shore, which the sea had loosened, and which the winds and water rolled by degrees to the land.

This wholly diverted my thoughts from the design of removing my habitation; and I busied my self mightily that day especially, in searching whether I could make any way into the ship, but I found nothing was to be expected of that kind, for that all the in-side of the ship was choaked up with sand. However, as I had learned not to despair of any thing, I resolved to pull every thing to pieces that I could of the ship, concluding that every thing I could get from her would be of some use or other to me.

May 3. I began with my saw and cut a piece of beam thro', which I thought held some of the upper part or quarter-deck together, and when I had cut it thro', I cleared away the sand as well as I could from the side which lay highest; but the tide coming in, I was obliged to give over for that time.

May 4. I went a fishing, but caught not one fish that I durst eat of, till I was weary of my sport, when just going to leave off, I caught a young dolphin. I had made me a long line of some rope yarn, but I had no hooks, yet I frequently caught fish enough, as much as I cared to eat; all which I dry'd in the sun, and eat them dry.

May 5. Worked on the wreck, cut another beam asunder, and brought three great fir planks off from the decks, which I ty'd together, and made swim on shore when the tide of flood came on.

May 6. Worked on the wreck, got several iron bolts out of her, and other pieces of iron work; worked very hard, and came home very much tyred, and had thoughts of giving it over.

May 7. Went to the wreck again, but with an intent not to work, but found the weight of the wreck had broke itself down, the beams being cut, that several pieces of the ship seemed to lie loose, and the in-side of the hold lay so open that I could see into it, but almost full of water and sand.

May 8. Went to the wreck, and carry'd an iron crow to wrench up the deck, which lay now quite clear of the water or sand; I wrenched open two planks, and brought them on shore also with the tide; I left the iron crow in the wreck for next day.

May 9. Went to the wreck, and with the crow made way into the body of the wreck, and felt several casks, and loosened them with the crow, but could not break them up; I felt also the roll of English lead, and could stir it, but it was too heavy to remove.

May 10, 11, 12, 13, 14. Went every day to the wreck, and got a great deal of pieces of timber, and boards, or plank, and 2 or 300 weight of iron.

May 15. I carry'd two hatchets to try if I could not cut a piece off of the roll of lead, by placing the edge of one hatchet, and driving it with the other; but as it lay about a foot and a half in the water, I could not make any blow to drive the hatchet.

May 16. It had blowed hard in the night, and the wreck appeared more broken by the force of the water; but I stayed so long in the woods to get pidgeons for food, that the tide prevented me going to the wreck that day.

May 17. I saw some pieces of the wreck blown on shore, at a great distance, near two miles off me, but resolved to see what they were, and found it was a piece of the head, but too heavy for me to bring away.

May 24. Every day to this day I worked on the wreck, and with hard labour I loosened some things so much with the crow, that the first blowing tide several casks floated out, and two of the seamens chests; but the wind blowing from the shore, nothing came to land that day but pieces of timber and a hogshead which had some Brazil pork in it, but the salt-water and the sand had spoiled it.

I continued this work every day to the 15th of June, except the time necessary to get food, which I always appointed, during this part of my employment, to be when the tide was up, that I might be ready when it was ebbed out, and by this time I had gotten timber, and plank, and iron-work enough to have builded a good boat, if I had known how; and also I got, at several times and in several pieces, near 100 weight of the sheet-lead.

June 16. Going down to the sea-side, I found a large tortoise or turtle; this was the first I had seen, which it seems was only my misfortune, not any defect of the place, or scarcity; for had I happened to be on the other side of the island, I might have had hundreds of them every day, as I found afterwards; but perhaps had paid dear enough for them.

June 17. I spent in cooking the turtle; I found in her three-score eggs, and her flesh was to me at that time the most savoury and pleasant that ever I tasted in my life, having had no flesh, but of goats and fowls, since I landed in this horrid place.

June 18. Rained all day, and stay'd within. I thought at this time the rain felt cold, and I was something chilly, which I knew was not usual in that latitude.

June 19. Very ill, and shivering, as if the weather had been cold.

June 20. No rest all night, violent pains in my head, and feaverish.

June 21. Very ill, frighted almost to death with the apprehensions of my sad condition, to be sick, and no help: prayed to God for the first time since the storm off of Hull, but scarce knew what I said, or why; my thoughts being all confused.

June 22. A little better, but under dreadful apprehensions of sickness.

June 23. Very bad again, cold shivering, and then a violent head-ach.

June 24. Much better.

June 25. An ague very violent; the fit held me seven hours, cold fit and hot, with faint sweats after it.

June 26. Better; and having no victuals to eat, took my gun, but found my self very weak; however, I killed a she-goat, and with much difficulty got it home, and broiled some of it and eat; I wou'd fain have stewed it and made some broth, but had no pot.

June 27. The ague again so violent that I lay a-bed all day, and neither eat or drank. I was ready to perish for thirst, but so weak, I had not strength to stand up, or to get my self any water to drink: prayed to God again, but was light-headed, and when I was not, I was so ignorant that I knew not what to say; only I lay and cry'd, 'Lord look upon me, Lord pity me, Lord have mercy upon me.' I suppose I did nothing else for two or three hours, till the fit wearing off, I fell asleep, and did not wake till far in the night; when I waked, I found my self much refreshed, but weak, and exceeding thirsty. However, as I had no water in my whole habitation, I was forced to lie till morning, and went to sleep again. In this second sleep, I had this terrible dream.

I thought that I was sitting on the ground on the outside of my wall, where I sat when the storm blew after the earthquake, and that I saw a man descend from a great black cloud, in a bright flame of fire, and light upon the ground. He was all over as bright as a flame, so that I could just bear to look towards him; his countenance was most inexpressibly dreadful, impossible for words to describe; when he stepped upon the ground with his feet, I thought the earth trembled, just as it had done before in the earthquake, and all the air looked, to my apprehension, as if it had been filled with flashes of fire.

He was no sooner landed upon the earth, but he moved forward towards me, with a long spear or weapon in his hand, to kill me; and when he came to a rising ground, at some distance, he spoke to me, or I heard a voice so terrible, that it is impossible to express the terror of it; all that I can say I understood, was this: 'Seeing all these things have not brought thee to repentance, now thou shalt die'; at which words, I thought he lifted up the spear that was in his hand, to kill me.

No one that shall ever read this account will expect that I should be able to describe the horrors of my soul at this terrible vision; I mean, that even while it was a dream, I even dreamed of those horrors; nor is it any more possible to describe the impression that remained upon my mind when I awaked and found it was but a dream.

I had, alas! no divine knowledge; what I had received by the good instruction of my father was then worn out by an uninterrupted series, for 8 years, of seafaring wickedness, and a constant conversation with nothing but such as were like my self, wicked and prophane to the last degree. I do not remember that I had in all that time one thought that so much as tended either to looking upwards toward God, or inwards towards a reflection upon my own ways; but a certain stupidity of soul, without desire of good or conscience of evil, had entirely overwhelmed me, and I was all that the most hardned, unthinking, wicked creature among our common sailors can be supposed to be, not having the least sense, either of the fear of God in danger, or of thankfulness to God in deliverances.

In the relating what is already past of my story, this will be the more easily believed, when I shall add, that thro' all the variety of miseries that had to this day befallen me, I never had so much as one thought of it being the hand of God, or that it was a just punishment for my sin; my rebellious behaviour against my father, or my present sins which were great; or so much as a punishment for the general course of my wicked life. When I was on the desperate expedition on the desart shores of Africa, I never had so much as one thought of what would become of me; or one wish to God to direct me whither I should go, or to keep me from the danger which apparently surrounded me, as well from voracious creatures as cruel savages : but I was meerly thoughtless of a God or a providence; acted like a meer brute from the principles of nature, and by the dictates of common sense only, and indeed hardly that.

When I was delivered and taken up at sea by the Portugal captain, well used, and dealt justly and honourably with, as well as charitably, I had not the least thankfulness on my thoughts. When again I was shipwrecked, ruined, and in danger of drowning on this island, I was as far from remorse, or looking on it as a judgment; I only said to my self often, that I was an unfortunate dog, and born to be always miserable.

It is true, when I got on shore first here, and found all my ship's crew drowned, and my self spared, I was surprized with a kind of extasie, and some transports of soul, which, had the grace of God assisted, might have come up to true thankfulness; but it ended where it begun, in a meer common flight of joy, or as I may say, being glad I was alive, without the least reflection upon the distinguishing goodness of the hand which had preserved me, and had singled me out to be preserved, when all the rest were destroyed; or an enquiry why Providence had been thus merciful to me; even just the same common sort of joy which seamen generally have after they are got safe ashore from a shipwreck, which they drown all in the next bowl of punch, and forget almost as soon at it is over; and all the rest of my life was like it.

Even when I was afterwards, on due consideration, made sensible of my condition, how I was cast on this dreadful place, out of the reach of humane kind, out of all hope of relief or prospect of redemption, as soon as I saw but a prospect of living, and that I should not starve and perish for hunger, all the sense of my affliction wore off, and I begun to be very easy, apply'd my self to the works proper for my preservation and supply, and was far enough from being afflicted at my condition, as a judgment from heaven, or as the hand of God against me; there were thoughts which very seldom entered into my head.

The growing up of the corn, as is hinted in my journal, had at first some little influence upon me, and began to affect me with seriousness, as long as I thought it had something miraculous in it; but as soon as ever that part of the thought was removed, all the impression which was raised from it wore off also, as I have noted already.

Even the earthquake, tho' nothing could be more terrible in its nature, or more immediately directing to the invisible power which alone directs such things, yet no sooner was the first fright over, but the impression it had made went off also. I had no more sense of God or His judgments, much less of the present affliction of my circumstances being from His hand, than if I had been in the most prosperous condition of life.

But now when I began to be sick, and a leisurely view of the miseries of death came to place itself before me, when my spirits began to sink under the burthen of a strong distemper, and nature was exhausted with the violence of the feaver, conscience, that had slept so long, begun to awake, and I began to reproach my self with my past life, in which I had so evidently, by uncommon wickedness, provoked the justice of God to lay me under uncommon strokes, and to deal with me in so vindictive a manner.

These reflections oppressed me for the second or third day of my distemper, and in the violence, as well of the feaver as of the dreadful reproaches of my conscience, extorted some words from me, like praying to God, tho' I cannot say they were either a prayer attended with desires or with hopes; it was rather the voice of meer fright and distress; my thoughts were confused, the convictions great upon my mind, and the horror of dying in such a miserable condition raised vapours into my head with the meer apprehensions; and in these hurries of my soul, I know not what my tongue might express: but it was rather exclamation, such as, 'Lord! what a miserable creature am I? If I should be sick, I shall certainly die for want of help, and what will become of me!' Then the tears burst out of my eyes, and I could say no more for a good while.

In this interval, the good advice of my father came to my mind, and presently his prediction which I mentioned at the beginning of this story, viz. that if I did take this foolish step, God would not bless me, and I would have leisure hereafter to reflect upon having neglected His counsel, when there might be none to assist in my recovery. 'Now,' said I aloud, 'my dear father's words are come to pass: God's justice has overtaken me, and I have none to help or hear me: I rejected the voice of Providence, which had mercifully put me in a posture or station of life wherein I might have been happy and easy; but I would neither see it my self, or learn to know the blessing of it from my parents; I left them to mourn over my folly, and now I am left to mourn under the consequences of it; I refused their help and assistance who wou'd have lifted me into the world, and wou'd have made every thing easy to me, and now I have difficulties to struggle with, too great even for nature itself to support, and no assistance, no help, no comfort, no advice.' Then I cry'd out, 'Lord, be my help, for I am in great distress.'

This was the first prayer, if I may call it so, that I had made for many years. But I return to my journal.

June 28. Having been somewhat refreshed with the sleep I had had, and the fit being entirely off, I got up; and tho' the fright and terror of my dream was very great, yet I considered that the fit of the ague wou'd return again the next day, and now was my time to get something to refresh and support my self when I should be ill; and the first thing I did, I filled a large square case bottle with water, and set it upon my table, in reach of my bed; and to take off the chill or aguish disposition of the water, I put about a quarter of a pint of rum into it, and mixed them together; then I got me a piece of the goat's flesh, and broiled it on the coals, but could eat very little; I walked about, but was very weak, and withal very sad and heavy-hearted in the sense of my miserable condition; dreading the return of my distemper the next day; at night I made my supper of three of the turtle's eggs, which I roasted in the ashes, and eat, as we call it, in the shell; and this was the first bit of meat I had ever asked God's blessing to, even as I cou'd remember, in my whole life.

After I had eaten, I try'd to walk, but found my self so weak that I cou'd hardly carry the gun (for I never went out without that), so I went but a little way, and sat down upon the ground, looking out upon the sea, which was just before me, and very calm and smooth. As I sat here, some such thoughts as these occurred to me.

What is this earth and sea of which I have seen so much? Whence is it produced? And what am I and all the other creatures, wild and tame, humane and brutal? Whence are we?

Sure we are all made by some secret power, who formed the earth and sea, the air and sky; and who is that?

Then it followed most naturally, It is God that has made it all. Well, but then it came on strangely, if God has made all these things, He guides and governs them all, and all things that concern them; for the power that could make all things must certainly have power to guide and direct them.

If so, nothing can happen in the great circuit of His works, either without His knowledge or appointment.

And if nothing happens without His knowledge, He knows that I am here, and am in this dreadful condition; and if nothing happens without His appointment, He has appointed all this to befal me.

Nothing occurred to my thought to contradict any of these conclusions; and therefore it rested upon me with the greater force that it must needs be, that God had appointed all this to befal me; that I was brought to this miserable circumstance by His direction, He having the sole power, not of me only, but of every thing that happened in the world. Immediately it followed:

Why has God done this to me? What have I done to be thus used?

My conscience presently checked me in that enquiry, as if I had blasphemed, and methought it spoke to me like a voice: 'WRETCH! dost thou ask what thou hast done? Look back upon a dreadful misspent life, and ask thy self what thou hast *not* done; ask, Why is it that thou wert not long ago destroyed? Why wert thou not drowned in Yarmouth roads? killed in the fight when the ship was taken by the Sallee man of war? devoured by the wild beasts on the coast of Africa? or drowned *here*, when all the crew perished but thy self? Dost thou ask, "What have I done?"'

I was struck dumb with these reflections, as one astonished, and had not a word to say, no, not to answer to my self, but rose up pensive and sad, walked back to my retreat, and went up over my wall, as if I had been going to bed, but my thoughts were sadly disturbed, and I had no inclination to sleep; so I sat down in my chair and lighted my lamp, for it began to be dark. Now as the apprehension of the return of my distemper terrify'd me very much, it occurred to my thought, that the Brasilians take no physick but their tobacco for almost all distempers; and I had a piece of a roll of tobacco in one of the chests which was quite cured, and some also that was green and not quite cured.

I went, directed by Heaven, no doubt; for in this chest I found a cure, both for soul and body. I opened the chest and found what I looked for, viz. the tobacco; and as the few books I had saved lay there too, I took out one of the Bibles which I mentioned before, and which to this time I had not found leisure, or so much as inclination, to look into; I say, I took it out, and brought both that and the tobacco with me to the table.

What use to make of the tobacco I knew not, as to my distemper, or whether it was good for it or no; but I try'd several experiments with it, as if I was resolved it should hit one way or other. I first took a piece of a leaf, and chewed it in my mouth, which indeed at first almost stupify'd my brain, the tobacco being green and strong, and that I had not been much used to it; then I took some and steeped it an hour or two in some rum, and resolved to take a dose of it when I lay down; and lastly, I burnt some upon a pan of coals, and held my nose close over the smoke of it as long as I could bear it, as well for the heat as almost for suffocation.

In the interval of this operation, I took up the Bible and began to read, but my head was too much disturbed with the tobacco to bear reading, at least that time; only having opened the book casually, the first words that occur'd to me were these: *Call on me in the day of trouble, and I will deliver, and thou shalt glorify me.*

The words were very apt to my case, and made some impression upon my thoughts at the time of reading them, tho' not so much as they did afterwards; for as for being delivered, the word had no sound, as I may say, to me; the thing was so remote, so impossible in my apprehension of things, that I began to say as the children of Israel did, when they were promised flesh to eat: *Can*

God spread a table in the wilderness? so I began to say, 'Can God Himself deliver me from this place?' and as it was not for many years that any hope appeared, this prevailed very often upon my thoughts; but, however, the words made a great impression upon me, and I mused upon them very often. It grew now late, and the tobacco had, as I said, dozed my head so much, that I inclined to sleep; so I left my lamp burning in the cave, least I should want any thing in the night, and went to bed; but before I lay down, I did what I never had done in all my life, I kneeled down and prayed to God to fulfil the promise to me, that if I called upon Him in the day of trouble, He would deliver me; after my broken and imperfect prayer was over, I drunk the rum in which I had steeped the tobacco, which was so strong and rank of the tobacco, that indeed I could scarce get it down; immediately upon this I went to bed. I found presently it flew up in my head violently, but I fell into a sound sleep, and waked no more 'till by the sun it must necessarily be near three a-clock in the afternoon the next day; nay, to this hour, I'm partly of the opinion that I slept all the next day and night, and 'till almost three that day after; for otherwise I knew not how I should lose a day out of my reckoning in the days of the week, as it appeared some years after I had done: for if I had lost it by crossing and re-crossing the line, I should have lost more than one day. But certainly I lost a day in my accompt, and never knew which way.

Be that, however, one way or th' other, when I awaked I found my self exceedingly refreshed, and my spirits lively and chearful; when I got up, I was stronger than I was the day before, and my stomach better, for I was hungry; and in short, I had no fit the next day, but continued much altered for the better; this was the 29th.

The 30th was my well day of course, and I went abroad with my gun, but did not care to travel too far. I killed a sea fowl or two, something like a brand goose, and brought them home, but was not very forward to eat them; so I ate some more of the turtle's eggs, which were very good. This evening I renewed the medicine which I had supposed did me good the day before, viz. the tobacco steeped in rum, only I did not take so much as before, nor did I chew any of the leaf, or hold my head over the smoke; however I was not so well the next day, which was the first of July, as I hoped I shou'd have been; for I had a little spice of the cold fit, but it was not much.

July 2. I renewed the medicine all the three ways, and dozed my self with it as at first; and doubled the quantity which I drank.

3. I missed the fit for good and all, tho' I did not recover my full strength for some weeks after; while I was thus gathering strength, my thoughts run exceedingly upon this scripture, I *will deliver thee*, and the impossibility of my deliverance lay much upon my mind in barr of my ever expecting it. But as I was discouraging my self with such thoughts, it occurred to my mind that I pored so much upon my deliverance from the main affliction, that I disregarded the deliverance I had received; and I was, as it were, made to ask my self such questions as these, viz. Have I not been delivered, and wonderfully too, from sickness? from the most distressed condition that could be, and that was so frightful to me? and what notice had I taken of it? Had I done my part? God had delivered me, but I had not glorify'd Him; that is to say, I had not owned and been thankful for that as a deliverance, and how cou'd I expect greater deliverance?

This touched my heart very much, and immediately I kneeled down and gave God thanks aloud for my recovery from my sickness.

July 4. In the morning I took the Bible, and beginning at the New Testament, I began seriously to read it, and imposed upon my self to read a while every morning and every night, not tying my self to the number of chapters, but as long as my thoughts shou'd engage me. It was not long after I set seriously to this work, but I found my heart more deeply and sincerely affected with the wickedness of my past life. The impression of my dream revived, and the words, *All these things have not brought thee to repentance*, ran seriously in my thought. I was earnestly begging of God to give me repentance, when it happened providentially the very day that reading the scripture, I came to these words, *He is exalted a Prince and a Saviour, to give repentance, and to give remission.* I threw down the book, and with my heart as well as my hands lifted up to heaven, in a kind of extasy of joy, I cry'd out aloud, 'Jesus, thou son of David, Jesus, thou exalted Prince and Saviour, give me repentance!'

This was the first time that I could say, in the true sense of the words, that I prayed in all my life; for now I prayed with a sense of my condition, and with a true scripture view of hope founded on the encouragement of the word of God; and from this time, I may say, I began to have hope that God would hear me.

Now I began to construe the words mentioned above, *Call on me, and I will deliver you,* in a different sense from what I had ever done before; for then I had no notion of any thing being called deliverance, but my being delivered from the captivity I was in; for tho' I was indeed at large in the place, yet the island was certainly a prison to me, and that in the worst sense in the world; but now I learned to take it in another sense. Now I looked back upon my past life with such horrour, and my sins appeared so dreadful, that my soul sought nothing of God but deliverance from the load of guilt that bore down all my comfort: as for my solitary life, it was nothing; I did not so much as pray to be delivered from it, or think of it; it was all of no consideration in comparison to this. And I add this part here, to hint to whoever shall read it, that whenever they come to a true sense of things, they will find deliverance from sin a much greater blessing than deliverance from affliction.

But leaving this part, I return to my journal.

My condition began now to be, tho' not less miserable as to my way of living, yet much easier to my mind; and my thoughts being directed, by a constant reading the scripture and praying to God, to things of a higher nature, I had a great deal of comfort within, which till now I knew nothing of; also, as my health and strength returned, I bestirred my self to furnish my self with every thing that I wanted, and make my way of living as regular as I could.

From the 4th of July to the 14th, I was chiefly employed in walking about with my gun in my hand, a little and a little at a time, as a man that was gathering up his strength after a fit of sickness; for it is hardly to be imagined how low I was, and to what weakness I was reduced. The application which I made use of was perfectly new, and perhaps what had never cured an ague before, neither can I recommend it to any one to practise, by this experiment; and tho' it did carry off the fit, yet it rather contributed to weakening me; for I had frequent convulsions in my nerves and limbs for some time.

I learned from it also this in particular, that being abroad in the rainy season was the most pernicious thing to my health that could be, especially in those rains which came attended with storms and hurricanes of wind; for as the rain which came in the dry season was always most accompany'd with such storms, so I found that rain was much more dangerous than the rain which fell in September and October.

I had been now in this unhappy island above 10 months; all possibility of deliverance from this condition seemed to be entirely taken from me; and I firmly believed that no humane shape had ever set foot upon that place. Having now secured my habitation, as I thought, fully to my mind, I had a great desire to make a more perfect discovery of the island, and to see what other productions I might find, which I yet knew nothing of.

It was the 15th of July that I began to take a more particular survey of the island it self. I went up the creek first, where, as I hinted, I brought my rafts on shore; I found, after I came about two miles up, that the tide did not flow any higher, and that it was no more than a little brook of running water, and very fresh and good; but this being the dry season, there was hardly any water in some parts of it, at least not enough to run in any stream so as it could be perceived.

On the bank of this brook I found many pleasant savana's or meadows, plain, smooth, and covered with grass; and on the rising parts of them next to the higher grounds, where the water, as it might be supposed, never overflowed, I found a great deal of tobacco, green, and growing to a great and very strong stalk; there were divers other plants which I had no notion of, or understanding about, and might perhaps have vertues of their own, which I could not find out.

I searched for the cassava root, which the Indians in all that climate make their bread of, but I could find none. I saw large plants of alloes, but did not then understand them. I saw several sugar canes, but wild and, for want of cultivation, imperfect.[29] I contented my self with these discoveries for this time, and came

back musing with my self what course I might take to know
the vertue and goodness of any of the fruits or plants which I
should discover; but could bring it to no conclusion; for, in
short, I made so little observation while I was in the Brasils,
that I knew little of the plants in the field, at least very little
that might serve me to any purpose now in my distress.

The next day, the 16th, I went up the same way again, and
after going something farther than I had gone the day before, I
found the brook, and the savana's began to cease, and the country
became more woody than before; in this part I found different
fruits, and particularly I found mellons upon the ground in
great abundance, and grapes upon the trees; the vines had
spread indeed over the trees, and the clusters of grapes were just
now in their prime, very ripe and rich. This was a surprising
discovery, and I was exceeding glad of them; but I was warned
by my experience to eat sparingly of them, remembring that
when I was ashore in Barbary, the eating of grapes killed several
of our English men who were slaves there, by throwing them
into fluxes and feavers. But I found an excellent use for these
grapes, and that was to cure or dry them in the sun, and keep
them as dry'd grapes or raisins are kept, which I thought would
be, as indeed they were, as wholesom as agreeable to eat, when
no grapes might be to be had.

I spent all that evening there, and went not back to my habitation, which, by the way, was the first night, as I might say, I
had lain from home. In the night I took my first contrivance, and
got up into a tree, where I slept well, and the next morning
proceeded upon my discovery, travelling near four miles, as I
might judge by the length of the valley, keeping still due north,
with a ridge of hills on the south and north-side of me.

At the end of this march I came to an opening, where the
country seemed to descend to the west, and a little spring of fresh
water, which issued out of the side of the hill by me, run the
other way, that is, due east; and the country appeared so fresh,
so green, so flourishing, every thing being in a constant verdure
or flourish of spring, that it looked like a planted garden.

I descended a little on the side of that delicious vale, surveying
it with a secret kind of pleasure (tho' mixt with my other afflict-

ing thoughts) to think that this was all my own, that I was king and lord of all this country indefeasibly, and had a right of possession; and if I could convey it, I might have it in inheritance as compleatly as any lord of a mannor in England. I saw here abundance of cocoa trees, orange, and lemon, and citron trees; but all wild, and very few bearing any fruit, at least not then. However, the green limes that I gathered were not only pleasant to eat, but very wholesome; and I mixed their juice afterwards with water, which made it very wholesome, and very cool and refreshing.

I found now I had business enough to gather and carry home; and I resolved to lay up a store, as well of grapes as limes and lemons, to furnish my self for the wet season, which I knew was approaching.

In order to this, I gathered a great heap of grapes in one place, and a lesser heap in another place, and a great parcel of limes and lemons in another place; and taking a few of each with me, I travelled homeward, and resolved to come again, and bring a bag or sack, or what I could make, to carry the rest home.

Accordingly, having spent three days in this journey, I came home; so I must now call my tent and my cave. But, before I got thither, the grapes were spoiled; the richness of the fruits and the weight of the juice having broken them and bruised them, they were good for little or nothing; as to the limes, they were good, but I could bring but a few.

The next day, being the 19th, I went back, having made me two small bags to bring home my harvest; but I was surprized, when coming to my heap of grapes, which were so rich and fine when I gathered them, I found them all spread about, trod to pieces, and dragged about, some here, some there, and abundance eaten and devoured. By this I concluded there were some wild creatures thereabouts which had done this; but what they were I knew not.

However, as I found that there was no laying them up on heaps, and no carrying them away in a sack, but that one way they would be destroyed, and the other way they would be crushed with their own weight, I took another course; for I gathered a large quantity of the grapes, and hung them up upon the out branches of the trees, that they might cure and dry in the sun; and as for the limes and lemons, I carry'd as many back as I could well stand under.

When I came home from this journey, I contemplated with great pleasure the fruitfulness of that valley and the pleasantness of the situation, the security from storms on that side of the water, and the wood, and concluded that I had pitched upon a place to fix my abode, which was by far the worst part of the country. Upon the whole I began to consider of removing my habitation; and to look out for a place equally safe as where I now was, scituate, if possible, in that pleasant fruitful part of the island.

This thought run long in my head, and I was exceeding fond of it for some time, the pleasantness of the place tempting me; but when I came to a nearer view of it, and to consider I was now by the sea-side, where it was at least possible that something might happen to my advantage, and by the same ill fate that brought me hither, might bring some other unhappy wretches to the same place; and tho' it was scarce probable that any such thing should ever happen, yet to enclose my self among the hills and woods, in the center of the island, was to anticipate my bondage, and to render such an affair not only improbable, but impossible; and that therefore I ought not by any means to remove.

However, I was so enamoured of this place, that I spent much of my time there for the whole remaining part of the month of July; and tho' upon second thoughts I resolved as above, not to remove, yet I built me a little kind of a bower, and surrounded it at a distance with a strong fence, being a double hedge, as high as I could reach, well staked, and filled between with brushwood; and here I lay very secure, sometimes two or three nights together, always going over it with a ladder, as before; so that I fancy'd now I had my country-house, and my sea-coast-house: and this work took me up to the beginning of August.

I had but newly finished my fence, and began to enjoy my labour, but the rains came on, and made me stick close to my first habitation; for tho' I had made me a tent like the other, with a piece of a sail, and spread it very well, yet I had not the shelter of a hill to keep me from storms, nor a cave behind me to retreat into, when the rains were extraordinary.

About the beginning of August, as I said, I had finished my bower, and began to enjoy my self. The third of August, I found the grapes I had hung up were perfectly dry'd, and indeed were excellent good raisins of the sun, so I began to take them down from the trees, and it was very happy that I did so; for the rains which followed would have spoiled them, and I had lost the best part of my winter food; for I had above two hundred large bunches of them. No sooner had I taken them all down, and carry'd most of them home to my cave, but it began to rain, and from hence, which was the fourteenth of August, it rained more or less, every day, till the middle of October; and sometimes so violently that I could not stir out of my cave for several days.

In this season I was much surprized with the increase of my family. I had been concerned for the loss of one of my cats, who run away from me, or, as I thought, had been dead, and I heard no more tale or tidings of her, till to my astonishment she came home about the end of August, with three kittens; this was the more strange to me, because tho' I had killed a wild cat, as I called it, with my gun, yet I thought it was a quite differing kind from our European cats; yet the young cats were the same kind of house breed like the old one; and both my cats being females, I thought it very strange. But from these three cats, I afterwards came to be so pestered with cats, that I was forced to kill them like vermine, or wild beasts, and to drive them from my house as much as possible.

From the fourteenth of August to the twenty sixth, incessant rain, so that I could not stir, and was now very careful not to be much wet. In this confinement I began to be straitned for food, but venturing out twice, I one day killed a goat, and the last day, which was the twenty sixth, found a very large tortoise, which was a treat to me, and my food was regulated thus: I eat a bunch of raisins for my breakfast, a piece of the goat's flesh or of the turtle for my dinner, broiled; for, to my great misfortune, I had no vessel to boil or stew any thing; and two or three of the turtle's eggs for my supper.

During this confinement in my cover by the rain, I worked daily two or three hours at enlarging my cave, and by degrees worked it on towards one side, till I came to the out-side of the hill, and made a door or way out, which came beyond my fence or wall, and so I came in and out this way; but I was not perfectly easy at lying so open; for as I had managed my self before, I was in a perfect enclosure, whereas now I thought I lay exposed, and open for any thing to come in upon me; and yet I could not perceive that there was any living thing to fear, the biggest creature that I had yet seen upon the island being a goat.

September the thirtieth, I was now come to the unhappy anniversary of my landing. I cast up the notches on my post, and found I had been on shore three hundred and sixty five days. I kept this day as a solemn fast, setting it apart to religious exercise, prostrating my self on the ground with the most serious humiliation, confessing my sins to God, acknowledging His righteous judgments upon me, and praying to Him to have mercy on me, through Jesus Christ; and having not tasted the least refreshment for twelve hours, even till the going down of the sun, I then eat a bisket cake and a bunch of grapes, and went to bed, finishing the day as I began it.

I had all this time observed no Sabbath-day; for as at first I had no sense of religion upon my mind, I had after some time omitted to distinguish the weeks, by making a longer notch than ordinary for the Sabbath day, and so did not really know what any of the days were; but now having cast up the days, as above, I found I had been there a year; so I divided it into weeks, and set apart every seventh day for a Sabbath; though I found at the end of my account I had lost a day or two in my reckoning.

A little after this my ink began to fail me, and so I contented my self to use it more sparingly, and to write down only the most remarkable events of my life, without continuing a daily memorandum of other things.

The rainy season and the dry season began now to appear regular to me, and learned to divide them, so as to provide for them accordingly. But I bought all my experience before I had it; and this I am going to relate, was one of the most discouraging experiments that I had made at all. I have mentioned that I had saved the few ears of barley and rice, which I had so surprizingly found spring up, as I thought, of themselves, and believe there was about thirty stalks of rice, and about twenty of barley; and now I thought it a proper time to sow it after the rains, the sun being in its southern position, going from me.

Accordingly I dug up a piece of ground as well as I could with my wooden spade, and dividing it into two parts, I sowed my grain; but as I was sowing, it casually occurred to my thoughts that I would not sow it all at first, because I did not know when was the proper time for it; so I sowed about two thirds of the seed, leaving about a handful of each.

It was a great comfort to me afterwards that I did so, for not one grain of that I sowed this time came to any thing; for the dry months following, the earth having had no rain after the seed was sown, it had no moisture to assist its growth, and never came up at all till the wet season had come again, and then it grew as if it had been but newly sown.

Finding my first seed did not grow, which I easily imagined was by the drought, I sought for a moister piece of ground to make another trial in, and I dug up a piece of ground near my new bower and sowed the rest of my seed in February, a little before the vernal equinox; and this, having the rainy months of March and April to water it, sprung up very pleasantly, and yielded a very good crop; but having part of the seed left only, and not daring to sow all that I had, I had but a small quantity at last, my whole crop not amounting to above half a peck of each kind.

But by this experiment I was made master of my business, and knew exactly when the proper season was to sow; and that I might expect two seed times and two harvests every year.

While this corn was growing, I made a little discovery which was of use to me afterwards. As soon as the rains were over, and the weather began to settle, which was about the month of November, I made a visit up the country to my bower, where though I had not been some months, yet I found all things just as I left them. The circle or double hedge that I had made was not only firm and entire, but the stakes which I had cut out of some trees that grew thereabouts were all shot out and grown with long branches, as much as a willow-tree usually shoots the first year after lopping its head. I could not tell what tree to call it, that these stakes were cut from. I was surprized, and yet very well pleased, to see the young trees grow; and I pruned them, and led them up to grow as much alike as I could; and it is scarce credible how beautiful a figure they grew into in three years; so that though the hedge made a circle of about twenty five yards in diameter, yet the trees, for such I might now call them, soon covered it; and it was a compleat shade, sufficient to lodge under all the dry season.

This made me resolve to cut some more stakes, and make me a hedge like this in a semicircle round my wall; I mean that of my first dwelling, which I did; and placing the trees or stakes in a double row, at about eight yards distance from my first fence, they grew presently, and were at first a fine cover to my habitation, and afterwards served for a defence also, as I shall observe in its order.

I found now that the seasons of the year might generally be divided, not into summer and winter, as in Europe, but into the rainy seasons and the dry seasons, which were generally thus:

Half February March Half April	Rainy, the sun being then on or near the equinox.
Half April May June July Half August	Dry, the sun being then to the north of the line.
Half August September Half October	Rainy, the sun being then come back.
Half October November December January Half February	Dry, the sun being then to the south of the line.

The rainy season sometimes held longer or shorter, as the winds happened to blow; but this was the general observation I made. After I had found by experience the ill consequence of being abroad in the rain, I took care to furnish my self with provisions before hand, that I might not be obliged to go out; and I sat within doors as much as possible during the wet months.

This time I found much employment (and very suitable also to the time), for I found great occasion of many things which I had no way to furnish my self with, but by hard labour and constant application; particularly, I try'd many ways to make my self a basket, but all the twigs I could get for the purpose proved so brittle that they would do nothing. It proved of excellent advantage to me now, that when I was a boy, I used to take great delight in standing at a basket-makers in the town where my father lived, to see them make their wicker-ware; and being, as boys usually are, very officious to help, and a great observer of the manner how they worked those things, and sometimes lending a hand, I had by this means full knowledge of the methods of it, that I wanted nothing but the materials; when it came into my mind that the twigs of that tree from whence I cut my stakes that grew, might possibly be as tough as the sallows and willows and osiers in England, and I resolved to try.

Accordingly the next day, I went to my country-house, as I called it, and cutting some of the smaller twigs, I found them to my purpose as much as I could desire; whereupon I came the next time prepared with an hatchet to cut down a quantity, which I soon found, for there was great plenty of them; these I set up to dry within my circle or hedge, and when they were fit for use, I carry'd them to my cave, and here during the next season, I employed my self in making, as well as I could, a great many baskets, both to carry earth, or to carry or lay up any thing as I had occasion; and tho' I did not finish them very handsomly, yet I made them sufficiently serviceable for my purpose; and thus afterwards I took care never to be without them; and as my wicker-ware decayed, I made more; especially I made strong deep baskets to place my corn in, instead of sacks, when I should come to have any quantity of it.

Having mastered this difficulty, and employed a world of

time about it, I bestirred my self to see if possible how to supply two wants. I had no vessels to hold any thing that was liquid, except two runlets which were almost full of rum, and some glass-bottles, some of the common size, and others which were case-bottles, square, for the holding of waters, spirits, &c. I had not so much as a pot to boil any thing, except a great kettle, which I saved out of the ship, and which was too big for such use as I desired it, viz. to make broth and stew a bit of meat by it self. The second thing I would fain have had, was a tobacco-pipe, but it was impossible to make one; however, I found a contrivance for that too at last.

I employed my self in planting my second rows of stakes or piles, and in this wicker working, all the summer or dry season, when another business took me up more time than it could be imagined I could spare.

I mentioned before that I had a great mind to see the whole island, and that I had travelled up the brook, and so on to where I built my bower, and where I had an opening quite to the sea on the other side of the island. I now resolved to travel quite cross to the sea-shore on that side; so taking my gun, a hatchet, and my dog, and a larger quantity of powder and shot than usual, with two bisket cakes and a great bunch of raisins in my pouch for my store,[30] I began my journey. When I had passed the vale where my bower stood as above, I came within view of the sea, to the west, and it being a very clear day, I fairly descry'd land, whether an island or a continent, I could not tell; but it lay very high, extending from the west to the w.s.w. at a very great distance; by my guess it could not be less than fifteen or twenty leagues off.

I could not tell what part of the world this might be, otherwise than that I knew it must be part of America, and, as I concluded by all my observations, must be near the Spanish dominions, and perhaps was all inhabited by savages, where if I should have landed, I had been in a worse condition than I was now; and therefore I acquiesced in the dispositions of Providence, which I began now to own and to believe ordered every thing for the best; I say, I quieted my mind with this, and left afflicting my self with fruitless wishes of being there.

Besides, after some pause upon this affair, I considered that if this land was the Spanish coast, I should certainly, one time or other, see some vessel pass or repass one way or other; but if not, then it was the savage coast between th Spanish country and Brasils, which are indeed the worst of savages; for they are cannibals, or men-eaters, and fail not to murther and devour all the humane bodies that fall into their hands.

With these considerations I walked leisurely forward, I found that side of the island where I now was much pleasanter than mine, the open or savanna fields sweet, adorned with flowers and grass, and full of very fine woods. I saw abundance of parrots, and fain I would have caught one, if possible, to have kept it to be tame, and taught it to speak to me. I did, after some pains taking, catch a young parrot, for I knocked it down with a stick, and having recovered it, I brought it home; but it was some years before I could make him speak: however, at last I taught him to call me by my name very familiarly. But the accident that followed, tho' it be a trifle, will be very diverting in its place.

I was exceedingly diverted with this journey. I found in the low grounds hares, as I thought them to be, and foxes, but they differed greatly from all the other kinds I had met with; nor could I satisfy my self to eat them, tho' I killed several. But I had no need to be ventrous; for I had no want of food, and of that which was very good too; especially these three sorts, viz. goats, pidgeons, and turtle or tortoise; which, added to my grapes, Leaden-hall Market [31] could not have furnished a table better than I, in proportion to the company; and tho' my case was deplorable enough, yet I had great cause for thankfulness, that I was not driven to any extremities for food; but rather plenty, even to dainties.

I never travelled in this journey above two miles outright in a day, or thereabouts; but I took so many turns and returns to see what discoveries I could make, that I came weary enough to the place where I resolved to sit down for all night; and then I either reposed my self in a tree, or surrounded my self with a row of stakes set upright in the ground, either from one tree to another, or so as no wild creature could come at me without waking me.

As soon as I came to the sea shore, I was surprized to see that I had taken up my lot on the worst side of the island; for here indeed the shore was covered with innumerable turtles, whereas on the other side I had found but three in a year and half. Here was also an infinite number of fowls of many kinds, some which I had seen and some which I had not seen before, and many of them very good meat; but such as I knew not the names of, except those called penguins.

I could have shot as many as I pleased, but was very sparing of my powder and shot: and therefore had more mind to kill a she goat, if I could, which I could better feed on; and though there were many goats here more than on my side the island, yet it was with much more difficulty that I could come near them, the country being flat and even, and they saw me much sooner than when I was on the hill.

I confess this side of the country was much pleasanter than mine, but yet I had not the least inclination to remove; for as I was fixed in my habitation, it became natural to me, and I seemed all the while I was here to be as it were upon a journey, and from home. However, I travelled along the shore of the sea towards the east, I suppose about twelve miles; and then setting up a great pole upon the shore for a mark, I concluded I would go home again; and that the next journey I took should be on the other side of the island, east from my dwelling, and so round till I came to my post again: of which in its place.

I took another way to come back than that I went, thinking I could easily keep all the island so much in my view that I could not miss finding my first dwelling by viewing the country; but I found my self mistaken; for being come about two or three miles, I found my self descended into a very large valley; but so surrounded with hills, and those hills covered with wood, that I could not see which was my way by any direction but that of the sun, nor even then, unless I knew very well the position of the sun at that time of the day.

It happened to my farther misfortune, that the weather proved hazey for three or four days while I was in this valley; and not being able to see the sun, I wandered about very uncomfortably, and at last was obliged to find out the sea side, look for my post, and come back the same way I went; and then by easy journies I turned homeward, the weather being exceeding hot, and my gun, ammunition, hatchet, and other things very heavy.

In this journey my dog surprized a young kid, and seized upon it, and I running in to take hold of it, caught it, and saved it alive from the dog. I had a great mind to bring it home if I could; for I had often been musing whether it might not be possible to get a kid or two, and so raise a breed of tame goats, which might supply me when my powder and shot should be all spent.

I made a collar to this little creature, and with a string which I made of some rope-yarn, which I always carry'd about me, I led him along, tho' with some difficulty, till I came to my bower, and there I enclosed him and left him; for I was very impatient to be at home, from whence I had been absent above a month.

I cannot express what a satisfaction it was to me, to come into my old hutch,[32] and lye down in my hamock-bed. This little wandring journey, without settled place of abode, had been so unpleasant to me, that my own house, as I called it to my self, was a perfect settlement to me, compared to that; and it rendred every thing about me so comfortable, that I resolved I would never go a great way from it again, while it should be my lot to stay on the island.

I reposed my self here a week, to rest and regale my self after my long journey; during which, most of the time was taken up in the weighty affair of making a cage for my Poll, who began now to be a meer domestick, and to be mighty well acquainted with me. Then I began to think of the poor kid, which I had penned in within my little circle, and resolved to go and fetch it home, or give it some food; accordingly I went, and found it where I left it, for indeed it could not get out, but almost starved for want of food. I went and cut bows of trees, and branches of such shrubs as I could find, and threw it over, and having fed it, I ty'd it as I did before, to lead it away; but it was so tame with being hungry, that I had no need to have ty'd it; for it followed me like a dog; and as I continually fed it, the creature became so loving, so gentle, and so fond, that it became from that time one of my domesticks also, and would never leave me afterwards.

The rainy season of the autumnal equinox was now come, and I kept the 30th of September in the same solemn manner as before, being the anniversary of my landing on the island, having now been there two years, and no more prospect of being delivered than the first day I came there. I spent the whole day in humble and thankful acknowledgments of the many wonderful mercies which my solitary condition was attended with, and without which it might have been infinitely more miserable. I gave humble and hearty thanks that God had been pleased to discover to me, even that it was possible I might be more happy in this solitary condition, than I should have been in a liberty of society, and in all the pleasures of the world; that He could fully make up to me the deficiencies of my solitary state, and the want of humane society, by His presence and the communications of His grace to my soul, supporting, comforting, and encouraging me to depend upon His providence here, and hope for His eternal presence hereafter.

It was now that I began sensibly to feel how much more happy this life I now led was, with all its miserable circumstances, than the wicked, cursed, abominable life I led all the past part of my days; and now I changed both my sorrows and my joys; my very desires altered, my affections changed their gusts, and my delights were perfectly new from what they were at my first coming, or indeed for the two years past.

Before, as I walked about, either on my hunting, or for viewing the country, the anguish of my soul at my condition would break out upon me on a sudden, and my very heart would die within me, to think of the woods, the mountains, the desarts I was in; and how I was a prisoner, locked up with the eternal bars and bolts of the ocean, in an uninhabited wilderness, without redemption. In the midst of the greatest composures of my mind, this would break out upon me like a storm, and make me wring my hands and weep like a child. Sometimes it would take me in the middle of my work, and I would immediately sit down and sigh, and look upon the ground for an hour or two together; and this was still worse to me; for if I could burst out into tears, or vent my self by words, it would go off, and the grief having exhausted it self would abate.

But now I began to exercise my self with new thoughts; I daily read the word of God, and apply'd all the comforts of it to my present-state. One morning, being very sad, I opened the Bible upon these words, *I will never, never leave thee, nor forsake thee;*[33] immediately it occurred that these words were to me; why else should they be directed in such a manner, just at the moment when I was mourning over my condition, as one forsaken of God and man? 'Well then,' said I, 'if God does not forsake me, of what ill consequence can it be, or what matters it, though the world should all forsake me, seeing, on the other hand, if I had all the world, and should lose the favour and blessing of God, there wou'd be no comparison in the loss?'

From this moment I began to conclude in my mind that it was possible for me to be more happy in this forsaken, solitary condition than it was probable I should ever have been in any other particular state in the world; and with this thought I was going to give thanks to God for bringing me to this place.

I know not what it was, but something shocked my mind at that thought, and I durst not speak the words. 'How canst thou be such a hypocrite,' said I, even audibly, 'to pretend to be thankful for a condition, which however thou may'st endeavour to be contented with, thou would'st rather pray heartily to be delivered from?' So I stopped there; but though I could not say I thanked God for being there, yet I sincerely gave thanks to God for opening my eyes, by whatever afflicting providences, to see the former condition of my life, and to mourn for my wickedness, and repent. I never opened the Bible, or shut it, but my very soul within me blessed God for directing my friend in England, without any order of mine, to pack it up among my goods; and for assisting me afterwards to save it out of the wreck of the ship.

Thus, and in this disposition of mind, I began my third year; and tho' I have not given the reader the trouble of so particular account of my works this year as the first, yet in general it may be observed that I was very seldom idle; but having regularly divided my time, according to the several daily employments that were before me, such as, first, my duty to God, and the reading the scriptures, which I constantly set apart some time for thrice every day; secondly, the going abroad with my gun for food.

which generally took me up three hours in every morning, when it did not rain; thirdly, the ordering, curing, preserving, and cooking what I had killed or catched for my supply; these took up great part of the day; also it is to be considered that the middle of the day, when the sun was in the zenith, the violence of the heat was too great to stir out; so that about four hours in the evening was all the time I could be supposed to work in; with this exception, that sometimes I changed my hours of hunting and working, and went to work in the morning, and abroad with my gun in the afternoon.

To this short time allowed for labour, I desire may be added the exceeding laboriousness of my work; the many hours which, for want of tools, want of help, and want of skill, every thing I did took up out of my time. For example, I was full two and forty days making me a board for a long shelf, which I wanted in my cave; whereas two sawyers, with their tools and a saw-pit, would have cut six of them out of the same tree in half a day.

My case was this: It was to be a large tree which was to be cut down, because my board was to be a broad one. This tree I was three days a cutting down, and two more cutting off the bows, and reducing it to a log or piece of timber. With inexpressible hacking and hewing I reduced both sides of it into chips, till it begun to be light enough to move; then I turned it, and made one side of it smooth and flat as a board from end to end; then turning that side downward, cut the other side, till I brought the plank to be about three inches thick, and smooth on both sides. Any one may judge the labour of my hands in such a piece of work: but labour and patience carry'd me through that and many other things. I only observe this in particular, to shew the reason why so much of my time went away with so little work, viz. that what might be a little to be done with help and tools, was a vast labour, and required a prodigious time to do alone and by hand.

But notwithstanding this, with patience and labour I went through many things; and indeed every thing that my circumstances made necessary to me to do, as will appear by what follows.

I was now, in the months of November and December, expecting my crop of barley and rice. The ground I had manured or dug up for them was not great; for as I observed, my seed of each was not above the quantity of half a peck; for I had lost one whole crop by sowing in the dry season; but now my crop promised very well, when on a sudden I found I was in danger of losing it all again by enemies of several sorts, which it was scarce possible to keep from it; as first, the goats, and wild creatures which I called hares, who tasting the sweetness of the blade, lay in it night and day, as soon as it came up, and eat it so close that it could get no time to shoot up into stalk.

This I saw no remedy for, but by making an enclosure about it with a hedge, which I did with a great deal of toil; and the more, because it required speed. However, as my arable land was but small, suited to my crop, I got it totally well fenced in about three weeks time; and shooting some of the creatures in the day time, I set my dog to guard it in the night, tying him up to a stake at the gate, where he would stand and bark all night long; so in a little time the enemies forsook the place, and the corn grew very strong and well, and began to ripen apace.

But as the beasts ruined me before, while my corn was in the blade, so the birds were as likely to ruin me now, when it was in the ear; for going along by the place to see how it throve, I saw my little crop surrounded with fowls of I know not how many sorts, who stood as it were watching till I should be gone. I immediately let fly among them (for I always had my gun with me). I had no sooner shot, but there rose up a little cloud of fowls, which I had not seen at all, from among the corn it self.

This touched me sensibly, for I foresaw that in a few days they would devour all my hopes, that I should be starved, and never be able to raise a crop at all, and what to do I could not tell. However, I resolved not to lose my corn, if possible, tho' I should watch it night and day. In the first place, I went among it to see what damage was already done, and found they had spoiled a good deal of it, but that as it was yet too green for them, the loss was not so great, but that the remainder was like to be a good crop if it could be saved.

I staid by it to load my gun, and then coming away I could

easily see the thieves sitting upon all the trees about me, as if they only waited till I was gone away, and the event proved it to be so; for as I walked off as if I was gone, I was no sooner out of their sight, but they dropt down one by one into the corn again. I was so provoked that I could not have patience to stay till more came on, knowing that every grain that they eat now, was, as it might be said, a peck-load to me in the consequence; but coming up to the hedge I fired again, and killed three of them. This was what I wished for; so I took them up, and served them as we serve notorious thieves in England, viz. hanged them in chains for a terror to others. It is impossible to imagine almost, that this should have such an effect as it had; for the fowls wou'd not only not come at the corn, but in short they forsook all that part of the island, and I could never see a bird near the place as long as my scare-crows hung there.

This I was very glad of, you may be sure, and about the latter end of December, which was our second harvest of the year, I reaped my crop.

I was sadly put to it for a scythe or a sicle to cut it down, and all I could do was to make one as well as I could out of one of the broad swords or cutlasses, which I saved among the arms out of the ship. However, as my first crop was but small, I had no great difficulty to cut it down; in short, I reaped it my way, for I cut nothing off but the ears, and carry'd it away in a great basket which I had made, and so rubbed it out with my hands; and at the end of all my harvesting, I found that out of my half peck of seed, I had near two bushels of rice, and above two bushels and half of barley; that is to say, by my guess, for I had no measure at that time.

However, this was a great encouragement to me, and I foresaw that in time it wou'd please God to supply me with bread. And yet here I was perplexed again, for I neither knew how to grind or make meal of my corn, or indeed how to clean it and part it; nor if made into meal, how to make bread of it; and if how to make it, yet I knew not how to bake it. These things being added to my desire of having a good quantity for store, and to secure a constant supply, I resolved not to taste any of this crop, but to preserve it all for seed against the next season, and in the mean time to employ all my study and hours of working to accomplish this great work of providing my self with corn and bread.

It might be truly said, that now I worked for my bread; 'tis a little wonderful, and what I believe few people have thought much upon, viz. the strange multitude of little things necessary in the providing, producing, curing, dressing, making, and finishing this one article of bread.

I that was reduced to a meer state of nature, found this to my daily discouragement, and was made more and more sensible of it every hour, even after I had got the first handful of seed-corn, which, as I have said, came up unexpectedly, and indeed to a surprize.

First, I had no plow to turn up the earth, no spade or shovel to dig it. Well, this I conquered, by making a wooden spade, as I observed before; but this did my work in but a wooden manner, and tho' it cost me a great many days to make it, yet for want of iron it not only wore out the sooner, but made my work the harder, and made it be performed much worse.

However, this I bore with, and was content to work it out with patience, and bear with the badness of the performance. When the corn was sowed, I had no harrow, but was forced to go over it my self and drag a great heavy bough of a tree over it, to scratch it, as it may be called, rather than rake or harrow it.

When it was growing and grown, I have observed already how many things I wanted, to fence it, secure it, mow or reap it, cure and carry it home, thrash, part it from the chaff, and save it. Then I wanted a mill to grind it, sieves to dress it, yeast and salt to make it into bread, and an oven to bake it, and yet all these things I did without, as shall be observed; and yet the corn was an inestimable comfort and advantage to me too. All this, as I said, made every thing laborious and tedious to me, but that there was no help for; neither was my time so much loss to me, because, as I had divided it, a certain part of it was every day appointed to these works; and as I resolved to use none of the corn for bread till I had a greater quantity by me; I had the next six months to apply my self wholly by labour and invention to furnish my self with utensils proper for the performing all the operations necessary for the making the corn (when I had it) fit for my use.

But first, I was to prepare more land, for I had now seed enough to sow above an acre of ground. Before I did this, I had a weeks-work at least to make me a spade, which when it was done was but a sorry one indeed, and very heavy, and required double labour to work with it; however, I went thro' that, and sowed my seed in two large flat pieces of ground, as near my house as I could find them to my mind, and fenced them in with a good hedge, the stakes of which were all cut of that wood which I had set before, and knew it would grow, so that in one year's time I knew I should have a quick or living-hedge, that would want but little repair. This work was not so little as to take me up less than three months, because great part of that time was of the wet season, when I could not go abroad.

Within doors, that is, when it rained, and I could not go out, I found employment on the following occasions; always observing, that all the while I was at work I diverted my self with talking to my parrot, and teaching him to speak, and I quickly learned him to know his own name, and at last to speak it out pretty loud, POLL, which was the first word I ever heard spoken in the island by any mouth but my own. This, therefore, was not my work, but an assistant to my work, for now, as I said, I had a great employment upon my hands, as follows, viz. I had long study'd, by some means or other, to make my self some earthen vessels, which indeed I wanted sorely, but knew not where to come at them. However, considering the heat of the climate, I did not doubt but if I could find out any such clay, I might botch up some such pot as might, being dry'd in the sun, be hard enough and strong enough to bear handling, and to hold any thing that was dry and required to be kept so; and as this was necessary in the preparing corn, meal, &c., which was the thing I was upon, I resolved to make some as large as I could, and fit only to stand like jarrs to hold what should be put into them.

It would make the reader pity me, or rather laugh at me, to tell how many awkward ways I took to raise this paste, what odd mishapen ugly things I made, how many of them fell in, and how many fell out, the clay not being stiff enough to bear its own weight; how many cracked by the over violent heat of the sun, being set out too hastily; and how many fell in pieces with only removing, as well before as after they were dry'd; and in a word, how after having laboured hard to find the clay, to dig it, to temper it, to bring it home and work it, I could not make above two large earthen ugly things, I cannot call them jarrs, in about two months labour.

However, as the sun baked these two very dry and hard, I lifted them very gently up, and set them down again in two great wicker-baskets which I had made on purpose for them, that they might not break, and as between the pot and the basket there was a little room to spare, I stuffed it full of the rice and barley straw, and these two pots being to stand always dry, I thought would hold my dry corn, and perhaps the meal, when the corn was bruised.

Tho' I miscarried so much in my design for large pots, yet I made several smaller things with better success, such as little round pots, flat dishes, pitchers and pipkins, and any things my hand turned to, and the heat of the sun baked them strangely hard.

But all this would not answer my end, which was to get an earthen pot to hold what was liquid, and bear the fire, which none of these could do. It happened after some time, making a pretty large fire for cooking my meat, when I went to put it out after I had done with it, I found a broken piece of one of my earthen-ware vessels in the fire, burnt as hard as a stone, and red as a tile. I was agreeably surprised to see it, and said to my self, that certainly they might be made to burn whole if they would burn broken.

This set me to studying how to order my fire, so as to make it burn me some pots. I had no notion of a kiln, such as the potters burn in, or of glazing them with lead, tho' I had some lead to do it with; but I placed three large pipkins and two or three pots in a pile one upon another, and placed my fire-wood all round it with a great heap of embers under them; I ply'd the fire with fresh fuel round the out-side, and upon the top, till I saw the pots in the inside red hot quite thro', and observed that they did not crack at all; when I saw them clear red, I let them stand in that heat about 5 or 6 hours, till I found one of them, tho' it did not crack, did melt or run, for the sand which was mixed with the clay melted by the violence of the heat, and would have run into glass if I had gone on; so I slacked my fire gradually till the pots began to abate of the red colour, and watching them all night, that I might not let the fire abate too fast, in the morning I had three very good, I will not say handsome, pipkins, and two other earthen pots, as hard burnt as cou'd be desired; and one of them perfectly glazed with the running of the sand.

After this experiment, I need not say that I wanted no sort of earthen ware for my use; but I must needs say, as to the shapes of them, they were very indifferent, as any one may suppose, when I had no way of making them but as the children make dirt-pies, or as a woman would make pies that never learned to raise paste.

No joy at a thing of so mean a nature was ever equal to mine, when I found I had made an earthen pot that would bear the fire; and I had hardly patience to stay till they were cold, before I set one upon the fire again, with some water in it, to boil me some meat, which it did admirably well; and with a piece of a kid I made some very good broth, though I wanted oatmeal, and several other ingredients requisite to make it so good as I would have had it been.

My next concern was to get me a stone mortar, to stamp or beat some corn in; for as to the mill, there was no thought at arriving to that perfection of art with one pair of hands. To supply this want I was at a great loss; for, of all trades in the world, I was as perfectly unqualify'd for a stone-cutter as for any whatever; neither had I any tools to go about it with. I spent many a day to find out a great stone big enough to cut hollow and make fit for a mortar, and could find none at all; except what was in the solid rock, and which I had no way to dig or cut out; nor indeed were the rocks in the island of hardness sufficient, but were all of a sandy crumbling stone, which neither would bear the weight of a heavy pestle, [n]or would break the corn without filling it with sand; so after a great deal of time lost in searching for a stone, I gave it over, and resolved to look out for a great block of hard wood, which I found indeed much easier; and getting one as big as I had strength to stir, I rounded it, and formed it in the out-side with my axe and hatchet, and then with the help of fire, and infinite labour, made a hollow place in it, as the Indians in Brasil make their canoes. After this, I made a great heavy pestle or beater, of the wood called the iron-wood, and this I prepared and laid by against I had my next crop of corn, when I proposed to my self to grind, or rather pound, my corn into meal to make my bread.

My next difficulty was to make a sieve, or search, to dress my meal, and to part it from the bran and the husk, without which I did not see it possible I could have any bread. This was a most difficult thing, so much as but to think on; for to be sure I had nothing like the necessary thing to make it; I mean fine thin canvas, or stuff, to search the meal through. And here I was at a full stop for many months; nor did I really know what to do; linnen I had none left, but what was meer rags; I had goats hair, but neither knew I how to weave it or spin it; and had I known how, here was no tools to work it with; all the remedy that I found for this was, that at last I did remember I had among the seamens cloaths which were saved out of the ship, some neck-cloths of callicoe or muslin; and with some pieces of these I made three small sieves, but proper enough for the work; and thus I made shift for some years; how I did afterwards, I shall shew in its place.

The baking part was the next thing to be considered, and how I should make bread when I came to have corn; for first I had no yeast; as to that part, as there was no supplying the want, so I did not concern my self much about it; but for an oven, I was indeed in great pain. At length I found out an experiment for that also, which was this: I made some earthen vessels, very broad, but not deep; that is to say, about two foot diameter, and not above nine inches deep; these I burnt in the fire, as I had done the other, and laid them by; and when I wanted to bake, I made a great fire upon my hearth, which I had paved with some square tiles of my own making and burning also; but I should not call them square.

When the fire-wood was burnt pretty much into embers, or live coals, I drew them forward upon this hearth so as to cover it all over, and there I let them lye till the hearth was very hot; then sweeping away all the embers, I set down my loaf or loaves, and whelming down the earthen pot upon them, drew the embers all round the out-side of the pot, to keep in, and add to the heat; and thus, as well as in the best oven in the world, I baked my barley loaves, and became in little time a meer pastry-cook into the bargain; for I made my self several cakes of the rice, and puddings; indeed I made no pies, neither had I any thing to put into them, supposing I had, except the flesh either of fowls or goats.

It need not be wondred at, if all these things took me up most part of the third year of my abode here; for it is to be observed that in the intervals of these things, I had my new harvest and husbandry to manage; for I reaped my corn in its season, and carry'd it home as well as I could, and laid it up in the ear in my large baskets, till I had time to rub it out; for I had no floor to thrash it on, or instrument to thrash it with.

And now indeed, my stock of corn increasing, I really wanted to build my barns bigger. I wanted a place to lay it up in; for the increase of the corn now yielded me so much, that I had of the barley about twenty bushels, and of the rice as much, or more; insomuch that now I resolved to begin to use it freely; for my bread had been quite gone a great while; also I resolved to see what quantity would be sufficient for me a whole year, and to sow but once a year.

Upon the whole, I found that the forty bushels of barley and rice was much more than I could consume in a year; so I resolved to sow just the same quantity every year that I sowed the last, in hopes that such a quantity would fully provide me with bread, &c.

All the while these things were doing, you may be sure my thoughts run many times upon the prospect of land which I had seen from the other side of the island, and I was not without secret wishes that I were on shore there, fancying the seeing the main land, and in an inhabited country I might find some way or other to convey myself farther, and perhaps at last find some means of escape.

But all this while I made no allowance for the dangers of such a condition, and how I might fall into the hands of savages, and perhaps such as I might have reason to think far worse than the lions and tigers of Africa; that if I once came into their power, I should run a hazard more than a thousand to one of being killed, and perhaps of being eaten; for I had heard that the people of the Carribean coast were canibals, or man-eaters; and I knew by the latitude that I could not be far off from that shore. That suppose they were not canibals, yet that they might kill me, as many Europeans who had fallen into their hands had been served, even when they had been ten or twenty together; much more I that was but one, and could make little or no defence. All these things, I say, which I ought to have considered well of, and did cast up in my thoughts afterwards, yet took up none of my apprehensions at first; but my head run mightily upon the thought of getting over to the shore.

Now I wished for my boy Xury, and the long boat with the shoulder of mutton sail, with which I sailed above a thousand miles on the coast of Africk; but this was in vain. Then I thought I would go and look at our ship's boat, which, as I have said, was blown up upon the shore, a great way in the storm, when we were first cast away. She lay almost where she did at first, but not quite; and was turned by the force of the waves and the winds almost bottom upward, against a high ridge of beachy rough sand; but no water about her as before.

If I had had hands to have refitted her, and to have launched her into the water, the boat would have done well enough, and I might have gone back into the Brasils with her easily enough; but I might have foreseen that I could no more turn her and set her upright upon her bottom, than I could remove the island. However, I went to the woods, and cut levers and rollers, and brought them to the boat, resolved to try what I could do, suggesting to my self that if I could but turn her down, I might easily repair the damage she had received, and she would be a very good boat, and I might go to sea in her very easily.

I spared no pains, indeed, in this piece of fruitless toil, and spent, I think, three or four weeks about it; at last, finding it impossible to heave it up with my little strength, I fell to digging away the sand, to undermine it, and so to make it fall down, setting pieces of wood to thrust and guide it right in the fall.

But when I had done this, I was unable to stir it up again, or to get under it, much less to move it forward towards the water; so I was forced to give it over; and yet, though I gave over the hopes of the boat, my desire to venture over for the main increased, rather than decreased, as the means for it seem'd impossible.

This at length put me upon thinking whether it was not possible to make myself a canoe, or periagua, such as the natives of those climates make, even without tools, or, as I might say, without hands, viz. of the trunk of a great tree. This I not only thought possible, but easy, and pleased my self extreamly with the thoughts of making it, and with my having much more convenience for it than any of the negroes or Indians; but not at all considering the particular inconveniences which I lay under, more than the Indians did, viz. want of hands to move it, when it was made, into the water, a difficulty much harder for me to surmount than all the consequences of want of tools could be to them; for what was it to me, that when I had chosen a vast tree in the woods, I might with much trouble cut it down, if after I might be able with my tools to hew and dub the out-side into the proper shape of a boat, and burn or cut out the inside to make it hollow, so to make a boat of it, if, after all this, I must leave it just there where I found it, and was not able to launch it into the water?

One would have thought I could not have had the least reflection upon my mind of my circumstance while I was making this boat, but I should have immediately thought how I should get it into the sea; but my thoughts were so intent upon my voyage over the sea in it, that I never once considered how I should get it off of the land; and it was really in its own nature more easy for me to guide it over forty five miles of sea, than about forty five fathom of land, where it lay, to set it a float in the water.

I went to work upon this boat the most like a fool that ever man did, who had any of his senses awake. I pleased my self with the design, without determining whether I was ever able to undertake it; not but that the difficulty of launching my boat came often into my head; but I put a stop to my own enquiries into it, by this foolish answer which I gave myself, 'Let's first make it, I'll warrant I'll find some way or other to get it along, when 'tis done.'

This was a most preposterous method; but the eagerness of my fancy prevailed, and to work I went. I felled a cedar tree: I question much whether Solomon ever had such a one for the building of the temple at Jerusalem. It was five foot ten inches diameter at the lower part next the stump, and four foot eleven inches diameter at the end of twenty two foot, after which it lessened for a while, and then parted into branches. It was not without infinite labour that I felled this tree; I was twenty days hacking and hewing at it at the bottom; I was fourteen more getting the branches and limbs and the vast spreading head of it cut off, which I hacked and hewed through with axe and hatchet, and inexpressible labour; after this, it cost me a month to shape it, and dub it to a proportion, and to something like the bottom of a boat, that it might swim upright as it ought to do. It cost me near three months more to clear the in-side, and work it out so as to make an exact boat of it. This I did indeed without fire, by meer malett and chissel, and by the dint of hard labour, till I had brought it to be a very handsome periagua, and big enough to have carry'd six and twenty men, and consequently big enough to have carry'd me and all my cargo.

When I had gone through this work, I was extremely delighted with it. The boat was really much bigger than I ever saw a canoe or periagua, that was made of one tree, in my life. Many a weary stroke it had cost, you may be sure; and there remained nothing but to get it into the water; and had I gotten it into the water, I make no question but I should have began the maddest voyage, and the most unlikely to be performed, that ever was undertaken.

But all my devices to get it into the water failed me; tho' they cost me infinite labour too. It lay about one hundred yards from the water, and not more. But the first inconvenience was, it was up hill towards the creek; well, to take away this discouragement, I resolved to dig into the surface of the earth, and so make a declivity. This I begun, and it cost me a prodigious deal of pains; but who grutches pains, that have their deliverance in view? But when this was worked through, and this difficulty managed, it was still much at one; for I could no more stir the canoe than I could the other boat.

Then I measured the distance of ground, and resolved to cut a dock or canal, to bring the water up to the canoe, seeing I could not bring the canoe down to the water. Well, I began this work, and when I began to enter into it, and calculate how deep it was to be dug, how broad, how the stuff to be thrown out, I found that by the number of hands I had, being none but my own, it must have been ten or twelve years before I should have gone through with it : for the shore lay high, so that at the upper end it must have been at least twenty foot deep; so at length, tho' with great reluctancy, I gave this attempt over also.

This grieved me heartily, and now I saw, tho' too late, the folly of beginning a work before we count the cost, and before we judge rightly of our own strength to go through with it.

In the middle of this work, I finished my fourth year in this place, and kept my anniversary with the same devotion, and with as much comfort as ever before; for by a constant study and serious application of the word of God, and by the assistance of His grace, I gained a different knowledge from what I had before. I entertained different notions of things. I looked now upon the world as a thing remote, which I had nothing to do with, no expectation from, and indeed no desires about : in a word, I had nothing indeed to do with it, nor was ever like to have; so I thought it looked as we may perhaps look upon it hereafter, viz. as a place I had lived in, but was come out of it; and well might I say, as Father Abraham to Dives, *Between me and thee is a great gulph fix'd.* [34]

In the first place, I was removed from all the wickedness of the world here. I had neither *the lust of the flesh, the lust of the eye, or the pride of life.* [35] I had nothing to covet; for I had all that I was now capable of enjoying; I was lord of the whole manor; or if I pleased, I might call my self king or emperor over the whole country which I had possession of. There were no rivals; I had no competitor, none to dispute sovereignty or command with me. I might have raised ship loadings of corn; but I had no use for it; so I let as little grow as I thought enough for my occasion. I had tortoise or turtles enough; but now and then one was as much as I could put to any use. I had timber enough to have built a fleet of ships. I had grapes enough to have made wine, or to have cured into raisins, to have loaded that fleet when they had been built.

But all I could make use of was all that was valuable. I had enough to eat and to supply my wants, and what was all the rest to me? If I killed more flesh than I could eat, the dog must eat it, or the vermin. If I sowed more corn than I could eat, it must be spoiled. The trees that I cut down were lying to rot on the ground. I could make no more use of them than for fewel; and that I had no occasion for, but to dress my food.

In a word, the nature and experience of things dictated to me, upon just reflection, that all the good things of this world are no farther good to us than they are for our use; and that whatever we may heap up indeed to give others, we enjoy just as much as we can use and no more. The most covetous griping miser in the world would have been cured of the vice of covetousness, if he had been in my case; for I possessed infinitely more than I knew what to do with. I had no room for desire, except it was of things which I had not, and they were but trifles, though indeed of great use to me. I had, as I hinted before, a parcel of money, as well gold as silver, about thirty six pounds sterling. Alas! there the nasty sorry useless stuff lay; I had no manner of business for it; and I often thought with my self that I would have given a handful of it for a gross of tobacco-pipes, or for a hand-mill to grind my corn; nay, I would have given it all for sixpennyworth of turnip and carrot seed out of England, or for a handful of pease and beans, and a bottle of ink. As it was, I had not the least advantage by it, or benefit from it; but there it lay in a drawer, and grew mouldy with the damp of the cave in the wet season; and if I had had the drawer full of diamonds, it had been the same case; and they had been of no manner of value to me, because of no use.

I had now brought my state of life to be much easier in itself than it was at first, and much easier to my mind, as well as to my body. I frequently sat down to my meat with thankfulness, and admired the hand of God's providence, which had thus spread my table in the wilderness. I learned to look more upon the bright side of my condition, and less upon the dark side, and to consider what I enjoyed, rather than what I wanted; and this gave me sometimes such secret comforts, that I cannot express them; and which I take notice of here, to put those discontented people in mind of it, who cannot enjoy comfortably what God has given them; because they see and covet something that He has not given them. All our discontents about what we want appeared to me to spring from the want of thankfulness for what we have.

Another reflection was of great use to me, and doubtless would be so to any one that should fall into such distress as mine was; and this was, to compare my present condition with what I at first expected it should be; nay, with what it would certainly have been, if the good providence of God had not wonderfully ordered the ship to be cast up nearer to the shore, where I not only could come at her, but could bring what I got out of her to the shore, for my relief and comfort; without which, I had wanted for tools to work, weapons for defence, or gun-powder and shot for getting my food.

I spent whole hours, I may say whole days, in representing to my self in the most lively colours how I must have acted if I had got nothing out of the ship; how I could not have so much as got any food except fish and turtles; and that as it was long before I found any of them, I must have perished first; that I should have lived, if I had not perished, like a meer savage; that if I had killed a goat or a fowl, by any contrivance, I had no way to flea or open them, or part the flesh from the skin and the bowels, or to cut it up; but must gnaw it with my teeth and pull it with my claws like a beast.

These reflections made me very sensible of the goodness of Providence to me, and very thankful for my present condition, with all its hardships and misfortunes; and this part also I cannot but recommend to the reflection of those who are apt in their misery to say, 'Is any affliction like mine!' Let them consider how much worse the cases of some people are, and their case might have been, if Providence had thought fit.

I had another reflection which assisted me also to comfort my mind with hopes; and this was, comparing my present condition with what I had deserved, and had therefore reason to expect from the hand of Providence. I had lived a dreadful life, perfectly destitute of the knowledge and fear of God. I had been well instructed by father and mother; neither had they been wanting to me, in their early endeavours, to infuse a religious awe of God into my mind, a sense of my duty, and of what the nature and end of my being required of me. But alas! falling early into the seafaring life, which of all the lives is the most destitute of the fear of God, though His terrors are always before them; I say, falling early into the seafaring life, and into seafaring company, all that little sense of religion which I had entertained was laughed out of me by my mess-mates, by a hardened despising of dangers, and the views of death, which grew habitual to me by my long absence from all manner of opportunities to converse with any thing but what was like my self, or to hear any thing that was good or tended towards it.

So void was I of every thing that was good, or of the least sense of what I was, or was to be, that in the greatest deliverances I enjoyed, such as my escape from Sallee, my being taken up by the Portuguese master of the ship, my being planted so well in the Brasils, my receiving the cargo from England, and the like, I never had once the word, 'Thank God,' so much as on my mind, or in my mouth; nor in the greatest distress, had I so much as a thought to pray to Him, or so much as to say, 'Lord have mercy upon me'; no, nor to mention the name of God, unless it was to swear by and blaspheme it.

I had terrible reflections upon my mind for many months, as I have already observed, on the account of my wicked and hardned life past; and when I looked about me and considered what particular providences had attended me since my coming into this place, and how God had dealt bountifully with me; had not only punished me less than my iniquity had deserved, but had so plentifully provided for me; this gave me great hopes that my repentance was accepted, and that God had yet mercy in store for me.

With these reflections I worked my mind up, not only to resignation to the will of God in the present disposition of my circumstances, but even to a sincere thankfulness for my con-

dition, and that I, who was yet a living man, ought not to complain, seeing I had not the due punishment of my sins; that I
enjoyed so many mercies which I had no reason to have expected
in that place; that I ought never more to repine at my condition,
but to rejoyce, and to give daily thanks for that daily bread which
nothing but a croud of wonders could have brought. That I ought
to consider I had been fed even by miracle, even as great as that
of feeding Elijah by ravens,[36] nay, by a long series of miracles; and
that I could hardly have named a place in the unhabitable part
of the world where I could have been cast more to my advantage;
a place where, as I had no society, which was my affliction on
one hand, so I found no ravenous beast, no furious wolves or
tygers to threaten my life, no venomous creatures, or poisonous,
which I might feed on to my hurt, no savages to murther and
devour me.

In a word, as my life was a life of sorrow one way, so it was
a life of mercy another; and I wanted nothing to make it a life
of comfort, but to be able to make my sence of God's goodness to
me, and care over me in this condition, be my daily consolation;
and after I did make a just improvement of these things, I went
away and was no more sad.

I had now been here so long that many things which I brought
on shore for my help were either quite gone or very much wasted
and near spent.

My ink, as I observed, had been gone some time, all but a
very little, which I eeked out with water a little and a little, till
it was so pale it scarce left any appearance of black upon the
paper. As long as it lasted, I made use of it to minute down the
days of the month on which any remarkable thing happened to
me. And first by casting up times past, I remember that there
was a strange concurrence of days in the various providences
which befel me; and which, if I had been superstitiously inclined
to observe days as fatal or fortunate, I might have had reason to
have looked upon with a great deal of curiosity.

First, I had observed that the same day that I broke away from
my father and my friends, and run away to Hull, in order to go
to sea, the same day afterwards I was taken by the Sallee man
of war, and made a slave.

The same day of the year that I escaped out of the wreck of that ship in Yarmouth roads, that same day-year afterwards I made my escape from Sallee in the boat.

The same day of the year I was born on, viz. the 30th of September, that same day I had my life so miraculously saved twenty-six year after, when I was cast on shore in this island, so that my wicked life and my solitary life begun both on a day.

The next thing to my ink's being wasted, was that of my bread, I mean the bisket which I brought out of the ship; this I had husbanded to the last degree, allowing my self but one cake of bread a day for above a year, and yet I was quite without bread for near a year before I got any corn of my own, and great reason I had to be thankful that I had any at all, the getting it being, as has been already observed, next to miraculous.

My cloaths began to decay too, mightily: as to linnen, I had had none a good while, except some chequered shirts which I found in the chests of the other seamen, and which I carefully preserved, because many times I could bear no other cloaths on but a shirt; and it was a very great help to me that I had among all the men's cloaths of the ship almost three dozen of shirts. There were also several thick watch-coats of the seamen's, which were left indeed, but they were too hot to wear; and tho' it is true that the weather was so violent hot that there was no need of cloaths, yet I could not go quite naked; no, tho' I had been inclined to it, which I was not, nor could not abide the thoughts of it, tho' I was all alone.

The reason why I could not go quite naked was, I could not bear the heat of the sun so well when quite naked as with some cloaths on; nay, the very heat frequently blistered my skin; whereas with a shirt on, the air itself made some motion and, whistling under that shirt, was twofold cooler than without it: no more could I ever bring my self to go out in the heat of sun without a cap or a hat; the heat of the sun, beating with such violence as it does in that place, would give me the head-ach presently, by darting so directly on my head, without a cap or hat on, so that I could not bear it, whereas, if I put on my hat, it would presently go away.

Upon those views I began to consider about putting the few

rags I had, which I called cloaths, into some order; I had worn
out all the wast-coats I had, and my business was now to try if I
could not make jackets out of the great watch-coats which I had
by me, and with such other materials as I had; so I set to work
a taylering, or rather indeed a botching, for I made most piteous
work of it. However, I made shift to make two or three new wast-
coats, which I hoped wou'd serve me a great while; as for
breeches or drawers, I made but a very sorry shift indeed, till
afterward.

I have mentioned that I saved the skins of all the creatures
that I killed, I mean four-footed ones, and I had hung them up
stretched out with sticks in the sun, by which means some of
them were so dry and hard that they were fit for little, but others,
it seems, were very useful. The first thing I made of these was a
great cap for my head, with the hair on the out side to shoot off
the rain; and this I performed so well, that after this I made me
a suit of cloaths wholly of these skins, that is to say, a wastcoat, and breeches open at knees, and both loose, for they were
rather wanting to keep me cool than to keep me warm. I must
not omit to acknowledge that they were wretchedly made;
for if I was a bad carpenter, I was a worse tayler. However,
they were such as I made very good shift with; and when I was
abroad, if it happened to rain, the hair of my wastcoat and cap
being outermost, I was kept very dry.

After this I spent a great deal of time and pains to make me
an umbrella; I was indeed in great want of one, and had a great
mind to make one; I had seen them made in the Brasils, where
they are very useful in the great heats which are there; and I felt
the heats every jot as great here, and greater too, being nearer the
equinox; besides, as I was obliged to be much abroad, it was a
most useful thing to me, as well for the rains as the heats. I
took a world of pains at it, and was a great while before I could
make anything likely to hold; nay, after I thought I had hit the
way, I spoiled two or three before I made one to my mind; but at
last I made one that answered indifferently well. The main difficulty I found was to make it to let down. I could make it to
spread, but if it did not let down too, and draw in, it was not
portable for me any way but just over my head, which wou'd

not do. However, at last, as I said, I made one to answer, and covered it with skins, the hair upwards, so that it cast off the rains like a penthouse, and kept off the sun so effectually that I could walk out in the hottest of the weather with greater advantage than I could before in the coolest, and when I had no need of it, cou'd close it and carry it under my arm.

Thus I lived mighty comfortably, my mind being entirely composed by resigning to the will of God, and throwing my self wholly upon the disposal of His providence. This made my life better than sociable, for when I began to regret the want of conversation, I would ask my self whether thus conversing mutually with my own thoughts, and, as I hope I may say, with even God Himself by ejaculations, was not better than the utmost enjoyment of humane society in the world.

I cannot say that after this, for five years, any extraordinary thing happened to me, but I lived on in the same course, in the same posture and place, just as before; the chief things I was employed in, besides my yearly labour of planting my barley and rice, and curing my raisins, of both which I always kept up just enough to have sufficient stock of one year's provisions beforehand; I say, besides this yearly labour, and my daily labour of going out with my gun, I had one labour, to make me a canoe, which at last I finished; so that by digging a canal to it of six foot wide and four foot deep, I brought it into the creek, almost half a mile. As for the first, which was so vastly big, as I made it without considering before hand, as I ought to do, how I should be able to launch it; so, never being able to bring it to the water, or bring the water to it, I was obliged to let it lye where it was, as a memorandum to teach me to be wiser next time: indeed, the next time, tho' I could not get a tree proper for it, and in a place where I could not get the water to it at any less distance than, as I have said, nearly half a mile, yet as I saw it was practicable at last, I never gave it over; and though I was near two years about it, yet I never grutched my labour, in hopes of having a boat to go off to sea at last.

However, though my little periagua was finished, yet the size of it was not at all answerable to the design which I had in view when I made the first; I mean, of venturing over to the terra firma, where it was above forty miles broad; accordingly, the smallness of my boat assisted to put an end to that design, and now I thought no more of it: but as I had a boat, my next design was to make a tour round the island; for as I had been on the other side in one place, crossing, as I have already described it, over the land, so the discoveries I made in that little journey made me very eager to see other parts of the coast; and now I had a boat, I thought of nothing but sailing round the island.

For this purpose, that I might do every thing with discretion and consideration, I fitted up a little mast to my boat, and made a sail to it out of some of the pieces of the ship's sail, which lay in store, and of which I had a great stock by me.

Having fitted my mast and sail, and try'd the boat, I found she would sail very well. Then I made little lockers, or boxes, at either end of my boat, to put provisions, necessaries, and ammunitions, &c., into, to be kept dry, either from rain or the sprye of the sea; and a little long hollow place I cut in the in-side of the boat, where I could lay my gun, making a flap to hang down over it to keep it dry.

I fixed my umbrella also in a step at the stern, like a mast, to stand over my head, and keep the heat of the sun off of me like an auning; and thus I every now and then took a little voyage upon the sea, but never went far out, nor far from the little creek; but at last, being eager to view the circumference of my little kingdom, I resolved upon my tour, and accordingly I victualled my ship for the voyage, putting in two dozen of my loaves (cakes I should rather call them) of barley bread, an earthen pot full of parched rice, a food I eat a great deal of, a little bottle of rum, half a goat, and powder and shot for killing more, and two large watch-coats, of those which, as I mentioned before, I had saved out of the seamen's chests; these I took, one to lye upon, and the other to cover me in the night.

It was the sixth of November, in the sixth year of my reign, or my captivity, which you please, that I set out on this voyage, and I found it much longer than I expected; for though the island it self was not very large, yet when I came to the east side of it, I found a great ledge of rocks lye out above two leagues into the sea, some above water, some under it; and beyond that, a shoal of sand, lying dry half a league more; so that I was obliged to go a great way out to sea to double the point.

When first I discovered them, I was going to give over my enterprise, and come back again, not knowing how far it might oblige me to go out to sea; and above all, doubting how I should get back again; so I came to an anchor; for I had made me a kind of an anchor with a piece of a broken graplin which I got out of the ship.

Having secured my boat, I took my gun and went on shore, climbing up upon a hill which seemed to overlook that point, where I saw the full extent of it, and resolved to venture.

In my viewing the sea from that hill where I stood, I perceived a strong, and indeed a most furious current, which run to the east, and even came close to the point; and I took the more notice of it, because I saw there might be some danger; that when I came into it, I might be carry'd out to sea by the strength of it, and not be able to make the island again; and indeed, had I not gotten first up upon this hill, I believe it would have been so; for there was the same current on the other side the island, only that it set off at a farther distance; and I saw there was a strong eddy under the shore; so I had nothing to do but to get in out of the first current, and I should presently be in an eddy.

I lay here, however, two days; because the wind blowing pretty fresh at E.S.E., and that being just contrary to the said current, made a great breach of the sea upon the point; so that it was not safe for me to keep too close to the shore for the breach, nor to go too far off because of the stream.

The third day in the morning, the wind having abated over night, the sea was calm, and I ventured; but I am a warning piece again to all rash and ignorant pilots; for no sooner was I come to the point, when even I was not my boat's length from the shore, but I found my self in a great depth of water, and a current like the sluice of a mill: it carry'd my boat along with it with such violence that all I could do could not keep her so much as on the edge of it; but I found it hurry'd me farther and farther out from the eddy, which was on my left hand. There was no wind stirring to help me, and all I could do with my paddlers signify'd nothing, and now I began to give my self over for lost;

for as the current was on both sides the island, I knew in a few leagues distance they must joyn again, and then I was irrecoverably gone; nor did I see any possibility of avoiding it; so that I had no prospect before me but of perishing, not by the sea, for that was calm enough, but of starving for hunger. I had indeed found a tortoise on the shore, as big almost as I could lift, and had tossed it into the boat; and I had a great jar of fresh water, that is to say, one of my earthen pots; but what was all this to being driven into the vast ocean, where, to be sure, there was no shore, no main land or island, for a thousand leagues at least?

And now I saw how easy it was for the providence of God to make the most miserable condition mankind could be in, *worse*. Now I looked back upon my desolate solitary island as the most pleasant place in the world, and all the happiness my heart could wish for was to be but there again. I stretched out my hands to it with eager wishes. 'O happy desart,' said I, 'I shall never see thee more. O miserable creature,' said I, 'whither am I going?' Then I reproached my self with my unthankful temper, and how I had repined at my solitary condition; and now what would I give to be on shore there again! Thus we never see the true state of our condition till it is illustrated to us by its contraries, nor know how to value what we enjoy, but by the want of it. It is scarce possible to imagine the consternation I was now in, being driven from my beloved island (for so it appeared to me now to be) into the wide ocean, almost two leagues, and in the utmost despair of ever recovering it again. However, I worked hard, till indeed my strength was almost exhausted, and kept my boat as much to the northward, that is, towards the side of the current which the eddy lay on, as possibly I could; when about noon, as the sun passed the meridian, I thought I felt a little breeze of wind in my face, springing up from the s.s.e. This cheared my heart a little, and especially when in about half an hour more it blew a pretty small gentle gale. By this time I was gotten at a frightful distance from the island, and had the least cloud of haizy weather intervened, I had been undone another way too; for I had no compass on board, and should never have known how to have steered towards the island, if I had but once lost sight of it; but the weather continuing clear, I apply'd my self to get up my mast again, and spread my sail, standing away to the north as much as possible, to get out of the current.

Just as I had set my mast and sail, and the boat began to stretch away, I saw even by the clearness of the water some alteration of the current was near; for where the current was so strong, the water was foul; but perceiving the water clear, I found the current abate, and presently I found to the east, at about half a mile, a breach of the sea upon some rocks; these rocks I found caused the current to part again, and as the main stress of it ran away more southerly, leaving the rocks to the north-east, so the other returned by the repulse of the rocks, and made a strong eddy, which run back again to the north-west, with a very sharp stream.

They who know what it is to have a reprieve brought to them upon the ladder, or to be rescued from thieves just a going to murther them, or who have been in such like extremities, may guess what my present surprise of joy was, and how gladly I put my boat into the stream of this eddy, and the wind also fresh-ning, how gladly I spread my sail to it, running chearfully before the wind, and with a strong tide or eddy under foot.

This eddy carry'd me about a league in my way back again directly towards the island, but about two leagues more to the northward than the current which carried me away at first; so that when I came near the island, I found my self open to the northern shore of it, that is to say, the other end of the island oposite to that which I went out from.

When I had made something more than a league of way by the help of this current or eddy, I found it was spent and served me no farther. However, I found that being between the two great currents, viz. that on the south side which had hurried me away, and that on the north which lay about a league on the other side; I say, between these two, in the wake of the island, I found the water at least still and running no way, and having still a breeze of wind fair for me, I kept on steering directly for the island, tho' not making such fresh way as I did before.

About four a-clock in the evening, being then within about a league of the island, I found the point of the rocks which occasioned this disaster, stretching out as is described before to the south-ward, and casting off the current more southwardly, had of course made another eddy to the north, and this I found very strong, but not directly setting the way my course lay, which was due west, but almost full north. However, having a fresh gale, I stretched a-cross this eddy slanting north-west, and in about an hour came within about a mile of the shore, where it being smooth water, I soon got to land.

When I was on shore I fell on my knees and gave God thanks for my deliverance, resolving to lay aside all thoughts of my deliverance by my boat; and refreshing my self with such things as I had, I brought my boat close to the shore in a little cove that I had spy'd under some trees, and lay'd me down to sleep, being quite spent with the labour and fatigue of the voyage.

I was now at a great loss which way to get home with my boat. I had run so much hazard, and knew too much [of] the case, to think of attempting it by the way I went out, and what might be at the other side (I mean the west side) I knew not, nor had I any mind to run any more ventures; so I only resolved in the morning to make my way westward along the shore and to see if there was no creek where I might lay up my frigate in safety, so as to have her again if I wanted her; in about three mile or thereabout, coasting the shore, I came to a very good inlet or bay about a mile over, which narrowed till it came to a very little rivulet or brook, where I found a very convenient harbour for my boat, and where she lay as if she had been in a little dock made on purpose for her. Here I put in, and having stowed my boat very safe, I went on shore to look about me and see where I was.

I soon found I had but a little past by the place where I had been before, when I travelled on foot to that shore; so taking nothing out of my boat but my gun and my umbrella, for it was exceeding hot, I began my march. The way was comfortable enough after such a voyage as I had been upon, and I reached my old bower in the evening, where I found every thing standing as I left it; for I always kept it in good order, being, as I said before, my country house.

I got over the fence, and laid me down in the shade to rest my limbs, for I was very weary, and fell asleep. But judge you, if you can, that read my story, what a surprize I must be in, when I was waked out of my sleep by a voice calling me by my name several times, 'Robin, Robin, Robin Crusoe, poor Robin Crusoe, where are you, Robin Crusoe? Where are you? Where have you been?'

I was so dead asleep at first, being fatigued with rowing, or paddling, as it is called, the first part of the day, and with walking the latter part, that I did not wake thoroughly, but dozing between sleeping and waking, thought I dreamed that some body spoke to me: but as the voice continued to repeat 'Robin Crusoe, Robin Crusoe', at last I began to wake more perfectly, and was at first dreadfully frighted, and started up in the utmost consternation. But no sooner were my eyes open, than I saw my Poll sitting on the top of the hedge, and immediately knew that it was he that spoke to me; for just in such bemoaning language I had used to talk to him and teach him; and he had learned it so perfectly, that he would sit upon my finger, and lay his bill close to my face, and cry, 'Poor Robin Crusoe, where are you? Where have you been? How come you here?' and such things as I had taught him.

However, even though I knew it was the parrot, and that indeed it could be no body else, it was a good while before I could compose my self. First, I was amazed how the creature got thither, and then, how he should just keep about the place, and no where else: but as I was well satisfied it could be no body but honest Poll, I got it over; and holding out my hand, and calling him by his name, Poll, the sociable creature came to me, and sat upon my thumb, as he used to do, and continued talking to me, 'Poor Robin Crusoe! and how did I come here? and where had I been?' just as if he had been overjoyed to see me again; and so I carry'd him home along with me.

I had now had enough of rambling to sea for some time, and had enough to do for many days to sit still, and reflect upon the danger I had been in. I would have been very glad to have had my boat again on my side of the island; but I knew not how it was practicable to get it about. As to the east side of the island, which I had gone round, I knew well enough there was no venturing that way; my very heart would shrink, and my very blood run chill, but to think of it: and as to the other side of the island, I did not know how it might be there; but supposing the current

ran with the same force against the shore at the east as it passed
by it on the other, I might run the same risk of being driven
down the stream, and carry'd by the island, as I had been before
of being carry'd away from it; so with these thoughts I contented my self to be without any boat, though it had been the
product of so many months labour to make it, and of so many
more to get it unto the sea.

In this government of my temper I remained near a year, lived
a very sedate, retired life, as you may well suppose; and my
thoughts being very much composed as to my condition, and
fully comforted in resigning my self to the dispositions of Providence, I thought I lived really very happily in all things, except
that of society.

I improved my self in this time in all the mechanick exercises
which my necessities put me upon applying my self to, and I
believe cou'd, upon occasion, make a very good carpenter, especially considering how few tools I had.

Besides this, I arrived at an unexpected perfection in my
earthen ware, and contrived well enough to make them with a
wheel, which I found infinitely easyer and better; because I made
things round and shapable, which before were filthy things indeed to look on. But I think I was never more vain of my own
performance, or more joyful for any thing I found out, than for
my being able to make a tobacco-pipe. And tho' it was a very
ugly clumsy thing when it was done, and only burnt red like
other earthen ware, yet as it was hard and firm, and would draw
the smoke, I was exceedingly comforted with it, for I had been
always used to smoke, and there were pipes in the ship, but I
forgot them at first, not knowing that there was tobacco in the
island; and afterwards, when I searched the ship again, I could
not come at any pipes at all.

In my wicker ware also I improved much, and made abundance
of necessary baskets, as well as my invention shewed me, tho' not
very handsome, yet they were such as were very handy and convenient for my laying things up in, or fetching things home in.
For example, if I killed a goat abroad, I could hang it up in a
tree, flea it and dress it, and cut it in pieces, and bring it home
in a basket; and the like by a turtle; I could cut it up, take out

the eggs and a piece or two of the flesh, which was enough for me, and bring them home in a basket, and leave the rest behind me. Also large deep baskets were my receivers for my corn, which I always rubbed out as soon as it was dry, and cured, and kept it in great baskets.

I began now to perceive my powder abated considerably, and this was a want which it was impossible for me to supply, and I began seriously to consider what I must do when I should have no more powder; that is to say, how I should do to kill any goat. I had, as is observed in the third year of my being here, kept a young kid, and bred her up tame, and I was in hope of getting a he-goat, but I could not by any means bring it to pass, 'till my kid grew an old goat; and I could never find it in my heart to kill her, till she dy'd at last of meer age.

But being now in the eleventh year of my residence and, as I have said, my ammunition growing low, I set my self to study some art to trap and snare the goats, to see whether I could not catch some of them alive, and particularly I wanted a she-goat great with young.

To this purpose I made snares to hamper them, and I do believe they were more than once taken in them, but my tackle was not good, for I had no wire, and I always found them broken, and my bait devoured.

At length I resolved to try a pit-fall; so I dug several large pits in the earth, in places where I had observed the goats used to feed, and over these pits I placed hurdles, of my own making too, with a great weight upon them; and several times I put ears of barley, and dry rice, without setting the trap, and I could easily perceive that the goats had gone in and eaten up the corn, for I could see the mark of their feet. At length I set three traps in one night, and going the next morning I found them all standing, and yet the bait eaten and gone; this was very discouraging. However, I altered my trap, and, not to trouble you with particulars, going one morning to see my trap, I found in one of them a large old he-goat, and in one of the other three kids, a male and two females.

As to the old one, I knew not what to do with him, he was so fierce I durst not go into the pit to him; that is to say, to go about to bring him away alive, which was what I wanted. I could have killed him, but that was not my business, nor would it answer my end. So I e'en let him out, and he ran away as if he had been frighted out of his wits: but I had forgot then what I learned afterwards, that hunger will tame a lyon. If I had let him stay there three or four days without food, and then have carry'd him some water to drink, and then a little corn, he would have been as tame as one of the kids, for they are mighty sagacious, tractable creatures where they are well used.

However, for the present I let him go, knowing no better at that time; then I went to the three kids, and taking them one by one, I tyed them with strings together, and with some difficulty brought them all home.

It was a good while before they wou'd feed, but throwing them some sweet corn, it tempted them and they began to be tame; and now I found that if I expected to supply my self with goat-flesh when I had no powder or shot left, breeding some up tame was my only way, when perhaps I might have them about my house like a flock of sheep.

But then it presently occurred to me, that I must keep the tame from the wild, or else they would always run wild when they grew up, and the only way for this was to have some enclosed piece of ground, well fenced either with hedge or pale, to keep them in so effectually, that those within might not break out, or those without break in.

This was a great undertaking for one pair of hands; yet as I saw there was an absolute necessity of doing it, my first piece of work was to find out a proper piece of ground, viz. where there was likely to be herbage for them to eat, water for them to drink, and cover to keep them from the sun.

Those who understand such enclosures will think I had very little contrivance, when I pitched upon a place very proper for all these, being a plain open piece of meadow-land, or savanna (as our people call it in the western collonies), which had two or three little drills of fresh water in it, and at one end was very woody; I say, they will smile at my forecast, when I shall tell them I began my enclosing of this piece of ground in such a manner that my hedge or pale must have been at least two mile about. Nor was the madness of it so great as to the compass, for if it was ten mile about I was like to have time enough to do it in. But I did not consider that my goats would be as wild in so much compass as if they had had the whole island, and I should have so much room to chace them in, that I should never catch them.

My hedge was begun and carry'd on, I believe, about fifty yards, when this thought occurred to me; so I presently stopt short, and for the first beginning I resolved to enclose a piece of about 150 yards in length and 100 yards in breadth, which as it would maintain as many as I should have in any reasonable time, so, as my flock encreased, I could add more ground to my enclosure.

This was acting with some prudence, and I went to work with courage. I was about three months hedging in the first piece, and till I had done it I tethered the three kids in the best part of it, and used them to feed as near me as possible to make them familiar; and very often I would go and carry them some ears of barley, or a handful of rice, and feed them out of my hand; so that after my enclosure was finished, and I let them loose, they would follow me up and down, bleating after me for a handful of corn.

This answered my end, and in about a year and a half I had a flock of about twelve goats, kids and all; and in two years more I had three and forty, besides several that I took and killed for my food. And after that I enclosed five several pieces of ground to feed them in, with little pens to drive them into, to take them as I wanted, and gates out of one piece of ground into another.

But this was not all, for now I not only had goat's flesh to feed on when I pleased, but milk too, a thing which indeed in my beginning I did not so much as think of, and which, when it came into my thoughts, was really an agreeable surprize. For now I set up my dairy, and had sometimes a gallon or two of milk in a day. And as nature, who gives supplies of food to every creature, dictates even naturally how to make use of it; so I that had never milked a cow, much less a goat, or seen butter or cheese made, very readily and handily, tho' after a great many essays and miscarriages, made me both butter and cheese at last, and never wanted it afterwards.

How mercifully can our great Creator treat His creatures, even in those conditions in which they seemed to be overwhelmed in destruction! How can He sweeten the bitterest providences, and give us cause to praise Him for dungeons and prisons! What a table was here spread for me in a wilderness, where I saw nothing at first but to perish for hunger!

It would have made a stoick smile to have seen me and my little family sit down to dinner; there was my majesty the prince and lord of the whole island; I had the lives of all my subjects at my absolute command; I could hang, draw, give liberty, and take it away, and no rebels among all my subjects.

Then to see how like a king I dined too, all alone, attended by my servants. Poll, as if he had been my favourite, was the only person permitted to talk to me. My dog, who was now grown very old and crazy,[37] and had found no species to multiply his kind upon, sat always at my right hand, and two cats, one on one side the table, and one on the other, expecting now and then a bit from my hand, as a mark of special favour.

But these were not the two cats which I brought on shore at first, for they were both of them dead, and had been interred near my habitation by my own hand; but one of them having multiply'd by I know not what kind of creature, these were two which I had preserved tame, whereas the rest run wild in the woods, and became indeed troublesom to me at last; for they would often come into my house, and plunder me too, till at last I was obliged to shoot them, and did kill a great many; at length they left me. With this attendance and in this plentiful manner I lived; neither could I be said to want any thing but society, and of that, in some time after this, I was like to have too much.

I was something impatient, as I have observed, to have the use of my boat; though very loath to run any more hazards; and therefore sometimes I sat contriving ways to get her about the island, and at other times I sat my self down contented enough without her. But I had a strange uneasiness in my mind to go down to the point of the island, where, as I have said, in my last ramble, I went up the hill to see how the shore lay, and how the current set, that I might see what I had to do. This inclination encreased upon me every day, and at length I resolved to travel thither by land, following the edge of the shore. I did so: but had any one in England been to meet such a man as I was, it must either have frighted them, or raised a great deal of laughter; and as I frequently stood still to look at my self, I could not but smile at the notion of my travelling through Yorkshire with such an equipage, and in such a dress. Be pleased to take a sketch of my figure, as follows.

I had a great high shapeless cap, made of a goat's skin, with a flap hanging down behind, as well to keep the sun from me as to shoot the rain off from running into my neck; nothing being so hurtful in these climates as the rain upon the flesh under the cloaths.

I had a short jacket of goat-skin, the skirts coming down to about the middle of my thighs, and a pair of open-kneed breeches of the same; the breeches were made of the skin of an old he-goat, whose hair hung down such a length on either side that like pantaloons it reached to the middle of my legs; stockings and shoes I had none, but had made me a pair of somethings, I scarce know what to call them, like buskins, to flap over my legs and lace on either side like spatter-dashes;[38] but of a most barbarous shape, as indeed were all the rest of my cloaths.

I had on a broad belt of goat's-skin dry'd, which I drew together with two thongs of the same, instead of buckles, and in a kind of a frog on either side of this, instead of a sword and a dagger, hung a little saw and a hatchet, one on one side, one on the other. I had another belt not so broad, and fastened in the same manner, which hung over my shoulder; and at the end of it, under my left arm, hung two pouches, both made of goat's-skin too; in one of which hung my powder, in the other my shot. At my back I carry'd my basket, on my shoulder my gun, and over my head a great clumsy ugly goat-skin umbrella, but which, after all, was the most necessary thing I had about me, next to my gun. As for my face, the colour of it was really not so moletta-like[39] as one might expect from a man not at all careful of it, and living within nine or ten degrees of the equinox. My beard I had once suffered to grow till it was about a quarter

of a yard long; but as I had both scissars and razors sufficient, I
had cut it pretty short, except what grew on my upper lip, which
I had trimmed into a large pair of Mahometan whiskers, such as
I had seen worn by some Turks who I saw at Sallee; for the
Moors did not wear such, tho' the Turks did; of these mustachioes
or whiskers I will not say they were long enough to hang my
hat upon them; but they were of a length and shape monstrous enough, and such as in England would have passed for
frightful.

But all this is by the by; for as to my figure, I had so few to
observe me that it was of no manner of consequence; so I say
no more to that part. In this kind of figure I went my new
journey, and was out five or six days. I travelled first along the
sea shore, directly to the place where I first brought my boat to an
anchor, to get up upon the rocks; and having no boat now to
take care of, I went over the land a nearer way to the same
height that I was upon before, when looking forward to the
point of the rocks which lay out, and which I was obliged to
double with my boat, as is said above, I was surprized to see the
sea all smooth and quiet, no ripling, no motion, no current, any
more there than in other places.

I was at a strange loss to understand this, and resolved to spend
some time in the observing it, to see if nothing from the sets of
the tide had occasioned it; but I was presently convinced how it
was, viz. that the tide of ebb setting from the west, and joyning
with the current of waters from some great river on the shore,
must be the occasion of this current; and that according as the
wind blew more forcibly from the west or from the north, this
current came nearer or went farther from the shore; for waiting
thereabouts till evening, I went up to the rock again, and then
the tide of ebb being made, I plainly saw the current again as
before, only that it run farther off, being near half a league from
the shore; whereas in my case, it set close upon the shore, and
hurry'd me and my canoe along with it, which at another time
it would not have done.

This observation convinced me that I had nothing to do but to
observe the ebbing and the flowing of the tide, and I might very
easily bring my boat about the island again: but when I began

to think of putting it in practice, I had such a terror upon my spirit at the remembrance of the danger I had been in, that I could not think of it again with any patience; but on the contrary, I took up another resolution which was more safe, though more laborious; and this was that I would build, or rather make me, another periagua or canoe; and so have one for one side of the island and one for the other.

You are to understand that now I had, as I may call it, two plantations in the island; one my little fortification or tent, with the wall about it under the rock, with the cave behind me, which by this time I had enlarged into several apartments or caves, one within another. One of these, which was the dryest and largest, and had a door out beyond my wall or fortification, that is to say, beyond where my wall joyned to the rock, was all filled up with the large earthen pots, of which I have given an account, and with fourteen or fifteen great baskets, which would hold five or six bushels each, where I laid up my stores of provision, especially my corn, some in the ear cut off short from the straw, and the other rubbed out with my hand.

As for my wall, made, as before, with long stakes or piles, those piles grew all like trees, and were by this time grown so big, and spread so very much, that there was not the least appearance to any one's view of any habitation behind them.

Near this dwelling of mine, but a little farther within the land, and upon lower ground, lay my two pieces of corn-ground, which I kept duly cultivated and sowed, and which duly yielded me their harvest in its season; and whenever I had occasion for more corn, I had more land adjoyning as fit as that.

Besides this, I had my country seat, and I had now a tollerable plantation there also; for first, I had my little bower, as I called it, which I kept in repair; that is to say, I kept the hedge which circled it in constantly fitted up to its usual height, the ladder standing always in the inside; I kept the trees, which at first were no more than my stakes, but were now grown very firm and tall; I kept them always so cut, that they might spread and grow thick and wild, and make the more agreeable shade, which they did effectually to my mind. In the middle of this I had my tent always standing, being a piece of a sail spread over poles set up for that purpose, and which never wanted any repair or renewing; and under this I had made me a squab or couch, with the skins of the creatures I had killed, and with other soft things, and a blanket laid on them, such as belonged to our sea-bedding, which I had saved, and a great watch-coat to cover me; and here, whenever I had occasion to be absent from my chief seat, I took up my country habitation.

Adjoyning to this I had my enclosures for my cattle, that is to say, my goats. And as I had taken an inconceivable deal of pains to fence and enclose this ground, so I was so uneasy to see it kept entire, lest the goats should break thro', that I never left off till with infinite labour I had stuck the out-side of the hedge so full of small stakes, and so near to one another, that it was rather a pale than a hedge, and there was scarce room to 'put a hand thro' between them, which afterwards when those stakes grew, as they all did in the next rainy season, made the enclosure strong like a wall, indeed stronger than any wall.

This will testify for me that I was not idle, and that I spared no pains to bring to pass whatever appeared necessary for my comfortable support; for I considered the keeping up a breed of tame creatures thus at my hand would be a living magazine of flesh, milk, butter, and cheese for me as long as I lived in the place, if it were to be forty years; and that keeping them in my reach depended entirely upon my perfecting my enclosures to such a degree that I might be sure of keeping them together; which by this method indeed I so effectually secured that, when these little stakes began to grow, I had planted them so very thick, I was forced to pull some of them up again.

In this place also I had my grapes growing, which I principally depended on for my winter store of raisins, and which I never failed to preserve very carefully, as the best and most agreeable dainty of my whole diet; and indeed they were not agreeable only, but physical,[40] wholesome, nourishing, and refreshing to the last degree.

As this was also about half way between my other habitation and the place where I had laid up my boat, I generally stayed and lay here in my way thither; for I used frequently to visit my boat, and I kept all things about or belonging to her in very good order; sometimes I went out in her to divert my self, but no more hazardous voyages would I go, nor scarce ever above a stone's cast or two from the shore, I was so apprehensive of being hurry'd out of my knowledge again by the currents, or winds, or any other accident. But now I come to a new scene of my life.

It happened one day about noon going towards my boat, I was exceedingly surprized with the print of a man's naked foot on the shore, which was very plain to be seen in the sand. I stood like one thunder-struck, or as if I had seen an apparition; I listened, I looked round me, I could hear nothing, nor see any thing; I went up to a rising ground to look farther; I went up the shore and down the shore, but it was all one, I could see no other impression but that one. I went to it again to see if there were any more, and to observe if it might not be my fancy; but there was no room for that, for there was exactly the very print of a foot, toes, heel, and every part of a foot; how it came thither I knew not, nor could in the least imagine. But after innumerable fluttering thoughts, like a man perfectly confused and out of my self, I came home to my fortification, not feeling, as we say, the ground I went on, but terrify'd to the last degree, looking behind me at every two or three steps, mistaking every bush and tree, and fancying every stump at a distance to be a man; nor is it possible to describe how many various shapes affrighted imagination represented things to me in, how many wild ideas were found every moment in my fancy, and what strange unaccountable whimsies came into my thoughts by the way.

When I came to my castle, for so I think I called it ever after this, I fled into it like one pursued; whether I went over by the ladder as first contrived, or went in at the hole in the rock which I called a door, I cannot remember; no, nor could I remember the next morning, for never frighted hare fled to cover, or fox to earth, with more terror of mind than I to this retreat.

I slept none that night; the farther I was from the occasion of my fright, the greater my apprehensions were, which is something contrary to the nature of such things, and especially to the usual practice of all creatures in fear: but I was so embarrassed with my own frightful ideas of the thing, that I formed nothing but dismal imaginations to my self, even tho' I was now a great way off of it. Sometimes I fancy'd it must be the devil; and reason joyned in with me upon this supposition; for how should any other thing in human shape come into the place? Where was the vessel that brought them? What marks was there of any other footsteps? And how was it possible a man should come there? But then to think that Satan should take human shape upon him in such a place where there could be no manner of occasion for it, but to leave the print of his foot behind him, and that even for no purpose too, for he could not be sure I should see it; this was an amusement the other way; I considered that the devil might have found out abundance of other ways to have terrify'd me than this of the single print of a foot; that as I lived quite on the other side of the island, he would never have been so simple to leave a mark in a place where 'twas ten thousand to one whether I should ever see it or not, and in the sand too, which the first surge of the sea upon a high wind would have defaced entirely. All this seemed inconsistent with the thing it self, and with all the notions we usually entertain of the subtilty of the devil.

Abundance of such things as these assisted to argue me out of all apprehensions of its being the devil; and I presently concluded then, that it must be some more dangerous creature, viz. that it must be some of the savages of the main land over-against me, who had wandered out to sea in their canoes, and, either driven by the currents or by contrary winds, had made the island; and had been on shore, but were gone away again to sea, being as loth, perhaps, to have stayed in this desolate island as I would have been to have had them.

While these reflections were rowling upon my mind, I was very thankful in my thoughts that I was so happy as not to be thereabouts at that time, or that they did not see my boat, by which they would have concluded that some inhabitants had been in the place, and perhaps have searched farther for me. Then terrible thoughts racked my imagination about their having found my boat, and that there were people here; and that if so, I should certainly have them come again in greater numbers, and devour me; that if it should happen so that they should not find me, yet they would find my enclosure, destroy all my corn, carry away all my flock of tame goats, and I should perish at last for meer want.

Thus my fear banished all my religious hope; all that former confidence in God, which was founded upon such wonderful experience as I had had of His goodness, now vanished, as if He that had fed me by miracle hitherto, could not preserve by His power the provision which He had made for me by His goodness. I reproached myself with my easiness, that would not sow any more corn one year than would just serve me till the next season, as if no accident could intervene to prevent my enjoying the crop that was upon the ground; and this I thought so just a reproof, that I resolved for the future to have two or three years corn beforehand, so that whatever might come, I might not perish for want of bread.

How strange a chequer work of providence is the life of man! and by what secret differing springs are the affections hurry'd about as differing circumstances present! To day we love what to morrow we hate; to day we seek what to morrow we shun; to day we desire what to morrow we fear, nay, even tremble at the apprehensions of; this was exemplify'd in me at this time in the most lively manner imaginable; for I whose only affliction was, that I seemed banished from human society, that I was alone, circumscribed by the boundless ocean, cut off from mankind, and condemned to what I called silent life; that I was as one who Heaven thought not worthy to be numbered among the living, or to appear among the rest of His creatures; that to have seen one of my own species would have seemed to me a raising from death to life, and the greatest blessing that Heaven it self, next to the supreme blessing of salvation, could bestow; I say, that I should now tremble at the very apprehensions of seeing a man, and was ready to sink into the ground at but the shadow or silent appearance of a man's having set his foot in the island.

Such is the uneven state of human life; and it afforded me a great many curious speculations afterwards, when I had a little recovered my first surprize; I considered that this was the station of life the infinitely wise and good providence of God had determined for me, that as I could not foresee what the ends of divine wisdom might be in all this, so I was not to dispute His sovereignty, who, as I was His creature, had an undoubted right by creation to govern and dispose of me absolutely as He thought fit; and who, as I was a creature who had offended Him, had likewise a judicial right to condemn me to what punishment He thought fit; and that it was my part to submit to bear His indignation, because I had sinned against Him.

I then reflected that God, who was not only righteous but omnipotent, as He had thought fit thus to punish and afflict me, so He was able to deliver me; that if He did not think fit to do it, 'twas my unquestioned duty to resign my self absolutely and entirely to His will; and on the other hand, it was my duty also to hope in Him, pray to Him, and quietly to attend the dictates and directions of His daily providence.

These thoughts took me up many hours, days, nay, I may say weeks and months; and one particular effect of my cogitations on this occasion I cannot omit, viz. One morning early, lying in my bed, and filled with thought about my danger from the appearance of savages, I found it discomposed me very much, upon which those words of the scripture came into my thoughts, *Call upon me in the day of trouble, and I will deliver, and thou shalt glorify me.*

Upon this, rising chearfully out of my bed, my heart was not only comforted, but I was guided and encouraged to pray earnestly to God for deliverance. When I had done praying, I took up my Bible, and opening it to read, the first words that presented to me were, *Wait on the Lord, and be of good cheer, and he shall strengthen thy heart; wait, I say, on the Lord.*[41] It is impossible to express the comfort this gave me. In answer, I thankfully laid down the book, and was no more sad, at least, not on that occasion.

In the middle of these cogitations, apprehensions, and reflections, it came into my thought one day, that all this might be a meer chimera of my own, and that this foot might be the print of my own foot, when I came on shore from my boat. This cheared me up a little too, and I began to perswade my self it was all a delusion; that it was nothing else but my own foot, and why might not I come that way from the boat, as well as I was going that way to the boat? Again I considered also that I could by no means tell for certain where I had trod, and where I had not; and that if at last this was only the print of my own foot, I had played the part of those fools who strive to make stories of spectres and apparitions, and then are frighted at them more than any body.

Now I began to take courage, and to peep abroad again; for I had not stirred out of my castle for three days and nights; so that I began to starve for provision; for I had little or nothing within doors but some barley cakes and water. Then I knew that my goats wanted to be milked too, which usually was my evening diversion; and the poor creatures were in great pain and inconvenience for want of it; and indeed, it almost spoiled some of them, and almost dry'd up their milk.

Heartning my self therefore with the belief that this was nothing but the print of one of my own feet, and so I might be truly said to start at my own shadow, I began to go abroad again, and went to my country house to milk my flock; but to see with what fear I went forward, how often I looked behind me, how I was ready every now and then to lay down my basket and run for my life, it would have made any one have thought I was haunted with an evil conscience, or that I had been lately most terribly frighted, and so indeed I had.

However, as I went down thus two or three days, and having seen nothing, I began to be a little bolder, and to think there was really nothing in it but my own imagination: but I cou'd not perswade my self fully of this till I should go down to the shore again, and see this print of a foot, and measure it by my own, and see if there was any similitude or fitness, that I might be assured it was my own foot. But when I came to the place, *First*, it appeared evidently to me, that when I laid up my boat, I could not possibly be on shore any where there about; *Secondly*, when I came to measure the mark with my own foot, I found my foot not so large by a great deal. Both these things filled my head with new imaginations, and gave me the vapours again to the highest degree; so that I shook with cold, like one in an ague; and I went home again, filled with the belief that some man or men had been on shore there; or in short, that the island was inhabited, and I might be surprized before I was aware; and what course to take for my security I knew not.

O what ridiculous resolution men take, when possessed with fear! It deprives them of the use of those means which reason offers for their relief. The first thing I proposed to my self was, to throw down my enclosures and turn all my tame cattle wild into the woods, that the enemy might not find them, and then frequent the island in prospect of the same, or the like booty; then to the simple thing of digging up my two corn fields, that they might not find such a grain there, and still be prompted to frequent the island; then to demolish my bower and tent, that they might not see any vestages of habitation, and be prompted to look farther, in order to find out the persons inhabiting.

These were the subject of the first night's cogitation, after I was come home again, while the apprehensions which had so overrun my mind were fresh upon me, and my head was full of vapours, as above. Thus fear of danger is ten thousand times more terrifying than danger it self when apparent to the eyes; and we find the burthen of anxiety greater by much than the evil which we are anxious about; and, which was worse than all this, I had not that relief in this trouble from the resignation I used to practise, that I hoped to have. I looked, I thought, like Saul,[42] who complained not only that the Philistines were upon him, but that God had forsaken him; for I did not now take due ways to compose my mind, by crying to God in my distress, and resting upon His providence, as I had done before, for my defence and deliverance; which if I had done, I had at least been more cheerfully supported under this new surprise, and perhaps carry'd through it with more resolution.

This confusion of my thoughts kept me waking all night; but in the morning I fell asleep, and having, by the amusement of my mind, been as it were tyred, and my spirits exhausted, I slept very soundly, and waked much better composed than I had ever been before; and now I began to think sedately; and upon the utmost debate with my self, I concluded that this island, which was so exceeding pleasant, fruitful, and no farther from the main land than as I had seen, was not so entirely abandoned as I might imagine; that altho' there were no stated inhabitants who lived on the spot, yet that there might sometimes come boats off from the shore, who either with design, or perhaps never but when they were driven by cross winds, might come to this place.

That I had lived here fifteen years now, and had not met with the least shadow or figure of any people yet; and that if at any time they should be driven here, it was probable they went away again as soon as ever they could, seeing they had never thought fit to fix there upon any occasion, to this time.

That the most I cou'd suggest any danger from, was from any such casual accidental landing of straggling people from the main, who, as it was likely if they were driven hither, were here against their wills, so they made no stay here, but went off again with all possible speed, seldom staying one night on shore, least they should not have the help of the tides and day-light back again; and that therefore I had nothing to do but to consider of some safe retreat, in case I should see any savages land upon the spot.

Now I began sorely to repent that I had dug my cave so large as to bring a door through again, which door, as I said, came out beyond where my fortification joyned to the rock; upon maturely considering this therefore, I resolved to draw me a second fortification, in the same manner of a semicircle, at a distance from my wall just where I had planted a double row of trees about twelve years before, of which I made mention. These trees having been planted so thick before, they wanted but a few piles to be driven between them, that they should be thicker and stronger, and my wall would be soon finished.

So that I had now a double wall, and my outer wall was thickned with pieces of timber, old cables, and every thing I could think of, to make it strong; having in it seven little holes, about as big as I might put my arm out at. In the in-side of this, I thickned my wall to above ten foot thick, with continual bringing earth out of my cave, and laying it at the foot of the wall, and walking upon it; and through the seven holes I contrived to plant the musquets, of which I took notice that I got seven on shore out of the ship; these, I say, I planted like my cannon, and fitted them into frames that held them like a carriage, that so I could fire all the seven guns in two minutes time. This wall

I was many a weary month a finishing, and yet never thought my self safe till it was done.

When this was done, I stuck all the ground without my wall, for a great way every way, as full with stakes or sticks of the osier-like wood, which I found so apt to grow, as they could well stand; insomuch that I believe I might set in near twenty thousand of them, leaving a pretty large space between them and my wall, that I might have room to see an enemy, and they might have no shelter from the young trees, if they attempted to approach my outer wall.

Thus in two years time I had a thick grove, and in five or six years time I had a wood before my dwelling, growing so monstrous thick and strong, that it was indeed perfectly impassable; and no men of what kind soever would ever imagine that there was any thing beyond it, much less a habitation. As for the way which I proposed to my self to go in and out, for I left no avenue, it was setting two ladders, one to a part of the rock, which was low, and then broke in, and left room to place another ladder upon that; so when the two ladders were taken down, no man living could come down to me without mischieving himself; and if they had come down they were still on the out-side of my outer wall.

Thus I took all the measures humane prudence could suggest for my own preservation; and it will be seen at length that they were not altogether without just reason; though I foresaw nothing at that time, more than my meer fear suggested to me.

While this was doing, I was not altogether careless of my other affairs; for I had a great concern upon me for my little herd of goats; they were not only a present supply to me upon every occasion, and began to be sufficient to me without the expence of powder and shot, but also without the fatigue of hunting after the wild ones, and I was loth to lose the advantage of them, and to have them all to nurse up over again.

To this purpose, after long consideration, I could think of but two ways to preserve them; one was to find another convenient place to dig a cave under-ground, and to drive them into it every night; and the other was to enclose two or three little bits of land remote from one another and as much concealed as I could, where I might keep about half a dozen young goats in each place: so that if any disaster happened to the flock in general, I might be able to raise them again with little trouble and time: and this, tho' it would require a great deal of time and labour, I thought was the most rational design.

Accordingly I spent some time to find out the most retired parts of the island; and I pitched upon one which was as private indeed as my heart could wish for; it was a little damp piece of ground in the middle of the hollow and thick woods, where, as is observed, I almost lost my self once before, endeavouring to come back that way from the eastern part of the island. Here I found a clear piece of land near three acres, so surrounded with woods that it was almost an enclosure by nature, at least it did not want near so much labour to make it so as the other pieces of ground I had worked so hard at.

I immediately went to work with this piece of ground, and in less than a month's time I had so fenced it round, that my flock or herd, call it which you please, who were not so wild now as at first they might be supposed to be, were well enough secured in it. So, without any farther delay, I removed ten young she-goats and two he-goats to this piece; and when they were there, I continued to perfect the fence till I had made it as secure as the other, which, however, I did at more leisure, and it took me up more time by a great deal.

All this labour I was at the expence of, purely from my apprehensions on the account of the print of a man's foot which I had seen; for as yet I never saw any human creature come near the island, and I had now lived two years under these uneasinesses, which indeed made my life much less comfortable than it was before; as may well be imagined by any who know what it is to live in the constant snare of the fear of man; and this I must observe with grief too, that the discomposure of my mind had too great impressions also upon the religious part of my thoughts, for the dread and terror of falling into the hands of savages and canibals lay so upon my spirits, that I seldom found my self in a due temper for application to my Maker, at least not with the sedate calmness and resignation of soul which I was wont to do; I rather prayed to God as under great affliction and

pressure of mind, surrounded with danger, and in expectation
every night of being murthered and devoured before morning; and
I must testify from my experience, that a temper of peace, thankfulness, love, and affection is much more the proper frame for
prayer than that of terror and discomposure; and that under the
dread of mischief impending, a man is no more fit for a comforting performance of the duty of praying to God, than he is for
repentance on a sick bed : for these discomposures affect the mind
as the others do the body; and the discomposure of the mind must
necessarily be as great a disability as that of the body, and much
greater, praying to God being properly an act of the mind, not of
the body.

But to go on. After I had thus secured one part of my little
living stock, I went about the whole island, searching for another private place, to make such another deposit; when wandring
more to the west point of the island than I had ever gone yet,
and looking out to sea, I thought I saw a boat upon the sea, at a
great distance; I had found a prospective glass or two in one of
the seamen's chests, which I saved out of our ship; but I had it
not about me, and this was so remote that I could not tell what
to make of it, though I looked at it till my eyes were not able
to hold to look any longer; whether it was a boat or not, I do
not know; but as I descended from the hill, I could see no more
of it, so I gave it over; only I resolved to go no more out without
a prospective glass in my pocket.

When I was come down the hill to the end of the island, where
indeed I had never been before, I was presently convinced that
the seeing the print of a man's foot was not such a strange thing
in the island as I imagined; and but that it was a special providence that I was cast upon the side of the island where the
savages never came, I should easily have known that nothing
was more frequent than for the canoes from the main, when they
happened to be a little too far out at sea, to shoot over to that
side of the island for harbour; likewise as they often met and
fought in their canoes, the victors, having taken any prisoners,
would bring them over to this shore, where according to their
dreadful customs, being all canibals, they would kill and eat
them; of which hereafter.

When I was come down the hill to the shore, as I said above, being the s.w. point of the island, I was perfectly confounded and amazed; nor is it possible for me to express the horror of my mind, at seeing the shore spread with skulls, hands, feet, and other bones of humane bodies; and particularly I observed a place where there had been a fire made, and a circle dug in the earth, like a cockpit, where it is supposed the savage wretches had sat down to their inhumane feastings upon the bodies of their fellow-creatures.

I was so astonished with the sight of these things, that I entertained no notions of any danger to my self from it for a long while; all my apprehensions were bury'd in the thoughts of such a pitch of inhuman, hellish brutality, and the horror of the degeneracy of human nature; which, though I had heard of often, yet I never had so near a view of before; in short, I turned away my face from the horrid spectacle; my stomach grew sick, and I was just at the point of fainting, when nature discharged the disorder from my stomach, and having vomited with an uncommon violence, I was a little relieved, but cou'd not bear to stay in the place a moment; so I gat me up the hill again with all the speed I cou'd, and walked on towards my own habitation.

When I came a little out of that part of the island, I stood still a while as amazed; and then recovering my self, I looked up with the utmost affection of my soul, and with a flood of tears in my eyes, gave God thanks that had cast my first lot in a part of the world where I was distinguished from such dreadful creatures as these; and that, though I had esteemed my present condition very miserable, had yet given me so many comforts in it, that I had still more to give thanks for than to complain of; and this above all, that I had even in this miserable condition been comforted with the knowledge of Himself, and the hope of His blessing, which was a felicity more than sufficiently equivalent to all the misery which I had suffered, or could suffer.

In this frame of thankfulness, I went home to my castle, and began to be much easier now, as to the safety of my circumstances, than ever I was before; for I observed that these wretches never came to this island in search of what they could get; perhaps not seeking, not wanting, or not expecting any thing here; and having often, no doubt, been up in the covered woody part of it, without finding any thing to their purpose. I knew I had been here now almost eighteen years, and never saw the least foot-steps of humane creature there before; and I might be here eighteen more, as entirely concealed as I was now, if I did not discover my self to them, which I had no manner of occasion to do, it being my only business to keep my self entirely concealed where I was, unless I found a better sort of creatures than canibals to make my self known to.

Yet I entertained such an abhorrence of the savage wretches that I have been speaking of, and of the wretched inhuman custom of their devouring and eating one another up, that I continued pensive and sad, and kept close within my own circle for almost two years after this. When I say my own circle, I mean by it my three plantations, viz. my castle, my country seat, which I called my bower, and my enclosure in the woods; nor did I look after this for any other use than as an enclosure for my goats; for the aversion which nature gave me to these hellish wretches was such, that I was fearful of seeing them as of seeing the devil himself; nor did I so much as go to look after my boat in all this time, but began rather to think of making me another; for I cou'd not think of ever making any more attempts to bring the other boat round the island to me, least I should meet with some of these creatures at sea, in which if I had happened to have fallen into their hands, I knew what would have been my lot.

Time, however, and the satisfaction I had that I was in no danger of being discovered by these people, began to wear off my uneasiness about them; and I began to live just in the same composed manner as before; only with this difference, that I used more caution, and kept my eyes more about me than I did before, least I should happen to be seen by any of them; and particularly, I was more cautious of firing my gun, least any of them being on the island should happen to hear of it : and it was therefore a very good providence to me, that I had furnished my self with a tame breed of goats, that I needed not hunt any more about the woods, or shoot at them; and if I did catch any of them after this, it was by traps and snares, as I had done before; so that for two years after this, I believe I never fired my gun once off, though I never went out without it; and, which was more, as I had saved three pistols out of the ship, I always carry'd them out with me, or at least two of them, sticking them in my goat-skin belt; also I furbished up one of the great cut-lashes that I had out of the ship, and made me a belt to put it on also; so that I was now a most formidable fellow to look at when I went abroad, if you add to the former description of my self, the particular of two pistols, and a great broad sword hanging at my side in a belt, but without a scabbard.

Things going on thus, as I have said, for some time, I seemed, excepting these cautions, to be reduced to my former calm, sedate way of living. All these things tended to shewing me more and more how far my condition was from being miserable, compared to some others; nay, to many other particulars of life, which it might have pleased God to have made my lot. It put me upon reflecting how little repining there would be among mankind at any condition of life, if people would rather compare their condition with those that are worse, in order to be thankful, than be always comparing them with those which are better, to assist their murmurings and complainings.

As in my present condition there were not really many things which I wanted, so indeed I thought that the frights I had been in about these savage wretches, and the concern I had been in for my own preservation, had taken off the edge of my invention for my own conveniences; and I had dropped a good design, which I had once bent my thoughts too much upon; and that was, to try if I could not make some of my barley into malt, and then try to brew my self some beer. This was really a whimsical thought, and I reproved my self often for the simplicity of it; for I presently saw there would be the want of several things necessary to the making my beer, that it would be impossible for me to supply; as first, casks to preserve it in, which was a thing that, as I have observed already, I cou'd never compass; no, though I spent not many days, but weeks, nay, months in attempting it, but to no purpose. In the next place, I had no hops to make it keep, no yeast to make it work, no copper or kettle to make it boil; and yet all these things notwithstanding, I verily believe, had not these things intervened, I mean the frights and terrors I was in about the savages, I had undertaken it, and perhaps brought it to pass too; for I seldom gave any thing over without accomplishing it, when I once had it in my head enough to begin it.

But my invention now run quite another way; for night and day I could think of nothing but how I might destroy some of these monsters in their cruel bloody entertainment, and, if possible, save the victim they should bring hither to destroy. It would take up a larger volume than this whole work is intended to be, to set down all the contrivances I hatched, or rather brooded upon in my thought, for the destroying these creatures, or at least frightening them, so as to prevent their coming hither any more; but all was abortive, nothing could be possible to take effect, unless I was to be there to do it my self; and what could one man do among them, when perhaps there might be twenty or thirty of them together, with their darts, or their bows and arrows, with which they could shoot as true to a mark as I could with my gun?

Sometimes I contrived to dig a hole under the place where they made their fire, and put in five or six pound of gun-powder, which when they kindled their fire, would consequently take fire, and blow up all that was near it; but as in the first place I should be very loth to wast so much powder upon them, my store being now within the quantity of one barrel, so neither could I be sure of its going off at any certain time, when it might surprise them; and at best, that it would do little more than just blow the fire about their ears and fright them; but not sufficient to make them forsake the place; so I laid it aside, and then proposed that I would place my self in ambush in some convenient place, with my three guns, all double loaded, and, in the middle of their bloody ceremony, let fly at them, when I should be sure to kill or wound perhaps two or three at every shoot; and then falling in upon them with my three pistols and my sword, I made no doubt but that if there was twenty I should kill them all. This fancy pleased my thoughts for some weeks, and I was so full of it that I often dreamed of it, and sometimes that I was just going to let fly at them in my sleep.

I went so far with it in my imagination, that I employed my self several days to find out proper places to put my self in ambuscade, as I said, to watch for them; and I went frequently to the place it self, which was now grown more familiar to me; and especially while my mind was thus filled with thoughts of revenge, and of a bloody putting twenty or thirty of them to the sword, as I may call it, the horror I had at the place, and at the signals of the barbarous wretches devouring one another, abated my malice.

Well, at length I found a place in the side of the hill, where I was satisfy'd I might securely wait till I saw any of their boats coming, and might then, even before they would be ready to come on shore, convey my self unseen into thickets of trees, in one of which there was a hollow large enough to conceal me entirely; and where I might sit and observe all their bloody doings, and take my full aim at their heads, when they were so close together as that it would be next to impossible that I should miss my shoot, or that I could fail wounding three or four of them at the first shoot.

In this place then I resolved to fix my design, and accordingly I prepared two muskets and my ordinary fowling piece. The two muskets I loaded with a brace of slugs each, and four or five smaller bullets, about the size of pistol bullets; and the fowling piece I loaded with near a handful of swan-shot, of the largest size; I also loaded my pistols with about four bullets each; and in this posture, well provided with ammunition for a second and third charge, I prepared my self for my expedition.

After I had thus laid the scheme of my design, and in my imagination put it in practice, I continually made my tour every morning up to the top of the hill, which was from my castle, as I called it, about three miles or more, to see if I cou'd observe any boats upon the sea, coming near the island, or standing over towards it; but I began to tire of this hard duty, after I had for two or three months constantly kept my watch, but came always back without any discovery, there having not in all that time been the least appearance, not only on or near the shore, but not on the whole ocean, so far as my eyes or glasses could reach every way.

As long as I kept up my daily tour to the hill to look out, so long also I kept up the vigour of my design, and my spirits seemed to be all the while in a suitable form for so outragious an execution as the killing twenty or thirty naked savages, for an offence which I had not at all entred into a discussion of in my thoughts, any farther than my passions were at first fired by the horror I conceived at the unnatural custom of that people of the country, who it seems had been suffered by Providence, in His wide disposition of the world, to have no other guide than that of their own abominable and vitiated passions; and consequently were left, and perhaps had been so for some ages, to act such horrid things, and receive such dreadful customs, as nothing but nature entirely abandoned of Heaven, and acted by some hellish degeneracy, could have run them into. But now, when, as I have said, I began to be weary of the fruitless excursion, which I had made so long, and so far, every morning in vain, so my opinion of the action it self began to alter, and I began with cooler and calmer thoughts to consider what it was I was going to engage in; what authority or call I had, to pretend to be judge and executioner upon these men as criminals, whom Heaven had thought fit for so many ages to suffer unpunished, to go on, and to be, as it were, the executioners of His judgments one upon another; how far these people were offenders against me, and what right I had to engage in the quarrel of that blood which they shed promiscuously one upon another. I debated this very often with my self thus: How do I know what God Himself judges in this particular case? It is certain these people either do not commit this as a crime; it is not against their own consciences reproving, or their light reproaching them. They do not know it be an offence, and then commit it in defiance of divine justice, as we do in almost all the sins we commit. They think it no more a crime to kill a captive taken in war, than we do to kill an ox; nor to eat humane flesh, than we do to eat mutton.

When I had considered this a little, it followed necessarily that I was certainly in the wrong in it, that these people were not murtherers in the sense that I had before condemned them in my thoughts; any more than those Christians were murtherers who often put to death the prisoners taken in battle; or more frequently, upon many occasions, put whole troops of men to the sword, without giving quarter, though they threw down their arms and submitted.

In the next place it occurred to me, that albeit the usage they thus gave one another was thus brutish and inhumane, yet it was really nothing to me: these people had done me no injury. That if they attempted me, or I saw it necessary for my immediate preservation to fall upon them, something might be said for it; but that as I was yet out of their power, and they had really no knowledge of me, and consequently no design upon me; and therefore it could not be just for me to fall upon them. That this would justify the conduct of the Spaniards in all their barbarities practised in America, where they destroyed millions of these people, who, however they were idolaters and barbarians, and had several bloody and barbarious rites in their customs, such as sacrificing human bodies to their idols, were yet, as to the Spaniards, very innocent people; and that the rooting them out of the country is spoken of with the utmost abhorrence and detestation by even the Spaniards themselves at this time, and by all other Christian nations of Europe, as a meer butchery, a bloody and unnatural piece of cruelty, unjustifiable either to God or man; and such, as for which the very name of a Spaniard is reckoned to be frightful and terrible to all people of humanity, or of Christian compassion; as if the kingdom of Spain were particularly eminent for the product of a race of men who were without principles of tenderness, or the common bowels of pity to the miserable, which is reckoned to be a mark of generous temper in the mind.

These considerations really put me to a pause, and to a kind of a full-stop; and I began by little and little to be off of my design, and to conclude I had taken wrong measures in my resolutions to attack the savages; that it was not my business to meddle with them, unless they first attacked me, and this it was my business if possible to prevent; but that if I were discovered and attacked, then I knew my duty.

On the other hand, I argued with my self, that this really was the way not to deliver my self, but entirely to ruin and destroy my self; for unless I was sure to kill every one that not only should be on shore at that time, but that should ever come on shore afterwards, if but one of them escaped to tell their country people what had happened, they would come over again by thousands to revenge the death of their fellows, and I should only bring upon my self a certain destruction, which at present I had no manner of occasion for.

Upon the whole I concluded that neither in principle or in policy, I ought one way or other to concern my self in this affair. That my business was by all possible means to conceal my self from them, and not to leave the least signal to them to guess by, that there were any living creatures upon the island; I mean of humane shape.

Religion joyned in with this prudential, and I was convinced now many ways, that I was perfectly out of my duty when I was laying all my bloody schemes for the destruction of innocent creatures, I mean innocent as to me. As to the crimes they were guilty of towards one another, I had nothing to do with them; they were national,[43] and I ought to leave them to the justice of God, who is the governour of nations, and knows how by national punishments to make a just retribution for national offences; and to bring publick judgments upon those who offend in a publick manner, by such ways as best pleases Him.

This appeared so clear to me now, that nothing was a greater satisfaction to me, than that I had not been suffered to do a thing which I now saw so much reason to believe would have been no less a sin than that of wilful murther, if I had committed it; and I gave most humble thanks on my knees to God; that had thus delivered me from blood-guiltiness; beseeching Him to grant me the protection of His providence, that I might not fall into the hands of the barbarians; or that I might not lay my hands upon them, unless I had a more clear call from Heaven to do it, in defence of my own life.

In this disposition I continued for near a year after this; and so far was I from desiring an occasion for falling upon these wretches, that in all that time I never once went up the hill to see whether there were any of them in sight, or to know whether any of them had been on shore there or not, that I might not be tempted to renew any of my contrivances against them, or be provoked by any advantage which might present it self, to fall upon them; only this I did, I went and removed my boat, which I had on the other side the island, and carry'd it down to the east end of the whole island, where I ran it into a little cove which I found under some high rocks, and where I knew, by reason of the currents, the savages durst not, at least would not come with their boats, upon any account whatsoever.

With my boat I carry'd away every thing that I had left there belonging to her, though not necessary for the bare going thither, viz. a mast and sail which I had made for her, and a thing like an anchor, but indeed which could not be called either anchor or grapling; however, it was the best I could make of its kind. All this I removed, that there might not be the least shadow of any discovery, or any appearance of any boat or of any human habitation upon the island.

Besides this, I kept my self, as I said, more retired than ever, and seldom went from my cell, other than upon my constant employment, viz. to milk my she-goats, and manage my little flock in the wood; which, as it was quite on the other part of the island, was quite out of danger; for certain it is, that these savage people who sometimes haunted this island never came with any thoughts of finding any thing here; and consequently never wandred off from the coast; and I doubt not, but they might have been several times on shore after my apprehensions of them had made me cautious, as well as before; and indeed, I looked back with some horror upon the thoughts of what my condition would have been, if I had chop'd upon them[44] and been discovered before that, when naked and unarmed, except with one gun, and that loaden often only with small shot, I walked every where peeping and peeping about the island to see what I could get; what a surprise should I have been in, if when I discovered the print of a man's foot, I had instead of that seen fifteen or twenty savages, and found them pursuing me, and by the swiftness of their running, no possibility of my escaping them.

The thoughts of this sometimes sunk my very soul within me,

and distressed my mind so much, that I could not soon recover it, to think what I should have done, and how I not only should not have been able to resist them, but even should not have had presence of mind enough to do what I might have done; much less, what now after so much consideration and preparation I might be able to do. Indeed, after serious thinking of these things, I should be very melancholy; and sometimes it would last a great while; but I resolved it at last all into thankfulness to that Providence, which had delivered me from so many unseen dangers, and had kept me from those mischiefs which I could no way have been the agent in delivering my self from; because I had not the least notion of any such thing depending, or the least supposition of it being possible.

This renewed a contemplation which often had come to my thoughts in former time, when first I began to see the merciful dispositions of Heaven in the dangers we run through in this life; how wonderfully we are delivered when we know nothing of it; how when we are in a quandary, as we call it, a doubt or hesitation, whether to go this way or that way, a secret hint shall direct us this way, when we intended to go that way; nay, when sense, our own inclination, and perhaps business has called to go the other way, yet a strange impression upon the mind, from we know not what springs, and by we know not what power, shall over-rule us to go this way; and it shall afterwards appear that had we gone that way which we should have gone, and even to our imagination ought to have gone, we should have been ruined and lost. Upon these and many like reflections, I afterwards made it a certain rule with me, that whenever I found those secret hints or pressings of my mind, to doing or not doing any thing that presented, or to going this way or that way, I never failed to obey the secret dictate; though I knew no other reason for it than that such a pressure or such a hint hung upon my mind. I could give many examples of the success of this conduct in the course of my life; but more especially in the latter part of my inhabiting this unhappy island; besides many occasions which it is very likely I might have taken notice of, if I had seen with the same eyes then, that I saw with now. But 'tis never too late to be wise; and I cannot but advise all considering men, whose lives are attended with such extraordinary incidents as mine, or even though not so extraordinary, not to slight such secret intimations of providence, let them come from what invisible intelligence they will, that I shall not discuss, and perhaps cannot account for; but certainly they are a proof of the converse of spirits, and the secret communication between those embody'd and those unembody'd; and such a proof as can never be withstood. Of which I shall have occasion to give some very remarkable instances in the remainder of my solitary residence in this dismal place.

I believe the reader of this will not think [it] strange if I confess that these anxieties, these constant dangers I lived in, and the concern that was now upon me, put an end to all invention, and to all the contrivances that I had laid for my future accommodations and conveniences. I had the care of my safety more now upon my hands than that of my food. I cared not to drive a nail or chop a stick of wood now, for fear the noise I should make should be heard; much less would I fire a gun, for the same reason; and above all, I was intollerably uneasy at making any fire, least the smoke which is visible at a great distance in the day should betray me; and for this reason I removed that part of my business which required fire, such as burning of pots and pipes, etc., into my new apartment in the woods, where, after I had been some time, I found, to my unspeakable consolation, a meer natural cave in the earth,[45] which went in a vast way, and where, I dare say, no savage, had he been at the mouth of it, would be so hardy as to venture in, nor indeed would any man else, but one who, like me, wanted nothing so much as a safe retreat.

The mouth of this hollow was at the bottom of a great rock, where by meer accident (I would say, if I did not see abundant reason to ascribe all such things now to providence) I was cutting down some thick branches of trees, to make charcoal; and before I go on, I must observe the reason of my making this charcoal; which was thus:

I was afraid of making a smoke about my habitation, as I said before; and yet I could not live there without baking my bread, cooking my meat, &c., so I contrived to burn some wood here, as I had seen done in England, under turf, till it became chark, or dry coal; and then putting the fire out, I preserved the coal to carry home, and perform the other services which fire was wanting for at home without danger of smoke.

But this is by the by. While I was cutting down some wood here, I perceived that behind a very thick branch of low brushwood, or underwood, there was a kind of hollow place; I was curious to look into it, and getting with difficulty into the mouth of it, I found it was pretty large; that is to say, sufficient for me to stand upright in it, and perhaps another with me; but I must confess to you, I made more hast out than I did in, when looking farther into the place, and which was perfectly dark, I saw two broad shining eyes of some creature, whether devil or man I knew not, which twinkled like two stars, the dim light from the cave's mouth shining directly in and making the reflection.

However, after some pause, I recovered my self, and began to call my self a thousand fools, and tell my self, that he that was afraid to see the devil was not fit to live twenty years in an island all alone; and that I durst to believe there was nothing in this cave that was more frightful than my self; upon this, plucking up my courage, I took up a great firebrand, and in I rushed again, with the stick flaming in my hand. I had not gone three steps in, but I was almost as much frighted as I was before; for I heard a very loud sigh, like that of a man in some pain, and it was followed by a broken noise, as if words half expressed, and then a deep sigh again. I stepped back, and was indeed struck with such a surprize, that it put me into a cold sweat; and if I had had a hat on my head, I will not answer for it, that my hair might not have lifted it off. But still plucking up my spirits as well as I could, and encouraging my self a little with considering that the power and presence of God was every where, and was able to protect me; upon this I stepped forward again, and by the light of the fire-brand, holding it up a little over my head, I saw lying on the ground a most monstrous frightful old he-goat, just making his will, as we say, and gasping for life, and dying indeed of meer old age.

I stirred him a little to see if I could get him out, and he essayed to get up, but was not able to raise himself; and I thought with my self, he might even lie there; for if he had frighted me so, he would certainly fright any of the savages, if any of them should be so hardy as to come in there, while he had any life in him.

I was now recovered from my surprize, and began to look round me, when I found the cave was but very small, that is to say, it might be about twelve foot over, but in no manner of shape, either round or square, no hands having ever been employed in making it but those of meer nature. I observed also, that there was a place at the farther side of it, that went in farther, but was so low that it required me to creep upon my hands and knees to go into it, and whither I went I knew not; so having no candle, I gave it over for some time; but resolved to come again the next day, provided with candles and a tinder-box, which I had made of the lock of one of the muskets, with some wild-fire in the pan.

Accordingly, the next day I came provided with six large candles of my own making; for I made very good candles now of goat's tallow; and going into this low place, I was obliged to creep upon all fours, as I have said, almost ten yards; which, by the way, I thought was a venture bold enough, considering that I knew not how far it might go, nor what was beyond it. When I was got through the strait, I found the roof rose higher up, I believe near twenty foot; but never was such a glorious sight seen in the island, I dare say, as it was to look round the sides and roof of this vault or cave; the walls reflected 100 thousand lights to me from my two candles; what it was in the rock, whether diamonds, or any other precious stones, or gold, which I rather supposed it to be, I knew not.

The place I was in was a most delightful cavity or grotto of its kind, as could be expected, though perfectly dark; the floor was dry and level, and had a sort of small loose gravel upon it, so that there was no nauseous or venomous creature to be seen, neither was there any damp or wet on the sides or roof. The only difficulty in it was the entrance, which, however, as it was a place of security, and such a retreat as I wanted, I thought that was a convenience; so that I was really rejoyced at the discovery, and resolved without any delay to bring some of those things which I was most anxious about, to this place; particularly, I resolved to bring hither my magazine of powder, and all my spare arms, viz. two fowling-pieces, for I had three in all; and three muskets, for of them I had eight in all; so I kept at my castle only five, which stood ready mounted like pieces of cannon on my out-most fence, and were ready also to take out upon any expedition.

Upon this occasion of removing my ammunition, I took occasion to open the barrel of powder which I took up out of the sea, and which had been wet; and I found that the water had penetrated about three or four inches into the powder on every side, which caking and growing hard, had preserved the inside like a kernel in a shell; so that I had near sixty pound of very good powder in the center of the cask, and this was an agreeable discovery to me at that time; so I carry'd all away thither, never keeping above two or three pound of powder with me in my castle, for fear of a surprize of any kind : I also carried thither all the lead I had left for bullets.

I fancy'd my self now like one of the ancient giants, which are said to live in caves and holes in the rocks, where none could come at them; for I perswaded my self while I was here, if five hundred savages were to hunt me, they could never find me out; or if they did, they would not venture to attack me here.

The old goat who I found expiring, dy'd in the mouth of the cave, the next day after I made this discovery; and I found it much easier to dig a great hole there, and throw him in and cover him with earth, than to drag him out; so I interred him there, to prevent the offence to my nose.

I was now in my twenty third year of residence in this island, and was so naturalized to the place, and to the manner of living, that could I have but enjoyed the certainty that no savages would come to the place to disturb me, I could have been content to have capitulated for spending the rest of my time there, even to the last moment, till I had laid me down and dy'd, like the old goat in the cave. I had also arrived to some little diversions and amusements, which made the time pass more pleasantly with me a great deal than it did before; as first, I had taught my Poll, as I noted before, to speak; and he did it so familiarly and talked so articulately and plain, that it was very pleasant to me; and he lived with me no less than six and twenty years: how long he might live afterwards, I know not; though I know they have a notion in the Brasils that they live a hundred years; perhaps poor Poll may be alive there still, calling after poor Robin Crusoe to this day. I wish no English man the ill luck to come there and hear him; but if he did, he would certainly believe it was the devil. My dog was a very pleasant and loving companion to me for no less than sixteen years of my time, and then dy'd of meer old age; as for my cats, they multiply'd as I have observed to that degree, that I was obliged to shoot several of them at first, to keep them from devouring me and all I had; but at length, when the two old ones I had brought with me were gone, and after some time continually driving them from me, and letting them have no provision with me, they all ran wild into the woods, except two or three favourites, which I kept tame, and whose young, when they had any, I always drowned; and these were part of my family. Besides these, I always kept two or three houshold kids about me, who I taught to feed out of my hand; and I had two more parrots which talked pretty well, and would all call Robin Crusoe; but none like my first; nor indeed did I take the pains with any of them that I had done with him. I had also several tame sea-fowls, whose names I know not, who I caught upon the shore, and cut their wings; and the little stakes which I had planted before my castle wall being now grown up to a good thick grove, these fowls all lived among these low trees, and bred there, which was very agreeable to me; so that, as I said above, I began to be very well contented with the life I led, if it might but have been secured from the dread of the savages.

But it was otherwise directed; and it may not be amiss for all people who shall meet with my story, to make this just observation from it, viz. how frequently, in the course of our lives, the evil which in it self we seek most to shun, and which when we are fallen into it the most dreadful to us, is oftentimes the very means or door of our deliverance, by which alone we can be raised again from the affliction we are fallen into. I cou'd give many examples of this in the course of my unaccountable life; but in nothing was it more particularly remarkable, than in the circumstances of my last years of solitary residence in this island.

It was now the month of December, as I said above, in my twenty third year; and this being the southern solstice, for winter I cannot call it, was the particular time of my harvest, and required my being pretty much abroad in the fields; when going out pretty early in the morning, even before it was thorow day-light, I was surprized with seeing a light of some fire upon the shore, at a distance from me of about two mile towards the end of the island, where I had observed some savages had been as before; but not on the other side; but to my great affliction, it was on my side of the island.

I was indeed terribly surprized at the sight, and stopped short within my grove, not daring to go out, least I might be surprized; and yet I had no more peace within, from the apprehensions I had that if these savages, in rambling over the island, should find my corn standing or cut, or any of my works and improvements, they would immediately conclude that there were people in the place, and would then never give over till they had found me out. In this extremity I went back directly to my castle, pulled up the ladder after me, and made all things without look as wild and natural as I could.

Then I prepared my self within, putting my self in a posture of defence; I loaded all my cannon, as I called them, that is to say, my muskets which were mounted upon my new fortification, and all my pistols, and resolved to defend my self to the last gasp, not forgetting seriously to commend my self to the divine protection, and earnestly to pray to God to deliver me out of the hands of the barbarians; and in this posture I continued about two hours; but began to be mighty impatient for intelligence abroad, for I had no spies to send out.

After sitting a while longer, and musing what I should do in this case, I was not able to bear sitting in ignorance any longer; so setting up my ladder to the side of the hill, where there was a flat place, as I observed before, and then pulling the ladder up after me, I set it up again, and mounted to the top of the hill; and pulling out my perspective glass, which I had taken on purpose, I laid me down flat on my belly on the ground, and began to look for the place; I presently found there was no less than nine naked savages, sitting round a small fire they had made, not to warm them, for they had no need of that, the weather being extreme hot; but, as I supposed, to dress some of their barbarous diet of humane flesh, which they had brought with them, whether alive or dead I could not know.

They had two canoes with them, which they had haled up upon the shore; and as it was then tide of ebb, they seemed to me to wait for the return of the flood, to go away again; it is not easy to imagine what confusion this sight put me into, especially seeing them come on my side the island, and so near me too; but when I observed their coming must always be with the current of the ebb, I began afterwards to be more sedate in my mind, being satisfy'd that I might go abroad with safety all the time of the tide of flood, if they were not on shore before: and having made this observation, I went abroad about my harvest work with the more composure.

As I expected, so it proved; for as soon as the tide made to the westward, I saw them all take boat, and row (or paddle as we call it) all away. I should have observed, that for an hour and more before they went off, they went to dancing, and I could easily discern their postures and gestures by my glasses: I could not perceive, by my nicest observation, but that they were stark naked, and had not the least covering upon them; but whether they were men or women, that I could not distinguish.

As soon as I saw them shipped and gone, I took two guns upon my shoulders, and two pistols at my girdle, and my great sword by my side, without a scabbard, and with all the speed I was able to make, I went away to the hill, where I had discovered the first appearance of all; and as soon as I gat thither, which was not less than two hours (for I could not go apace, being so loaden with arms as I was), I perceived there had been three canoes more of savages on that place; and looking out farther, I saw they were all at sea together, making over for the main.

This was a dreadful sight to me, especially when going down to the shore, I could see the marks of horror which the dismal work they had been about had left behind it, viz. the blood, the bones, and part of the flesh of humane bodies, eaten and devoured by those wretches, with merriment and sport. I was so filled with indignation at the sight, that I began now to premeditate the destruction of the next that I saw there, let them be who or how many soever.

It seemed evident to me that the visits which they thus make to this island are not very frequent; for it was above fifteen months before any more of them came on shore there again; that is to say, I neither saw them, or any footsteps or signals of them, in all that time; for as to the rainy seasons, then they are sure not to come abroad, at least not so far; yet all this while I lived uncomfortably, by reason of the constant apprehensions I was in of their coming upon me by surprize; from whence I observe, that the expectation of evil is more bitter than the suffering, especially if there is no room to shake off that expectation or those apprehensions.

During all this time I was in the murthering humour; and took up most of my hours, which should have been better employed, in contriving how to circumvent and fall upon them, the very next time I should see them; especially if they should be divided, as they were the last time, into two parties; nor did I consider at all, that if I killed one party, suppose ten or a dozen, I was still the next day, or week, or month, to kill another, and so another, even *ad infinitum*, till I should be at length no less a murtherer than they were in being man-eaters; and perhaps much more so.

I spent my days now in great perplexity and anxiety of mind, expecting that I should one day or other fall into the hands of these merciless creatures; and if I did at any time venture abroad, it was not without looking round me with the greatest care and caution imaginable; and now I found, to my great comfort, how happy it was that I provided for a tame flock or herd of goats; for I durst not upon any account fire my gun, especially near that side of the island where they usually came, least I should alarm the savages; and if they had fled from me now, I was sure to have them come back again, with perhaps two or three hundred canoes with them, in a few days, and then I knew what to expect.

However, I wore out a year and three months more, before I

ever saw any more of the savages, and then I found them again, as I shall soon observe. It is true, they might have been there once or twice; but either they made no stay, or at least I did not hear them; but in the month of May, as near as I could calculate, and in my four and twentieth year, I had a very strange encounter with them, of which in its place.

The perturbation of my mind, during this fifteen or sixteen months' interval, was very great; I slept unquiet, dreamed always frightful dreams, and often started out of my sleep in the night: in the day great troubles overwhelmed my mind, and in the night I dreamed often of killing the savages, and of the reasons why I might justify the doing of it; but to wave all this for a while, it was in the middle of May, on the sixteenth day I think, as well as my poor wooden calendar would reckon; for I markt all upon the post still; I say, it was the sixteenth of May, that it blew a very great storm of wind all day, with a great deal of lightning and thunder, and a very foul night it was after it; I know not what was the particular occasion of it, but as I was reading in the Bible, and taken up with very serious thoughts about my present condition, I was surprized with a noise of a gun, as I thought, fired at sea.

This was to be sure a surprize of a quite different nature from any I had met with before; for the notions this put into my thoughts were quite of another kind. I started up in the greatest hast imaginable, and in a trice clapt my ladder to the middle place of the rock, and pulled it after me, and mounting it the second time, got to the top of the hill the very moment that a flash of fire bid me listen for a second gun, which accordingly in about half a minute I heard, and by the sound knew that it was from that part of the sea where I was driven down the current in my boat.

I immediately considered that this must be some ship in distress, and that they had some comrade, or some other ship in company, and fired these guns for signals of distress, and to obtain help. I had this presence of mind at that minute, as to think that though I could not help them, it may be they might help me; so I brought together all the dry wood I could get at hand, and making a good handsome pile, I set it on fire upon the hill; the wood was dry, and blazed freely; and though the wind blew very hard, yet it burnt fairly out; that I was certain, if there was any such thing as a ship, they must needs see it, and no doubt they did; for as soon as ever my fire blazed up, I heard another gun, and after that several others, all from the same quarter; I ply'd my fire all night long, till day broke; and when it was broad day, and the air cleared up, I saw something at a great distance at sea, full east of the island, whether a sail or a hull I could not distinguish, no, not with my glasses, the distance was so great, and the weather still something haizy also; at least it was so out at sea.

I looked frequently at it all that day, and soon perceived that it did not move; so I presently concluded that it was a ship at an anchor, and being eager, you may be sure, to be satisfy'd, I took my gun in my hand, and run toward the south side of the island, to the rocks where I had formerly been carry'd away with the current; and getting up there, the weather by this time being perfectly clear, I could plainly see, to my great sorrow, the wreck of a ship cast away in the night upon those concealed rocks which I found when I was out in my boat; and which rocks, as they checked the violence of the stream and made a kind of counter-stream or eddy, were the occasion of my recovering from the most desperate hopeless condition that ever I had been in in all my life.

Thus what is one man's safety is another man's destruction; for it seems these men, whoever they were, being out of their know-ledge, and the rocks being wholly under water, had been driven upon them in the night, the wind blowing hard at E. and E.N.E. Had they seen the island, as I must necessarily suppose they did not, they must, as I thought, have endeavoured to have saved themselves on shore by the help of their boat; but their firing of guns for help, especially when they saw, as I imagined, my fire, filled me with many thoughts. First, I imagined that upon seeing my light, they might have put themselves into their boat, and have endeavoured to make the shore; but that the sea going very high, they might have been cast away; other times I imagined they might have lost their boat before, as might be the case many ways; as particularly by the breaking of the sea upon their ship, which many times obliges men to stave or take in pieces their boat, and sometimes to throw it over-board with their own hands; other times I imagined they had some other ship or ships in company, who, upon the signals of distress they had made, had taken them up and carry'd them off; other whiles I fancy'd they were all gone off to sea in their boat, and being hurry'd away by the current that I had been formerly in, were carry'd out into the great ocean, where there was nothing but misery and perishing; and that perhaps they might by this time think of starving, and of being in a condition to eat one another.

As all these were but conjectures at best, so in the condition I was in, I could do no more than look upon the misery of the poor men, and pity them, which had still this good effect on my side that it gave me more and more cause to give thanks to God who had so happily and comfortably provided for me in my desolate condition; and that of two ships' companies who were now cast away upon this part of the world, not one life should be spared but mine. I learned here again to observe, that it is very rare that the providence of God casts us into any condition of life so low, or to any misery so great, but we may see something or other to be thankful for, and may see others in worse circumstances than our own.

Such certainly was the case of these men, of whom I could not so much as see room to suppose any of them were saved; nothing could make it rational so much as to wish or expect that they did not all perish there; except the possibility only of their being taken up by another ship in company, and this was but meer possibility indeed; for I saw not the least signal or appearance of any such thing.

I cannot explain by any possible energy of words what a strange longing or hankering of desires I felt in my soul upon this sight; breaking out sometimes thus: 'O that there had been but one or two; nay, or but one soul saved out of this ship, to have escaped to me, that I might but have had one companion, one fellow-creature to have spoken to me, and to have conversed with!' In all the time of my solitary life, I never felt so earnest, so strong a desire after the society of my fellow-creatures, or so deep a regret at the want of it.

There are some secret moving springs in the affections, which when they are set a going by some object in view, or be it some object, though not in view, yet rendred present to the mind by the power of imagination, that motion carries out the soul by its impetuosity to such violent eager embracings of the object, that the absence of it is insupportable.

Such were these earnest wishings that but one man had been saved! 'O that it had been but one!' I believe I repeated the words, 'O that it had been but one!' a thousand times; and the desires were so moved by it, that when I spoke the words, my hands would clinch together, and my fingers press the palms of my hands, that if I had had any soft thing in my hand, it would have crusht it involuntarily; and my teeth in my head wou'd strike together, and set against one another so strong, that for some time I could not part them again.

Let the naturalists explain these things, and the reason and manner of them; all I can say to them is, to describe the fact, which was even surprising to me when I found it; though I knew not from what it should proceed; it was doubtless the effect of ardent wishes, and of strong ideas formed in my mind, realizing the comfort which the conversation of one of my fellow-Christians would have been to me.

But it was not to be; either their fate or mine, or both, forbid it; for till the last year of my being on this island, I never knew whether any were saved out of that ship or no; and had only the affliction, some days after, to see the corps of a drownded boy come on shore, at the end of the island which was next the ship-wreck. He had on no cloaths but a seaman's wastcoat, a pair of open kneed linnen drawers, and a blew linnen shirt; but nothing to direct me so much as to guess what nation he was of. He had nothing in his pocket but two pieces of eight, and a tobacco-pipe; that last was to me of ten times more value than the first.

It was now calm, and I had a great mind to venture out in my boat to this wreck; not doubting but I might find something on board that might be useful to me; but that did not altogether press me so much as the possibility that there might yet be some living creature on board, whose life I might not only save, but might, by saving that life, comfort my own to the last degree;

and this thought clung so to my heart, that I could not be quiet, night or day, but I must venture out in my boat on board this wreck; and committing the rest to God's providence, I thought the impression was so strong upon my mind, that it could not be resisted, that it must come from some invisible direction, and that I should be wanting to my self if I did not go.

Under the power of this impression, I hastened back to my castle, prepared every thing for my voyage, took a quantity of bread, a great pot for fresh water, a compass to steer by, a bottle of rum, for I had still a great deal of that left, a basket full of raisins; and thus loading my self with every thing necessary, I went down to my boat, got the water out of her, and got her afloat, loaded all my cargo in her, and then went home again for more; my second cargo was a great bag full of rice, the umbrella to set up over my head for shade, another large pot full of fresh water, and about two dozen of my small loaves or barley cakes, more than before, with a bottle of goat's-milk and a cheese; all which, with great labour and sweat, I brought to my boat; and praying to God to direct my voyage, I put out, and rowing or padling the canoe along the shore, I came at last to the utmost point of the island on that side, viz. N.E. And now I was to launch out into the ocean, and either to venture, or not to venture. I looked on the rapid currents which ran constantly on both sides of the island at a distance, and which were very terrible to me, from the remembrance of the hazard I had been in before, and my heart began to fail me; for I foresaw that if I was driven into either of those currents, I should be carry'd a vast way out to sea, and perhaps out of my reach, or sight of the island again; and that then, as my boat was but small, if any little gale of wind should rise, I should be inevitably lost.

These thoughts so oppressed my mind that I began to give over my enterprize, and having haled my boat into a little creek on the shore, I stept out and sat me down upon a little rising bit of ground, very pensive and anxious, between fear and desire about my voyage; when, as I was musing, I could perceive that the tide was turned, and the flood come on, upon which my going was for so many hours impracticable; upon this presently it occurred to me that I should go up to the highest piece of ground I could find, and observe, if I could, how the sets of the tide or currents lay when the flood came in, that I might judge whether, if I was driven one way out, I might not expect to be driven another way home, with the same rapidness of the currents. This thought was no sooner in my head, but I cast my eye upon a little hill, which sufficiently overlooked the sea both ways, and from whence I had a clear view of the currents, or sets of the tide, and which way I was to guide my self in my return; here I found, that as the current of the ebb set out close by the south point of the island, so the current of the flood set in close by the shore of the north side, and that I had nothing to do but to keep to the north of the island in my return, and I should do well enough.

Encouraged with this observation, I resolved the next morning to set out with the first of the tide; and reposing my self for the night in the canoe, under the great watch-coat I mentioned, I launched out. I made first a little out to sea full north, till I began to feel the benefit of the current, which set eastward, and which carry'd me at a great rate, and yet did not so hurry me as the southern side current had done before, and so as to take from me all government of the boat; but having a strong steerage with my paddle, I went at a great rate directly for the wreck, and in less than two hours I came up to it.

It was a dismal sight to look at: the ship, which by its building was Spanish, stuck fast, jammed in between two rocks; all the stern and quarter of her was beaten to pieces with the sea; and as her forecastle, which stuck in the rocks, had run on with great violence, her mainmast and foremast were brought by the board, that is to say, broken short off; but her boltsprit was sound and the head and bow appeared firm. When I came close to her, a dog appeared upon her, who seeing me coming, yelped and cry'd; and as soon as I called him, jumped into the sea, to come to me, and I took him into the boat, but found him almost dead from hunger and thirst. I gave him a cake of my bread, and he eat it like a ravenous wolf, that had been starving a fortnight in the snow. I then gave the poor creature some fresh water, with which, if I would have let him, he would have burst himself.

After this I went on board: but the first sight I met with was two men drowned in the cook-room or forecastle of the ship, with their arms fast about one another. I concluded, as is indeed probable, that when the ship struck, it being in a storm, the sea broke so high and continually over her, that the men were not able to bear it, and were strangled with the constant rushing in of the water, as much as if they had been under water. Besides the dog, there was nothing left in the ship that had life; nor any goods that I could see, but what were spoiled by the water. There were some casks of liquor, whether wine or brandy I knew not, which lay lower in the hold, and which, the water being ebbed out, I could see; but they were too big to meddle with. I saw several chests, which I believed belonged to some of the seamen; and I got two of them into the boat, without examining what was in them.

Had the stern of the ship been fixed, and the forepart broken off, I am perswaded I might have made a good voyage; for by what I found in these two chests, I had room to suppose the ship had a great deal of wealth on board; and if I may guess by the course she steered, she must have been bound from the Buenos Ayres, or the Rio de la Plata, in the south part of America, beyond the Brasils, to the Havana, in the Gulph of Mexico, and so perhaps to Spain. She had no doubt a great treasure in her, but of no use at the time to any body; and what became of the rest of her people, I then knew not.

I found, besides these chests, a little cask full of liquor, of about twenty gallons, which I got into my boat with much difficulty; there were several muskets in a cabin, and a great powder-horn, with about 4 pounds of powder in it; as for the muskets, I had no occasion for them; so I left them, but took the powder-horn. I took a fire shovel and tongs, which I wanted extremely; as also two little brass kettles, a copper pot to make chocolate, and a gridiron; and with this cargo, and the dog, I came away, the tide beginning to make home again; and the same evening, about an hour within night, reached the island again, weary and fatigued to the last degree.

I reposed that night in the boat, and in the morning I resolved to harbour what I had gotten in my new cave, not to carry it

home to my castle. After refreshing my self, I got all my cargo on
shore, and began to examine the particulars. The cask of liquor I
found to be a kind of rum, but not such as we had at the Brasils;
and in a word, not at all good; but when I came to open the
chèsts, I found several things of great use to me: for example, I
found in one a fine case of bottles, of an extraordinary kind, and
filled with cordial waters, fine and very good; the bottles held
about three pints each, and were tipped with silver: I found two
pots of very good succades or sweetmeats, so fastened also on top
that the salt water had not hurt them; and two more of the
same, which the water had spoiled: I found some very good shirts,
which were very welcome to me; and about a dozen and half of
linnen white handkerchiefs and coloured neckcloths; the former
were also very welcome, being exceeding refreshing to wipe my
face in a hot day. Besides this, when I came to the till in the
chest, I found there three great bags of pieces of eight, which
held about eleven hundred pieces in all; and in one of them,
wrapt up in a paper, six doubloons of gold, and some small
bars or wedges of gold; I suppose they might all weigh near a
pound.

The other chest I found had some cloaths in it, but of little
value; but by the circumstances it must have belonged to the
gunner's mate; though there was no powder in it but about two
pound of fine glazed powder,[46] in three small flasks, kept, I suppose, for charging their fowling-pieces on occasion. Upon the
whole, I got very little by this voyage that was of any use to
me; for as to the money, I had no manner of occasion for it:
'twas to me as the dirt under my feet; and I would have given it
all for three or four pair of English shoes and stockings, which
were things I greatly wanted, but had not had on my feet now
for many years: I had indeed gotten two pair of shoes now,
which I took off of the feet of the two drowned men who I saw in
the wreck; and I found two pair more in one of the chests, which
were very welcome to me; but they were not like our English
shoes, either for ease or service; being rather what we call pumps
than shoes. I found in this seaman's chest about fifty pieces of
eight in ryals, but no gold; I suppose this belonged to a poorer
man than the other, which seemed to belong to some officer.

Well, however, I lugged this money home to my cave, and laid it up, as I had done that before which I brought from our own ship; but it was great pity, as I said, that the other part of this ship had not come to my share; for I am satisfy'd I might have loaded my canoe several times over with money, which, if I had ever escaped to England, would have lain here safe enough, till I might have come again and fetched it.

Having now brought all my things on shore, and secured them, I went back to my boat, and rowed or paddled her along the shore to her old harbour, where I laid her up, and made the best of my way to my old habitation, where I found everything safe and quiet; so I began to repose my self, live after my old fashion, and take care of my family affairs; and for a while, I lived easy enough; only that I was more vigilant than I used to be, looked out oftner, and did not go abroad so much; and if at any time I did stir with any freedom, it was always to the east part of the island, where I was pretty well satisfy'd the savages never came, and where I could go without so many precautions, and such a load of arms and ammunition as I always carry'd with me if I went the other way.

I lived in this condition near two years more; but my unlucky head, that was always to let me know it was born to make my body miserable, was all this two years filled with projects and designs, how, if it were possible, I might get away from this island; for sometimes I was for making another voyage to the wreck, though my reason told me that there was nothing left there worth the hazard of my voyage; sometimes for a ramble one way, sometimes another; and I believe verily, if I had had the boat that I went from Sallee in, I should have ventured to sea, bound any where, I knew not whither.

I have been in all my circumstances a memento to those who are touched with the general plague of mankind, whence, for ought I know, one half of their miseries flow; I mean that of not being satisfy'd with the station wherein God and nature has placed them; for not to look back upon my primitive condition, and the excellent advice of my father, the opposition to which was, as I may call it, my original sin, my subsequent mistakes of the same kind had been the means of my coming into this miserable condition; for had that providence, which so happily had seated me at the Brasils as a planter, blessed me with confined desires, and I could have been contented to have gone on gradually, I might have been by this time (I mean, in the time of my being in this island) one of the most considerable planters in the Brasils; nay, I am perswaded that by the improvements I had made in that little time I lived there, and the encrease I should probably have made if I had stayed, I might have been worth an hundred thousand moydors; and what business had I to leave a settled fortune, a well stocked plantation, improving and encreasing, to turn supra-cargo to Guinea, to fetch negroes, when patience and time would have so encreased our stock at home, that we could have bought them at our own door, from those whose business it was to fetch them? and though it had cost us something more, yet the difference of that price was by no means worth saving at so great a hazard.

But as this is ordinarily the fate of young heads, so reflection upon the folly of it is as ordinarily the exercise of more years, or of the dear bought experience of time; and so it was with me now; and yet so deep had the mistake taken root in my temper, that I could not satisfy my self in my station, but was continually poring upon the means and possibility of my escape from this place; and that I may, with the greater pleasure to the reader, bring on the remaining part of my story, it may not be improper to give some account of my first conceptions on the subject of this foolish scheme for my escape; and how, and upon what foundation I acted.

I am now to be supposed retired into my castle, after my late voyage to the wreck, my frigate laid up and secured under water, as usual, and my condition restored to what it was before. I had more wealth indeed than I had before, but was not at all the richer; for I had no more use for it than the Indians of Peru had before the Spaniards came there.

It was one of the nights in the rainy season in March, the four and twentieth year of my first setting foot in this island of solitariness; I was lying in my bed, or hammock, awake, very well in health, had no pain, no distemper, no uneasiness of body; no, nor any uneasiness of mind, more than ordinary; but could by no means close my eyes, that is, so as to sleep; no, not a wink all night long, otherwise than as follows:

It is as impossible as needless to set down the innumerable crowd of thoughts that whirled through that great thorow-fare of the brain, the memory, in this night's time: I run over the whole history of my life in miniature, or by abridgement, as I may call it, to my coming to this island, and also of the part of my life since I came to this island. In my reflections upon the state of my case since I came on shore on this island, I was comparing the happy posture of my affairs in the first years of my habitation here, compared to the life of anxiety, fear, and care which I had lived ever since I had seen the print of a foot in the sand; not that I did not believe the savages had frequented the island even all the while, and might have been several hundreds of them at times on shore there; but I had never known it, and was incapable of any apprehesions about it; my satisfaction was perfect, though my danger was the same; and I was as happy in not knowing my danger, as if I had never really been exposed to it. This furnished my thoughts with many very profitable reflections, and particularly this one, how infinitely good that providence is, which has provided in its government of mankind such narrow bounds to his sight and knowledge of things; and though he walks in the midst of so many thousand dangers, the sight of which, if discovered to him, would distract his mind and sink his spirits, he is kept serene and calm, by having the events of things hid from his eyes, and knowing nothing of the dangers which surround him.

After these thoughts had for some time entertained me, I came to reflect seriously upon the real danger I had been in for so many years, in this very island; and how I had walked about in the greatest security, and with all possible tranquillity; even when perhaps nothing but a brow of a hill, a great tree, or the casual approach of night had been between me and the worst kind of destruction, viz. that of falling into the hands of cannibals and savages, who would have seized on me with the same view as I did of a goat or a turtle, and have thought it no more a crime to kill and devour me, than I did of a pigeon or a curlieu. I would unjustly slander my self, if I should say I was not sincerely thankful to my great Preserver, to whose singular protection I acknowledged, with great humility, that all these unknown deliverances were due; and without which, I must inevitably have fallen into their merciless hands.

When these thoughts were over, my head was for some time taken up in considering the nature of these wretched creatures, I mean the savages; and how it came to pass in the world, that the wise Governour of all things should give up any of His creatures to such inhumanity, nay, to something so much below even brutality itself, as to devour its own kind; but as this ended in some (at that time fruitless) speculations, it occurred to me to enquire what part of the world these wretches lived in; how far off the coast was from whence they came; what they ventured over so far from home for; what kind of boats they had; and why I might not order my self and my business so, that I might be as able to go over thither as they were to come to me.

I never so much as troubled my self to consider what I should do with my self when I came thither; what would become of me, if I fell into the hands of the savages; or how I should escape from them, if they attempted me; no, nor so much as how it was possible for me to reach the coast, and not to be attempted by some or other of them, without any possibility of delivering my self; and if I should not fall into their hands, what I should do for provision, or whither I should bend my course; none of these thoughts, I say, so much as came in my way; but my mind was wholly bent upon the notion of passing over in my boat to the main land. I looked back upon my present condition as the most miserable that could possibly be, that I was not able to throw my self into any thing but death, that could be called worse; that if I reached the shore of the main, I might perhaps meet with relief, or I might coast along, as I did on the shore of Africk, till I came to some inhabited country, and where I might find some relief; and after all, perhaps I might fall in with some Christian ship that might take me in; and if the worse came to the worst, I could but die, which would put an end to all these miseries at once. Pray note, all this was the fruit of a disturbed mind, an impatient temper, made as it were desperate by the long continuance of my troubles and the disappointments I had met in the wreck I had been on board of; and where I had been so near the obtaining what I so earnestly longed for, viz. some-body to speak to, and to learn some knowledge from of the place where I was, and of the probable means of my deliverance; I say, I was agitated wholly by these thoughts. All my calm of mind in my resignation to providence, and waiting the issue of the dispositions of Heaven, seemed to be suspended, and I had, as it were, no power to turn my thoughts to any thing, but to the project of a voyage to the main, which came upon me with such force, and such an impetuosity of desire, that it was not to be resisted.

When this had agitated my thoughts for two hours or more, with such violence, that it set my very blood into a ferment, and my pulse beat as high as if I had been in a feaver, meerly with the extraordinary fervour of my mind about it; nature, as if I had been fatigued and exhausted with the very thought of it, threw me into a sound sleep; one would have thought I should have dreamed of it, but I did not, nor of any thing relating to it; but I dreamed that as I was going out in the morning as usual from my castle, I saw upon the shore two canoes and eleven savages coming to land, and that they brought with them another savage, who they were going to kill, in order to eat him; when on a sudden, the savage that they were going to kill, jumpt away, and ran for his life; and I thought, in my sleep, that he came running into my little thick grove before my fortification, to hide himself; and that I seeing him alone, and not perceiving that the other sought him that way, showed my self to him, and smiling upon him, encouraged him; that he kneeled down to me, seeming to pray me to assist him; upon which I shewed my ladder, made him go up, and carry'd him into my cave, and he became my servant; and that as soon as I had gotten this man, I said to my self, 'Now I may certainly venture to the main land; for this fellow will serve me as a pilot, and will tell me what to do, and whether to go for provisions; and whether not to go for fear of being devoured, what places to venture into, and what to escape.' I waked with this thought, and was under such inexpressible impressions of joy at the prospect of my escape in my dream, that the disappointments which I felt upon coming to my self and finding it was no more than a dream, were equally extravagant the other way, and threw me into a very great dejection of spirit.

Upon this, however, I made this conclusion, that my only way to go about an attempt for an escape was, if possible, to get a savage into my possession; and if possible, it should be one of their prisoners, who they had condemned to be eaten, and should bring thither to kill; but these thoughts still were attended with this difficulty, that it was impossible to effect this, without attacking a whole caravan of them, and killing them all; and this was not only a very desperate attempt, and might miscarry; but on the other hand, I had greatly scrupled the lawfulness of it to me; and my heart trembled at the thoughts of shedding so much blood, tho' it was for my deliverance. I need not repeat the arguments which occurred to me against this, they being the same mentioned before; but tho' I had other reasons to offer now, viz. that those men were enemies to my life, and would devour me, if they could; that it was self-preservation in the highest degree, to deliver my self from this death of a life, and was acting in my own defence as much as if they were actually assaulting me, and the like; I say, tho' these things argued for it, yet the thoughts of shedding humane blood for my deliverance were very terrible to me, and such as I could by no means reconcile my self to, a great while.

However, at last, after many secret disputes with my self, and after great perplexities about it, for all these arguments one way and another struggled in my head a long time, the eager prevailing desire of deliverance at length mastered all the rest; and I resolved, if possible, to get one of those savages into my hands, cost what it would. My next thing then was to contrive how to do it, and this indeed was very difficult to resolve on. But as I could pitch upon no probable means for it, so I resolved to put my self upon the watch, to see them when they came on shore, and leave the rest to the event, taking such measures as the opportunity should present, let be what would be.

With these resolutions in my thoughts, I set my self upon the scout as often as possible, and indeed so often till I was heartily tired of it, for it was above a year and a half that I waited, and for great part of that time went out to the west end, and to the south west corner of the island, almost every day, to see for canoes, but none appeared. This was very discouraging, and began to trouble me much, tho' I cannot say that it did in this case, as it had done some time before that, viz. wear off the edge of my desire to the thing. But the longer it seemed to be delay'd, the more eager I was for it; in a word, I was not at first so careful to shun the sight of these savages, and avoid being seen by them, as I was now eager to be upon them.

Besides, I fancied my self able to manage one, nay, two or three savages, if I had them, so as to make them entirely slaves to me, to do whatever I should direct them, and to prevent their being able at any time to do me any hurt. It was a great while that I pleased my self with this affair, but nothing still presented; all my fancies and schemes came to nothing, for no savages came near me for a great while.

About a year and a half after I had entertained these notions, and, by long musing, had as it were resolved them all into nothing, for want of an occasion to put them in execution, I was surprized one morning early, with seeing no less than five canoes all on shore together on my side the island; and the people who belonged to them all landed, and out of my sight. The number of them broke all my measures, for seeing so many, and knowing that they always came four or six, or sometimes more in a boat, I could not tell what to think of it, or how to take my measures to attack twenty or thirty men single handed; so I lay still in my castle, perplexed and discomforted; however, I put my self into all the same postures for an attack that I had formerly provided, and was just ready for action, if any thing had presented. Having waited a good while, listening to hear if they made any noise, at length, being very impatient, I set my guns at the foot of my ladder, and clambered up to the top of the hill, by my two stages as usual; standing so, however, that my head did not appear above the hill, so that they could not perceive me by any means; here I observed, by the help of my perspective glass, that they were no less than thirty in number, that they had a fire kindled, that they had had meat dressed. How they cooked it, that I knew not, or what it was; but they were all dancing in I know not how many barbarous gestures and figures, their own way, round the fire.

While I was thus looking on them, I perceived by my perspective two miserable wretches dragged from the boats, where it seems they were laid by, and were now brought out for the slaughter. I perceived one of them immediately fell, being knocked down, I suppose with a club or wooden sword, for that was their way, and two or three others were at work immediately cutting him open for their cookery, while the other victim was left standing by himself, till they should be ready for him. In that very moment this poor wretch seeing himself a little at liberty, nature inspired him with hopes of life, and he started away from them, and ran with incredible swiftness along the sands directly towards me, I mean towards that part of the coast where my habitation was.

I was dreadfully frighted (that I must acknowledge) when I perceived him to run my way, and especially when, as I thought, I saw him pursued by the whole body; and now I expected that part of my dream was coming to pass, and that he would certainly take shelter in my grove; but I could not depend by any means upon my dream for the rest of it, viz. that the other savages would not pursue him thither, and find him there. However, I kept my station, and my spirits began to recover when I found that there was not above three men that followed him, and still more was I encouraged when I found that he outstrip'd them exceedingly in running, and gained ground of them, so that if he could but hold it for half an hour, I saw easily he would fairly get away from them all.

There was between them and my castle the creek which I mentioned often at the first part of my story, when I landed my cargoes out of the ship; and this, I saw plainly, he must necessarily swim over, or the poor wretch would be taken there. But when the savage escaping came thither, he made nothing of it, tho' the tide was then up, but plunging in, swam thro' in about thirty strokes or thereabouts, landed, and ran on with exceeding strength and swiftness; when the three persons came to the creek, I found that two of them could swim, but the third cou'd not, and that standing on the other side, he looked at the other, but went no further, and soon after went softly back again, which, as it happened, was very well for him in the main.

I observed that the two who swam were yet more than twice as long swimming over the creek as the fellow was that fled from them. It came now very warmly upon my thoughts, and indeed irresistibly, that now was my time to get me a servant, and perhaps a companion or assistant; and that I was called plainly by Providence to save this poor creature's life; I immediately run down the ladders with all possible expedition, fetched my two guns, for they were both but at the foot of the ladders, as I observed above; and getting up again, with the same haste, to the top of the hill, I crossed toward the sea; and having a very short cut, and all down hill, clapped my self in the way between the pursuers and the pursued; hallowing aloud to him that fled, who looking back, was at first perhaps as much frighted at me as at them; but I beckoned with my hand to him to come back; and in the mean time, I slowly advanced towards the two that followed; then rushing at once upon the foremost, I knocked him down with the stock of my piece; I was loath to fire, because I would not have the rest hear; though at that distance it would not have been easily heard, and being out of sight of the smoke too, they wou'd not have easily known what to make of it. Having knocked this fellow down, the other who pursued with him stopped, as if he had been frighted; and I advanced a-pace towards him; but as I came nearer, I perceived presently he had a bow and arrow, and was fitting it to shoot at me; so I was then necessitated to shoot at him first, which I did, and killed him at the first shoot; the poor savage who fled, but had stopped, though he saw both his enemies fallen and killed, as he thought, yet was so frighted with the fire and noise of my piece, that he stood stock still, and neither came forward or went backward, tho' he seemed rather enclined to fly still than to come on; I hollowed again to him, and made signs to come forward, which he easily understood, and came a little way, then stopped again, and then a little further, and stopped again, and I cou'd then perceive that he stood trembling, as if he had been taken prisoner, and had just been to be killed, as his two enemies were. I beckoned him again to come to me, and gave him all the signs of encouragement that I could think of, and he came nearer and nearer, kneeling down every ten or twelve steps in token of acknowledgement for my saving his life. I smiled at him, and looked pleasantly, and beckoned to him to come still nearer; at length he came close to me, and then he kneeled down again, kissed the ground, and laid his head upon the ground, and taking me by the foot, set my foot upon his head; this it seems was in token of swearing to be my slave for ever; I took him up, and made much of him, and encouraged him all I could. But there was more work to do yet, for I perceived the savage who I knocked down was not killed, but stunned with the blow, and began to come to himself; so I pointed to him, and showing him the savage, that he was not dead; upon this he spoke some words to me, and though I could not understand them, yet I thought they were pleasant to hear, for they were the first sound of a man's voice that I had heard, my own excepted, for above twenty five years. But there was no time for such reflections now; the savage who was knocked down recovered himself so far as to sit up upon the ground, and I perceived that my savage began to be afraid; but when I saw that, I presented my other piece at the man, as if I would shoot him; upon this my savage, for so I call him now, made a motion to me to lend him my sword, which hung naked in a belt by my side; so I did: he no sooner had it, but he runs to his enemy, and at one blow cut off his head as cleverly, no executioner in Germany could have done it sooner or better; which I thought very strange, for one who I had reason to believe never saw a sword in his life before, except their own wooden swords; however, it seems, as I learned afterwards, they make their wooden swords so sharp, so heavy, and the wood is so hard, that they will cut off heads even with them, ay and arms, and that at one blow too; when he had done this, he comes laughing to me in sign of triumph, and brought me the sword again, and with abundance of gestures which I did not understand, laid it down with the head of the savage that he had killed, just before me.

But that which astonished him most, was to know how I had killed the other Indian so far off; so pointing to him, he made signs to me to let him go to him, so I bad him go, as well as I could; when he came to him, he stood like one amazed, looking at him, turned him first on one side, then on t'other, looked at the wound the bullet had made, which it seems was just in his breast, where it had made a hole, and no great quantity of blood had followed, but he had bled inwardly, for he was quite dead. He took up his bow and arrows, and came back, so I turned to go away, and beckoned to him to follow me, making signs to him that more might come after them.

Upon this he signed to me that he should bury them with sand, that they might not be seen by the rest if they followed; and so I made signs again to him to do so; he fell to work, and in an instant he had scraped a hole in the sand with his hands, big enough to bury the first in, and then dragged him into it, and covered him, and did so also by the other; I believe he had bury'd them both in a quarter of an hour; then calling him away, I carry'd him not to my castle, but quite away to my cave, on the farther part of the island; so I did not let my dream come to pass in that part, viz. that he came into my grove for shelter.

Here I gave him bread, and a bunch of raisins to eat, and a draught of water, which I found he was indeed in great distress for, by his running; and having refreshed him, I made signs for him to go lie down and sleep; pointing to a place where I had laid a great parcel of rice straw, and a blanket upon it, which I used to sleep upon my self sometimes; so the poor creature laid down, and went to sleep.

He was a comely handsome fellow, perfectly well made; with straight strong limbs, not too large; tall and well shaped, and, as I reckon, about twenty six years of age. He had a very good countenance, not a fierce and surly aspect; but seemed to have something very manly in his face, and yet he had all the sweetness and softness of an European in his countenance too, especially when he smiled. His hair was long and black, not curled like wool; his forehead very high and large, and a great vivacity and sparkling sharpness in his eyes. The colour of his skin was not quite black, but very tawny; and yet not of an ugly yellow nauseous tawny, as the Brasilians, and Virginians, and other natives of America are; but of a bright kind of a dun olive colour, that had in it something very agreeable, tho' not very easy to describe. His face was round and plump; his nose small, not flat like the negroes, a very good mouth, thin lips, and his fine teeth well set, and white as ivory. After he had slumbered, rather than slept, about half an hour, he waked again, and comes out of the cave to me; for I had been milking my goats, which I had in the enclosure just by; when he espy'd me, he came running to me, laying himself down again upon the ground, with all the possible signs of an humble thankful disposition, making a many antick gestures to show it. At last he lays his head flat upon the ground, close to my foot, and sets my other foot upon his head, as he had done before; and after this, made all the signs to me of subjection, servitude, and submission imaginable, to let me know how he would serve me as long as he lived. I understood him in many things, and let him know I was very well pleased with him; in a little time I began to speak to him, and teach him to speak to me; and first, I made him know his name should be Friday, which was the day I saved his life; I called him so for the memory of the time; I likewise taught him to say Master, and then let him know, that was to be my name; I likewise taught him to say yes and no, and to know the meaning of them; I gave him some milk in an earthen pot, and let him see me drink it before him, and sop my bread in it; and I gave him a cake of bread to do the like, which he quickly comply'd with, and made signs that it was very good for him.

I kept there with him all that night; but as soon as it was day, I beckoned to him to come with me, and let him know I would give him some cloaths, at which he seemed very glad, for he was stark naked. As we went by the place where he had bury'd the two men, he pointed exactly to the place, and shewed me the marks that he had made to find them again, making signs to me that we should dig them up again, and eat them; at this I appeared very angry, expressed my abhorrence of it, made as if I would vomit at the thoughts of it, and beckoned with my hand to him to come away, which he did immediately, with great submission. I then led him up to the top of the hill, to see if his enemies were gone; and pulling out my glass, I looked, and saw plainly the place where they had been, but no appearance of them, or of their canoes; so that it was plain they were gone, and had left their two comrades behind them, without any search after them.

But I was not content with this discovery; but having now more courage, and consequently more curiosity, I took my man Friday with me, giving him the sword in his hand, with the bow and arrows at his back, which I found he could use very dextrously, making him carry one gun for me, and I two for my self, and away we marched to the place where these creatures had been; for I had a mind now to get some fuller intelligence of them. When I came to the place, my very blood ran chill in my veins, and my heart sunk within me, at the horror of the spectacle: indeed it was a dreadful sight, at least it was so to me; though Friday made nothing of it. The place was covered with humane bones, the ground dy'd with their blood, great pieces of flesh left here and there, half eaten, mangled and scorched; and in short, all the tokens of the triumphant feast they had been making there, after a victory over their enemies. I saw three skulls, five hands, and the bones of three or four legs and feet, and abundance of other parts of the bodies; and Friday, by his signs, made me understand that they brought over four prisoners to feast upon; that three of them were eaten up, and that he, pointing to himself, was the fourth; that there had been a great battle between them and their next king, whose subjects it seems he had been one of; and that they had taken a great number of prisoners, all which were carry'd to several places by those that had taken them in the fight, in order to feast upon them, as was done here by these wretches upon those they brought hither.

I caused Friday to gather all the skulls, bones, flesh, and whatever remained, and lay them together on a heap, and make a great fire upon it, and burnt them all to ashes: I found Friday had still a hankering stomach after some of the flesh, and was still a cannibal in his nature; but I discovered so much abhorrence at the very thoughts of it, and at the least appearance of it, that he durst not discover it; for I had by some means let him know that I would kill him if he offered it.

When we had done this, we came back to our castle, and there I fell to work for my man Friday; and first of all, I gave him a pair of linnen drawers, which I had out of the poor gunner's chest

I mentioned, and which I found in the wreck; and which with a little alteration fitted him very well; then I made him a jerkin of goat's-skin, as well as my skill would allow; and I was now grown a tollerable good taylor; and I gave him a cap, which I had made of a hare-skin, very convenient, and fashionable enough; and thus he was cloathed for the present, tollerably well, and was mighty well pleased to see himself almost as well cloathed as his master. It is true, he went awkwardly in these things at first; wearing the drawers was very awkward to him, and the sleeves of the wastcoat galled his shoulders and the inside of his arms; but a little easing them where he complained they hurt him, and using himself to them, at length he took to them very well.

The next day after I came home to my hutch with him, I began to consider where I should lodge him; and that I might do well for him, and yet be perfectly easy my self, I made a little tent for him in the vacant place between my two fortifications, in the inside of the last, and in the outside of the first; and as there was a door or entrance there into my cave, I made a formal framed door case, and a door to it of boards, and set it up in the passage, a little within the entrance; and causing the door to open on the inside, I barred it up in the night, taking in my ladders too; so that Friday could no way come at me in the inside of my innermost wall, without making so much noise in getting over, that it must needs waken me; for my first wall had now a compleat roof over it of long poles, covering all my tent, and leaning up to the side of the hill, which was again laid cross with smaller sticks instead of laths, and then thatched over a great thickness with the rice straw, which was strong like reeds; and at the hole or place which was left to go in or out by the ladder, I had placed a kind of trap-door, which if it had been attempted on the outside, would not have opened at all, but would have fallen down and made a great noise; and as to weapons, I took them all in to my side every night.

But I needed none of all this precaution; for never man had a more faithful, loving, sincere servant, than Friday was to me; without passions, sullenness, or designs, perfectly obliged and engaged; his very affections were ty'd to me, like those of a child to a father; and I dare say he would have sacrificed his life for the saving mine upon any occasion whatsoever; the many testimonies he gave me of this, put it out of doubt, and soon convinced me that I needed to use no precautions as to my safety on his account.

This frequently gave me occasion to observe, and that with wonder, that however it had pleased God, in His providence, and in the government of the works of His hand, to take from so great a part of the world of His creatures, the best uses to which their faculties and the powers of their souls are adapted; yet that He has bestowed upon them the same powers, the same reason, the same affections, the same sentiments of kindness and obligation, the same passions and resentments of wrongs, the same sense of gratitude, sincerity, fidelity, and all the capacities of doing good and receiving good, that He has given to us; and that when He pleases to offer to them occasions of exerting these, they are as ready, nay more ready to apply them to the right uses for which they were bestowed, than we are: and this made me very melancholly sometimes, in reflecting as the several occasions presented, how mean a use we make of all these, even though we have these powers enlightened by the great lamp of instruction, the spirit of God, and by the knowledge of His word, added to our understanding; and why it has pleased God to hide the like saving knowledge from so many millions of souls, who, if I might judge by this poor savage, would make a much better use of it than we did.

From hence, I sometimes was led too far to invade the soverainty of Providence, and as it were arraign the justice of so arbitrary a disposition of things, that should hide that light from some, and reveal it to others, and yet expect a like duty from both. But I shut it up, and checked my thoughts with this conclusion, (1st) that we did not know by what light and law these should be condemned; but that as God was necessarily, and by the nature of His being, infinitely holy and just, so it could not be, but that if these creatures were all sentenced to absence from Himself, it was on account of sinning against that light which, as the scripture says, was a law to themselves, and by such rules as their consciences would acknowledge to be just, tho' the foundation was not discovered to us: and (2d) that still as we are all the clay in the hand of the potter, no vessel could say to Him, Why hast Thou formed me thus?

But to return to my new companion: I was greatly delighted with him, and made it my business to teach him every thing that was proper to make him useful, handy, and helpful; but especially to make him speak, and understand me when I spake, and he was the aptest schollar that ever was, and particularly was so merry, so constantly diligent, and so pleased, when he cou'd but understand me, or make me understand him, that it was very pleasant to me to talk to him; and now my life began to be so easy, that I began to say to my self, that could I but have been safe from more savages, I cared not if I was never to remove from the place while I lived.

After I had been two or three days returned to my castle, I thought that, in order to bring Friday off from his horrid way of feeding, and from the relish of a cannibal's stomach, I ought to let him taste other flesh; so I took him out with me one morning to the woods. I went indeed intending to kill a kid out of my own flock, and bring him home and dress it; but as I was going, I saw a she goat lying down in the shade, and two young kids sitting by her. I catched hold of Friday. 'Hold,' says I, 'stand still,' and made signs to him not to stir; immediately I presented my piece, shot and killed one of the kids. The poor creature, who had at a distance seen me kill the savage his enemy, but did not know or could imagine how it was done, was sensibly surprized, trembled and shook, and looked so amazed that I thought he would have sunk down. He did not see the kid I shot at, or perceive I had killed it, but ripped up his wastcoat to feel if he was not wounded, and as I found, presently thought I was resolved to kill him; for he came and kneeled down to me, and embraceing my knees, said a great many things I did not understand; but I could easily see that the meaning was to pray me not to kill him.

I soon found a way to convince him that I would do him no harm, and taking him up by the hand, laughed at him, and pointed to the kid which I had killed, beckoned to him to run and fetch it, which he did; and while he was wondering and looking to see how the creature was killed, I loaded my gun again, and by and by I saw a great fowl like a hawk sit upon a tree within shot; so to let Friday understand a little what I would do, I called him to me again, pointed at the fowl, which was indeed a parrot, tho' I thought it had been a hawk; I say, pointing to the parrot, and to my gun, and to the ground under the parrot, to let him see I would make it fall, I made him understand that I would shoot and kill that bird; according I fired and bad him look, and immediately he saw the parrot fall, he stood like one frighted again, notwithstanding all I had said to him; and I found he was the more amazed because he did not see me put any thing into the gun; but thought that there must be some wonderful fund of death and destruction in that thing, able to kill man, beast, bird, or any thing near or far off, and the astonishment this created in him was such as could not wear off for a long time; and I believe, if I would have let him, he would have worshipped me and my gun. As for the gun it self, he would not so much as touch it for several days after; but would speak to it, and talk to it, as if it had answered him, when he was by himself; which, as I afterwards learned of him, was to desire it not to kill him.

Well, after his astonishment was a little over at this, I pointed to him to run and fetch the bird I had shot, which he did, but stayed some time; for the parrot, not being quite dead, was fluttered away a good way off from the place where she fell; however, he found her, took her up, and brought her to me; and as I had perceived his ignorance about the gun before, I took this advantage to charge the gun again, and not let him see me do it, that I might be ready for any other mark that might present; but nothing more offered at that time; so I brought home the kid, and the same evening I took the skin off, and cut it out as well as I could; and having a pot for that purpose, I boiled or stewed some of the flesh, and made some very good broth; and after I had begun to eat some, I gave some to my man, who seemed very glad of it, and liked it very well; but that which was strangest to him was to see me eat salt with it; he made a sign to me that salt was not good to eat, and putting a little into his own mouth, he seemed to nauseate it, and would spit and sputter at it, washing his mouth with fresh water after it; on the other hand, I took some meat in my mouth without salt, and I pretended to spit and sputter for want of salt, as fast as he had done at the salt; but it would not do, he would never care for salt with his meat or in his broth; at least not a great while, and then but a very little.

Having thus fed him with boiled meat and broth, I was re-solved to feast him the next day with roasting a piece of the kid; this I did by hanging it before the fire on a string, as I had seen many people do in England, setting two poles up, one on each side of the fire, and one cross on the top, and tying the string to the cross-stick, letting the meat turn continually. This Friday admired very much; but when he came to taste the flesh, he took so many ways to tell me how well he liked it, that I could not but understand him; and at last he told me he would never eat man's flesh any more, which I was very glad to hear.

The next day I set him to work to beating some corn out, and sifting it in the manner I used to do, as I observed before, and he soon understood how to do it as well as I, especially after he had seen what the meaning of it was, and that it was to make bread of; for after that I let him see me make my bread, and bake it too, and in a litle time Friday was able to do all the work for me, as well as I could do it myself.

I begun now to consider, that having two mouths to feed in-stead of one, I must provide more ground for my harvest, and plant a larger quantity of corn than I used to do; so I marked out a larger piece of land, and began the fence in the same man-ner as before, in which Friday not only worked very willingly and very hard, but did it very chearfully, and I told him what it was for; that it was for corn to make more bread, because he was now with me, and that I might have enough for him and my self too. He appeared very sensible of that part, and let me know that he thought I had much more labour upon me on his account than I had for my self; and that he would work the harder for me, if I would tell him what to do.

This was the pleasantest year of all the life I led in this place; Friday began to talk pretty well, and understand the names of almost every thing I had occasion to call for, and of every place I had to send him to, and talked a great deal to me; so that, in short, I began now to have some use for my tongue again, which indeed I had very little occasion for before; that is to say, about speech; besides the pleasures of talking to him, I had a singular satisfaction in the fellow himself; his simple unfeigned honesty appeared to me more and more every day, and I began really to love the creature; and on his side, I believe he loved me more than it was possible for him ever to love any thing before.

I had a mind once to try if he had any hankering inclination to his own country again, and having learned him English so well that he could answer me almost any questions, I asked him whether the nation that he belonged to never conquered in battle; at which he smiled, and said, 'Yes, yes, we always fight the better'; that is, he meant always get the better in fight; and so we began the following discourse: 'You always fight the better,' said I, 'how came you to be taken prisoner then, Friday?'

Friday. My nation beat much, for all that.

Master. How beat? if your nation beat them, how came you to be taken?

Friday. They more many than my nation in the place where me was; they take one, two, three, and me; my nation over-beat them in the yonder place, where me no was; there my nation take one, two, great thousand.

Master. But why did not your side recover you from the hands of your enemies then?

Friday. They run one, two, three, and me, and make go in the canoe; my nation have no canoe that time.

Master. Well, Friday, and what does your nation do with the men they take, do they carry them away and eat them, as these did?

Friday. Yes, my nation eat mans too, eat all up.

Master. Where do they carry them?

Friday. Go to other place where they think.

Master. Do they come hither?

Friday. Yes, yes, they come hither; come other else place.

Master. Have you been here with them?

Friday. Yes, I been here. [*points to the* N.W. *side of the island, which, it seems, was their side.*]

By this I understood, that my man Friday had formerly been

among the savages who used to come on shore on the farther part of the island, on the same man eating occasions that he was now brought for; and sometime after, when I took the courage to carry him to that side, being the same I formerly mentioned, he presently knew the place, and told me he was there once when they eat up twenty men, two women, and one child; he could not tell twenty in English; but he numbred them by laying so many stones on a row, and pointing to me to tell them over.

I have told this passage, because it introduces what follows; that after I had had this discourse with him, I asked him how far it was from our island to the shore, and whether the canoes were not often lost; he told me there was no danger, no canoes ever lost; but that after a little way out to the sea, there was a current, and wind, always one way in the morning, the other in the afternoon.

This I understood to be no more than the sets of the tide, as going out or coming in; but I afterwards understood it was occasioned by the great draft and reflux of the mighty river Oroonooko; in the mouth or the gulph of which river, as I found afterwards, our island lay; and this land which I perceived to the w. and n.w. was the great island Trinidad, on the north point of the mouth of the river. I asked Friday a thousand questions about the country, the inhabitants, the sea, the coast, and what nations were near; he told me all he knew with the greatest openness imaginable; I asked him the name of the several nations of his sort of people; but could get no other name than Caribs; from whence I easily understood that these were the Caribbees, which our maps place on the part of America which reaches from the mouth of the river Oroonooko to Guiana, and onwards to St. Martha.[47] He told me that up a great way beyond the moon, that was, beyond the setting of the moon, which must be w. from their country, there dwelt white bearded men, like me; and pointed to my great whiskers, which I mention'd before; and that they had killed 'much mans,' that was his word; by all which I understood, he meant the Spaniards, whose cruelties in America had been spread over the whole countries, and was remembered by all the nations from father to son.

I enquired if he could tell me how I might come from this

island, and get among those white men; he told me, yes, yes, I might go 'in two canoe'; I could not understand what he meant, or make him describe to me what he meant by 'two canoe', till last, with great difficulty, I found he meant it must be in a large great boat, as big as two canoes.

This part of Friday's discourse began to relish with me very well, and from this time I entertained some hopes, that one time or other, I might find an opportunity to make my escape from this place; and that this poor savage might be a means to help me to do it.

During the long time that Friday had now been with me, and that he began to speak to me and understand me, I was not wanting to lay a foundation of religious knowledge in his mind; particularly I asked him one time who made him. The poor creature did not understand me at all, but thought I had asked him who was his father; but I took it by another handle, and asked him who made the sea, the ground we walked on, and the hills, and woods; he told me it was one old Benamuckee, that lived beyond all. He could describe nothing of this great person, but that he was very old; much older, he said, than the sea or the land, than the moon or the stars. I asked him then, if this old person had made all things, why did not all things worship him; he looked very grave, and with a perfect look of innocence said, 'All things do say O to him.' I asked him if the people who die in his country went away any where. He said, yes, they all went to Benamuckee; then I asked him whether these they eat up went thither too. He said yes.

From these things I began to instruct him in the knowledge of the true God. I told him that the great Maker of all things lived up there, pointing up towards heaven; that He governs the world by the same power and providence by which He had made it; that He was omnipotent, could do every thing for us, give every thing to us, take every thing from us; and thus by degrees I opened his eyes. He listned with great attention, and received with pleasure the notion of Jesus Christ being sent to redeem us, and of the manner of making our prayers to God, and His being able to hear us, even into heaven. He told me one day, that if our God could hear us up beyond the sun, He must needs be a greater god than their Benamuckee, who lived but a little way off, and yet could not hear till they went up to the great mountains where he dwelt to speak to him. I asked him if ever he went thither to speak to him; he said no, they never went that were young men; none went thither but the old men, who he called their *oowocakee*, that is, as I made him explain it to me, their religious, or clergy, and that they went to say O (so he called saying prayers) and then came back, and told them what Benamuckee said. By this I observed that there is priestcraft even amongst the most blinded ignorant pagans in the world; and the policy of making a secret religion, in order to preserve the veneration of the people to the clergy, is not only to be found in the Roman, but perhaps among all religions in the world, even among the most brutish and barbarous savages.

I endeavoured to clear up this fraud to my man Friday, and told him that the pretence of their old men going up the mountains to say O to their god Benamuckee was a cheat, and their bringing word from thence what he said was much more so; that if they met with any answer, or spake with any one there, it must be with an evil spirit. And then I entred into a long discourse with him about the devil, the original of him, his rebellion against God, his enmity to man, the reason of it, his setting himself up the dark parts of the world to be worship'd instead of God, and as God; and the many stratagems he made use of to delude mankind to his ruine; how he had a secret access to our passions and to our affections, to adapt his snares so to our inclinations, as to cause us even to be our own tempters, and to run upon our destruction by our own choice.

I found it was not so easie to imprint right notions in his mind about the devil, as it was about the being of a God. Nature assisted all my arguments to evidence to him even the necessity of a great First Cause and over-ruling governing Power, a secret directing Providence, and of the equity and justice of paying homage to Him that made us, and the like. But there appeared nothing of all this in the notion of an evil spirit; of his original, his being, his nature, and above all of his inclination to do evil, and to draw us in to do so too; and the poor creature puzzled me once in such a manner, by a question meerly natural and innocent, that I scarce knew what to say to him. I had been talking a great deal to him of the power of God, His omnipotence, His dreadful nature to sin, His being a consuming fire to the workers of iniquity; how, as He had made us all, He could destroy us and all the world in a moment; and he listened with great seriousness to me all the while.

After this, I had been telling him how the devil was God's enemy in the hearts of men, and used all his malice and skill to defeat the good designs of Providence, and to ruine the kingdom of Christ in the world; and the like. 'Well,' says Friday, 'but you say, God is so strong, so great, is He not much strong, much might as the devil?' 'Yes, yes,' says I, 'Friday, God is stronger than the devil, God is above the devil, and therefore we pray to God to tread him down under our feet, and enable us to resist his temptations and quench his fiery darts.' 'But,' says he again, 'if God much strong, much might as the devil, why God no kill the devil, so make him no more do wicked?'

I was strangely surprized at his question, and after all, tho' I was now an old man, yet I was but a young doctor, and ill enough quallified for a casuist, or a solver of difficulties; and at first I could not tell what to say, so I pretended not to hear him, and asked him what he said. But he was too earnest for an answer to forget his question; so that he repeated it in the very same broken words, as above. By this time I had recovered my self a little, and I said, 'God will at last punish him severely; he is reserved for the judgment, and is to be cast into the bottomless-pit, to dwell with everlasting fire.' This did not satisfie Friday, but he returns upon me, repeating my words, 'Reserve, at last, me no understand; but why not kill the devil now, not kill great ago?' 'You may as well ask me,' said I, 'why God does not kill you and I, when we do wicked things here that offend Him. We are pre- served to repent and be pardoned.' He muses a while at this. 'Well, well,' says he, mighty affectionately, 'that well; so you, I, devil, all wicked, all preserve, repent, God pardon all.' Here I was run down again by him to the last degree, and it was a testimony to me, how the meer notions of nature, though they will guide reasonable creatures to the knowledge of a God, and of a worship or homage due to the supreme Being, of God as the consequence of our nature; yet nothing but divine revelation can form the knowledge of Jesus Christ, and of a redemption purchased for us, of a Mediator of the new covenant, and of an Intercessor at the foot-stool of God's throne; I say, nothing but a revelation from heaven can form these in the soul, and that therefore the gospel of our Lord and Saviour Jesus Christ, I mean, the word of God, and the spirit of God promised for the guide and sanctifier of His people, are the absolutely necessary instructors of the souls of men, in the saving knowledge of God, and the means of salvation.

I therefore diverted the present discourse between me and my man, rising up hastily, as upon some sudden occasion of going out; then sending him for something a good way off, I seriously prayed to God that He would enable me to instruct savingly this poor savage, assisting by His spirit the heart of the poor ignorant creature, to receive the light of the knowledge of God in Christ, reconciling him to Himself, and would guide me to speak so to him from the word of God, as his conscience might be convinced, his eyes opened, and his soul saved. When he came again to me, I entred into a long discourse with him upon the subject of the redemption of man by the Saviour of the world, and of the doctrine of the gospel preached from heaven, viz. of repentance towards God, and faith in our blessed Lord Jesus. I then explained to him, as well as I could, why our blessed Redeemer took not on Him the nature of angels, but the seed of Abraham, and how for that reason the fallen angels had no share in the redemption; that he came only to the lost sheep of the house of Israel, and the like.

I had, God knows, more sincerity than knowledge, in all the methods I took for this poor creature's instruction, and must acknowledge what I believe all that act upon the same principle will find, that in laying things open to him, I really informed and instructed myself in many things that either I did not know, or had not fully considered before, but which occurred naturally to my mind, upon my searching into them for the information of this poor savage; and I had more affection in my enquiry after things upon this occasion, than ever I felt before; so that whether this poor wild wretch was the better for me or no, I had great reason to be thankful that ever he came to me. My grief set lighter upon me, my habitation grew comfortable to me beyond measure; and when I reflected that in this solitary life which I had been confined to, I had not only been moved my self to look up to heaven, and to seek to the hand that had brought me there, but was now to be made an instrument under Providence to save the life, and, for ought I knew, the soul of a poor savage, and bring him to the true knowledge of religion, and of the Christian doctrine, that he might know Christ Jesus, to know whom is life eternal; I say, when I reflected upon all these things, a secret joy run through every part of my soul, and I frequently rejoyced that ever I was brought to this place, which I had so often thought the most dreadful of all afflictions that could possibly have befallen me.

In this thankful frame I continued all the remainder of my time, and the conversation which employed the hours between Friday and I was such as made the three years which we lived there together perfectly and compleatly happy, if any such thing as compleat happiness can be formed in a sublunary state. The savage was now a good Christian, a much better than I; though I have reason to hope, and bless God for it, that we were equally penitent, and comforted restored penitents; we had here the word of God to read, and no farther off from His spirit to instruct, than if we had been in England.

I always apply'd my self in reading the scripture, to let him know, as well as I could, the meaning of what I read; and he again, by his serious enquiries and questionings, made me, as I said before, a much better scholar in the scripture knowledge than I should ever have been by my own private meer reading. Another thing I cannot refrain from observing here also from experience, in this retired part of my life, viz. how infinite and inexpressible a blessing it is, that the knowledge of God, and of the doctrine of salvation by Christ Jesus, is so plainly laid down in the word of God, so easy to be received and understood, that as the bare reading the scripture made me capable of understanding enough of my duty to carry me directly on to the great work of sincere repentance for my sins, and laying hold of a Saviour for life and salvation, to a stated reformation in practice, and obedience to all God's commands, and this without any teacher or instructer; I mean, humane; so the same plain instruction sufficiently served to the enlightning this savage creature, and bringing him to be such a Christian, as I have known few equal to him in my life.

As to all the disputes, wranglings, strife, and contention, which has happened in the world about religion, whether niceties in doctrines, or schemes of church government, they were all perfectly useless to us; as for ought I can yet see, they have been to all the rest of the world. We had the sure guide to heaven, viz. the word of God; and we had, blessed be God, comfortable views of the spirit of God teaching and instructing us by His word, leading us into all truth, and making us both willing and obedient to the instruction of His word, and I cannot see the least use that the greatest knowledge of the disputed points in religion which have made such confusions in the world would have been to us, if we could have obtained it; but I must go on with the historical part of things, and take every part in its order.

After Friday and I became more intimately acquainted, and that he could understand almost all I said to him, and speak fluently, though in broken English, to me, I acquainted him with my own story, or at least so much of it as related to my coming into the place, how I had lived there, and how long. I let him into the mystery, for such it was to him, of gunpowder and bullet, and taught him how to shoot; I gave him a knife, which he was wonderfully delighted with, and I made him a belt, with a frog hanging to it, such as in England we wear hangers in; and in the frog, instead of a hanger, I gave him a hatchet, which was not only as good a weapon in some cases, but much more useful upon other occasions.

I described to him the country of Europe, and particularly England, which I came from; how we lived, how we worshipped God, how we behaved to one another; and how we traded in ships to all parts of the world. I gave him an account of the wreck which I had been on board of, and shewed him as near as I could the place where she lay; but she was all beaten in pieces before, and gone.

I shewed him the ruins of our boat, which we lost when we escaped, and which I could not stir with my whole strength then, but was now fallen almost to pieces. Upon seeing this boat, Friday stood musing a great while, and said nothing; I asked him what it was he study'd upon; at last says he, 'Me see such boat like come to place at my nation.'

I did not understand him a good while; but at last, when I had examined farther into it, I understood by him that a boat, such as that had been, came on shore upon the country where he lived; that is, as he explained it, was driven thither by stress of weather. I presently imagined that some European ship must have been cast away upon their coast, and the boat might get loose, and drive a shore; but was so dull, that I never once thought of men making escape from a wreck thither, much less whence they might come; so I only inquired after a description of the boat.

Friday described the boat to me well enough; but brought me better to understand him, when he added with some warmth, 'We save the white mans from drown.' Then I presently asked him if there was any white mans, as he called them, in the boat. 'Yes,' he said, 'the boat full white mans.' I asked him how many; he told upon his fingers seventeen. I asked him then what become of them; he told me, 'They live, they dwell at my nation.'

This put new thoughts into my head; for I presently imagined that these might be the men belonging to the ship that was cast away in sight of my island, as I now call it; and who after the ship was struck on the rock, and they saw her inevitably lost, had saved themselves in their boat, and were landed upon that wild shore among the savages.

Upon this, I enquired of him more critically what was become of them. He assured me they lived still there; that they had been there about four years; that the savages let them alone, and gave them victuals to live. I asked him how it came to pass they did not kill them and eat them. He said, 'No, they make brother with them'; that is, as I understood him, a truce: and then he added, 'They no eat mans but when makes the war fight'; that is to say, they never eat any men but such as come to fight with them, and are taken in battle.

It was after this some considerable time, that being upon the top of the hill, at the east side of the island, from whence, as I have said, I had in a clear day discovered the main or continent of America; Friday, the weather being very serene, looks very earnestly towards the main land, and in a kind of surprise, falls a jumping and dancing, and calls out to me, for I was at some distance from him. I asked him what was the matter. 'O joy!' says he, 'O glad! There see my country, there my nation!'

I observed an extraordinary sense of pleasure appeared in his face, and his eyes sparkled, and his countenance discovered a strange eagerness, as if he had a mind to be in his own country again; and this observation of mine put a great many thoughts into me, which made me at first not so easy about my new man Friday as I was before; and I made no doubt but that if Friday could get back to his own nation again, he would not only forget all his religion, but all his obligation to me; and would be forward enough to give his countrymen an account of me, and come back perhaps with a hundred or two of them, and make a feast upon me, at which he might be as merry as he used to be with those of his enemies, when they were taken in war.

But I wronged the poor honest creature very much, for which I was very sorry afterwards. However, as my jealousy encreased, and held me some weeks, I was a little more circumspect, and not so familiar and kind to him as before; in which I was certainly in the wrong too, the honest grateful creature having no thought about it, but what consisted with the best principles, both as a religious Christian, and as a grateful friend, as appeared afterwards to my full satisfaction.

While my jealousy of him lasted, you may be sure I was every day pumping him to see if he would discover any of the new thoughts, which I suspected were in him; but I found every thing he said was so honest and so innocent, that I could find nothing to nourish my suspicion; and in spight of all my uneasiness he made me at last entirely his own again, nor did he in the least perceive that I was uneasie, and therefore I could not suspect him of deceit.

One day walking up the same hill, but the weather being haizy at sea, so that we could not see the continent, I called to him, and said, 'Friday, do not you wish your self in your own country, your own nation?' 'Yes,' he said, 'he be much O glad to be at his own nation.' 'What would you do there?' said I, 'would you turn wild again, eat mens flesh again, and be a savage as you were before?' He lookt full of concern, and shaking his head said, 'No, no, Friday tell them to live good, tell them to pray God, tell then to eat corn-bread, cattle-flesh, milk, no eat man again.' 'Why then,' said I to him, 'they will kill you.' He looked grave at that, and then said, 'No, they no kill me, they willing love learn.' He meant by this, they would be willing to learn. He added, they learned much of the bearded-mans that come in the boat. Then I asked him if he would go back to them. He smiled at that, and told me he could not swim so far. I told me I would make a canoe for him. He told me he would go, if I would go with him. 'I go!' says I, 'why, they will eat me if I come there.' 'No, no,' says he, 'me make they no eat you; me make they much love you.' He meant he would tell them how I had killed his enemies, and saved his life, and so he would make them love me; then he told me as well as he could, how kind they were to seventeen white-men, or bearded-men, as he called them, who came on shore there in distress.

From this time I confess I had a mind to venture over, and see if I could possibly joyn with these bearded-men, who I made no doubt were Spaniards or Portuguese; not doubting but if I could we might find some method to escape from thence; being upon the continent, and a good company together; better than I could from an island 40 miles off the shore, and alone without help. So after some days I took Friday to work again, by way of discourse, and told him I would give him a boat to go back to his nation; and accordingly I carry'd him to my frigate which lay on the other side of the island, and having cleared it of water, for I always kept it sunk in the water, I brought it out, shewed it him, and we both went into it.

I found he was a most dextrous fellow at managing it, would make it go almost as swift and fast again as I could; so when he was in, I said to him, 'Well, now, Friday, shall we go to your nation?' He looked very dull at my saying so, which it seems was because he thought the boat too small to go so far. I told him

then I had a bigger; so the next day I went to the place where the
first boat lay which I had made, but which I could not get into
water. He said that was big enough; but then as I had taken no
care of it, and it had lain two or three and twenty years there,
the sun had split and dry'd it, that it was in a manner rotten.
Friday told me such a boat would do very well, and would carry
'much enough vittle, drink, bread', that was his way of talking.

Upon the whole, I was by this time so fixed upon my design
of going over with him to the continent, that I told him we would
go and make one as big as that, and he should go home in it. He
answered not one word, but looked very grave and sad. I asked
him what was the matter with him. He asked me again thus,
'Why you angry mad with Friday, what me done?' I asked him
what he meant; I told him I was not angry with him at all. 'No
angry! No angry!' says he, repeating the words several times,
'why send Friday home away to my nation?' 'Why,' says I,
'Friday, did you not say you wished you were there?' 'Yes, yes,'
says he, 'wish be both there, no wish Friday there, no master
there.' In a word, he would not think of going there without me.
'I go there! Friday,' says I, 'what shall I do there?' He turned
very quick upon me at this: 'You do great deal much good,' says
he, 'you teach wild mans be good sober tame mans; you tell
them know God, pray God, and live new life.' 'Alas! Friday,'
says I, 'thou knowest not what thou sayest, I am but an ignorant
man myself.' 'Yes, yes,' says he, 'you teachee me good, you
teachee them good.' 'No, no, Friday,' says I, 'you shall go without
me, leave me here to live by my self, as I did before.' He looked
confused again at that word, and running to one of the hatchets
which he used to wear, he takes it up hastily, comes and gives it
me. 'What must I do with this?' says I to him. 'You take, kill
Friday,' says he. 'What must I kill you for?' said I again. He
returns very quick, 'What you send Friday away for? take, kill
Friday, no send Friday away?' This he spoke so earnestly, that
I saw tears stand in his eyes. In a word, I so plainly discovered
the utmost affection in him to me, and a firm resolution in him,
that I told him then, and often after, that I would never send him
away from me, if he was willing to stay with me.

Upon the whole, as I found by all his discourse a settled affection to me, and that nothing should part him from me, so I found all the foundation of his desire to go to his own country was laid in his ardent affection to the people, and his hopes of my doing them good; a thing which as I had no notion of my self, so I had not the least thought or intention or desire of undertaking it. But still I found a strong inclination to my attempting an escape as above, founded on the supposition gathered from the discourse, viz. that there were seventeen bearded men there; and therefore, without any more delay, I went to work with Friday to find out a great tree proper to fell, and make a large periagua or canoe to undertake the voyage. There were trees enough in the island to have built a little fleet, not of periaguas and canoes, but even of good large vessels. But the main thing I looked at, was to get one so near the water that we might launch it when it was made, to avoid the mistake I committed at first.

At last, Friday pitched upon a tree, for I found he knew much better than I what kind of wood was fittest for it, nor can I tell to this day what wood to call the tree we cut down, except that it was very like the tree we call fustic,[48] or between that and the Nicaragua wood,[49] for it was much the same colour and smell. Friday was for burning the hollow or cavity of this tree out to make it for a boat. But I shewed him how rather to cut it out with tools, which, after I had shewed him how to use, he did very handily, and in about a month's hard labour we finished it, and made it very handsome, especially when with our axes, which I shewed him how to handle, we cut and hewed the out-side into the true shape of a boat; after this, however, it cost us near a fortnight's time to get her along as it were inch by inch upon great rowlers into the water. But when she was in, she would have carry'd twenty men with great ease.

When she was in the water, and tho' she was so big, it amazed me to see with what dexterity and how swift my man Friday would manage her, turn her, and paddle her along; so I asked him if he would, and if we might venture over in her. 'Yes,' he said, 'he venture over in her very well, tho' great blow wind.' However, I had a farther design that he knew nothing of, and that was to make a mast and sail and to fit her with an anchor and cable. As to a mast, that was easy enough to get; so I pitched upon a strait young cedar-tree, which I found near the place, and which there was great plenty of in the island, and I set Friday to work to cut it down, and gave him directions how to shape and order it. But as to the sail, that was my particular care; I knew I had old sails, or rather pieces of old sails enough; but as I had had them now six and twenty years by me, and had not been very careful to preserve them, not imagining that I should ever have this kind of use for them, I did not doubt but they were all rotten, and indeed most of them were so; however, I found two pieces which appeared pretty good, and with these I went to work, and with a great deal of pains, and awkward tedious stitching (you may be sure) for want of needles, I at length made a three cornered ugly thing, like what we call in England a shoulder of mutton sail, to go with a boom at bottom, and a little short sprit at the top, such as usually our ships' long-boats sail with, and such as I best knew how to manage; because it was such a one as I had to the boat in which I made my escape from Barbary, as related in the first part of my story.

I was near two months performing this last work, viz. rigging and fitting my mast and sails; for I finished them very compleat, making a small stay, and a sail or fore-sail to it, to assist, if we should turn to windward; and which was more than all, I fixed a rudder to the stern of her, to steer with; and though I was but a bungling shipwright, yet as I knew the usefulness, and even necessity of such a thing, I apply'd my self with so much pains to do it, that at last I brought it to pass; though considering the many dull contrivances I had for it that failed, I think it cost me almost as much labour as making the boat.

After all this was done too, I had my man Friday to teach as to what belonged to the navigation of my boat; for though he knew very well how to paddle a canoe, he knew nothing what belonged to a sail and a rudder; and was the most amazed, when he saw me work the boat to and again in the sea by the rudder, and how the sail gybed, and filled this way or that way, as the course we sailed changed; I say, when he saw this, he stood like one astonished and amazed. However, with a little use, I made all these things familiar to him; and he became an expert sailor, except that as to the compass, I could make him understand very little of that. On the other hand, as there was very little cloudy weather, and seldom or never any fogs in those parts, there was the less occasion for a compass, seeing the stars were always to be seen by night, and the shore by day, except in the rainy seasons, and then no body cared to stir abroad, either by land or sea.

I was now entred on the seven and twentieth year of my captivity in this place; though the last three years that I had this creature with me ought rather to be left out of the account, my habitation being quite of another kind than in all the rest of the time. I kept the anniversary of my landing there with the same thankfulness to God for His mercies, as at first; and if I had such cause of acknowledgment at first, I had much more so now, having such additional testimonies of the care of Providence over me, and the great hopes I had of being effectually and speedily delivered; for I had an invincible impression upon my thoughts, that my deliverance was at hand, and that I should not be another year in this place. However, I went on with my husbandry, digging, planting, fencing, as usual; I gathered and cured my grapes, and did every necessary thing as before.

The rainy season was in the mean time upon me, when I kept more within doors than at other times; so I had stowed our new vessel as secure as we could, bringing her up into the creek, where as I said, in the beginning I landed my rafts from the ship, and haling her up to the shore at high water mark, I made my man Friday dig a little dock, just big enough to hold her, and just deep enough to give her water enough to fleet in; and then when the tide was out, we made a strong dam cross the end of it, to keep the water out; and so she lay dry, as to the tide from the sea; and to keep the rain off, we laid a great many boughs of trees, so thick that she was as well thatched as a house; and thus we waited for the month of November and December, in which I designed to make my adventure.

When the settled season began to come in, as the thought of my design returned with the fair weather, I was preparing daily for the voyage; and the first thing I did was to lay by a certain quantity of provisions, being the stores for our voyage; and intended, in a week or a fortnight's time, to open the dock and launch out our boat. I was busy one morning upon some thing of this kind, when I called to Friday, and bid him go to the sea shore, and see if he could find a turtle or tortoise, a thing which we generally got once a week, for the sake of the eggs as well as the flesh. Friday had not been long gone, when he came running back, and flew over my outer wall, or fence, like one that felt not the ground, or the steps he set his feet on; and before I had time to speak to him, he cries out to me, 'O master! O master! O sorrow! O bad!' 'What's the matter, Friday?' says I. 'O yonder, there,' says he, 'one, two, three canoe! one, two, three!' By his way of speaking, I concluded there were six; but on inquiry, I found it was but three. 'Well, Friday,' says I, 'do not be frighted'; so I heartned him up as well as I could. However, I saw the poor fellow was most terribly scared; for nothing ran in his head but that they were come to look for him, and would cut him in pieces and eat him; and the poor fellow trembled so, that I scarce knew what to do with him. I comforted him as well as I could, and told him I was in as much danger as he, and that they would eat me as well as him; 'but,' says I, 'Friday, we must resolve to fight them; can you fight, Friday?' 'Me shoot,' says he, 'but there come many great number.' 'No matter for that,' said I again, 'our guns will fright them that we do not kill'; so I asked him whether if I resolved to defend him, he would defend me, and stand by me, and do just as I bid him. He said, 'Me die, when you bid die, master'; so I went and fetched a good dram of rum, and gave him; for I had been so good a husband of my rum, that I had a great deal left. When he drank it, I made him take the two fowling-pieces, which we always carry'd, and load them with large swan-shot, as big as small pistol bullets; then I took four muskets, and loaded them with two slugs and five small bullets each; and my two pistols I loaded with a brace of bullets each; I hung my great sword as usual, naked by my side, and gave Friday his hatchet.

When I had thus prepared my self, I took my perspective-glass, and went up to the side of the hill, to see what I could discover; and I found quickly, by my glass, that there were one and twenty savages, three prisoners, and three canoes; and that their whole business seemed to be the triumphant banquet upon these three humane bodies (a barbarous feast indeed), but nothing more than as I had observed was usual with them.

I observed also, that they were landed not where they had done when Friday made his escape, but nearer to my creek, where the shore was low, and where a thick wood came close almost down to the sea. This, with the abhorrence of the inhumane errand these wretches came about, filled me with such indignation that I came down again to Friday, and told him I was resolved to go down to them, and kill them all; and asked him if he would stand by me. He was now gotten over his fright, and his spirits being a little raised with the dram I had given him, he was very chearful, and told me as before, he would die, when I bid die.

In this fit of fury, I took first and divided the arms which I had charged, as before, between us; I gave Friday one pistol to stick in his girdle, and three guns upon his shoulder; and I took one pistol and the other three my self; and in this posture we marched out. I took a small bottle of rum in my pocket, and gave Friday a large bag, with more powder and bullet; and as to orders, I charged him to keep close behind me, and not to stir, or shoot, or do any thing, till I bid him; and in the mean time, not to speak a word. In this posture I fetched a compass to my right-hand, of near a mile, as well to get over the creek as to get into the wood; so that I might come within shoot of them before I should be discovered, which I had seen by my glass it was easy to do.

While I was making this march, my former thoughts returning, I began to abate my resolution; I do not mean that I entertained any fear of their number; for as they were naked, unarmed wretches, 'tis certain I was superior to them; nay, though I had been alone; but it occurred to my thoughts, what call, what occasion, much less what necessity I was in to go and dip my hands in blood, to attack people who had neither done, or intended me any wrong, who as to me were innocent, and whose barbarous customs were their own disaster, being in them a token indeed of God's having left them, with the other nations of that part of the world, to such stupidity, and to such inhumane courses; but did not call me to take upon me to be a judge of their actions, much less an executioner of His justice; that whenever He thought fit, He would take the cause into His own hands, and by national vengeance punish them as a people, for national crimes; but that in the mean time, it was none of my business; that it was true, Friday might justify it, because he was a declared enemy, and in a state of war with those very particular people; and it was lawful for him to attack them; but I could not say the same with respect to me. These things were so warmly pressed upon my thoughts, all the way as I went, that I resolved I would only go and place my self near them, that I might observe their barbarous feast, and that I would act then as God should direct; but that unless something offered that was more a call to me than yet I knew of, I would not meddle with them.

With this resolution I entered the wood, and with all possible wariness and silence, Friday following close at my heels, I marched till I came to the skirt of the wood, on the side which was next to them; only that one corner of the wood lay between me and them; here I called softly to Friday, and shewing him a great tree, which was just at the corner of the wood, I bad him go to the tree, and bring me word if he could see there plainly what they were doing; he did so, and came immediately back to me, and told me they might be plainly viewed there; that they were all about their fire, eating the flesh of one of their prisoners; and that another lay bound upon the sand, a little from them, which he said they would kill next, and which fired all the very soul within me; he told me it was not one of their nation, but one of the bearded men, who he had told me of, that came to their country in the boat. I was filled with horror at the very naming the white bearded man, and going to the tree, I saw plainly by my glass a white man who lay upon the beach of the sea, with his hands and his feet ty'd, with flags, or things like rushes; and that he was an European, and had cloaths on.

There was another tree, and a little thicket beyond it, about fifty yards nearer to them than the place where I was, which by going a little way about, I saw I might come at undiscovered, and that then I should be within half shot of them; so I with-held my passion, though I was indeed enraged to the highest degree, and going back about twenty paces, I got behind some bushes, which held all the way till I came to the other tree; and then I came to a little rising ground, which gave me a full view of them, at the distance of about eighty yards.

I had now not a moment to lose; for nineteen of the dreadful wretches sat upon the ground, all close huddled together, and had just sent the other two to butcher the poor Christian, and bring him perhaps limb by limb to their fire, and they were stooped down to untie the bands at his feet; I turned to Friday. 'Now, Friday,' said I, 'do as I bid thee'; Friday said he would; 'Then, Friday,' says I, 'do exactly as you see me do, fail in nothing'; so I set down one of the muskets and the fowling-piece upon the ground, and Friday did the like by his; and with the other musket I took my aim at the savages, bidding him do the like; then asking him if he was ready, he said yes. 'Then fire at them,' said I; and the same moment I fired also.

Friday took his aim so much better than I, that on the side that he shot, he killed two of them, and wounded three more; and on my side, I killed one, and wounded two. They were, you may be sure, in a dreadful consternation; and all of them, who were not hurt, jumped up upon their feet, but did not immediately know which way to run, or which way to look: for they knew not from whence their destruction came. Friday kept his eyes close upon me, that as I had bid him, he might observe what I did; so as soon as the first shot was made, I threw down the piece, and took up the fowling-piece, and Friday did the like; he sees me cock and present, he did the same again. 'Are you ready, Friday?' said I; 'Yes,' says he; 'Let fly then,' says I, 'in the name of God,' and with that I fired again among the amazed wretches, and so did Friday; and as our pieces were now loaden with what I called swan-shot, or small pistol bullets, we found only two drop; but so many were wounded, that they run about yelling and skreaming like mad creatures, all bloody, and miserably wounded, most of them; whereof three more fell quickly after, though not quite dead.

'Now, Friday,' says I, laying down the discharged pieces, and taking up the musket which was yet loaden, 'follow me,' says I; which he did, with a great deal of courage; upon which I rushed out of the wood, and shewed my self, and Friday close at my foot; as soon as I perceived they saw me, I shouted as loud as I could, and bad Friday do so too; and running as fast as I could, which by the way, was not very fast, being loaden with arms as I was, I made directly towards the poor victim, who was, as I said, lying upon the beach or shore, between the place where they sat and the sea. The two butchers who were just going to work with him, had left him at the surprize of our first fire, and fled in a terrible fright to the sea side, and had jumped into a canoe, and three more of the rest made the same way; I turned to Friday, and bid him step forwards, and fire at them; he understood me immediately, and running about forty yards to be near them, he shot at them, and I thought he had killed them all; for I see them all fall of a heap into the boat; though I saw two of them up again quickly: however, he killed two of them, and wounded the third; so that he lay down in the bottom of the boat, as if he had been dead.

While my man Friday fired at them, I pulled out my knife, and cut the flags that bound the poor victim, and loosing his hands and feet, I lifted him up, and asked him in the Portuguese tongue what he was. He answered in Latin, 'Christianus'; but was so weak and faint, that he could scarce stand or speak; I took my bottle out of my pocket, and gave it him, making signs that he should drink, which he did; and I gave him a piece of bread, which he eat; then I asked him what countryman he was, and he said, 'Espagniole'; and being a little recovered, let me know by all the signs he could possibly make, how much he was in my debt for his deliverance. 'Seignior,' said I, with as much Spanish as I could make up, 'we will talk afterwards; but we must fight now; if you have any strength left, take this pistol and sword, and lay about you.' He took them very thankfully, and no sooner had he the arms in his hands, but as if they had put new vigour into him, he flew upon his murtherers like a fury, and had cut two of them in pieces in an instant; for the truth is, as the whole was a surprize to them, so the poor creatures were so much frighted with the noise of our pieces, that they fell down for meer amazement and fear; and had no more power to attempt their own escape, than their flesh had to resist our shot; and that was the case of those five that Friday shot at in the boat; for as three of them fell with the hurt they received, so the other two fell with the fright.

I kept my piece in my hand still, without firing, being willing to keep my charge ready, because I had given the Spaniard my pistol and sword; so I called to Friday, and bad him run up to the tree from whence we first fired, and fetch the arms which lay there, that had been discharged, which he did with great swiftness; and then giving him my musket, I sat down my self to load all the rest again, and bad them come to me when they wanted. While I was loading these pieces, there happened a fierce engagement between the Spaniard and one of the savages, who made at him with one of their great wooden swords, the same weapon that was to have killed him before, if I had not prevented it. The Spaniard, who was as bold and as brave as could be imagined, though weak, had fought this Indian a good while, and had cut him two great wounds on his head; but the savage being a stout lusty fellow, closing in with him, had thrown him down (being faint) and was wringing my sword out of his hand, when the Spaniard, tho' undermost, wisely quitting the sword, drew the pistol from his girdle, shot the savage through the body, and killed him upon the spot, before I, who was running to help him, could come near him.

Friday, being now left to his liberty, pursued the flying wretches with no weapon in his hand but his hatchet; and with that he dispatched those three who, as I said before, were wounded at first and fallen, and all the rest he could come up with, and the Spaniard coming to me for a gun, I gave him one of the fowling-pieces, with which he pursued two of the savages, and wounded them both; but as he was not able to run, they both got from him into the wood, where Friday pursued them, and killed one of them; but the other was too nimble for him, and though he was wounded, yet had plunged himself into the sea, and swam with all his might off to those who were left in the canoe, which three in the canoe, with one wounded, who we know not whether he dy'd or no, were all that escaped our hands of one and twenty. The account of the rest is as follows:

3 killed at our first shot from the tree.
2 killed at the next shot.
2 killed by Friday in the boat.
2 killed by ditto, of those at first wounded.
1 killed by ditto, in the wood.
3 killed by the Spaniard.
4 killed, being found dropped here and there of their wounds, or killed by Friday in his chase of them.
4 escaped in the boat, whereof one wounded if not dead.

—

21 in all.

—

Those that were in the canoe worked hard to get out of gun-shot; and though Friday made two or three shot at them, I did not find that he hit any of them. Friday would fain have had me took one of their canoes, and pursued them; and indeed I was very anxious about their escape, least carrying the news home to their people, they should come back perhaps with two or three hundred of their canoes, and devour us by meer multitude; so I consented to pursue them by sea, and running to one of their canoes, I jumped in, and bad Friday follow me; but when I was in the canoe, I was surprized to find another poor creature lye there alive, bound hand and foot, as the Spaniard was, for the slaughter, and almost dead with fear, not knowing what the matter was; for he had not been able to look up over the side of the boat, he was ty'd so hard, neck and heels, and had been ty'd so long that he had really but little life in him.

I immediately cut the twisted flags or rushes which they had bound him with, and would have helped him up; but he could not stand or speak, but groaned most piteously, believing it seems still that he was only unbound in order to be killed.

When Friday came to him, I bade him speak to him, and tell him of his deliverance, and pulling out my bottle, made him give the poor wretch a dram, which, with the news of his being delivered, revived him, and he sat up in the boat; but when Friday came to hear him speak, and look in his face, it would have moved any one to tears, to have seen how Friday kissed him, embraced him, hugged him, cry'd, laughed, hollowed, jumped about, danced, sung, and then cry'd again, wrung his hands, beat his own face and head, and then sung and jumped about again, like a distracted creature. It was a good while before I could make him speak to me, or tell me what was the matter; but when he came a little to himself, he told me that it was his father.

It is not easy for me to express how it moved me to see what extasy and filial affection had worked in this poor savage, at the sight of his father, and of his being delivered from death; nor indeed can I describe half the extravagancies of his affection after this; for he went into the boat and out of the boat a great many times. When he went in to him, he would sit down by him, open his breast, and hold his father's head close to his bosom, half an hour together, to nourish it; then he took his arms and ankles, which were numbed and stiff with the binding, and chaffed and rubbed them with his hands, and I perceiving what the case was, gave him some rum out of my bottle to rub them with, which did them a great deal of good.

This action put an end to our pursuit of the canoe with the other savages, who were now gotten almost out of sight; and it was happy for us that we did not; for it blew so hard within two hours after, and before they could be gotten a quarter of their way, and continued blowing so hard all night, and that from the north-west, which was against them, that I could not suppose their boat could live, or that they ever reached to their own coast.

But to return to Friday, he was so busy about his father, that I could not find in my heart to take him off for some time: but after I thought he could leave him a little, I called him to me, and he came jumping and laughing, and pleased to the highest extream; then I asked him if he had given his father any bread. He shook his head, and said, 'None: ugly dog eat all up self'; so I gave him a cake of bread out of a little pouch I carry'd on purpose; I also gave him a dram for himself, but he would not taste it, but carry'd it to his father. I had in my pocket also two or three bunches of my raisins, so I gave him a handful of them for his father. He had no sooner given his father these raisins, but I saw him come out of the boat, and run away, as if he had been bewitched, he run at such a rate; for he was the swiftest fellow of his foot that ever I saw; I say, he run at such a rate, that he was out of sight, as it were, in an instant; and though I called, and hollowed too, after him, it was all one, away he went, and in a quarter of an hour I saw him come back again, though not so fast as he went; and as he came nearer, I found his pace was slacker because he had something in his hand.

When he came up to me, I found he had been quite home for an earthen jugg or pot to bring his father some fresh water, and that he had got two more cakes or loaves of bread: the bread he gave me, but the water he carry'd to his father: however, as I was very thirsty too, I took a little sup of it. This water revived his father more than all the rum or spirits I had given him; for he was just fainting with thirst.

When his father had drank, I called to him to know if there was any water left; he said yes; and I bad him give it to the poor Spaniard, who was in as much want of it as his father; and I sent one of the cakes, that Friday brought, to the Spaniard too, who was indeed very weak, and was reposing himself upon a green place under the shade of a tree; and whose limbs were also very stiff, and very much swelled with the rude bandage he had been ty'd with. When I saw that upon Friday's coming to him with the water, he sat up and drank, and took the bread, and began to eat, I went to him and gave him a handful of raisins; he looked up in my face with all the tokens of gratitude and thankfulness that could appear in any countenance; but he was so weak, notwithstanding he had so exerted himself in the fight, that he could not stand up upon his feet; he try'd to do it two or three times, but was really not able, his ankles were so swelled and so painful to him; so I bad him sit still, and caused Friday to rub his ankles, and bathe them with rum, as he had done his father's.

I observed the poor affectionate creature every two minutes, or perhaps less, all the while he was here, turned his head about, to see if his father was in the same place and posture as he left him sitting; and at last he found he was not to be seen; at which he started up, and without speaking a word, flew with that swiftness to him, that one could scarce perceive his feet to touch the ground as he went. But when he came, he only found he had laid himself down to ease his limbs; so Friday came back to me presently, and I then spoke to the Spaniard to let Friday help him up if he could, and lead him to the boat, and then he should carry him to our dwelling, where I would take care of him. But Friday, a lusty strong fellow, took the Spaniard quite up upon his back, and carry'd him away to the boat, and set him down softly upon the side or gunnel of the canoe, with his feet in the inside of it, and then lifted him quite in, and set him close to his father, and presently stepping out again, launched the boat off, and paddled it along the shore faster than I could walk, tho' the wind blew pretty hard too; so he brought them both safe into our creek; and leaving them in the boat, runs away to fetch the other canoe. As he passed me, I spoke to him, and asked him whither he went; he told me, 'Go fetch more boat'; so away he went like the wind; for sure never man or horse run like him, and he had the other canoe in the creek, almost as soon as I got to it by land; so he wafted me over, and then went to help our new guests out of the boat, which he did; but they were neither of them able to walk; so that poor Friday knew not what to do.

To remedy this, I went to work in my thought, and calling to Friday to bid them sit down on the bank while he came to me, I soon made a kind of hand-barrow to lay them on, and Friday and I carry'd them up both together upon it between us. But when we got them to the outside of our wall or fortification, we were at a worse loss than before; for it was impossible to get them over; and I was resolved not to break it down: so I set to work again; and Friday and I, in about 2 hours time, made a very handsom tent, covered with old sails, and above that with boughs of trees, being in the space without our outward fence, and between that and the grove of young wood which I had planted: and here we made them two beds of such things as I had, viz. of good rice-straw, with blankets laid upon it to lye on, and another to cover them on each bed.

My island was now peopled, and I thought my self very rich in subjects; and it was a merry reflection which I frequently made, how like a king I looked. First of all, the whole country was my own meer property; so that I had an undoubted right of dominion. 2dly, my people were perfectly subjected: I was absolute lord and lawgiver; they all owed their lives to me, and were ready to lay down their lives, if there had been occasion of it, for me. It was remarkable too, we had but three subjects, and they were of three different religions. My man Friday was a Protestant, his father was a pagan and a cannibal, and the Spaniard was a Papist: however, I allowed liberty of conscience throughout my dominions. But this is by the way.

As soon as I had secured my two weak rescued prisoners, and given them shelter, and a place to rest them upon, I began to think of making some provision for them. And the first thing I did, I ordered Friday to take a yearling goat, betwixt a kid and a goat, out of my particular flock, to be killed, when I cut off the hinder quarter, and chopping it into small pieces, I set Friday to work to boiling and stewing, and made them a very good dish, I assure you, of flesh and broth, having put some barley and rice also into the broth; and as I cooked it without doors, for I made no fire within my inner wall, so I carry'd it all into the new tent; and having set a table there for them, I sat down and eat my own dinner also with them, and, as well as I could, cheared them and encouraged them; Friday being my interpreter, especially to his father, and indeed to the Spaniard too; for the Spaniard spoke the language of the savages pretty well.

After we had dined, or rather supped, I ordered Friday to take one of the canoes, and go and fetch our muskets and other firearms, which for want of time we had left upon the place of battle, and the next day I ordered him to go and bury the dead bodies of the savages, which lay open to the sun, and would presently be offensive; and I also ordered him to bury the horrid remains of their barbarous feast, which I knew were pretty much, and which I could not think of doing my self; nay, I could not bear to see them, if I went that way: all which he punctually performed, and defaced the very appearance of the savages being there; so that when I went again, I could scarce know where it was, otherwise than by the corner of the wood pointing to the place.

I then began to enter into a little conversation with my two new subjects; and first I set Friday to enquire of his father, what he thought of the escape of the savages in that canoe, and whether we might expect a return of them with a power too great for us to resist. His first opinion was, that the savages in the boat never could live out the storm, which blew that night they went off, but must of necessity be drowned or driven south to those other shores, where they were as sure to be devoured as they were to be drowned if they were cast away; but as to what they would do if they came safe on shore, he said he knew not; but it was his opinion that they were so dreadfully frighted with the manner of their being attacked, the noise and the fire, that he believed they would tell their people they were all killed by thunder and lightning, not by the hand of man, and that the two which appeared, viz. Friday and me, were two heavenly spirits or furies, come down to destroy them, and not men with weapons. This he said he knew, because he heard them all cry out so in their language to one another, for it was impossible to them to conceive that a man could dart fire, and speak thunder, and kill at a distance without lifting up the hand, as was done now. And this old savage was in the right, for, as I understood since by other hands, the savages never attempted to go over to the island afterwards; they were so terrified with the accounts given by those four men (for it seems they did escape the sea), that they believed whoever went to that enchanted island would be destroyed with fire from the gods.

This however I knew not, and therefore was under continual apprehensions for a good while, and kept always upon my guard, me and all my army; for as we were now four of us, I would have ventured upon a hundred of them fairly in the open field at any time.

In a little time, however, no more canoes appearing, the fear of their coming wore off, and I began to take my former thoughts of a voyage to the main into consideration, being likewise assured by Friday's father, that I might depend upon good usage from their nation on his account, if I would go.

But my thoughts were a little suspended when I had a serious discourse with the Spaniard, and when I understood that there were sixteen more of his countrymen and Portuguese, who having been cast away, and made their escape to that side, lived there at peace indeed with the savages, but were very sore put to it for necessaries, and indeed for life. I asked him all the particulars of their voyage, and found they were a Spanish ship bound from the Rio de la Plata to the Havana, being directed to leave their loading there, which was chiefly hides and silver, and to bring back what European goods they could meet with there; that they had five Portuguese seamen on board, who they took out of another wreck; that five of their own men were drowned when the first ship was lost, and that these escaped thro' infinite dangers and hazards, and arrived almost starved on the cannibal coast, where they expected to have been devoured every moment.

He told me they had some arms with them, but they were perfectly useless, for that they had neither powder or ball, the washing of the sea having spoiled all their powder but a little, which they used at their first landing to provide themselves some food.

I asked him what he thought would become of them there, and if they had formed no design of making any escape. He said they had many consultations about it, but that having neither vessel, or tools to build one, or provisions of any kind, their councils always ended in tears and despair.

I asked him how he thought they would receive a proposal from me, which might tend towards an escape, and whether, if they were all here, it might not be done. I told him with freedom, I feared mostly their treachery and ill usage of me, if I put my life in their hands; for that gratitude was no inherent virtue in the nature of man; nor did men always square their dealings by the obligations they had received, so much as they did by the advantages they expected. I told him it would be very hard that I should be the instrument of their deliverance, and that they should afterwards make me their prisoner in New Spain, where an English man was certain to be made a sacrifice, what necessity, or what accident soever, brought him thither; and that I had rather be delivered up to the savages, and be devoured alive, than fall into the merciless claws of the priests, and be carry'd into the Inquisition. I added, that otherwise I was perswaded, if they were all here, we might, with so many hands, build a bark large enough to carry us all away, either to the Brasils south-ward, or to the islands or Spanish coast north-ward; but that if in requital they should, when I had put weapons into their hands, carry me by force among their own people, I might be ill used for my kindness to them, and make my case worse than it was before.

He answered with a great deal of candor and ingenuity, that their condition was so miserable, and they were so sensible of it, that he believed they would abhor the thought of using any man unkindly that should contribute to their deliverance; and that, if I pleased, he would go to them with the old man, and discourse with them about it, and return again, and bring me their answer: that he would make conditions with them upon their solemn oath, that they should be absolutely under my lead-ing, as their commander and captain, and that they should swear upon the holy sacraments and the Gospel, to be true to me, and to go to such Christian country as that I should agree to, and no other; and to be directed wholly and absolutely by my orders, 'till they were landed safely in such country as I intended; and that he would bring a contract from under their hands for that purpose.

Then he told me he would first swear to me himself that he would never stir from me as long as he lived, 'till I gave him orders; and that he would take my side to the last drop of his blood, if there should happen the least breach of faith among his country-men.

He told me they were all of them very civil honest men, and they were under the greatest distress imaginable, having neither weapons or cloaths, nor any food, but at the mercy and discretion of the savages; out of all hopes of ever returning to their own country; and that he was sure, if I would undertake their relief, they would live and die by me.

Upon these assurances, I resolved to venture to relieve them, if possible, and to send the old savage and this Spaniard over to them to treat. But when we had gotten all things in a readiness to go, the Spaniard himself started an objection, which had so much prudence in it on one hand, and so much sincerity on the other hand, that I could not but be very well satisfy'd in it; and by his advice, put off the deliverance of his comerades for at least half a year. The case was thus:

He had been with us now about a month; during which time I had let him see in what manner I had provided, with the assistance of Providence, for my support; and he saw evidently what stock of corn and rice I had laid up; which as it was more than sufficient for my self, so it was not sufficient, at least without good husbandry, for my family, now it was encreased to number four: but much less would it be sufficient, if his country-men, who were, as he said, fourteen still alive, should come over. And least of all should it be sufficient to victual our vessel, if we should build one, for a voyage to any of the Christian colonies of America. So he told me, he thought it would be more advisable to let him and the two others dig and cultivate some more land, as much as I could spare seed to sow; and that we should wait another harvest, that we might have a supply of corn for his country-men when they should come; for want might be a temptation to them to disagree, or not to think themselves delivered, otherwise than out of one difficulty into another. 'You know,' says he, 'the children of Israel, though they rejoyced at first for their being delivered out of Egypt, yet rebelled even against God Himself that delivered them, when they came to want bread in the wilderness.'

His caution was so seasonable, and his advice so good, that I could not but be very well pleased with his proposal, as well as I was satisfy'd with his fidelity. So we fell to digging all four of us, as well as the wooden tools we were furnished with permitted; and in about a month's time, by the end of which it was seed time, we had gotten as much land cured and trim'd up, as we sowed 22 bushels of barley on, and 16 jars of rice, which was in short all the seed we had to spare; nor indeed did we leave our selves barley sufficient for our own food, for the six months that we had to expect our crop, that is to say, reckoning from the time we set our seed aside for sowing; for it is not to be supposed it is six months in the ground in that country.

Having now society enough, and our number being sufficient to put us out of fear of the savages, if they had come, unless their number had been very great, we went freely all over the island,

where-ever we found occasion; and as here we had our escape or
deliverance upon our thoughts, it was impossible, at least for me,
to have the means of it out of mine; to this purpose, I marked
out several trees which I thought fit for our work, and I set
Friday and his father to cutting them down; and then I caused
the Spaniard, to whom I imparted my thought on that affair, to
oversee and direct their work. I shewed them with what in-
defatigable pains I had hewed a large tree into single planks, and
I caused them to do the like, till they had made about a dozen
large planks of good oak, near 2 foot broad, 35 foot long, and
from 2 inches to 4 inches thick: what prodigious labour it took
up, any one may imagine.

At the same time I contrived to encrease my little flock of tame
goats as much as I could; and to this purpose, I made Friday and
the Spaniard go out one day, and my self with Friday the next
day; for we took our turns: and by this means we got above 20
young kids to breed up with the rest; for when-ever we shot the
dam, we saved the kids, and added them to our flock. But above
all, the season for curing the grapes coming on, I caused such a
prodigious quantity to be hung up in the sun, that I believe, had
we been at Alicant,[50] where the raisins of the sun are cured, we
could have filled 60 or 80 barrels; and these with our bread was
a great part of our food, and very good living too, I assure you;
for it is an exceeding nourishing food.

It was now harvest, and our crop in good order; it was not the
most plentiful encrease I had seen in the island, but, however, it
was enough to answer our end; for from our 22 bushels of barley
we brought in and thrashed out above 220 bushels; and the like
in proportion of the rice, which was store enough for our food
to the next harvest, tho' all the 16 Spaniards had been on shore
with me; or if we had been ready for a voyage, it would very
plentifully have victualled our ship, to have carry'd us to any
part of the world, that is to say, of America.

When we had thus housed and secured our magazine of corn,
we fell to work to make more wicker work, viz. great baskets in
which we kept it; and the Spaniard was very handy and dexterous at this part, and often blamed me that I did not make some
things, for defence, of this kind of work; but I saw no need of it.

And now having a full supply of food for all the guests I expected, I gave the Spaniard leave to go over to the main, to see what he could do with those he had left behind him there. I gave him a strict charge in writing not to bring any man with him, who would not first swear in the presence of himself and of the old savage that he would no way injure, fight with, or attack the person he should find in the island, who was so kind to send for them in order to their deliverance; but that they would stand by and defend him against all such attempts, and where-ever they went, would be entirely under and subjected to his commands; and that this should be put in writing, and signed with their hands. How we were to have this done, when I knew they had neither pen or ink, that indeed was a question which we never asked.

Under these instructions, the Spaniard and the old savage, the father of Friday, went away in one of the canoes, which they might be said to come in, or rather were brought in, when they came as prisoners to be devoured by the savages.

I gave each of them a musket with a firelock on it, and about eight charges of powder and ball, charging them to be very good husbands of both, and not to use either of them but upon urgent occasion.

This was a chearful work, being the first measures used by me in view of my deliverance for now 27 years and some days. I gave them provisions of bread, and of dry'd grapes, sufficient for themselves for many days, and sufficient for all their country-men for about eight days time; and wishing them a good voyage, I see them go, agreeing with them about a signal they should hang out at their return, by which I should know them again, when they came back, at a distance, before they came on shore.

They went away with a fair gale on the day that the moon was at full by my account, in the month of October: but as for an exact reckoning of days, after I had once lost it, I could never recover it again; nor had I kept even the number of years so punctually as to be sure that I was right, tho' as it proved, when I afterwards examined my account, I found I had kept a true reckoning of years.

It was no less than eight days I had waited for them, when a

strange and unforeseen accident intervened, of which the like
has not perhaps been heard of in history. I was fast asleep in my
hutch one morning, when my man Friday came running in to
me, and called aloud, 'Master, master, they are come, they are
come.'

I jumped up, and regardless of danger, I went out, as soon as I
could get my cloaths on, thro' my little grove, which by the way
was by this time grown to be a very thick wood; I say, regardless
of danger, I went without my arms, which was not my custom
to do : but I was surprized, when turning my eyes to the sea, I
presently saw a boat at about a league and an half's distance,
standing in for the shore, with a shoulder of mutton sail, as they
call it; and the wind blowing pretty fair to bring them in; also
I observed presently that they did not come from that side which
the shore lay on, but from the southernmost end of the island.
Upon this I called Friday in, and bid him lie close, for these were
not the people we looked for, and that we might not know yet
whether they were friends or enemies.

In the next place, I went in to fetch my perspective glass, to see
what I could make of them; and having taken the ladder out, I
climbed up to the top of the hill, as I used to do when I was
apprehensive of any thing, and to take my view the plainer without being discovered.

I had scarce set my foot on the hill, when my eye plainly discovered a ship lying at an anchor, at about two leagues and an
half's distance from me south-south-east, but not above a league
and an half from the shore. By my observation it appeared plainly
to be an English ship, and the boat appeared to be an English
long-boat.

I cannot express the confusion I was in, tho' the joy of seeing
a ship, and one who I had reason to believe was manned by my
own country-men, and consequently friends, was such as I cannot describe; but yet I had some secret doubts hung about me,
I cannot tell from whence they came, bidding me keep upon my
guard. In the first place, it occurred to me to consider what business an English ship could have in that part of the world, since
it was not the way to or from any part of the world where the
English had any traffick; and I knew there had been no storms

to drive them in there, as in distress; and that if they were English really, it was most probable that they were here upon no good design; and that I had better continue as I was, than fall into the hands of thieves and murtherers.

Let no man despise the secret hints and notices of danger, which sometimes are given him, when he may think there is no possibility of its being real. That such hints and notices are given us, I believe few that have made any observations of things can deny; that they are certain discoveries of an invisible world, and a converse of spirits, we cannot doubt; and if the tendency of them seems to be to warn us of danger, why should we not suppose they are from some friendly agent, whether supreme, or inferior, and subordinate, is not the question; and that they are given for our good?

The present question abundantly confirms me in the justice of this reasoning; for had I not been made cautious by this secret admonition, come it from whence it will, I had been undone inevitably, and in a far worse condition than before, as you will see presently.

I had not kept my self long in this posture, but I saw the boat draw near the shore, as if they looked for a creek to thrust in at for the convenience of landing; however, as they did not come quite far enough, they did not see the little inlet where I formerly landed my rafts; but run their boat on shore upon the beach, at about half a mile from me, which was very happy for me; for otherwise they would have landed just, as I may say, at my door, and would soon have beaten me out of my castle, and perhaps have plundered me of all I had.

When they were on shore I was fully satisfy'd that they were English men; at least, most of them; one or two I thought were Dutch, but it did not prove so. There were in all eleven men, whereof three of them I found were unarmed, and, as I thought, bound; and when the first four or five of them were jumped on shore, they took those three out of the boat as prisoners. One of the three I could perceive using the most passionate gestures of entreaty, affliction, and despair, even to a kind of extravagance; the other two I could perceive lifted up their hands sometimes, and appeared concerned indeed, but not to such a degree as the first.

I was perfectly confounded at the sight, and knew not what the meaning of it should be. Friday called out to me in English, as well as he could, 'O master ! you see English mans eat prisoner as well as savage mans.' 'Why,' says I, 'Friday, do you think they are a going to eat them then?' 'Yes,' says Friday, 'they will eat them.' 'No, no,' says I, 'Friday, I am afraid they will murther them indeed, but you may be sure they will not eat them.'

All this while I had no thought of what the matter really was, but stood trembling with the horror of the sight, expecting every moment when the three prisoners should be killed; nay, once I saw one of the villains lift up his arm with a great cutlash, as the seamen call it, or sword, to strike one of the poor men; and I expected to see him fall every moment, at which all the blood in my body seemed to run chill in my veins.

I wished heartily now for my Spaniard, and the savage that was gone with him; or that I had any way to have come undiscovered within shot of them, that I might have rescued the three men; for I saw no fire arms they had among them; but it fell out to my mind another way.

After I had observed the outrageous usage of the three men by the insolent seamen, I observed the fellows run scattering about the land, as if they wanted to see the country. I observed that the three other men had liberty to go also where they pleased; but they sat down all three upon the ground, very pensive, and looked like men in despair.

This put me in mind of the first time when I came on shore, and began to look about me; how I gave my self over for lost; how wildly I looked round me; what dreadful apprehensions I had; and how I lodged in the tree all night for fear of being devoured by wild beasts.

As I knew nothing that night of the supply I was to receive by the providential driving of the ship nearer the land, by the storms and tide, by which I have since been so long nourished and supported; so these three poor desolate men knew nothing how certain of deliverance and supply they were, how near it was to them, and how effectually and really they were in a condition of safety, at the same time that they thought themselves lost, and their case desperate.

So little do we see before us in the world, and so much reason
have we to depend chearfully upon the great Maker of the
world, that He does not leave his creatures so absolutely destitute,
but that in the worst circumstances they have always something
to be thankful for, and sometimes are nearer their deliverance
than they imagine; nay, are even brought to their deliverance by
the means by which they seem to be brought to their destruction.

It was just at the top of high-water when these people came
on shore, and while partly they stood parlying with the prisoners
they brought, and partly while they rambled about to see what
kind of a place they were in, they had carelessly staid till the
tide was spent and the water was ebbed considerably away, leaving their boat a-ground.

They had left two men in the boat, who, as I found afterwards,
having drank a little too much brandy, fell a-sleep; however, one
of them waking sooner than the other, and finding the boat too
fast a-ground for him to stir it, hollowed for the rest who were
straggling about, upon which they all soon came to the boat; but
it was past all their strength to launch her, the boat being very
heavy, and the shore on that side being a soft ousy sand, almost
like a quick-sand.

In this condition, like true seamen who are perhaps the least of
all mankind given to fore-thought, they gave it over, and away
they strolled about the country again; and I heard one of them
say aloud to another, calling them off from the boat, 'Why, let
her alone, Jack, can't ye, she will float next tide'; by which I was
fully confirmed in the main enquiry, of what countrymen they
were.

All this while I kept myself very close, not once daring to stir
out of my castle, any farther than to my place of observation,
near the top of the hill; and very glad I was, to think how well
it was fortify'd. I knew it was no less than ten hours before the
boat could be on float again, and by that time it would be dark,
and I might be at more liberty to see their motions, and to hear
their discourse, if they had any.

In the mean time, I fitted my self up for a battle, as before;
though with more caution, knowing I had to do with another

kind of enemy than I had at first: I ordered Friday also, who I had made an excellent marksman with his gun, to load himself with arms: I took my self two fowling-pieces, and gave him three muskets. My figure indeed was very fierce; I had my formidable goat-skin coat on, with the great cap I have mentioned, a naked sword by my side, two pistols in my belt, and a gun upon each shoulder.

It was my design, as I said above, not to have made any attempt till it was dark: but about two a clock, being the heat of the day, I found that in short they were all gone straggling into the woods, and, as I thought, were laid down to sleep. The three poor distressed men, too anxious for their condition to get any sleep, were however set down under the shelter of a great tree, at about a quarter of a mile from me, and, as I thought, out of sight of any of the rest.

Upon this I resolved to discover my self to them, and learn something of their condition. Immediately I marched in the figure as above, my man Friday at a good distance behind me, as formidable for his arms as I, but not making quite so staring a spectre-like figure as I did.

I came as near them undiscovered as I could, and then, before any of them saw me, I called aloud to them in Spanish, 'What are ye, gentlemen?'

They started up at the noise, but were ten times more confounded when they saw me, and the uncouth figure that I made. They made no answer at all, but I thought I perceived them just going to fly from me, when I spoke to them in English: 'Gentlemen,' said I, 'do not be surprized at me; perhaps you may have a friend near you when you did not expect it.' 'He must be sent directly from heaven then,' said one of them very gravely to me, and pulling off his hat at the same time to me, 'for our condition is past the help of man.' 'All help is from heaven, sir,' said I. 'But can you put a stranger in the way how to help you, for you seem to me to be in some great distress? I saw you when you landed, and when you seemed to make applications to the brutes that came with you, I saw one of them lift up his sword to kill you.'

The poor man, with tears running down his face, and trembling, looking like one astonished, returned, 'Am I talking to god or man! Is it a real man, or an angel!' 'Be in no fear about that, sir,' said I, 'if God had sent an angel to relieve you, he would have come better cloathed, and armed after another manner than you see me in; pray lay aside your fears, I am a man, an Englishman, and disposed to assist you, you see; I have one servant only; we have arms and ammunition; tell us freely, can we serve you? — What is your case?'

'Our case,' said he, 'sir, is too long to tell you, while our murtherers are so near; but in short, sir, I was commander of that ship, my men have mutinied against me; they have been hardly prevailed on not to murther me, and at last have set me on shore in this desolate place, with these two men with me, one my mate, the other a passenger, where we expected to perish, believing the place to be uninhabited, and know not yet what to think of it.'

'Where are those brutes, your enemies,' said I, 'do you know where they are gone?' 'There they lye, sir,' said he, pointing to a thicket of trees; 'my heart trembles, for fear they have seen us, and heard you speak; if they have, they will certainly murther us all.'

'Have they any fire-arms?' said I. He answered they had only two pieces, and one which they left in the boat. 'Well then,' said I, 'leave the rest to me; I see they are all asleep, it is an easie thing to kill them all; but shall we rather take them prisoners?' He told me there were two desperate villains among them, that it was scarce safe to shew any mercy to; but if they were secured, he believed all the rest would return to their duty. I asked him which they were. He told me he could not at that distance describe them; but he would obey my orders in any thing I would direct. 'Well,' says I, 'let us retreat out of their view or hearing, least they awake,' and we will resolve further'; so they willingly went back with me, till the woods covered us from them.

'Look you, sir,' said I, 'if I venture upon your deliverance, are you willing to make two conditions with me?' He anticipated my proposals, by telling me that both he and the ship, if recovered, should be wholly directed and commanded by me in every thing; and if the ship was not recovered, he would live and dye with me in what part of the world soever I would send him; and the two other men said the same.

'Well,' says I, 'my conditions are but two. 1. That while you stay on this island with me, you will not pretend to any authority here; and if I put arms into your hands, you will upon all occasions give them up to me, and do no prejudice to me or mine upon this island, and in the mean time be governed by my orders.

'2. That if the ship is or may be recovered, you will carry me and my man to England passage free.'

He gave me all the assurances that the invention and faith of man could devise, that he would comply with these most reasonable demands, and besides would owe his life to me, and acknowledge it upon all occasions as long as he lived.

'Well then,' said I, 'here are three muskets for you, with powder and ball; tell me next what you think is proper to be done.' He shewed all the testimony of his gratitude that he was able; but offered to be wholly guided by me. I told him I thought it was hard venturing any thing; but the best method I could think of was to fire upon them at once, as they lay; and if any was not killed at the first volley, and offered to submit, we might save them, and so put it wholly upon God's providence to direct the shot.

He said very modestly, that he was loath to kill them, if he could help it, but that those two were incorrigible villains, and had been the authors of all the mutiny in the ship, and if they escaped, we should be undone still; for they would go on board, and bring the whole ship's company, and destroy us all. 'Well then,' says I, 'necessity legitimates my advice; for it is the only way to save our lives.' However, seeing him still cautious of shedding blood, I told him they should go themselves, and manage as they found convenient.

In the middle of this discourse, we heard some of them awake, and soon after we saw two of them on their feet. I asked him if either of them were of the men who he had said were the heads of the mutiny. He said, no. 'Well then,' said I, 'you may let them escape, and Providence seems to have wakned them on purpose to save themselves. Now,' says I, 'if the rest escape you, it is your fault.'

Animated with this, he took the musket I had given him in his hand and a pistol in his belt, and his two comerades with him, with each man a piece in his hand. The two men who were with him, going first, made some noise, at which one of the seamen who was awake turned about, and seeing them coming, cry'd out to the rest; but it was too late then; for the moment he cry'd out, they fired; I mean the two men, the captain wisely reserving his own piece. They had so well aimed their shot at the men they knew, that one of them was killed on the spot, and the other very much wounded; but not being dead, he started up upon his feet, and called eagerly for help to the other; but the captain stepping to him, told him, 'twas too late to cry for help, he should call upon God to forgive his villany, and with that word knocked him down with the stock of his musket, so that he never spoke more. There were three more in the company, and one of them was also slightly wounded. By this time I was come, and when they saw their danger, and that it was in vain to resist, they begged for mercy. The captain told them he would spare their lives, if they would give him any assurance of their abhorrence of the treachery they had been guilty of, and would swear to be faithful to him in recovering the ship, and afterwards in carrying her back to Jamaica, from whence they came. They gave him all the protestations of their sincerity that could be desired, and he was willing to believe them, and spare their lives, which I was not against, only that I obliged him to keep them bound hand and foot while they were upon the island.

While this was doing, I sent Friday with the captain's mate to the boat, with orders to secure her and bring away the oars and sail, which they did; and by and by, three straggling men that were (happily for them) parted from the rest, came back upon hearing the guns fired, and seeing their captain, who before was their prisoner, now their conqueror, they submitted to be bound also; and so our victory was compleat.

It now remained that the captain and I should enquire into one another's circumstances. I began first, and told him my whole history, which he heard with an attention even to amazement; and particularly at the wonderful manner of my being furnished with provisions and ammunition; and indeed, as my story is a whole collection of wonders, it affected him deeply; but when he

reflected from thence upon himself, and how I seemed to have
been preserved there on purpose to save his life, the tears ran
down his face, and he could not speak a word more.

After this communication was at an end, I carry'd him and
his two men into my apartment, leading them in just where I
came out, viz. at the top of the house, where I refreshed them
with such provisions as I had, and shewed them all the contrivances I had made during my long, long inhabiting that place.

All I shewed them, all I said to them, was perfectly amazing;
but above all, the captain admired my fortification, and how perfectly I had concealed my retreat with a grove of trees, which
having been now planted near twenty years, and the trees growing much faster than in England, was become a little wood, and
so thick that it was unpassable in any part of it, but at that one
side where I had reserved my little winding passage into it. I told
him this was my castle and my residence, but that I had a seat
in the country, as most princes have, whither I could retreat
upon occasion, and I would shew him that too another time; but
at present our business was to consider how to recover the ship.
He agreed with me as to that; but told me he was perfectly at a
loss what measures to take; for that there were still six and
twenty hands on board, who having entred into a cursed conspiracy, by which they had all forfeited their lives to the law,
would be hardened in it now by desperation; and would carry it
on, knowing that if they were reduced, they should be brought
to the gallows, as soon as they came to England, or to any of the
English colonies; and that therefore there would be no attacking
them with so small a number as we were.

I mused for some time upon what he had said, and found it
was a very rational conclusion; and that therefore something was
to be resolved on very speedily, as well to draw the men on board
into some snare for their surprize, as to prevent their landing
upon us, and destroying us; upon this it presently occurred to
me, that in a little while the ship's crew, wondring what was
become of their comrades and of the boat, would certainly come
on shore in their other boat, to see for them, and that then perhaps they might come armed, and be too strong for us; this he
allowed was rational.

Upon this, I told him the first thing we had to do was to stave the boat which lay upon the beach, so that they might not carry her off; and taking everything out of her, leave her so far useless as not to be fit to swim; accordingly we went on board, took the arms which were left on board out of her, and whatever else we found there, which was a bottle of brandy, and another of rum, a few bisket cakes, a horn of powder, and a great lump of sugar in a piece of canvas; the sugar was five or six pounds; all which was very welcome to me, especially the brandy and sugar, of which I had had none left for many years.

When we had carry'd all these things on shore (the oars, mast, sail, and rudder of the boat were carry'd away before, as above) we knocked a great hole in her bottom, that if they had come strong enough to master us, yet they could not carry off the boat.

Indeed, it was not much in my thoughts that we could be able to recover the ship; but my view was that if they went away without the boat, I did not much question to make her fit again, to carry us away to the Leeward Islands, and call upon our friends, the Spaniards, in my way, for I had them still in my thoughts.

While we were thus preparing our designs, and had first by main strength heaved the boat up upon the beach, so high that the tide would not fleet her off at high-water-mark; and besides, had broke a hole in her bottom, too big to be quickly stopped, and were sat down musing what we should do; we heard the ship fire a gun, and saw her make a waft with her antient, as a signal for the boat to come on board; but no boat stirred; and they fired several times, making other signals for the boat.

At last, when all their signals and firing proved fruitless, and they found the boat did not stir, we saw them, by the help of my glasses, hoist another boat out, and row towards the shore; and we found as they approached that there was no less than ten men in her, and that they had fire-arms with them.

As the ship lay almost two leagues from the shore, we had a full view of them as they came, and a plain sight of the men, even of their faces, because the tide having set them a little to the east of the other boat, they rowed up under shore, to come to the same place where the other had landed, and where the boat lay.

By this means, I say, we had a full view of them, and the captain knew the persons and characters of all the men in the boat, of whom he said that there were three very honest fellows, who he was sure were led into this conspiracy by the rest, being over-powered and frighted.

But that as for the boatswain, who it seems was the chief officer among them, and all the rest, they were as outragious as any of the ship's crew, and were no doubt made desperate in their new enterprize, and terribly apprehensive he was that they would be too powerful for us.

I smiled at him, and told him that men in our circumstances were past the operation of fear: that seeing almost every condition that could be, was better than that which we were supposed to be in, we ought to expect that the consequence, whether death or life, would be sure to be a deliverance. I asked him what he thought of the circumstances of my life, and whether a deliverance were not worth venturing for. 'And where, sir,' said I, 'is your belief of my being preserved here on purpose to save your life, which elevated you a little while ago? For my part,' said I, 'there seems to be but one thing amiss in all the prospect of it.' 'What's that?' says he. 'Why,' said I, ''tis that as you say, there are three or four honest fellows among them, which should be spared; had they been all of the wicked part of the crew, I should have thought God's providence had singled them out to deliver them into your hands; for depend upon it, every man of them that comes a-shore are our own, and shall die or live as they behave to us.'

As I spoke this with a raised voice and chearful countenance, I found it greatly encouraged him; so we set vigorously to our business. We had, upon the first appearance of the boat's coming from the ship, considered of separating our prisoners, and had indeed secured them effectually.

Two of them, of whom the captain was less assured than ordinary, I sent with Friday and one of the three (delivered men) to my cave, where they were remote enough, and out of danger of being heard or discovered, or of finding their way out of the woods, if they could have delivered themselves. Here they left them bound, but gave them provisions, and promised them if they continued there quietly, to give them their liberty in a day or two; but that if they attempted their escape, they should be put to death without mercy. They promised faithfully to bear their confinement with patience, and were very thankful that they had such good usage as to have provisions and a light left them; for Friday gave them candles (such as we made our selves) for their comfort; and they did not know but that he stood sentinel over them at the entrance.

The other prisoners had better usage; two of them were kept pinioned indeed, because the captain was not free to trust them; but the other two were taken into my service upon their captain's recommendation, and upon their solemnly engaging to live and die with us; so with them and the three honest men, we were seven men, well armed; and I made no doubt we shou'd be able to deal well enough with the ten that were a coming, considering that the captain had said there were three or four honest men among them also.

As soon as they got to the place where their other boat lay, they run their boat in to the beach, and came all on shore, haling the boat up after them, which I was glad to see; for I was afraid they would rather have left the boat at an anchor, some distance from the shore, with some hands in her to guard her; and so we should not be able to seize the boat.

Being on shore, the first thing they did, they ran all to their other boat, and it was easy to see that they were under a great surprize, to find her stripped as above, of all that was in her, and a great hole in her bottom.

After they had mused a while upon this, they set up two or three great shouts, hollowing with all their might, to try if they could make their companions hear; but all was to no purpose. Then they came all close in a ring, and fired a volley of their small arms, which indeed we heard, and the ecchos made the woods ring; but it was all one, those in the cave we were sure could not hear, and those in our keeping, though they heard it well enough, yet durst give no answer to them.

They were so astonished at the surprize of this, that as they told us afterwards, they resolved to go all on board again to their ship, and let them know that the men were all murthered, and the long-boat staved; accordingly they immediately launched their boat again, and gat all of them on board.

The captain was terribly amazed and even confounded at this, believing they would go on board the ship again, and set sail, giving their comrades for lost, and so he should still lose the ship, which he was in hopes we should have recovered; but he was quickly as much frighted the other way.

They had not been long put off with the boat, but we perceived them all coming on shore again; but with this new measure in their conduct, which it seems they consulted together upon, viz. to leave three men in the boat, and the rest to go on shore, and go up into the country to look for their fellows.

This was a great disappointment to us; for now we were at a loss what to do; for our seizing those seven men on shore would be no advantage to us, if we let the boat escape; because they would then row away to the ship, and then the rest of them would be sure to weigh and set sail, and so our recovering the ship would be lost.

However, we had no remedy but to wait and see what the issue of things might present. The seven men came on shore, and the three who remained in the boat put her off to a good distance from the shore, and came to an anchor to wait for them; so it was impossible for us to come at them in the boat.

Those that came on shore kept close together, marching towards the top of the little hill under which my habitation lay; and we could see them plainly, though they could not perceive us. We could have been very glad they would have come nearer to us, so that we might have fired at them, or that they would have gone farther off, that we might have come aboard.

But when they were come to the brow of the hill, where they could see a great way into the valleys and woods, which lay towards the north-east part, and where the island lay lowest, they shouted and hollowed till they were weary; and not caring it seems to venture far from the shore, nor far from one another, they sat down together under a tree, to consider of it. Had they thought fit to have gone to sleep there, as the other party of them had done, they had done the jobb for us; but they were too full of apprehensions of danger to venture to go to sleep, though they could not tell what the danger was they had to fear neither.

The captain made a very just proposal to me, upon this consultation of theirs, viz. that perhaps they would all fire a volley again, to endeavour to make their fellows hear, and that we should all sally upon them, just at the juncture when their pieces were all discharged, and they would certainly yield, and we should have them without blood-shed. I liked the proposal, provided it was done while we were near enough to come up to them, before they could load their pieces again.

But this event did not happen, and we lay still a long time, very irresolute what course to take; at length I told them, there would be nothing to be done in my opinion till night, and then if they did not return to the boat, perhaps we might find a way to get between them and the shore, and so might use some stratagem with them in the boat to get them on shore.

We waited a great while, though very impatient for their removing; and were very uneasy, when after long consultations, we saw them start all up and march down toward the sea. It seems they had such dreadful apprehensions upon them of the danger of the place, that they resolved to go on board the ship again, give their companions over for lost, and so go on with their intended voyage with the ship.

As soon as I perceived them go towards the shore, I imagined it to be as it really was, that they had given over their search, and were for going back again; and the captain, as soon as I told him my thoughts, was ready to sink at the apprehensions of it; but I presently thought of a stratagem to fetch them back again, and which answered my end to a tittle.

I ordered Friday and the captain's mate to go over the little creek westward, towards the place where the savages came on shore when Friday was rescued; and as soon as they came to a little rising ground, at about half a mile distance, I bad them hollow as loud as they could, and wait till they found the seamen heard them; that as soon as ever they heard the seamen answer them, they should return it again, and then keeping out of sight, take a round, always answering when the other hollowed, to draw them as far into the island, and among the woods, as possible, and then wheel about again to me, by such ways as I directed them.

They were just going into the boat, when Friday and the mate hollowed, and they presently heard them, and answering, run along the shore westward, towards the voice they heard, where they were presently stopped by the creek, where the water being up, they could not get over, and called for the boat to come up and set them over, as indeed I expected.

When they had set themselves over, I observed that the boat being gone a good way into the creek, and as it were, in a harbour within the land, they took one of the three men out of her to go along with them, and left only two in the boat, having fastned her to the stump of a little tree on the shore.

This was what I wished for, and immediately leaving Friday and the captain's mate to their business, I took the rest with me, and crossing the creek out of their sight, we surprized the two men before they were aware; one of them lying on shore, and the other being in the boat; the fellow on shore was between sleeping and waking, and going to start up; the captain, who was foremost, ran in upon him and knocked him down, and then called out to him in the boat, to yield, or he was a dead man.

There needed very few arguments to perswade a single man to yield, when he saw five men upon him, and his comrade knocked down; besides, this was, it seems, one of the three who were not so hearty in the mutiny as the rest of the crew, and therefore was easily perswaded, not only to yield, but afterwards to joyn very sincerely with us.

In the mean time, Friday and the captain's mate so well managed their business with the rest, that they drew them by hollowing and answering, from one hill to another, and from one wood to another, till they not only heartily tyred them, but left them where they were very sure they could not reach back to the boat before it was dark; and indeed they were heartily tyred themselves also by the time they came back to us.

We had nothing now to do but to watch for them in the dark, and to fall upon them, so as to make sure work with them.

It was several hours after Friday came back to me, before they came back to their boat; and we could hear the foremost of them long before they came quite up, calling to those behind to come along, and could also hear them answer and complain how lame and tyred they were, and not able to come any faster, which was very welcome news to us.

At length they came up to the boat; but 'tis impossible to express their confusion, when they found the boat fast a-ground in the creek, the tide ebbed out, and their two men gone. We could hear them call to one another in a most lamentable manner, telling one another they were gotten into an inchanted island; that either there were inhabitants in it, and they should all be murthered, or else there were devils and spirits in it, and they should be all carry'd away and devoured.

They hallowed again, and called their two comerades by their names a great many times, but no answer. After some time, we could see them, by the little light there was, run about wringing their hands like men in despair; and that sometimes they would go and sit down in the boat to rest themselves, then come ashore again, and walk about again, and so over the same thing again.

My men would fain have me give them leave to fall upon them at once in the dark; but I was willing to take them at some advantage, so to spare them, and kill as few of them as I could; and especially I was unwilling to hazard the killing any of our own men, knowing the other were very well armed. I resolved to wait to see if they did not separate; and therefore to make sure of them, I drew my ambuscade nearer, and ordered Friday and the captain to creep upon their hands and feet as close to the ground as they could that they might not be discovered, and get as near them as they could possibly, before they offered to fire.

They had not been long in that posture, but that the boatswain, who was the principal ringleader of the mutiny, and had now shewn himself the most dejected and dispirited of all the rest, came walking towards them with two more of their crew; the captain was so eager, as having this principal rogue so much in his power, that he could hardly have patience to let him come so near as to be sure of him; for they only heard his tongue before: but when they came nearer, the captain and Friday, starting up on their feet, let fly at them.

The boatswain was killed upon the spot, the next man was shot into the body and fell just by him, tho' he did not die 'till an hour or two after; and the third run for it.

At the noise of the fire, I immediately advanced with my whole army, which was now 8 men, viz. my self *generalissimo*, Friday my lieutenant-general, the captain and his two men, and the three prisoners of war, who we had trusted with arms.

We came upon them indeed in the dark, so that they could not see our number; and I made the man we had left in the boat, who was now one of us, call to them by name, to try if I could bring them to a parley, and so might perhaps reduce them to terms, which fell out just as we desired : for indeed it was easy to think, as their condition then was, they would be very willing to capitulate; so he calls out as loud as he could, to one of them, 'Tom Smith, Tom Smith!' Tom Smith answered immediately, 'Who 's that, Robinson?' for it seems he knew his voice. T'other answered, 'Ay, ay; for God's sake, Tom Smith, throw down your arms and yield, or you are all dead men this moment.'

'Who must we yield to? where are they?' says Smith again. 'Here they are,' says he, 'here 's our captain, and fifty men with him, have been hunting you this two hours; the boatswain is killed, Will Frye is wounded, and I am a prisoner; and if you do not yield, you are all lost.'

'Will they give us quarter then,' says Tom Smith, 'and we will yield?' 'I 'll go and ask, if you promise to yield,' says Robinson; so he asked the captain, and the captain then calls himself out, 'You, Smith, you know my voice, if you lay down your arms immediately, and submit, you shall have your lives all but Will. Atkins.'

Upon this, Will. Atkins cry'd out, 'For God's sake, captain, give me quarter, what have I done? They have been all as bad as I'; which by the way was not true neither; for it seems this Will. Atkins was the first man that laid hold of the captain, when they first mutiny'd, and used him barbarously, in tying his hands and giving him injurious language. However, the captain told him he must lay down his arms at discretion, and trust to the governour's mercy, by which he meant me; for they all called me governour.

In a word, they all laid down their arms, and begged their
lives; and I sent the man that had parley'd with them, and two
more, who bound them all; and then my great army of 50 men,
which, particularly with those three, were all but eight, came
up and seized upon them all, and upon their boat, only that I
kept my self and one more out of sight, for reasons of state.

Our next work was to repair the boat, and think of seizing
the ship; and as for the captain, now he had leisure to parley
with them, he expostulated with them upon the villany of their
practices with him, and at length upon the farther wickedness of
their design, and how certainly it must bring them to misery and
distress in the end, and perhaps to the gallows.

They all appeared very penitent, and begged hard for their
lives; as for that, he told them, they were none of his prisoners,
but the commander's of the island; that they thought they had
set him on shore in a barren uninhabited island, but it had
pleased God so to direct them, that the island was inhabited, and
that the governour was an English man; that he might hang
them all there, if he pleased; but as he had given them all quarter,
he supposed he would send them to England to be dealt with
there as justice required, except Atkins, who he was commanded by the governour to advise to prepare for death; for that
he would be hanged in the morning.

Though this was all a fiction of his own, yet it had its desired
effect; Atkins fell upon his knees to beg the captain to inter-
ceed with the governour for his life; and all the rest beg'd of him
for God's sake, that they might not be sent to England.

It now occurred to me that the time of our deliverance was
come, and that it would be a most easy thing to bring these
fellows in to be hearty in getting possession of the ship; so I
retired in the dark from them, that they might not see what kind
of a governour they had, and called the captain to me; when I
called, as at a good distance, one of the men was ordered to speak
again, and say to the captain, 'Captain, the commander calls for
you'; and presently the captain reply'd, 'Tell his Excellency, I
am just a coming.' This more perfectly amused them; and they
all believed that the commander was just by with his fifty men.

Upon the captain's coming to me, I told him my project for

seizing the ship, which he liked of wonderfully well, and resolved to put it in execution the next morning.

But in order to execute it with more art, and secure of success, I told him we must divide the prisoners, and that he should go and take Atkins and two more of the worst of them, and send them pinioned to the cave where the others lay: this was committed to Friday and the two men who came on shore with the captain.

They conveyed them to the cave, as to a prison; and it was indeed a dismal place, especially to men in their condition.

The other I ordered to my bower, as I called it, of which I have given a full description; and as it was fenced in, and they pinioned, the place was secure enough, considering they were upon their behaviour.

To these in the morning I sent the captain, who was to enter into a parley with them, in a word to try them, and tell me whether he thought they might be trusted or no, to go on board and surprize the ship. He talked to them of the injury done him; of the condition they were brought to; and that though the governour had given them quarter for their lives as to the present action, yet that if they were sent to England, they would all be hanged in chains, to be sure; but that if they would join in so just an attempt as to recover the ship, he would have the governour's engagement for their pardon.

Any one may guess how readily such a proposal would be accepted by men in their condition; they fell down on their knees to the captain, and promised, with the deepest imprecations, that they would be faithful to him to the last drop, and that they should owe their lives to him, and would go with him all over the world, that they would own him for a father to them as long as they lived.

'Well,' says the captain, 'I must go and tell the governor what you say, and see what I can do to bring him to consent to it.' So he brought me an account of the temper he found them in; and that he verily believed they would be faithful.

However, that we might be very secure, I told him he should go back again, and choose out those five and tell them, they might see that he did not want men, that he would take out those five to be his assistants, and that the governour would keep the other two, and the three that were sent prisoners to the castle (my cave), as hostages for the fidelity of those five; and that if they proved unfaithful in the execution, the five hostages should be hanged in chains alive upon the shore.

This looked severe, and convinced them that the governour was in earnest; however, they had no way left them but to accept it; and it was now the business of the prisoners, as much as of the captain, to perswade the other five to do their duty.

Our strength was now thus ordered for the expedition: 1. The captain, his mate, and passenger. 2. Then the two prisoners of the first gang, to whom, having their characters from the captain, I had given their liberty, and trusted them with arms. 3. The other two who I had kept till now in my bower, pinioned; but upon the captain's motion, had now released. 4. These five released at last: so that they were twelve in all, besides five we kept prisoners in the cave, for hostages.

I asked the captain if he was willing to venture with these hands on board the ship; for as for me and my man Friday, I did not think it was proper for us to stir, having seven men left behind; and it was employment enough for us to keep them assunder and supply them with victuals.

As to the five in the cave, I resolved to keep them fast, but Friday went in twice a day to them, to supply them with necessaries; and I made the other two carry provisions to a certain distance, where Friday was to take it.

When I shewed my self to the two hostages, it was with the captain, who told them I was the person the governour had ordered to look after them, and that it was the governour's pleasure they should not stir any where, but by my direction; that if they did, they should be fetched into the castle, and be lay'd in irons; so that as we never suffered them to see me as governour, so I now appeared as another person, and spoke of the governour, the garrison, the castle, and the like, upon all occasions.

The captain now had no difficulty before him, but to furnish his two boats, stop the breach of one, and man them. He made his passenger captain of one, with four other men; and himself, and his mate, and five more, went in the other: and they contrived their business very well; for they came up to the ship about midnight. As soon as they came within call of the ship, he made Robinson hale them, and tell them they had brought off the men and the boat, but that it was a long time before they had found them, and the like; holding them in a chat 'till they came to the ship's side; when the captain and the mate, entring first with their arms, immediately knocked down the second mate and carpenter with the but-end of their muskets, being very faithfully seconded by their men; they secured all the rest that were upon the main and quarter decks, and began to fasten the hatches to keep them down who were below, when the other boat and their men, entring at the fore chains, secured the forecastle of the ship, and the scuttle which went down into the cook-room, making three men they found there prisoners.

When this was done, and all safe upon deck, the captain ordered the mate with three men to break into the round-house where the new rebel captain lay, and having taken the alarm was gotten up, and with two men and a boy had gotten fire arms in their hands; and when the mate with a crow split open the door, the new captain and his men fired boldly among them, and wounded the mate with a musket ball, which broke his arm, and wounded two more of the men but killed no body.

The mate, calling for help, rushed however into the round-house, wounded as he was, and with his pistol shot the new captain thro' the head, the bullet entring at his mouth, and came out again behind one of his ears, so that he never spoke a word; upon which the rest yielded, and the ship was taken effectually, without any more lives lost.

As soon as the ship was thus secured, the captain ordered seven guns to be fired, which was the signal agreed upon with me, to give me notice of his success, which you may be sure I was very glad to hear, having sat watching upon the shore for it till near two of the clock in the morning.

Having thus heard the signal plainly, I laid me down; and it having been a day of great fatigue to me, I slept very sound, 'till I was something surprized with the noise of a gun; and presently starting up, I heard a man call me by the name of Governour,

Governour, and presently I knew the captain's voice, when climbing up to the top of the hill, there he stood, and pointing to the ship, he embraced me in his arms. 'My dear friend and deliverer,' says he, 'there 's your ship, for she is all yours, and so are we and all that belong to her.' I cast my eyes to the ship, and there she rode within little more than half a mile of the shore; for they had weighed her anchor as soon as they were masters of her; and the weather being fair, had brought her to an anchor just against the mouth of the little creek; and the tide being up, the captain had brought the pinnace in near the place where I at first landed my rafts, and so landed just at my door.

I was at first ready to sink down with the surprise. For I saw my deliverance indeed visibly put into my hands, all things easy, and a large ship just ready to carry me away whither I pleased to go. At first, for some time, I was not able to answer him one word; but as he had taken me in his arms, I held fast by him, or I should have fallen to the ground.

He perceived the surprize, and immediately pulls a bottle out of his pocket, and gave me a dram of cordial, which he had brought on purpose for me; after I had drank it, I sat down upon the ground; and though it brought me to my self, yet it was a good while before I could speak a word to him.

All this while the poor man was in as great an extasy as I, only not under any surprize, as I was; and he said a thousand kind tender things to me, to compose me and bring me to my self; but such was the flood of joy in my breast, that it put all my spirits into confusion; at last it broke out into tears, and in a little while after I recovered my speech.

Then I took my turn, and embraçed him as my deliverer; and we rejoyced together. I told him I looked upon him as a man sent from heaven to deliver me, and that the whole transaction seemed to be a chain of wonders; that such things as these were the testimonies we had of a secret hand of Providence governing the world, and an evidence that the eyes of an infinite power could search into the remotest corner of the world, and send help to the miserable whenever He pleased.

I forgot not to lift up my heart in thankfulness to Heaven;

and what heart could forbear to bless Him, who had not only in a miraculous manner provided for one in such a wilderness, and in such a desolate condition, but from whom every deliverance must always be acknowledged to proceed.

When we had talked a while the captain told me he had brought me some little refreshment, such as the ship afforded, and such as the wretches that had been so long his master had not plundered him of. Upon this he called aloud to the boat, and bid his men bring the things ashore that were for the governour; and indeed it was a present, as if I had been one not that was to be carry'd away along with them, but as if I had been to dwell upon the island still, and they were to go without me.

First, he had brought me a case of bottles full of excellent cordial waters, six large bottles of Madera wine; the bottles held two quarts a-piece; two pound of excellent good tobacco, twelve good pieces of the ship's beef, and six pieces of pork, with a bag of pease, and about a hundred weight of bisket.

He brought me also a box of sugar, a box of flower, a bag full of lemons, and two bottles of lime-juice, and abundance of other things. But besides these, and what was a thousand times more useful to me, he brought me six clean new shirts, six very good neckcloaths, two pair of gloves, one pair of shoes, a hat, and one pair of stockings, and a very good suit of cloaths of his own, which had been worn but very little: in a word he cloathed me from head to foot.

It was a very kind and agreeable present, as any one may imagine to one in my circumstances: but never was any thing in the world of that kind so unpleasant, awkward, and uneasy, as it was to me to wear such cloaths at their first putting on.

After these ceremonies past, and after all his good things were brought into my little apartment, we began to consult what was to be done with the prisoners we had; for it was worth considering, whether we might venture to take them away with us or no, especially two of them, who we knew to be incorrigible and refractory to the last degree; and the captain said, he knew they were such rogues, that there was no obliging them, and if he did carry them away, it must be done in irons, as malefactors to be delivered over to justice at the first English colony he could come at; and I found that the captain himself was very anxious about it.

Upon this, I told him that if he desired it, I durst undertake to bring the two men he spoke of, to make it their own request that he should leave them upon the island. 'I should be very glad of that,' says the captain, 'with all my heart.'

'Well,' says I, 'I will send for them up, and talk with them for you'; so I caused Friday and the two hostages, for they were now discharged, their comrades having performed their promise; I say, I caused them to go to the cave, and bring up the five men pinioned, as they were, to the bower, and keep them there 'till I came.

After some time, I came thither dressed in my new habit, and now I was called govenour again; being all met, and the captain with me, I caused the men to be brought before me, and I told them I had had a full account of their villanous behaviour to the captain, and how they had run away with the ship, and were preparing to commit farther robberies, but that Providence had ensnared them in their own ways, and that they were fallen into the pit which they had digged for others.

I let them know that by my direction the ship had been seized, that she lay now in the road; and they might see by and by that their new captain had received the reward of his villany; for that they might see him hanging at the yard-arm.

That as to them, I wanted to know what they had to say, why I should not execute them as pirates taken in the fact, as by my commission they could not doubt I had authority to do.

One of them answered in the name of the rest, that they had nothing to say but this, that when they were taken, the captain promised them their lives, and they humbly implored my mercy; but I told them I knew not what mercy to shew them; for as for my self, I had resolved to quit the island with all my men, and had taken passage with the captain to go for England; and as for the captain, he could not carry them to England, other than as prisoners in irons to be try'd for mutiny and running away with the ship; the consequence of which, they must needs know, would be the gallows; so that I could not tell which was best for them, unless they had a mind to take their fate in the island;

if they desired that, I did not care, as I had liberty to leave it, I had some inclination to give them their lives, if they thought they could shift on shore.

They seemed very thankful for it, said they would much rather venture to stay there, than to be carry'd to England to be hanged, so I left it on that issue.

However, the captain seemed to make some difficulty of it, as if he durst not leave them there. Upon this I seemed a little angry with the captain, and told him that they were my prisoners, not his; and that seeing I had offered them so much favour, I would be as good as my word; and that if he did not think fit to consent to it, I would set them at liberty, as I found them; and if he did not like it, he might take them again if he could catch them.

Upon this they appeared very thankful, and I accordingly set them at liberty, and bad them retire into the woods to the place whence they came, as I would leave them some fire arms, some ammunition, and some directions how they should live very well, if they thought fit.

Upon this I prepared to go on board the ship, but told the captain that I would stay that night to prepare my things, and desired him to go on board in the mean time, and keep all right in the ship, and send the boat on shore the next day for me; ordering him in the mean time to cause the new captain who was killed to be hanged at the yard-arm that these men might see him.

When the captain was gone, I sent for the men up to me to my apartment, and entred seriously into discourse with them of their circumstances; I told them I thought they had made a right choice; that if the captain carry'd them away, they would certainly be hanged. I shewed them the new captain hanging at the yard-arm of the ship, and told them they had nothing less to expect.

When they had all declared their willingness to stay, I then told them I would let them into the story of my living there, and put them into the way of making it easy to them. Accordingly I gave them the whole history of the place, and of my coming to it; shewed them my fortifications, the way I made my bread, planted my corn, cured my grapes; and in a word, all that was necessary to make them easy. I told them the story also of the sixteen Spaniards that were to be expected; for whom I left a letter, and made them promise to treat them in common with themselves.

I left them my fire arms, viz. five muskets, three fowling pieces, and three swords. I had above a barrel and half of powder left; for after the first year or two, I used but little, and wasted none. I gave them a description of the way I managed the goats, and directions to milk and fatten them, and to make both butter and cheese.

In a word, I gave them every part of my own story; and I told them I would prevail with the captain to leave them two barrels of gun-powder more, and some garden-seeds, which I told them I would have been very glad of; also I gave them the bag of pease which the captain had brought me to eat, and bad them be sure to sow and encrease them.

Having done all this, I left them the next day, and went on board the ship: we prepared immediately to sail, but did not weigh that night. The next morning early, two of the five men came swimming to the ship's side, and making a most lamentable complaint of the other three, begged to be taken into the ship, for God's sake, for they should be murthered, and begged the captain to take them on board, tho' he hanged them immediately.

Upon this the captain pretended to have no power without me; but after some difficulty, and after their solemn promises of amendment, they were taken on board, and were some time after soundly whipped and pickled; after which, they proved very honest and quiet fellows.

Some time after this, the boat was ordered on shore, the tide being up, with the things promised to the men, to which the captain at my intercession caused their chests and cloaths to be added, which they took, and were very thankful for; I also encouraged them, by telling them that if it lay in my way to send any vessel to take them in, I would not forget them.

When I took leave of this island, I carry'd on board for reliques the great goat's-skin-cap I had made, my umbrella, and my parrot; also I forgot not to take the money I formerly mentioned, which had laid by me so long useless, that it was grown rusty, or tarnished, and could hardly pass for silver till it had been a little rubbed and handled; as also the money I found in the wreck of the Spanish ship.

And thus I left the island, the nineteenth of December as I found by the ship's account, in the year 1686, after I had been upon it eight and twenty years, two months, and 19 days; being delivered from this second captivity the same day of the month that I first made my escape in the barco-longo, from among the Moors of Sallee.

In this vessel, after a long voyage, I arrived in England, the eleventh of June, in the year 1687, having been thirty and five years absent.

When I came to England, I was as perfect a stranger to all the world, as if I had never been known there. My benefactor and faithful steward, who I had left in trust with my money, was alive, but had had great misfortunes in the world; was become a widow the second time, and very low in the world. I made her easy as to what she owed me, assuring her I would give her no trouble; but on the contrary, in gratitude to her former care and faithfulness to me, relieved her as my little stock would afford, which at that time would indeed allow me to do but little for her; but I assured her I would never forget her former kindness to me; nor did I forget her, when I had sufficient to help her, as shall be observed in its place.

I went down afterwards into Yorkshire; but my father was dead, and my mother, and all the family extinct, except that I found two sisters, and two of the children of one of my brothers; and as I had been long ago given over for dead, there had been no provision made for me; so that in a word, I found nothing to relieve or assist me; and that little money I had, would not do much for me, as to settling in the world.

I met with one piece of gratitude indeed, which I did not expect; and this was that the master of the ship, who I had so happily delivered, and by the same means saved the ship and cargo, having given a very handsome account to the owners of the manner how I had saved the lives of the men, and the ship, they invited me to meet them and some other merchants concerned, and altogether made me a very handsome compliment upon the subject, and a present of almost two hundred pounds sterling.

But after making several reflections upon the circumstances of my life, and how little way this would go towards settling me in the world, I resolved to go to Lisbon, and see if I might not come by some information of the state of my plantation in the Brasils, and of what was become of my partner, who I had reason to suppose had some years now given me over for dead.

With this view I took shipping for Lisbon, where I arrived in April following; my man Friday accompanying me very honestly in all these ramblings, and proving a most faithful servant upon all occasions.

When I came to Lisbon I found out by enquiry, and to my particular satisfaction, my old friend the captain of the ship, who first took me up at sea, off the shore of Africk. He was now grown old, and had left off the sea, having put his son, who was far from a young man, into his ship, and who still used the Brasil trade. The old man did not know me, and indeed, I hardly knew him; but I soon brought him to my remembrance, and as soon brought my self to his remembrance, when I told him who I was.

After some passionate expressions of the old acquaintance, I enquired, you may be sure, after my plantation and my partner. The old man told me he had not been in the Brasils for about nine years; but that he could assure me, that when he came away my partner was living, but the trustees, who I had joined with him to take cognizance of my part, were both dead; that however, he believed that I would have a very good account of the improvement of the plantation; for that upon the general belief of my being cast away and drowned, my trustees had given in the account of the produce of my part of the plantation, to the procurator fiscal, who had appropriated it, in case I never came to claim it; one third to the king, and two thirds to the monastery of St. Augustine, to be expended for the benefit of the poor, and for the conversion of the Indians to the Catholick faith; but that if I appeared, or any one for me, to claim the inheritance, it should be restored; only that the improvement, or annual production, being distributed to charitable uses, could not be restored; but he assured me, that the steward of the king's revenue (from lands) and the proviedor, or steward of the monastery, had taken great care all along, that the incumbent, that is to say my partner, gave every year a faithful account of the produce, of which they received duly my moiety.

I asked him if he knew to what height of improvement he had brought the plantation, and whether he thought it might be worth looking after, or whether on my going thither I should meet with no obstruction to my possessing my just right in the moiety.

He told me he could not tell exactly to what degree the plantation was improved; but this he knew, that my partner was grown exceeding rich upon the enjoying but one half of it; and that to the best of his remembrance, he had heard that the king's third of my part, which was it seems granted away to some other monastery or religious house, amounted to above two hundred moidores a year; that as to my being restored to a quiet possession of it, there was no question to be made of that, my partner being alive to witness my title, and my name being also enrolled in the register of the country; also he told me that the survivors of my two trustees were very fair honest people, and very wealthy; and he believed I would not only have their assistance for putting me in possession, but would find a very considerable sum of money in their hands, for my account; being the produce of the farm while their fathers held the trust, and before it was given up as above, which, as he remembered, was for about twelve years.

I shewed my self a little concerned and uneasy at this account, and enquired of the old captain how it came to pass that the trustees should thus dispose my effects, when he knew that I had made my will, and had made him, the Portuguese captain, my universal heir, &c.

He told me, that was true; but as there was no proof of my being dead, he could not act as executor, until some certain account should come of my death, and that besides, he was not willing to intermeddle with a thing so remote; that it was true he had registered my will, and put in his claim; and could he have given any account of my being dead or alive, he would have acted by procuration, and taken possession of the *ingenio*, so they called the sugar-house, and had given his son, who was now at the Brasils, order to do it.

'But,' says the old man, 'I have one piece of news to tell you, which perhaps may not be so acceptable to you as the rest, and that is, that believing you were lost, and all the world believing so also, your partner and trustees did offer to accompt to me in your name, for six or eight of the first years of profits, which I received; but there being at that time,' says he, 'great disbursements for encreasing the works, building an *ingenio*, and buying slaves, it did not amount to near so much as afterwards it produced: however,' says the old man, 'I shall give you a true account of what I have received in all, and how I have disposed of it.'

After a few days farther conference with this ancient friend, he brought me an account of the six first years income of my plantation, signed by my partner and the merchant trustees, being always delivered in goods, viz. tobacco in roll, and sugar in chests, besides rum, molossus, &c., which is the consequence of a sugar work; and I found by this account, that every year the income considerably encreased; but as above, the disbursement being large, the sum at first was small. However, the old man let me see that he was debtor to me 470 moidores of gold, besides 60 chests of sugar, and 15 double rolls of tobacco which were lost in his ship; he having been ship-wrecked coming home to Lisbon about 11 years after my leaving the place.

The good man then began to complain of his misfortunes, and how he had been obliged to make use of my money to recover his losses, and buy him a share in a new ship. 'However, my old friend,' says he, 'you shall not want a supply in your necessity; and as soon as my son returns, you shall be fully satisfy'd.'

Upon this, he pulls out an old pouch, and gives me 160 Portugal moidores in gold; and giving me the writing of his title to the ship, which his son was gone to the Brasils in, of which he was a quarter part owner, and his son another, he puts them both into my hands for security of the rest.

I was too much moved with the honesty and kindness of the poor man, to be able to bear this; and remembring what he had done for me, how he had taken me up at sea, and how generously he had used me on all occasions, and particularly, how sincere a friend he was now to me, I could hardly refrain weeping at what he said to me. Therefore, first I asked him if his circumstances admitted him to spare so much money at that time, and if it would not straiten him. He told me, he could not say but it might straiten him a little; but however it was my money, and I might want it more than he.

Every thing the good man said was full of affection, and I could hardly refrain from tears while he spoke. In short, I took 100 of the moidores, and called for a pen and ink to give him a receipt for them; then I returned him the rest, and told him, if ever I had possession of the plantation, I would return the other to him also, as indeed I afterwards did; and that as to the bill of sale of his part in his son's ship, I would not take it by any means; but that if I wanted the money, I found he was honest enough to pay me; and if I did not, but came to receive what he gave me reason to expect, I would never have a penny more from him.

When this was passed, the old man began to ask me if he should put me into a method to make my claim to my plantation. I told him I thought to go over to it my self. He said I might do so if I pleased; but that if I did not there were ways enough to secure my right, and immediately to appropriate the profits to my use; and as there were ships in the river of Lisbon, just ready to go away to Brasil, he made me enter my name in a publick register, with his affidavit, affirming upon oath that I was alive, and that I was the same person who took up the land for the planting the said plantation at first.

This being regularly attested by a notary, and a procuration affixed, he directed me to send it with a letter of his writing, to a merchant of his acquaintance at the place, and then proposed my staying with him till an account came of the return.

Never any thing was more honourable than the proceedings upon this procuration; for in less than seven months I received a large packet from the survivors of my trustees the merchants, for whose account I went to sea, in which were the following particular letters and papers enclosed.

First, there was the account current of the produce of my
farm or plantation, from the year when their fathers had bal-
lanced with my old Portugal captain, being for six years; the ballance appeared to be 1,174 moidores in my favour.

Secondly, there was the account of four years more while they
kept the effects in their hands, before the government claimed
the administration, as being the effects of a person not to be
found, which they called civil death; and the ballance of this,
the value of the plantation encreasing, amounted to [38,892]
cruisadoes, which made 3,241 moidores.

Thirdly, there was the prior of the Augustins' account, who
had received the profits for above fourteen years; but not being to
account for what was disposed to the hospital, very honestly
declared he had 872 moidores not distributed, when he acknowledged to my account; as to the king's part, that refunded
nothing.

There was a letter of my partner's, congratulating me very
affectionately upon my being alive, giving me an account how
the estate was improved, and what it produced a year, with a
particular of the number of squares or acres that it contained;
how planted, how many slaves there were upon it; and making
two and twenty crosses for blessings, told me he had said so
many *Ave Marias* to thank the blessed Virgin that I was alive;
inviting me very passionately to come over and take possession
of my own; and in the mean time to give him orders to whom
he should deliver my effects, if I did not come my self; concluding with a hearty tender of his friendship, and that of his
family, and sent me, as a present, seven fine leopards' skins,
which he had it seems received from Africa, by some other ship
which he had sent thither, and who it seems had made a better
voyage than I. He sent me also five chests of excellent sweetmeats, and an hundred pieces of gold uncoined, not quite so
large as moidores.

By the same fleet my two merchant trustees shipped me 1,200
chests of sugar, 800 rolls of tobacco, and the rest of the whole
accompt in gold.

I might well say, now indeed, that the latter end of Job was
better than the beginning. It is impossible to express here the

flutterings of my very heart, when I looked over these letters, and especially when I found all my wealth about me; for as the Brasil ships come all in fleets, the same ships which brought my letters brought my goods; and the effects were safe in the river before the letters came to my hand. In a word, I turned pale, and grew sick; and had not the old man run and fetched me a cordial, I believe the sudden surprize of joy had overset nature, and I had dy'd upon the spot.

Nay after that, I continued very ill, and was so some hours, 'till a physician being sent for, and something of the real cause of my illness being known, he ordered me to be let blood; after which I had relief, and grew well: but I verily believe, if it had not been eased by a vent given in that manner to the spirits, I should have dy'd.

I was now master, all on a sudden, of above 5,000l. sterling in money, and had an estate, as I might well call it, in the Brasils, of above a thousand pounds a year, as sure as an estate of lands in England: and in a word, I was in a condition which I scarce knew how to understand, or how to compose my self for the enjoyment of it.

The first thing I did was to recompense my original benefactor, my good old captain, who had been first charitable to me in my distress, kind to me in my beginning, and honest to me at the end. I shewed him all that was sent me; I told him, that next to the providence of Heaven, which disposes all things, it was owing to him; and that it now lay on me to reward him, which I would do a hundred fold. So I first returned to him the hundred moidores I had received of him, then I sent for a notary, and caused him to draw up a general release or discharge for the 470 moidores, which he had acknowledged he owed me, in the fullest and firmest manner possible; after which, I caused a procuration to be drawn, impowering him to be my receiver of the annual profits of my plantation, and appointing my partner to accompt to him, and make the returns by the usual fleets to him in my name; and a clause in the end, being a grant of 100 moidores a year to him, during his life, out of the effects, and 50 moidores a year to his son after him, for his life: and thus I requited my old man.

I was now to consider which way to steer my course next, and
what to do with the estate that Providence had thus put into my
hands; and indeed I had more care upon my head now, than I
had in my silent state of life in the island, where I wanted
nothing but what I had, and had nothing but what I wanted:
whereas I had now a great charge upon me, and my business was
how to secure it. I had ne'er a cave now to hide my money in,
or a place where it might lye without lock or key, 'till it grew
mouldy and tarnished before any body would meddle with it:
on the contrary, I knew not where to put it, or who to trust
with it. My old patron, the captain, indeed was honest, and that
was the only refuge I had.

In the next place my interest in the Brasils seemed to summon
me thither; but now I could not tell how to think of going
thither, 'till I had settled my affairs, and left my effects in some
safe hands behind me. At first I thought of my old friend the
widow, who I knew was honest and would be just to me, but
then she was in years, and but poor, and, for ought I knew,
might be in debt; so that in a word, I had no way but to go
back to England my self, and take my effects with me.

It was some months, however, before I resolved upon this; and
therefore, as I had rewarded the old captain fully, and to his satisfaction, who had been my former benefactor, so I began to think
of my poor widow, whose husband had been my first benefactor,
and she, whilst it was in her power, my faithful steward and
instructor. So the first thing I did, I got a merchant in Lisbon
to write to his correspondent in London, not only to pay a bill,
but to go find her out, and carry her in money an hundred pounds
from me, and to talk with her, and comfort her in her poverty, by
telling her she should, if I lived, have a further supply. At the
same time I sent my two sisters in the country each of them an
hundred pounds, they being, though not in want, yet not in very
good circumstances; one having been marry'd and left a widow,
and the other having a husband not so kind to her as he should be.

But among all my relations or acquaintances, I could not yet
pitch upon one to whom I durst commit the gross of my stock,
that I might go away to the Brasils, and leave things safe behind
me; and this greatly perplexed me.

I had once a mind to have gone to the Brasils, and have settled my self there; for I was, as it were, naturalized to the place; but I had some little scruple in my mind about religion, which insensibly drew me back, of which I shall say more presently. However, it was not religion that kept me from going there for the present; and as I had made no scruple of being openly of the religion of the country, all the while I was among them, so neither did I yet; only that now and then having of late thought more of it than formerly when I began to think of living and dying among them, I began to regret my having professed my self a Papist, and thought it might not be the best religion to die with.

But, as I have said, this was not the main thing that kept me from going to the Brasils, but that really I did not know with whom to leave my effects behind me; so I resolved at last to go to England with it, where, if I arrived, I concluded I should make some acquaintance or find some relations that would be faithful to me; and according I prepared to go for England with all my wealth.

In order to prepare things for my going home, I first, the Brasil fleet being just going away, resolved to give answers suitable to the just and faithful account of things I had from thence; and first to the prior of St. Augustine I wrote a letter full of thanks for their just dealings, and the offer of the 872 moidores which was indisposed of, which I desired might be given, 500 to the monastery and 372 to the poor, as the prior should direct, desiring the good padres prayers for me, and the like.

I wrote next a letter of thanks to my two trustees, with all the acknowledgment that so much justice and honesty called for; as for sending them any present, they were far above having any occasion of it.

Lastly, I wrote to my partner, acknowledging his industry in the improving the plantation, and his integrity in encreasing the stock of the works, giving him instructions for his future government of my part, according to the powers I had left with my old patron, to whom I desired him to send whatever became due to me, 'till he should hear from me more particularly; assuring him that it was my intention, not only to come to him, but to settle my self there for the remainder of my life. To this I added a very handsom present of some Italian silks for his wife and two daughters, for such the captain's son informed me he had; with two pieces of fine English broad cloath, the best I could get in Lisbon, five pieces of black bays, and some Flanders lace of a good value.

Having thus settled my affairs, sold my cargoe, and turned all my effects into good bills of exchange, my next difficulty was, which way to go to England. I had been accustomed enough to the sea, and yet I had a strange aversion to going to England by sea at that time; and though I could give no reason for it, yet the difficulty encreased upon me so much, that though I had once shipped my baggage in order to go, yet I altered my mind, and that not once, but two or three times.

It is true, I had been very unfortunate by sea, and this might be some of the reason; but let no man slight the strong impulses of his own thoughts in cases of such moment. Two of the ships which I had singled out to go in, I mean, more particularly singled out than any other, that is to say, so as in one of them to put my things on board, and in the other to have agreed with the captain; I say, two of these ships miscarry'd, viz. one was taken by the Algerines, and the other was cast away on the Start near Torbay, and all the people drowned except three; so that in either of those vessels I had been made miserable; and in which most, it was hard to say.

Having been thus harassed in my thoughts, my old pilot, to whom I communicated every thing, pressed me earnestly not to go by sea, but either to go by land to the Groyne,[51] and cross over the Bay of Biscay to Rochell, from whence it was but an easy and safe journey by land to Paris, and so to Calais and Dover; or to go up to Madrid, and so all the way by land thro' France.

In a word, I was so prepossessed against my going by sea at all, except from Calais to Dover, that I resolved to travel all the way by land; which as I was not in haste, and did not value the charge, was by much the pleasanter way; and to make it more so, my old captain brought an English gentleman, the son of a merchant in Lisbon, who was willing to travel with me: after which, we picked up two more English merchants also, and two young Portuguese gentlemen, the last going to Paris only; so that we were in all six of us, and five servants; the two merchants and the two Portuguese contenting themselves with one servant between two, to save the charge; and as for me, I got an English sailor to travel with me as a servant, besides my man Friday, who was too much a stranger to be capable of supplying the place of a servant on the road.

In this manner I set out from Lisbon; and our company being all very well mounted and armed, we made a little troop, whereof they did me the honour to call me captain, as well because I was the oldest man, as because I had two servants, and indeed was the original of the whole journey.

As I have troubled you with none of my sea-journals, so I shall trouble you now with none of my land-journal: but some adventures that happened to us in this tedious and difficult journey I must not omit.

When we came to Madrid, we being all of us strangers to Spain, were willing to stay some time to see the court of Spain, and to see what was worth observing; but it being the latter part of the summer, we hastened away, and set out from Madrid about the middle of October: but when we came to the edge of Navarre, we were alarmed at several towns on the way, with an account that so much snow has fallen on the French side of the mountains, that several travellers were obliged to come back to Pampeluna, after having attempted, at an extream hazard, to pass on.

When we came to Pampeluna it self, we found it so indeed; and to me that had been always used to a hot climate, and indeed to countries where we could scarce bear any cloaths on, the cold was insufferable; nor indeed was it more painful than it was surprising, to come but ten days before out of the Old Castile, where the weather was not only warm but very hot, and immediately to feel a wind from the Pyrenean mountains, so very keen, so severely cold, as to be intollerable, and to endanger benumbing and perishing of our fingers and toes.

Poor Friday was really frighted when he saw the mountains all covered with snow, and felt cold weather, which he had never seen or felt before in his life.

To mend the matter, when we came to Pampeluna, it continued snowing with so much violence, and so long, that the people said winter was come before its time, and the roads which were difficult before were now quite impassable : for in a word, the snow lay in some places too thick for us to travel; and being not hard frozen, as is the case in northern countries, there was no going without being in danger of being bury'd alive every step. We stayed no less than twenty days at Pampeluna; when (seeing the winter coming on, and no likelihood of its being better; for it was the severest winter all over Europe that had been known in the memory of man) I proposed that we should all go away to Fonterabia, and there take shipping for Bourdeaux, which was a very little voyage.

But while we were considering this, there came in four French gentlemen, who having been stopped on the French side of the passes, as we were on the Spanish, had found out a guide, who traversing the country near the head of Languedoc, had brought them over the mountains by such ways, that they were not much incommoded with the snow; and where they met with snow in any quantity, they said it was frozen hard enough to bear them and their horses.

We sent for this guide, who told us he would undertake to carry us the same way with no hazard from the snow, provided we were armed sufficiently to protect our selves from wild beasts; for he said, upon these great snows, it was frequent for some wolves to show themselves at the foot of the mountains, being made ravenous for want of food, the ground being covered with snow. We told him we were well enough prepared for such creatures as they were, if he would ensure us from a kind of two-legged wolves, which we were told we were in most danger from, especially on the French side of the mountains.

He satisfy'd us there was no danger of that kind in the way that we were to go; so we readily agreed to follow him, as did also twelve other gentlemen, with their servants, some French, some Spanish; who, as I said, had attempted to go, and were obliged to come back again.

Accordingly, we all set out from Pampeluna, with our guide, on the fifteenth of November; and indeed, I was surprized, when instead of going forward, he came directly back with us on the same road that we came from Madrid, above twenty miles; when being passed two rivers, and come into the plain country, we found our selves in a warm climate again, where the country was pleasant, and no snow to be seen; but on a sudden, turning to his left, he approached the mountains another way; and though it is true, the hills and precipices looked dreadful, yet he made so many tours, such meanders, and led us by such winding ways, that we were insensibly passed the height of the mountains, without being much incumbered with the snow; and all on a sudden he shewed us the pleasant fruitful provinces of Languedoc and Gascoign, all green and flourishing; tho' indeed it was at a great distance, and we had some rough way to pass yet.

We were a little uneasy, however, when we found it snowed one whole day and a night, so fast that we could not travel; but he bid us be easy, we should soon be past it all. We found indeed, that we began to descend every day, and to come more north than before; and so depending upon our guide, we went on.

It was about two hours before night, when our guide being something before us, and not just in sight, out rushed three monstrous wolves, and after them a bear, out of a hollow way, adjoyning to a thick wood; two of the wolves flew upon the guide, and had he been half a mile before us, he had been devoured indeed, before we could have helped him. One of them fastned upon his horse, and the other attacked the man with that violence, that he had not time, or not presence of mind enough, to draw his pistol, but hollowed and cry'd out to us most lustily; my man Friday being next me, I bid him ride up and see what was the matter; as soon as Friday came in sight of the man, he hollowed as loud as t'other, 'O master! O master!' but like a bold fellow, rode directly up to the poor man, and with his pistol shot the wolf that attacked him into the head.

It was happy for the poor man that it was my man Friday; for he having been used to that kind of creature in his country, had no fear upon him, but went close up to him, and shot him as above; whereas any of us would have fired at a farther distance, and have perhaps either missed the wolf, or endangered shooting the man.

But it was enough to have terrify'd a bolder man than I, and indeed it alarmed all our company, when with the noise of Friday's pistol, we heard on both sides the dismallest howling of wolves, and the noise redoubled by the eccho of the mountains, that it was to us as if there had been a prodigious multitude of them; and perhaps indeed there was not such a few, as that we had no cause of apprehensions.

However, as Friday had killed this wolf, the other, that had fastned upon the horse, left him immediately, and fled; having happily fastned upon his head, where the bosses of the bridle had stuck in his teeth, so that he had not done him much hurt. The man indeed was most hurt; for the raging creature had bit him twice, once on the arm, and the other time a little above his knee; and he was just as it were tumbling down by the disorder of his horse, when Friday came up and shot the wolf.

It is easy to suppose that at the noise of Friday's pistol, we all mended our pace, and rid up as fast as the way (which was very difficult) would give us leave, to see what was the matter; as soon as we came clear of the trees, which blinded us before, we saw clearly what had been the case, and how Friday had disengaged the poor guide; though we did not presently discern what kind of creature it was he had killed.

But never was a fight managed so hardily, and in such a surprizing manner, as that which followed between Friday and the bear, which gave us all (though at first we were surprized and afraid for him) the greatest diversion imaginable. As the bear is a heavy, clumsey creature, and does not gallop as the wolf does, who is swift and light; so he has two particular qualities, which generally are the rule of his actions. First, as to men, who are not his proper prey; I say, not his proper prey, because tho' I cannot say what excessive hunger might do, which was now their case, the ground being all covered with snow; but as to men, he does not usually attempt them, unless they first attack him : on the contrary, if you meet him in the woods, if you don't meddle with him, he won't meddle with you; but then you must take care to be very civil to him, and give him the road; for he is a very nice gentleman, he won't go a step out of his way for a prince; nay, if you are really afraid, your best way is to look

another way, and keep going on; for sometimes if you stop, and
stand still, and look steadily at him, he takes it for an affront;
but if you throw or toss any thing at him, and it hits him,
though it were but a bit of a stick as big as your finger, he takes
it for an affront, and sets all his other business aside to pursue
his revenge; for he will have satisfaction in point of honour;
that is his first quality. The next is, that if he be once affronted,
he will never leave you, night or day, till he has his revenge; but
follows at a good round rate, till he overtakes you.

My man Friday had delivered our guide, and when we came up
to him he was helping him off from his horse; for the man was
both hurt and frighted, and indeed the last more than the first;
when on the sudden we spy'd the bear come out of the wood, and
a vast monstrous one it was, the biggest by far that ever I saw.
We were all a little surprized when we saw him; but when
Friday saw him, it was easy to see joy and courage in the
fellow's countenance. 'O! O! O!' says Friday three times,
pointing to him; 'O master! You give me te leave! Me shakee te
hand with him: me make you good laugh.'

I was surprized to see the fellow so pleased. 'You fool you,' says
I, 'he will eat you up.' 'Eatee me up! Eatee me up!' says Friday,
twice over again; 'me eatee him up: me make you good laugh:
you all stay here, me show you good laugh'; so down he sits,
and gets his boots off in a moment, and put on a pair of pumps, as
we call the flat shoes they wear, and which he had in his pocket,
gives my other servant his horse, and with his gun away he flew
swift like the wind.

The bear was walking softly on, and offered to meddle with no
body, till Friday coming pretty near, calls to him, as if the bear
could understand him; 'Hark ye, hark ye,' says Friday, 'me
speakee wit you.' We followed at a distance; for now being come
down on the Gascoign side of the mountains, we were entred a
vast great forest, where the country was plain, and pretty open,
though many trees in it scattered here and there.

Friday, who had, as we say, the heels of the bear, came up with
him quickly, and takes up a great stone, and throws at him, and
hit him just on the head; but did him no more harm than if he
had thrown it against a wall; but it answered Friday's end; for

the rogue was so void of fear, that he did it purely to make the bear follow him, and show us some laugh as he called it.

As soon as the bear felt the stone and saw him, he turns about and comes after him, taking devilish long strides, and shuffling along at a strange rate, so as would have put a horse to a middling gallop; away runs Friday, and takes his course as if he run towards us for help; so we all resolved to fire at once upon the bear and deliver my man; though I was angry at him heartily for bringing the bear back upon us, when he was going about his own business another way; and especially I was angry that he had turned the bear upon us, and then run away; and I called out, 'You dog,' said I, 'is this your making us laugh? Come away, and take your horse, that we may shoot the creature.' He hears me, and crys out, 'No shoot, no shoot, stand still, you get much laugh.' And as the nimble creature run two foot for the beast's one, he turned on a sudden on one side of us, and seeing a great oak-tree, fit for his purpose, he beckoned to us to follow, and doubling his pace he gets nimbly up the tree, laying his gun down upon the ground, at about five or six yards from the bottom of the tree.

The bear soon came to the tree, and we followed at a distance; the first thing he did, he stopped at the gun, smelt to it, but let it lye, and up he scrambles into the tree, climbing like a cat, though so monstrously heavy. I was amazed at the folly, as I thought it, of my man, and could not for my life see any thing to laugh at yet, till seeing the bear get up the tree we all rode nearer to him.

When we came to the tree, there was Friday got out to the small end of a large limb of the tree, and the bear got about half way to him; as soon as the bear got out to that part where the limb of the tree was weaker, 'Ha,' says he to us, 'now you see me teachee the bear dance'; so he falls a jumping and shaking the bough, at which the bear began to totter, but stood still, and begun to look behind him, to see how he should get back; then indeed we did laugh heartily. But Friday had not done with him by a great deal; when he sees him stand still he calls out to him again, as if he had supposed the bear could speak English, 'What, you no come farther? pray you come farther'; so he left jumping and shaking the bough; and the bear, just as if he had understood what he said, did come a little further, then he fell a jumping again, and the bear stopped again.

We thought now was a good time to knock him on the head, and I called to Friday to stand still, and we would shoot the bear; but he cry'd out earnestly, 'O pray! O pray! No shoot, me shoot, by and then'; he would have said, 'by and by.' However, to shorten the story, Friday danced so much, and the bear stood so ticklish, that we had laughing enough indeed, but still could not imagine what the fellow would do; for first we thought he depended upon shaking the bear off; and we found the bear was too cunning for that too; for he would not go out far enough to be thrown down, but clings fast with his great broad claws and feet, so that we could not imagine what would be the end of it, and where the jest would be at last.

But Friday put us out of doubt quickly; for seeing the bear cling fast to the bough, and that he would not be perswaded to come any farther, 'Well, well,' says Friday, 'you no come farther, me go, me go; you no come to me, me go come to you'; and upon this, he goes out to the smallest end of the bough, where it would bend with his weight, and gently lets himself down by it, sliding down the bough, till he came near enough to jump down on his feet, and away he run to his gun, takes it up, and stands still.

'Well,' said I to him, 'Friday, what will you do now? Why don't you shoot him?' 'No shoot,' says Friday, 'no yet, me shoot now, me no kill; me stay, give you one more laugh'; and indeed so he did, as you will see presently; for when the bear see his enemy gone, he comes back from the bough where he stood; but did it mighty leisurely, looking behind him every step, and coming backward till he got into the body of the tree; then with the same hinder end foremost, he came down the tree, grasping it with his claws, and moving one foot at a time, very leisurely; at this juncture, and just before he could set his hind feet upon the ground, Friday stept up close to him, clapt the muzzle of his piece into his ear, and shot him dead as a stone.

Then the rogue turned about, to see if we did not laugh, and when he saw we were pleased by our looks, he falls a laughing himself very loud. 'So we kill bear in my country,' says Friday.

'So you kill them,' says I, 'why you have no guns.' 'No,' says he, 'no gun, but shoot great much long arrow.'

This was indeed a good diversion to us; but we were still in a wild place, and our guide very much hurt, and what to do we hardly knew; the howling of wolves run much in my head; and indeed, except the noise I once heard on the shore of Africa, of which I have said something already, I never heard any thing that filled me with so much horrour.

These things, and the approach of night, called us off, or else, as Friday would have had us, we should certainly have taken the skin of this monstrous creature off, which was worth saving; but we had three leagues to go, and our guide hastened us, so we left him, and went forward on our journey.

The ground was still covered with snow, tho' not so deep and dangerous as on the mountains, and the ravenous creatures, as we heard afterwards, were come down into the forest and plain country, pressed by hunger to seek for food; and had done a great deal of mischief in the villages, where they surprized the country people, killed a great many of their sheep and horses, and some people too.

We had one dangerous place to pass, which our guide told us, if there were any more wolves in the country, we should find them there; and this was in a small plain, surrounded with woods on every side, and a long narrow defile or lane, which we were to pass to get through the wood, and then we should come to the village where we were to lodge.

It was within half an hour of sun-set when we entred the first wood; and a little after sun-set when we came into the plain. We met with nothing in the first wood, except that in a little plain within the wood, which was not above two furlongs over, we saw five great wolves cross the road, full speed one after another, as if they had been in chase of some prey, and had it in view; they took no notice of us, and were gone and out of our sight in a few moments.

Upon this our guide, who by the way was a wretched faint-hearted fellow, bid us keep in a ready posture; for he believed there were more wolves a coming.

We kept our arms ready, and our eyes about us, but we saw

no more wolves, 'till we came thro' that wood, which was near half a league, and entred the plain; as soon as we came into the plain we had occasion enough to look about us. The first object we met with was a dead horse; that is to say, a poor horse which the wolves had killed, and at least a dozen of them at work; we could not say eating of him, but picking of his bones rather; for they had eaten up all the flesh before.

We did not think fit to disturb them at their feast, neither did they take much notice of us: Friday would have let fly at them, but I would not suffer him by any means; for I found we were like to have more business upon our hands than we were aware of. We were not gone half over the plain, but we began to hear the wolves howl in the wood on our left, in a frightful manner, and presently after we saw about a hundred coming on directly towards us, all in a body, and most of them in a line, as regularly as an army drawn up by experienced officers. I scarce knew in what manner to receive them; but found to draw ourselves in a close line was the only way: so we formed in a moment. But that we might not have too much interval, I ordered that only every other man should fire, and that the others who had not fired should stand ready to give them a second volley immediately, if they continued to advance upon us, and that then those who had fired at first should not pretend to load their fusees again, but stand ready with every one a pistol; for we were all armed with a fusee and a pair of pistols each man; so we were by this method able to fire six volleys, half of us at a time; however, at present we had no necessity; for upon firing the first volley, the enemy made a full stop, being terrify'd as well with the noise as with the fire; four of them being shot into the head, dropped; several others were wounded, and went bleeding off, as we could see by the snow. I found they stopped, but did not immediately retreat; whereupon remembring that I had been told that the fiercest creatures were terrify'd at the voice of a man, I caused all our company to hollow as loud as we could; and I found the notion not altogether mistaken; for upon our shout, they began to retire and turn about; then I ordered a second volley to be fired in their rear, which put them to the gallop, and away they went to the woods.

This gave us leisure to charge our pieces again, and that we might loose no time, we kept going; but we had but little more than loaded our fusees, and put ourselves into a readiness, when we heard a terrible noise in the same wood, on our left, only that it was farther onward the same way we were to go.

The night was coming on, and the light began to be dusky, which made it worse on our side; but the noise encreasing, we could easily perceive that it was the howling and yelling of those hellish creatures; and on a sudden, we perceived 2 or 3 troops of wolves, one on our left, one behind us, and one on our front; so that we seemed to be surrounded with 'em; however, as they did not fall upon us, we kept our way forward, as fast as we could make our horses go, which, the way being very rough, was only a good large trot; and in this manner we came in view of the entrance of a wood, through which we were to pass, at the farther side of the plain; but we were greatly surprized, when coming nearer the lane or pass, we saw a confused number of wolves standing just at the entrance.

On a sudden, at another opening of the wood, we heard the noise of a gun; and looking that way, out rushed a horse, with a saddle and a bridle on him, flying like the wind, and sixteen or seventeen wolves after him, full speed; indeed, the horse had the heels of them; but as we supposed that he could not hold it at that rate, we doubted not but they would get up with him at last, and no question but they did.

But here we had a most horrible sight; for riding up to the entrance where the horse came out, we found the carcass of another horse, and of two men, devoured by the ravenous creatures, and one of the men was no doubt the same who we heard fired the gun; for there lay a gun just by him, fired off; but as to the man, his head and the upper part of his body was eaten up.

This filled us with horror, and we knew not what course to take, but the creatures resolved us soon; for they gathered about us presently, in hopes of prey; and I verily believe there were three hundred of them. It happened very much to our advantage, that at the entrance into the wood, but a little way from it, there lay some large timber trees, which had been cut down the summer before, and I suppose lay there for carriage; I drew my little troop in among those trees, and placing our selves in a line behind one long tree, I advised them all to light, and keeping that tree before us for a breast work, to stand in a triangle, or three fronts, enclosing our horses in the center.

We did so, and it was well we did; for never was a more furious charge than the creatures made upon us in the place; they came on us with a growling kind of noise (and mounted the piece of timber, which, as I said, was our breast work) as if they were only rushing upon their prey; and this fury of theirs, it seems, was principally occasioned by their seeing our horses behind us, which was the prey they aimed at: I ordered our men to fire as before, every other man; and they took their aim so sure, that indeed they killed several of the wolves at the first volley; but there was a necessity to keep a continual firing; for they came on like devils, those behind pushing on those before.

When we had fired our second volley of our fusees, we thought they stopped a little, and I hoped they would have gone off; but it was but a moment; for others came forward again; so we fired two volleys of our pistols, and I believe in these four firings we had killed seventeen or eighteen of them, and lamed twice as many; yet they came on again.

I was loath to spend our last shot too hastily; so I called my servant, not my man Friday, for he was better employed; for with the greatest dexterity imaginable, he had charged my fusee and his own, while we were engaged; but as I said, I called my other man, and giving him a horn of powder, I bad him lay a train all along the piece of timber, and let it be a large train; he did so, and had but just time to get away, when the wolves came up to it, and some were got up upon it; when I, snapping an uncharged pistol close to the powder, set it on fire; those that were upon the timber were scorcht with it, and six or seven of them fell, or rather jumped in among us, with the force and fright of the fire; we dispatched these in an instant, and the rest were so frighted with the light, which the night, for it was now very dark, made more terrible, that they drew back a little.

Upon which I ordered our last pistol to be fired off in one volley, and after that we gave a shout; upon this, the wolves turned tail, and we sally'd immediately upon near twenty lame ones, who we found struggling on the ground, and fell a cutting them with our swords, which answered our expectation; for the crying and howling they made was better understood by their fellows, so that they all fled and left us.

We had, first and last, killed about three score of them; and had it been day-light, we had killed many more. The field of battle being thus cleared, we made forward again; for we had still near a league to go. We heard the ravenous creatures houl and yell in the woods as we went, several times; and sometimes we fancy'd we saw some of them, but the snow dazling our eyes, we were not certain; so in about an hour more, we came to the town where we were to lodge, which we found in a terrible fright, and all in arms; for it seems that the night before, the wolves and some bears had broke into the village in the night, and put them in a terrible fright; and they were obliged to keep guard night and day, but especially in the night, to preserve their cattle, and indeed their people.

The next morning our guide was so ill, and his limbs swelled with the rankling of his two wounds,[52] that he could go no farther; so we were obliged to take a new guide there, and go to Thoulouse, where we found a warm climate, a fruitful pleasant country, and no snow, no wolves, or any thing like them; but when we told our story at Thoulouse, they told us it was nothing but what was ordinary in the great forest at the foot of the mountains, especially when the snow lay on the ground : but they enquired much what kind of a guide we had gotten, that would venture to bring us that way in such a severe season; and told us it was very much we were not all devoured. When we told them how we placed our selves, and the horses in the middle, they blamed us exceedingly, and told us it was fifty to one but we had been all destroyed; for it was the sight of the horses which made the wolves so furious, seeing their prey; and that at other times they are really afraid of a gun; but the being excessive hungry, and raging on that account, the eagerness to come at the horses had made them sensless of danger; and that if we had not by the continued fire, and at last by the stratagem of the train of powder, mastered them, it had been great odds but that we had been torn to pieces; whereas had we been content to have sat still on horseback, and fired as horsemen, they would not have taken the horses for so much their own, when men were on their backs, as otherwise; and withal they told us, that at last, if we had stood altogether, and left our horses, they would have been so eager to have devoured them, that we might have come off safe, especially having our fire arms in our hands, and being so many in number.

For my part, I was never so sensible of danger in my life; for seeing above three hundred devils come roaring and open mouthed to devour us, and having nothing to shelter us, or retreat to, I gave my self over for lost; and as it was, I believe I shall never care to cross those mountains again; I think I would much rather go a thousand leagues by sea, though I were sure to meet with a storm once a week.

I have nothing uncommon to take notice of in my passage through France; nothing but what other travellers have given an account of, with much more advantage than I can. I travelled from Thoulouse to Paris, and without any considerable stay, came to Callais, and landed safe at Dover, the fourteenth of January, after having had a severely cold season to travel in.

I was now come to the center of my travels, and had in a little time all my new discovered estate safe about me, the bills of exchange which I brought with me having been very currently paid.

My principal guide and privy councellor was my good antient widow, who in gratitude for the money I had sent her, thought no pains too much, or care too great, to employ for me; and I trusted her so entirely with every thing, that I was perfectly easy as to the security of my effects; and indeed, I was very happy from my beginning, and now to the end, in the unspotted integrity of this good gentlewoman.

And now I began to think of leaving my effects with this woman, and setting out for Lisbon, and so to the Brasils; but now another scruple came in my way, and that was religion; for as I had entertained some doubts about the Roman religion, even while I was abroad, especially in my state of solitude; so I knew there was no going to the Brasils for me, much less going to settle there, unless I resolved to embrace the Roman Catholick religion, without any reserve; unless on the other hand I resolved to be a sacrifice to my principles, be a martyr for religion, and die in the Inquisition; so I resolved to stay at home, and if I could find means for it, to dispose of my plantation.

To this purpose I wrote to my old friend at Lisbon, who in return gave me notice that he could easily dispose of it there: but that if I thought fit to give him leave to offer it in my name to the two merchants, the survivors of my trustees, who lived in the Brasils, who must fully understand the value of it, who lived just upon the spot, and who I knew were very rich; so that he believed they would be fond of buying it; he did not doubt, but I should make 4 or 5,000 pieces of eight the more of it.

Accordingly I agreed, gave him order to offer it to them, and he did so; and in about 8 months more, the ship being then returned, he sent me account that they had accepted the offer, and had remitted 33,000 pieces of eight to a correspondent of theirs at Lisbon, to pay for it.

In return I signed the instrument of sale in the form which they sent from Lisbon, and sent it to my old man, who sent me bills of exchange for 32,800 pieces of eight, for the estate; reserving the payment of 100 moidores a year to him, the old man, during his life, and 50 moidores afterwards to his son for his life, which I had promised them, which the plantation was to make good as a rent-charge. And thus I have given the first part of a life of fortune and adventure, a life of Providence's chequer-work, and of a variety which the world will seldom be able to show the like of: beginning foolishly, but closing much more happily than any part of it ever gave me leave so much as to hope for.

Any one would think that in this state of complicated good fortune I was past running any more hazards; and so indeed I had been, if other circumstances had concurred; but I was inured to a wandring life, had no family, not many relations, nor, however rich, had I contracted much acquaintance; and though I had sold my estate in the Brasils, yet I could not keep the country out of my head, and had a great mind to be upon the wing again; especially I could not resist the strong inclination I had to see my island, and to know if the poor Spaniards were in being there, and how the rogues I left there had used them.

My true friend, the widow, earnestly diswaded me from it, and so far prevailed with me, that for almost seven years she prevented my running abroad; during which time I took my two nephews, the children of one of my brothers, into my care. The eldest having something of his own, I bred up as a gentleman, and gave him a settlement of some addition to his estate, after my decease; the other I put out to a captain of a ship; and after five years, finding him a sensible bold enterprising young fellow, I put him into a good ship, and sent him to sea: and this young fellow afterwards drew me in, as old as I was, to farther adventures my self.

In the mean time I in part settled my self here; for first of all I marry'd, and that not either to my disadvantage or dissatisfaction, and had three children, two sons and one daughter: but my wife dying, and my nephew coming home with good success from a voyage to Spain, my inclination to go abroad, and his importunity, prevailed and engaged me to go in his ship, as a private trader to the East Indies. This was in the year 1694.

In this voyage I visited my new collony in the island, saw my successors the Spaniards, had the whole story of their lives, and of the villains I left there; how at first they insulted the poor Spaniards, how they afterwards agreed, disagreed, united, separated, and how at last the Spaniards were obliged to use violence with them, how they were subjected to the Spaniards, how honestly the Spaniards used them; a history, if it were entred into, as full of variety and wonderful accidents as my own part; particularly also as to their battles with the Caribbeans, who landed several times upon the island, and as to the improvement they made upon the island it self, and how five of them made an attempt upon the main land, and brought away eleven men and five women prisoners, by which, at my coming, I found about twenty young children on the island.

Here I stayed about 20 days, left them supplies of all necessary things, and particularly of arms, powder, shot, cloaths, tools, and two workmen, which I brought from England with me, viz. a carpenter and a smith.

Besides this, I shared the island into parts with 'em, reserved to my self the property of the whole, but gave them such parts respectively as they agreed on; and having settled all things with them, and engaged them not to leave the place, I left them there.

From thence I touched at the Brasils, from whence I sent a bark, which I bought there, with more people to the island, and in it, besides other supplies, I sent seven women, being such as I found proper for service, or for wives to such as would take them. As to the English men, I promised them to send them some women from England, with a good cargoe of necessaries, if they would apply themselves to planting, which I afterwards perform'd. And the fellows proved very honest and diligent after they were mastered and had their properties set apart for them. I sent them also from the Brasils five cows, three of them being big with calf, some sheep, and some hogs, which, when I came again, were considerably encreased.

But all these things, with an account how 300 Caribbees came and invaded them, and ruined their plantations, and how they fought with that whole number twice, and were at first defeated, and three of them killed; but at last a storm destroying their enemies canoes, they famished or destroyed almost all the rest, and renewed and recovered the possession of their plantation, and still lived upon the island; all these things, with some very surprizing incidents in some new adventures of my own, for ten years more, I may perhaps give a farther account of hereafter.

APPENDIX: ALEXANDER SELKIRK

THE adventures of Crusoe on his island, the main part of Defoe's book, were based on the central incident in the life of an undisciplined Scot, Alexander Selkirk, or Selcraig (1676–1721), a tall, powerful, and skilled sailor from Largo in Fife. Crusoe's preliminary adventures with the Moors are of tangential interest to the island story, and the book tends to tail off with the rather slack account of his journey back to England. Although it is possible, and even likely, that Defoe met Selkirk before he wrote his book, he used only this one incident in the real sailor's turbulent history. In it he sees the kind of moral which many readers saw, for accounts of Selkirk were well-known and popular in the eighteenth century, culminating in Cowper's poem: 'I am monarch of all I survey'. Of course, Defoe uses the story in his own way, and tells the tale with his peculiar imaginative force. It is to compare different treatments of the story, not to point out the 'source' of the story, that the two accounts of Selkirk are included here. If Defoe hadn't found and used Selkirk's story, he would have found something else of the same kind.

At least two other cases of solitary survival on the island of Juan Fernandez are recorded. A Mosquito (Guyanese) Indian, Will, was abandoned there in January 1681, when a motley fleet of buccaneers fled at the approach of three unknown sail. Will was picked up alive and well in April 1684 by another buccaneer ship, the *Batchelor's Delight*. Also, the Spanish pilot of the ship which abandoned the Indian said that, many years before, the solitary survivor of a shipwreck lived on the island for five years before being rescued by buccaneers. William Dampier was a member of both these buccaneering expeditions and wrote the facts down.

In September 1703, the same William Dampier sailed in command of another privateering expedition (privately financed but with the approval of the government), the purpose of which was to harry the Spanish and Portuguese shipping off the estuary of the Plate. Failing that, they meant to sail round the Horn to try their fortune off the shore of Peru, or even as far north as to intercept the Acapulco galleon, laden with the produce of the Mexican mines. This expedition consisted of two ships. The *St George* carried twenty-six guns and displaced 120 tons. Alexander Selkirk mustered as the Sailing-Master (or first mate) in the *Cinque Ports*, with a crew of sixty-three.

During an unhappy voyage, Dampier handled some disaffection rather clumsily, and in fact put his own first mate ashore (with another seaman) in the Cape Verde Islands. The captains of the two ships could not agree, and when in February 1704 they reached the Juan Fernandez islands, three hundred and fifty miles off Valparaiso in Chile, any joint purpose had more or less been lost. The largest of the three islands (now called *Mas-a-Tierra*), the nearest to the mainland, was used by privateers for refitting after the arduous voyage round the Horn, so as to avoid the attention of the Spaniards. While the two ships were there, Dampier took the *St George* into an indecisive action with a French ship, having abandoned five men on the island in his haste to set sail. They were shortly afterwards picked up by some French ships. Finally, after some unsuccessful operations off Panama, the *St George* and the *Cinque Ports* parted company. Dampier's expedition fizzled out, and in September the *Cinque Ports* found herself back in Juan Fernandez to refit.

At the beginning of October 1714, Captain Stradling gave orders to sail. Selkirk protested violently, because the ship was not very seaworthy. The argument ended by the Sailing-Master demanding to be set ashore with his kit. Perhaps he expected to be followed by enough of the thoroughly disloyal crew to prevent the ship from sailing. Stradling was far from popular. No one, however, joined him and as the *Cinque Ports'* boat pulled away from the island, Selkirk lost his nerve, and shrieked to be taken back aboard, but in vain. Stradling no doubt hoped to use this incident as an example.

Four years and four months later, on 2 February 1709, Selkirk rejoined human society. Yet another privateering expedition of two vessels, the *Duke* and the *Dutchess*, under the command of Captain Woodes Rogers, picked him up. The indestructible Dampier was sailing as a pilot this time. Woodes Rogers' account of the rescue is as follows:

'Immediately our Pinnace return'd from the shore, and brought abundance of Craw-fish, with a Man cloth'd in Goat-Skins, who look'd wilder than the first Owners of them. He had been on the Island four Years and four Months, being left there by Capt. *Stradling* in the *Cinque-Ports*; his Name was *Alexander Selkirk* a *Scotch* Man, who had been Master of the *Cinque-Ports*, a Ship that came here last with Capt. *Dampier*, who told me that this was the best Man in her; so I immediately agreed with him to be a Mate on board our Ship. 'Twas he that made the Fire last night when he saw our Ships, which he judg'd to be *English*. During his stay here he saw several Ships pass by, but only two came in to anchor. As he went to view them, he found 'em to be *Spaniards*, and retir'd from 'em; upon which they shot at him. Had they been *French*, he would have submitted; but chose to risque his dying alone on the Island, rather than fall into the hands of the *Spaniards* in these parts, because he apprehended they would murder him, or make a Slave of him in the Mines, for he fear'd they would spare no Stranger that might be capable of discovering the *South-Sea*. The *Spaniards* had landed, before he knew what they were, and they came so near him that he had much ado to escape; for they not only shot at him but pursu'd him into the Woods, where he climb'd to the top of a Tree, at the foot of which they made water, and kill'd several Goats just by, but went off again without discovering him. He told us that he was born at *Largo* in the County of *Fife* in *Scotland*, and was bred a Sailor from his Youth. The reason of his being left here was a difference betwixt him and his Captain; which, together with the Ships being leaky, made him willing rather to stay here than go along with him at first; and when he was at last willing, the Captain would not receive him. He had been in the Island before to wood and water, when two of the Ships Company were left upon it for six Months till the Ship return'd, being chas'd thence by two *French South-Sea* Ships.

He had with him his Clothes and Bedding, with a Fire-lock, some Powder, Bullets, and Tobacco, a Hatchet, a Knife, a Kettle, a Bible, some practical Pieces, and his Mathematical Instruments and Books. He diverted and provided for himself as well as he could; but for the first eight months had much ado to bear up against Melancholy, and the Terror of being left alone in such a desolate place. He built two Hutts with Piemento Trees, cover'd them with long Grass, and lin'd them with the Skins of Goats, which he kill'd with his Gun as he wanted, so long as his Powder lasted, which was but a pound; and that being near spent, he got fire by rubbing two sticks of Piemento Wood together upon his knee. In the lesser Hutt, at some distance from the other, he dress'd his Victuals, and in the larger he slept, and employ'd himself in reading, singing Psalms, and praying; so that he said he was a better Christian while in this Solitude than ever he was before, or than, he was afraid, he should ever be again. At first he never eat anything till Hunger constrain'd him, partly for grief and partly for want of Bread and Salt; nor did he go to bed till he could watch no longer : the Piemento Wood, which burnt very clear, serv'd him both for Firing and Candle, and refresh'd him with its fragrant Smell.

He might have had Fish enough, but could not eat 'em for want of Salt, because they occasion'd a Looseness; except Crawfish, which are there as large as our Lobsters, and very good: These he sometimes broil'd, and at other times boil'd, as he did his Goats Flesh, of which he made very good Broth, for they are not so rank as ours : he kept an Account of 500 that he kill'd while there, and caught as many more, which he mark'd on the Ear and let go. When his Powder fail'd, he took them by speed of foot; for his way of living and continual Exercise of walking and running, clear'd him of all gross Humours, so that he ran with wonderful Swiftness thro the Woods and up the Rocks and Hills, as we perceiv'd when we employ'd him to catch Goats for us. We had a Bull-Dog, which we sent with several of our nimblest Runners to help him in catching Goats; but he distanc'd and tir'd both the Dog and the Men, catch'd the Goats, and brought 'em to us on his back. He told us that his Agility in pursuing a Goat had once like to have cost him his Life; he pursu'd it with so much Eagerness that he catch'd hold of it on the brink of a Precipice, of which he was not aware, the Bushes having hid it from him; so that he fell with the Goat down the said Precipice a great height, and was so stunn'd and bruised with the Fall, that he narrowly escap'd with his Life, and when he came to his Senses, found the Goat dead under him. He lay there about 24 hours, and was scarce able to crawl to his Hutt, which was about a mile distant, or to stir abroad again in ten days.

He came at last to relish his Meat well enough without Salt or Bread, and in the Season had plenty of good Turnips, which had been sow'd there by Capt. *Dampier's* Men, and have now overspread some Acres of Ground. He had enough of good Cabbage from the Cabbage-Trees, and season'd his Meat with the Fruit of the Piemento Trees, which is the same as the *Jamaica* Pepper, and smells deliciously. He found there also a black Pepper call'd *Malagita*, which was very good to expel Wind, and against Griping of the Guts.

He soon wore out all his Shoes and Clothes by running thro the Woods; and at last being forc'd to shift without them, his Feet became so hard, that he run everywhere without Annoyance: and it was some time before he could wear Shoes after we found him; for not being us'd to any so long, his Feet swell'd when he came first to wear 'em again.

After he had conquer'd his Melancholy, he diverted himself sometimes by cutting his Name on the Trees, and the Time of his being left and Continuance there. He was at first much pester'd with Cats and Rats, that had bred in great numbers from some of each Species which had got ashore from Ships that put in there to wood and water. The Rats gnaw'd his Feet and Clothes while asleep, which oblig'd him to cherish the Cats with his Goats-flesh; by which many of them became so tame, that they would lie about him in hundreds, and soon deliver'd him from the Rats. He likewise tamed some Kids, and to divert himself would now and then sing and dance with them and his Cats: so that by the Care of Providence and Vigour of his Youth, being now but about 30 years old, he came at last to conquer all the Inconveniences of his Solitude, and to be very easy. When his Clothes wore out, he made himself a Coat and Cap of Goat-Skins, which he stitch'd together with little Thongs of the same, that he cut with his Knife. He had no other Needle but a Nail; and when his Knife was wore to the back, he made others as well as he could of some Iron Hoops that were left ashore, which he beat thin and ground upon Stones. Having some Linen Cloth

by him, he sow'd himself Shirts with a Nail, and stitch'd 'em
with the Worsted of his old Stockings, which he pull'd out
on purpose. He had his last Shirt on when we found him on the
Island.

At his first coming on board with us, he had so much forgot his
Language for want of Use, that we could scarce understand him,
for he seem'd to speak his words by halves. We offer'd him a
Dram, but he would not touch it, having drank nothing but
Water since his being there, and 'twas some time before he could
relish our Victuals.

He could give us an account of no other Product of the Island
than what we have mention'd, except small black Plums, which
are very good, but hard to come at, the Trees which bear 'em
growing on high Mountains and Rocks. Piemento Trees are plenty
here, and we saw some of 60 foot high, and about two yards
thick; and Cotton Trees higher, and near four fathom round in
the Stock.

The Climate is so good, that the Trees and Grass are verdant
all the year. The Winter lasts no longer than *June* and *July*, and
is not then severe, there being only a small Frost and a little Hail,
but sometimes great Rains. The Heat of the Summer is equally
moderate, and there's not much Thunder or tempestuous Weather
of any sort. He saw no venomous or savage Creature on the
Island, nor any other sort of Beast but Goats, *etc.*, as above-
mentioned; the first of which had been put ashore here on purpose for a Breed by *Juan Fernando* a *Spaniard*, who settled there
with some Families for a time, till the Continent of *Chili* began
to submit to the *Spaniards*; which being more profitable, tempted
them to quit this Island, which is capable of maintaining a good
number of People, and of being made so strong that they could
not be easily dislodg'd.'

> Captain Woodes Rogers, A *Cruising Voyage Round the
> World*, edited by G. E. Manwaring from the original edition
> of 1712 (New York 1928, pp. 91–5).

To his great talents as a writer, Richard Steele, the founder of
the *Tatler* and co-founder of the *Spectator*, added a brilliant
journalist's gift for sensing the trends in public interest. He

apparently sought out Selkirk when he later returned to England in 1711, and their interviews formed the substance of an essay in his periodical *The Englishman*, no. 26 for 1–3 December 1713 :

Talia monstrabat relegens errata retrorsum. Virg.[53]
[Such things . . . he pointed out as he retraced his former wanderings.]

Under the Title of this Paper, I do not think it foreign to my Design, to speak of a Man born in Her Majesty's Dominions, and relate an Adventure in his Life so uncommon, that it's doubtful whether the like has happen'd to any other of human Race. The Person I speak of is *Alexander Selkirk*, whose Name is familiar to Men of Curiosity, from the Fame of his having lived four Years and four Months alone in the Island of *Juan Fernandez*. I had the pleasure frequently to converse with the Man soon after his Arrival in *England*, in the Year 1711. It was matter of great Curiosity to hear him, as he is a Man of good Sense, give an Account of the different Revolutions in his own Mind in that long Solitude. When we consider how painful Absence from Company for the space of but one Evening, is to the generality of Mankind, we may have a sense how painful this necessary and constant Solitude was to a Man bred a Sailor, and ever accustomed to enjoy and suffer, eat, drink, and sleep, and perform all Offices of Life, in Fellowship and Company. He was put ashore from a leaky Vessel, with the Captain of which he had had an irreconcileable difference; and he chose rather to take his Fate in this place, than in a crazy Vessel, under a disagreeable Commander. His Portion were a Sea-Chest, his wearing Cloaths and Bedding, a Fire-lock, a Pound of Gun-powder, a large quantity of Bullets, a Flint and Steel, a few Pounds of Tobacco, an Hatchet, a Knife, a Kettle, a Bible, and other Books of Devotion, together with Pieces that concerned Navigation, and his Mathematical Instruments. Resentment against his Officer, who had ill used him, made him look forward on this Change of Life, as the more eligible one, till the Instant in which he saw the Vessel put off; at which moment, his Heart yearned within him, and melted at the parting with his Comrades and all Human Society at once. He had in Provisions for the Sustenance of Life but the quantity of two Meals, the Island abounding only with wild Goats, Cats and Rats. He judged it most probable that he should find more immediate and easy Relief, by finding Shell-fish on the Shore, than seeking Game with his Gun. He accordingly found great quantities of Turtles, whose Flesh is extreamly delicious, and of which he frequently eat very plentifully on his first Arrival, till it grew disagreeable to his Stomach, except in Jellies. The Necessities of Hunger and Thirst, were his greatest Diversions from the Reflection on his lonely Condition. When those Appetites were satisfied, the Desire of Society was as strong a Call upon him, and he appeared to himself least necessitious when he wanted every thing; for the Supports of his Body were easily attained, but the eager Longings for seeing again the Face of Man during the Interval of craving bodily Appetites, were hardly suportable. He grew dejected, languid, and melancholy, scarce able to refrain from doing himself Violence, till by Degrees, by the Force of Reason, and frequent reading of the Scriptures, and turning his Thoughts upon the Study of Navigation, after the Space of eighteen Months, he grew thoroughly reconciled to his Condition. When he had made this Conquest, the Vigour of his Health, Disengagement from the World, a constant, chearful, serene Sky, and a temperate Air, made his Life one continual Feast, and his Being much more joyful than it had before been irksome. He now taking Delight in every thing, made the Hutt in which he lay, by Ornaments which he cut down from a spacious Wood, on the side of which it was situated, the most delicious Bower, fann'd with continual Breezes, and gentle Aspirations of Wind, that made his Repose after the Chase equal to the most sensual Pleasures.

I forgot to observe, that during the Time of his Dissatisfaction, Monsters of the Deep, which frequently lay on the Shore, added to the Terrors of his Solitude; the dreadful Howlings and Voices seemed too terrible to be made for human Ears; but upon the Recovery of his Temper, he could with Pleasure not only hear their Voices, but approach the Monsters themselves with great Intrepidity. He speaks of Sea-Lions, whose Jaws and Tails were capable of seizing or breaking the Limbs of a Man, if he approached them: But at that Time his Spirits and Life were so high, and he could act so regularly and unconcerned, that meerly

from being unruffled in himself, he killed them with the greatest
Ease imaginable: For observing, that though their Jaws and
Tails were so terrible, yet the Animals being mighty slow in
working themselves round, he had nothing to do but place himself exactly opposite to their Middle, and as close to them as
possible, and he dispatched them with his Hatchet at Will.

THE Precaution which he took against Want, in case of
Sickness, was to lame Kids when very young, so as that they
might recover their Health, but never be capable of Speed. These
he had in great Numbers about his Hutt; and when he was himself in full Vigour, he could take at full Speed the swiftest Goat
running up a Promontory, and never failed of catching them but
on a Descent.

His Habitation was extreamly pester'd with Rats, which
gnaw'd his Cloaths and Feet when sleeping. To defend him
against them, he fed and tamed Numbers of young Kitlings,
who lay about his Bed, and preserved him from the Enemy.
When his Cloaths were quite worn out, he dried and tacked
together the Skins of Goats, with which he cloathed himself,
and was enured to pass through Woods, Bushes, and Brambles
with as much Carelessness and Precipitance as any other Animal.
It happened once to him, that running on the Summit of a Hill,
he made a Stretch to seize a Goat, with which under him, he
fell down a Precipice, and lay sensless for the Space of three Days,
the Length of which Time he Measured by the Moon's Growth
since his last Observation. This manner of Life grew so ex-
quisitely pleasant, that he never had a Moment heavy upon his
Hands; his Nights were untroubled, and his Days joyous, from
the Practice of Temperance and Exercise. It was his Manner to
use stated Hours and Places for Exercises of Devotion, which he
performed aloud, in order to keep up the Faculties of Speech,
and to utter himself with greater Energy.

WHEN I first saw him, I thought, if I had not been let into
his Character and Story, I could have discerned that he had been
much separated from Company, from his Aspect and Gesture;
there was a strong but chearful Seriousness in his Look, and a
certain Disregard to the ordinary things about him, as if he had
been sunk in Thought. When the Ship which brought him off

the Island came in, he received them with the greatest Indifference, with relation to the Prospect of going off with them, but with great Satisfaction in an Opportunity to refresh and help them. The Man frequently bewailed his Return to the World, which could not, he said, with all its Enjoyments, restore him to the Tranquility of his Solitude. Though I had frequently conversed with him, after a few Months Absence he met me in the Street, and though he spoke to me, I could not recollect that I had seen him; familiar Converse in this Town had taken off the Loneliness of his Aspect, and quite altered the Air of his Face.

THIS plain Man's Story is a memorable Example, that he is happiest who confines his Wants to natural Necessities; and he that goes further in his Desires, increases his Wants in Proportion to his Acquisitions; or to use his own Expression, *I am now worth 800 Pounds, but shall never be so happy, as when I was not worth a Farthing.*

SELECT FURTHER READING

BIBLIOGRAPHY

THE starting point for identifying Defoe's work is J. R. Moore, *A Checklist of the Writings of Daniel Defoe* (Indiana University Press, Bloomington, Ind., 1960; repr. with additions, Hamden, Conn., 1971, listing 548 titles), but argument continues on inclusions and exclusions, e.g. P. Rogers, 'Addenda and Corrigenda to Moore's *Checklist*', P.B.S.A. 75 (1981); J. A. Stoler, *Daniel Defoe: An Annotated Bibliography of Modern Criticism, 1900–1980* (Garland Publishing, N.Y., 1984); M. E. Novak, 'Defoe' in A. E. Dyson (ed.), *The English Novel: Select Bibliographical Guides* (O.U.P., 1975), a good review essay and listing.

EDITIONS AND SELECTIONS

Pending the appearance of the 40 volumes of the Southern Illinois University Press *Collected Writings*, the only sets of Defoe's novels are still: G. A. Aitken (ed.), *Romances and Narratives by Daniel Defoe*, 16 vols. (1895), which includes *The Farther Adventures* [second part] *of Robinson Crusoe*; G. H. Maynadier (ed.), *The Works of Daniel Defoe*, 16 vols. (Boston, Mass., and N.Y., 1903–4), a modernized text adding *Serious Reflections* [third part of *RC*]; *Novels And Selected Writings of Daniel Defoe* [includes *RC* 1 and 2], 14 vols. (Shakespeare Head Edition, Oxford, 1927–8).

Individual novels available include: *Captain Singleton* (O.U.P., 1969); *Memoirs of a Cavalier* (O.U.P., 1972); *Colonel Jacque* (O.U.P., 1965); *Journal of the Plague Year* (Penguin, 1966; O.U.P., 1969), *Roxana* (O.U.P., 1964; repr. 1981); *Moll Flanders* (O.U.P., 1971; Norton Critical Editions, N.Y. [with background and critical pieces], 1973; Penguin, 1978).

Selections from Defoe's works including non-fiction may be found in: J. T. Boulton (ed.), *Daniel Defoe* (Batsford, 1965; repr. as *Selected Writings of Daniel Defoe*, Cambridge, 1975), with an

'Introduction' on Defoe's language; M. F. Shugrue (ed.), *Selected Poetry and Prose of Daniel Defoe* (Holt, Rinehart and Wilson, N.Y., 1968); L. A. Curtis (ed.), *The Versatile Defoe: An Anthology of Uncollected Writings of Daniel Defoe* (Rowman and Littlefield, Totowa, N.J., 1979), useful notes.

Non-fiction relevant to reading *RC* includes: A. W. Secord (ed.), *Defoe's Review*, 22 vols. (N.Y., 1938); W. L. Payne (ed.), *The Best of Defoe's Review* (N.Y., 1951); M. Schonhorn (ed.), *A General History of the Pyrates* (Dent, 1972), with a commentary; *A Tour through the Whole Island of Great Britain* (2 vols., Everyman Library, 1927; ed. and abridged by P. Rogers, Penguin, 1965); G. H. Healey (ed.), *Letters of Defoe* (O.U.P., 1955).

DEFOE AND HIS WORKS

F. Bastian, *Defoe's Early Life* [to 1703] (Macmillan, 1981), excellent documentation, conclusions arguable; M. Byrd (ed.), *Daniel Defoe: A Collection of* [12] *Critical Essays* (Prentice-Hall, Englewood Cliffs, N.J., 1976); Peter Earle, *The World of Defoe* (Weidenfeld and Nicolson, 1976), an excellent introduction; J. R. Moore, *Daniel Defoe, Citizen of the Modern World* (University of Chicago Press, Chicago, 1958), with a chronology, full notes and bibliography; M. E. Novak, *Defoe and the Nature of Man* (O.U.P., 1963) and *Economics and the Fiction of Defoe* (University of California Studies in English 24, Los Angeles, Cal., 1964); J. J. Richetti, *Defoe's Narratives: Situations and Structures* (O.U.P., 1975); P. Rogers (ed.), *Defoe: the Critical Heritage* (Routledge, 1972); M. Shinagel, *Defoe and Middle-Class Gentility* (Harvard University Press, Cambridge, Mass., 1968); G. Starr, *Defoe and Spiritual Autobiography* (Princeton University Press, Princeton, N.J., 1965; repr. N.Y., 1971); J. R. Sutherland, *Daniel Defoe: A Critical Study* (Harvard University Press, Cambridge, Mass., 1971), a useful introduction; I. Watt, *The Rise of the Novel* (Chatto & Windus, 1957; Peregrine Books, 1963) has a section on *RC* and *Moll Flanders*; E. Zimmerman, *Defoe and the Novel* (University of California Press, Los Angeles, Cal., 1975).

ROBINSON CRUSOE

In addition to the works listed in the section above, which all have substantial discussions of *RC*, the following may be particularly noted: H. C. Hutchins, *Robinson Crusoe and Its Printing: 1719–1731* (Columbia University Press, N.Y., 1925) puts the printing history of the book on a firm basis, supplemented by K. I. D. Maslen, 'The Printers of *RC*', *The Library* VII 1952; F. H. Ellis (ed.), *RC: A Collection of* [12] *Critical Essays* (Prentice-Hall, Englewood Cliffs, N.J., 1969); C. Hill, 'Robinson Crusoe', *History Workshop Journal* 10 (1980); J. Paul Hunter, *The Reluctant Pilgrim: Defoe's Emblematic Method and Quest for Form in Robinson Crusoe* (The John Hopkins Press, Baltimore, Md, 1966); R. L. Mégroz, *The Real Robinson Crusoe* (Cresset Press, 1939), an entertaining life of Alexander Selkirk; P. Rogers, *Robinson Crusoe* (Unwin Critical Library, 1979) informative, with a helpful bibliography.

NOTES

A Note on the Text:

The printing history of the *Life and Strange Surprising Adventures of Robinson Crusoe* is rather complicated. The present text is based on the copy of the first edition in the Library of the University of London, and incorporates the alterations made in the third edition. Some old printers' conventions differ from modern practice and these have been modified to make for easier reading. For example, the dialogue has been put inside inverted commas, instead of being (somewhat carelessly) italicized; the apostrophe before the final 'd' has been replaced by an 'e' in most cases, as in *reposed* for *repos'd*. Otherwise the spelling has been left unaltered. Defoe wrote a very loosely punctuated prose, often in paragraph-long units broken only by semi-colons and colons. This has been left unaltered; it fits in well with an old narrator recalling his past, but is characteristic of all Defoe's fiction. The old printer's text is clearly a little haphazard, and gross difficulties have in a very few cases been smoothed over and a few obvious errors rectified.

1. *dispatched*: all editions except the first two alter this to 'disputed', but it seems to mean that since all stories like this are to be read quickly, improvement is equally likely whether the story is true or a romance. It helps the reader's enjoyment and profit.
2. *wise man . . . riches*: 'Give me neither poverty nor riches': Proverbs 30:8.
3. *sheet anchor . . . end*: the *sheet anchor* was the largest of the Ship's anchors, used only in an emergency. *better end*: when a rope is 'veered out' (or paid out) to the 'bitter-end', that is the end round the bit which secures it to the ship, no more is left.
4. *at all adventures*: at hazard, recklessly.
5. *calenture*: from the Spanish *calentura* = a fever; a disease con-

tracted by sailors in the tropics, characterized by delirium and
hallucinations.

6. *a Turkish rover of Sallee*: Sallee (now Salé) was a port adjacent
to the present Rabat in Morocco and known as the haunt of
dreaded pirates.

7. *powder-chest*: primitive shells, made of wood filled with
gunpowder and stones or bullets.

8. *her antient and pendants out*: *antient* is a corrupt form of *ensign*
(usually found in the sixteenth century) and may be a deliberate
archaism on Defoe's part. *Pendant* is a form of pennant, the
long tapering flag flown from the topmast of a naval ship in
commission.

9. *case of bottles*: a set of heavy glass liquor bottles (usually
square), protected by a snug fitted box from being rattled and
broken in travelling.

10. *my arm under his twist*: twist is an old word for the crotch;
perhaps another deliberate archaism.

11. *lyons and tygers*: there are no *tigers* in Africa, but the word
was applied to the leopard, panther and animals of similar
kind.

12. *the Pico of Teneriffe*: the mountain in the centre of Teneriffe
(Canary Islands), one of the highest (12,190 feet) mountains
up to then scaled by man. It was often given absurd heights,
such as fifteen miles (*New Geographical Dictionary*, 1737).

13. *the River Gambia or Senegall*: the River Gambia is about 130
miles south of cape Verde, the River Senegal 130 miles north.

14. *offered me this medium*: *medium* = compromise. This sense is
apparently an introduction of Defoe's.

15. *Bay de Todos los Santos*: *Todo os Santos* is one of the finest and
largest deep-water harbours on the coast of Brazil, on which
is Salvador, then the capital.

16. *ingenio*: Spanish (and Portuguese) for a Sugar Mill and
refinery in the West Indies.

17. *Cape St. Augustino*: presumably either the Ponta do Colcan-
har, or Cap S. Rouge, on the right-hand shoulder of the South
American continent.

18. *Isle of Fernand de Noranha*: about 250 miles north east of the
above.

19. *within the circle of the Carribee-Islands*: the position given would put the ship just east of Trinidad. The Windward and Leeward Islands stretch thence in a semi-circle north and west to Puerto Rica, Hispaniola and Cuba. Barbados is north of Trinidad, and east of the Windwards.

20 *for sudden joys, like griefs, confound at first*: perhaps Defoe's adaptation of 'Great joys, like griefs, are silent', from Shackerley Marmion's popular comedy, *Holland's Leaguer* (1632).

21. *the ship was bulged*: damaged so as to breach the bilge.

22. *several spare yards*: a yard is a wooden spar strung by its centre from the mast, to support and stretch a sail.

23. *five or six gallons of rack*: arrack (from an Arabic word for price), a Levantine word for any distilled spirit.

24. *three large runlets of rum or spirits*: runlet is an archaic word for a cask of varying capacity.

25. *in the offing*: a position in the sea at a distance from the shore.

26. *two or three seals*: it does not seem likely that seals would be seen off the Orinoco, in the South Atlantic: these particular seals may have come from accounts of Juan Fernandez.

27. *load them with flaggs*: flags are coarse grass or sedge.

28. *of the same kind as our European, nay, as our English barley*: it does not seem that there is any distinction between *European* and *English* barley.

29. *several sugar canes, but wild*: the Sugar Cane, a giant grass, never grew wild in the West Indies or South America. The cultivated plant was introduced there by the Spaniards and Portuguese in the sixteenth century.

30. *for my store*: supplies, another archaism.

31. *Leaden-hall Market*: so called from the construction of its roof, a London meat and game market at the corner of Gracechurch street.

32. *into my old hutch*: a sordid hut or cabin, or, jocularly, a small house.

33. *I will never . . . thee*: Joshua 1:5.

34. *Father Abraham . . . fix'd*: Luke 16:26.

35. *the lust . . . life*: John 2.16.

36. *feeding Elijah by ravens*: 1 Kings 17:4–6.

37. *very old and crazy*: frail and infirm.

38. *spatter-dashes*: a kind of long leather or cloth gaiters. The O.E.D. gives 1687 as the earliest date of the word's use: later 'spats'.

39. *moletta*: mulatto.

40. *not agreeable only, but physical*: medicinal.

41. *Wait . . . Lord*: Psalms 27:14.

42. *Saul*: 1 Samuel 28:15.

43. *As to the crimes . . . they were national*: characteristic of the nation as a whole, therefore not a matter for individual choice.

44. *if I had chop'd upon them*: *chanced* upon them, perhaps from the nautical use of chop=to change direction.

45. *a meer natural cave in the earth*: completely natural.

46. *two pound of fine glazed powder*: the grains of the best gunpowder were glazed with graphite to slow down combustion, making it safe to use.

47. *St. Martha*: Santa Marta on the coast of Colombia.

48. *fustic*: *Cladrastis (Chlorophora, Maclura)*, a tree found in South America and the West Indies. The wood gives a yellow dye.

49. *Nicaragua wood*: a species of *Caesalpinia* (which yields a red dye), similar to Brazil wood.

50. *Alicant*: Alicante in Valencia.

51. *the Groyne*: La Coruña [Corunna] in Spain.

52. *with the rankling of his two wounds*: festering or ulcerating.

53. *Aeneid*, III, 690. The story has been told by 'Achaemenides, comrade of the luckless Ulysses', who had been marooned on the island of Ortygia and rescued by Aeneas. In the light of the motive for Crusoe's wandering, it is interesting to note that Achaemenides begins his story by saying, 'since my father Adamastus was poor – and would to heaven that fortune had so stayed – I set out for Troy.' Was *Defoe* recalling this episode in Virgil's poem?

GLOSSARY

of words and phrases with unfamiliar meanings and spellings

admiration (admire): astonishment (wonder at)

affection: feeling, love, devotion

amuse: to deceive or bamboozle; also *amused* = bamboozled; *amusement* = deceit

barco-longo: a low, undecked vessel; the term Crusoe applies to the pinnace in which he escapes from the Moors.

bays: baize; a coarse, long-napped woollen cloth

beachy: shingly, stony

brand goose: the *brant goose*, the smallest wild goose

conscience: consciousness

crowded to the utmost: as much sail as possible

cruisado: = *crusado*: a Portuguese coin bearing a cross worth about 2s. 3d. sterling [11p]

doubloon: a double pistole, a Spanish gold coin worth 35s. [£1.75]

dozed: made dull or drowsy, stupefied

drill: a trickling rivulet, a rill

flea = flay

forecast: plan, contrivance

fore-chains: lengths of chain on the ship's side, bracing the supports for the foremast (or bowsprit)

fusee, fuzee: (from the French *fusil*) a light musket, a fire-lock

graplin: = *grapnel*: a small three-fluked anchor

grutch: to grudge

gusts: individual tastes or likings

hanger: short sword

keep: to remain or stay for the time in a particular spot

main sheet: line or rope attached to one or other of the bottom corners of the mainsail

Maresco [It. *Moresco*; Sp. *Morisso*]: a Moor

meer: = mere, can mean 'complete', 'sheer', 'entire', as well as 'nothing more than' *mend it*: amend, improve it.

mischieve: do mischief to, injure

moidore, moydor: a Portuguese gold coin worth about 27s. sterling
   [£1.35]

molossus: an obsolete form of *molasses*

motion: an inward prompting or impulse

naturalist: one who studies natural as distinct from spiritual
   things, a physicist or 'natural philosopher'

periagua: a dug-out canoe, made from a single tree-trunk

perspective [*glass*]: telescope

physical: medicinal, curative

pickle: a nautical punishment of rubbing salt and vinegar on the
   back of a man who has been flogged

piece of eight: a Spanish dollar worth eight *ryals* (q.v.), worth 4s.
   sterling [20p]

presently: immediately

prudential: a prudential consideration

quarter: one of the two after parts of the ship's sides

ryal: =*real*: a small Spanish coin worth 6d. [2½p]

salvages: savages

search: = searce: a sieve or strainer (originally of hair cloth); also
   a verb, to sieve or strain

shoulder of mutton sail: a triangular, for-and-aft sail

stay: for-and-aft rigging support of a mast

Straits-mouth: The Straits of Gibraltar

FOR THE BEST IN PAPERBACKS, LOOK FOR THE

In every corner of the world, on every subject under the sun, Penguin represents quality and variety – the very best in publishing today.

For complete information about books available from Penguin – including Pelicans, Puffins, Peregrines and Penguin Classics – and how to order them, write to us at the appropriate address below. Please note that for copyright reasons the selection of books varies from country to country.

In the United Kingdom: For a complete list of books available from Penguin in the U.K., please write to *Dept E.P., Penguin Books Ltd, Harmondsworth, Middlesex, UB7 0DA*

In the United States: For a complete list of books available from Penguin in the U.S., please write to *Dept BA, Penguin, 299 Murray Hill Parkway, East Rutherford, New Jersey 07073*

In Canada: For a complete list of books available from Penguin in Canada, please write to *Penguin Books Canada Ltd, 2801 John Street, Markham, Ontario L3R 1B4*

In Australia: For a complete list of books available from Penguin in Australia, please write to the *Marketing Department, Penguin Books Australia Ltd, P.O. Box 257, Ringwood, Victoria 3134*

In New Zealand: For a complete list of books available from Penguin in New Zealand, please write to the *Marketing Department, Penguin Books (NZ) Ltd, Private Bag, Takapuna, Auckland 9*

In India: For a complete list of books available from Penguin, please write to *Penguin Overseas Ltd, 706 Eros Apartments, 56 Nehru Place, New Delhi, 110019*

In Holland: For a complete list of books available from Penguin in Holland, please write to *Penguin Books Nederland B.V., Postbus 195, NL–1380AD Weesp, Netherlands*

In Germany: For a complete list of books available from Penguin, please write to *Penguin Books Ltd, Friedrichstrasse 10 – 12, D–6000 Frankfurt Main 1, Federal Republic of Germany*

In Spain: For a complete list of books available from Penguin in Spain, please write to *Longman Penguin España, Calle San Nicolas 15, E–28013 Madrid, Spain*